Mortimer Blakely is Missing
Amanda Taylor

Published by Northern Heritage Publications
an imprint of Jeremy Mills Publishing Limited

113 Lidget Street
Lindley
Huddersfield
West Yorkshire HD3 3JR

www.jeremymillspublishing.co.uk

First published 2013
Text © Amanda Taylor

ISBN 978-1-906600-93-8

For Paul

Man is least himself when he talks in his own person.
Give him a mask, and he will tell you the truth.

Oscar Wilde (16th October 1854 – 30th November 1900)

Chapter One

'Where to put it. That was a major problem.'

"It." What did he mean by "it", I wondered. My vision struggled to adjust in the bad light. Finally seeing "it", I staggered back with shock. I could not stop myself, barely aware of Mr Brown's hand on my arm to steady me.

'Not such a taking sight for any man to behold, eh.' The warder's voice was full of contempt. 'Where would you put it? The men's or the women's block?'

'Hold your tongue,' ordered Brown.

The apparition – I have no better description for what I was seeing – crouched by the plank bed on the opposite wall of the small cell. The spectacle was grotesque. Painted and rouged in a soiled frilled dress, he, she, was neither man nor woman, an ugly ambiguity.

The eyes above the gash of mouth appealed for understanding in an all-absorbing expression I had not seen in a human being before; an expression that was prepared to consume any insult, any slight thrown at it for this… for this behaviour that was beyond all my previous experience and therefore was beyond my understanding.

Oh yes, I had goggled in fascination along with other punters at the half-man, half-woman freak show, a safe contained sideshow removed from real life. And, yes, I had heard of the hijras, the eunuchs of India, and our outlawing of their practices, and all the ongoing legislation attempting to eradicate them throughout the entire continent. But this…

"This is the Reverend George Hobb,' announced Brown. 'He would like you to act for him.'

'Reverend,' I repeated in disbelief. 'So where's his dog collar?'

'He prefers the dress,' replied Brown drily.

'I don't understand.'

'You had better ask *him* about the whys and the wherefores,' shrugged Brown.

'Building up quite a reputation aren't we, sir, for defending the bizarre?' whispered Martin Trotter, my clerk.

'Quiet,' I warned him.

'Well?' asked Brown.

'Well what?'

'Will you act for him or not?' asked the desperate solicitor.

'"Act", I think the Reverend is capable of doing that all on his own.' I nodded down to his cowering client. 'What are you accused of?' I asked Reverend Hobb directly. In answer he gave a defiant flounce and several layers of satin petticoats rustled in the dirt of the flagged floor.

'It isn't anything he's done. It's how others react to him,' explained Brown.

'Are you surprised?' whispered the serpent at my ear.

'Trotter, I'll not tell you again.' I shook my clerk off to move closer. Not only did the Reverend have a puffy black eye but both cheeks and his nose were badly swollen, and the unmistakable shadow of a beard had begun to form beneath his face powder.

'Nearly caused a riot at a public house he was drinking in,' admitted Brown reluctantly. 'A rabble outside started throwing stones at the windows.'

'And where was that?' I asked.

'The Star in Stonegate, I believe,' Brown explained shrugging his shoulders again. His apparent acceptance of his client's deviant behaviour was beginning to irritate me.

'Do you not have a voice of your own, sir?' I stooped on one knee next to the Reverend, fascination and abhorrence mixed.

'Hardly spoke a word since he's been in here,' said the warder, whose face was familiar to me though I couldn't remember exactly from where. 'Shock, I expect.'

'Who did this to you?' I asked the prisoner, watching a tear or two spill out from his good eye. Finally a genuine stream of emotion ran through the caked make-up, announcing to the body of men collected there with me that here was a fellow human being. Boots scuffed disconcertedly against the stone floor. I gently stroked my finger across his bristling cheek, breaking the stream. 'Never mind, we'll address all these matters later.'

'Thank you.' George Hobb spoke in a quiet voice, low and shockingly masculine for all his painted face and manner of dress.

'Isn't this the same cell that Daniel Robertshaw was contained in?' I turned to the warder.

'The same, sir.'

'Must be well over a year ago now. And you were brought in to replace that despicable Goater, weren't you?'

'I was, sir. Fancy, you remembering that,' said the warder, delighted.

'But Mr Robertshaw was held in solitary confinement accused of murder, not for wearing a dress.'

'Indeed, sir, but just as the police feared their station would be torn apart should he remain in their custody any longer, the governor could not assure Hobb's safety were he allowed to associate freely with other prisoners here.'

'So, all this is for his own good,' ridiculed Brown. 'A special case.'

'Tell me, is Goater still in the prison service?' I asked the warder, attempting to calm matters.

'No, sir. I believe he joined the constabulary shortly before the Robertshaw trial.'

'The constabulary. That was predictable.'

'Never mind this fellow Goater.' Trotter interjected impatiently. 'What are we doing here, sir?'

'Interviewing a prospective client,' I snapped back.

'This situation would be farcical if it wasn't so pathetic. Surely, impersonating a female is a misdemeanour, something for the magistrates' court, not a serious criminal offence for jury trial.'

'That's where you are wrong, Mr Trotter,' cut in Brown.

'But Mr Cairn is a top... You'll not take this, sir. You'll be laughed out of court.' Trotter sounded almost hysterical.

'Has he been before the magistrate yet?' I asked Brown.

'No. He was only arrested yesterday.'

'Ah, on Whit Monday, so the court will have an accumulation of cases.'

'I believe he is due to appear the day after tomorrow.'

'And what is he charged with? Do you know?'

'So far he is accused of causing a public mischief by drooping as a woman.'

'Well, perhaps Trotter is right then. Surely such a soft charge cannot warrant my involvement.'

'There is talk of an examination...' Brown hesitated as the lace round his client's wrists began to shake. '... by a police surgeon.'

'You'll resist of course.'

'I'll do my best but I fear they might regard any intervention on my part as a sign of my client's guilt. And if they insist...'

'Have the paperwork in my chambers in the morning at nine o'clock, and then we'll see,' I told him, swinging on my heels towards the cell door followed by the disgruntled Trotter. 'I like a challenge,' I said, frowning back at my clerk. 'And what is more, I'll not be dictated to by the likes of you as to what brief I will or will not take.'

* * * * *

'Must be a north-easterly coming across the plain of York today,' huffed and puffed Brown. 'And it's supposed to be spring.'

'Take a chair by the fire and warm yourself,' I told him. 'Bootham Chambers always has a welcoming fire burning whatever the season.'

'Yes, we can discuss matters just as well by the hearth.' Brown sank thankfully into one of my armchairs. He smiled at the embarrassing squeak of leather drawn by his trouser seat. 'Her Majesty is eighty today, I believe,' he said by way of diversion.

'Yes, I know,' I said, taking the chair opposite him. 'The old queen's reign is nearly at an end and we are on the cusp of a new century. So why are we still so primitive and warlike that they are having to discuss at this conference in the Hague whether or not soldiers should be allowed to lob projectiles and explosives at each other out of balloons?'

'Doesn't say a lot for mankind, does it, Cairn?'

'Darjeeling and macaroons,' I offered. Brown nodded enthusiastically, saying he had not had time to breakfast that morning. I rang for the girl who attended to all the culinary requirements of *Bingham, Leacock, Fawcett & Cairn* and made my order. She curtsied and Brown's eyes followed her out of the room. His expression was interested rather than lascivious.

'A new acquisition,' I explained. 'Very efficient, very well-trained.'

'Business must be brisk.'

'Since the Robertshaw trial we've never looked back.'

'Decent of you to take an interest in this case then,' said Brown, crossing his legs in a relaxed manner. I liked my solicitors to be relaxed, my clients rarely were.

'My clerk scolds me for having a penchant for the bizarre.' I smiled.

'I noticed.'

'Oh dear, did you? I'll have to reprimand Trotter over those stage whispers of his. You don't think the Reverend George Hobb heard Trotter's unprofessional comment as well, do you?' I had no intention of defending my clerk over something that was indefensible. Trotter had been acting above his station ever since *Regina v Robertshaw*. I would have to pull him into line.

'Trotter disapproved, we were to be discouraged. Your man only expressed the prejudice of most men.'

'But not yours, I've noticed.' I could not help regarding Brown's liberality with some curiosity.

'You know, Cairn, there is a lot more to George Hobb than the person you met yesterday.'

'Yes, I'm sure…' A knock on the door interrupted us. 'Thank you, Emma.' The girl gave her neat little curtsy again before placing the tea set of Leeds creamware on the table between us, accompanied by a plate full of large macaroons.'

Without further ado, hungry Mr Brown dived forward.

'Delicious,' he mumbled. 'The taste of sweet almond comes through perfectly.'

'You like almonds then.'

'I'm particularly partial to them.'

'Help yourself to as many as you want.' I offered the plate to him.

'Thank you.' Brown's delicate hand reached for another cake from the equally delicate openwork pottery. 'Mouth wateringly delicious,' he mumbled again.

'It appears that you have a proclivity for clients accused of causing an affray either inside or outside public houses.'

'Ah, you're talking about the King's Arms and John Barr now,' laughed Brown. 'You'll be interested to learn that Farmer Walker remained true to his word and has kept Barr's wife on as a milkmaid while her husband serves his time. She and her children remain in their tenanted cottage.'

'Well, that's really good to hear. It isn't their fault that the head of the family is such a self-centred rogue.'

'From what I gather they are all faring better without him. I hope she doesn't take him back.'

'"Drink, our old friend drink is the evil here, is it not?"' My impersonation of the presiding judge in the Barr case was reasonable enough, I thought, but all laughter had faded from the eyes of the man opposite me.

'George Hobb is a different man entirely from John Barr and something far more intoxicating than liquor is involved here.'

'How do you mean?'

'This impulse of his. He told me he's done it since childhood, first his sister's dresses and then...'

'Before you go any further, you'd better let me take a look at your written observations on the matter,' I interrupted.

Brown reached down into his case. 'Your clerk has a point though, Cairn. I do hope you know what you are getting involved in, if you decide to take this case. I fear the law is going to make an example of my client.'

'I don't like examples being made in law,' I responded quietly.

'And a man of the cloth's future is at stake.'

'Or, more appropriately, a man of the dress.'

'If you are not going to treat this matter with the gravity it deserves, Cairn...' Brown said, returning the papers to his case.

'Don't be so sensitive, man. Now tell me, I'm curious. How did you become involved in all this yourself?' I asked.

'I knew George years ago when I was at university in London. I knew him only as a man. A very fine man at that.'

'So what is he doing in York dressed as a woman?' The obvious question.

'I believe he was on a visit to the Archbishop's Palace.' Brown's unexpected answer.

'Not in drag, I hope.'

'"Drag?"'

'A theatrical term, I believe, in reference to the strange sensation experienced by female impersonators as their long skirts drag across the stage.'

'George told me he feels this compulsion to dress-up particularly during bouts of anxiety. He does it to relieve some tension within himself. He does it for himself alone. On occasions he might wish to test his womanhood in society but he has no desire to attract other men.'

'No, but if your "example" theory is correct, they will do their best to ensnare him under this newly created legislation of importuning. Am I not right?'

'You could be,' sighed Brown. 'But it's not true though. He isn't like that.'

I made no attempt to hide my scepticism. 'To whomever or whatever this compulsion is directed, men are sexual beings. I am a sexual being.'

'I'm really not sure George is though. He doesn't seem to have, never has had that sort of interest in other people. He is a spiritual man. He's more interested in saving other people's souls than occupying their bodies. That is why I was surprised when I heard he was…'

'Look,' I interrupted, 'I'll be perfectly honest with you, Mr Brown. I don't see this as a cause for your pal, the Reverend George Hobb, at all. If I do take it on, it will be more a legal test case for my chambers. A case to test last year's reformed Vagrancy Act, which my senior partner, Carlton-Bingham, and I regard as a pernicious and vague piece of legislation.'

'An act trumped up following the Wilde trial.'

'Partly. That we can agree on.'

'But don't you see, Cairn, George is a genuine unfortunate.'

'I'm not sure what I see when I see your client,' I admitted.

'Then perhaps you are in for some surprises.'

Chapter Two

Thursday morning – an hour earlier I had sent Trotter to view proceedings against Hobb at the magistrates' court.

'Come in,' I told the knock on the door, too soon to be my returned clerk. Instead the awesome figure of my head of chambers, Carlton-Bingham, filled the frame. Stepping forward a pace or two, he flung a wad of documents on my table.

'Don't look so worried,' he told me. 'I've located some material that might help you with the Hobb case.'

'You really think we should take it on then?' I asked, somewhat taken aback.

'Well, we both have concerns about the moral validity of the law involved. This is our opportunity to test it.'

'Trotter thinks if *Regina v Hobb* comes to a jury trial it will turn into a courtroom farce.'

'Ah,' pondered Carlton-Bingham. 'I expect Trotter has his own reasons for feeling like that.'

'What reasons?'

'Well, he is a man living on his own, is he not?'

'I live on my own,' I countered in astonishment.

'There you are, you see,' said Carlton-Bingham making for the door. 'Like Trotter you are afraid that your reputation will be sullied by association.' He paused for a second on the threshold and turned. 'Allow me to quote from one of your favourite authors, I believe, Samuel Langhorne Clemens alias Mark Twain, "Do the thing you fear most and the death of fear is certain".'

'Did you know Twain might be coming over to England next summer?' I asked, a little slow in regaining my composure. Carlton-Bingham was always intent on provoking me.

'I did hear something, a whisper that he could possibly be staying with a newspaper proprietor friend of mine at Dollis Hill House in London.'

'You are joking.'

'No, I am perfectly serious. And, yes, perhaps I will drop in on him and his guest should the great man materialise.'

'I wish you would take me with you then.'

'When I've time, I'll mention it to Gilzean-Reid.'

'You really are a friend of Hugh Gilzean-Reid?'

'You would be surprised at my connections, James. And regarding newspapermen, if this Hobb business makes it to a higher court we'd better ensure that they are all there, what? Like the Robertshaw trial.'

'Was it you who arranged for the nationals to be there?' I was incredulous. Carlton-Bingham had kept this piece of information very close to his chest until now.

'Never doubted you'd win that one for a moment, old boy.'

As Carlton-Bingham's Huckleberry guffaws subsided down the corridor, I was left with the decision of whether or not to take on Hobb's defence. I cannot deny that I felt very uncomfortable in the company of this pathetic female usurper. Self-awareness is one thing but I was about to wade into a world completely alien to me. Although somewhat bullied at school for my good looks, nevertheless I was a stalwart of the rugby fifteen at both school and university. Carlton-Bingham was right. I was afraid. But within the next hour something was about to happen to change all that.

I had well and truly dipped my toes into the murky waters of female impersonators, *Regina v Boulton, Park and others*, whose complex court reports Carlton-Bingham had thoughtfully dug out for my perusal, when Trotter burst in through the doorway. No knock, just the heavy oak door flung back on its hinges, and there he was without so much as a by-your-leave – the Fishergate cowboy.

'Thought I'd seen everything,' he blustered. 'But I've never seen such a carry on as I've just witnessed.'

'What are you talking about? And how dare you barge into my room without knocking? I could have had a client with me, a colleague, anyone,' I spluttered angrily.

'I'm sorry, Mr Cairn, but I've never seen a human being so humbled save for the Lord Jesus himself on his day of crucifixion.'

'Who, man, who has been humbled?'

'The Reverend George Hobb, sir, the gentleman you sent me to observe in the Police Court.'

'Hobb has suddenly been recognised as a gentleman by you, has he?'

'I'm that upset,' said Trotter. 'The crowds, sir, all there to jeer and gloat, you wouldn't believe it.'

'Try me,' I told him coolly.

'As you know, sir, the Reverend is such a slight fellow. A mob besieged him on Clifford Street pavement before he even got inside the court, dragging at his clothes, his wig, trying to lift his petticoats, and all the while the police swaggering around him, enjoying the show and doing nothing to stop them.'

'God! Brown didn't allow him to stand before the magistrate in that dreadful female get-up, did he?'

Trotter nodded, saying, 'I believe the Reverend insisted upon appearing so. Again he was mobbed inside the building, inside the court. Mr Turner was hard pressed to restore order.'

'I bet he was with Hobb all rouged up.'

'No, no, sir, there was no attempt to glamorise the Reverend. He wasn't winking around, enjoying the spectacle of it like other poofs I've heard of. He looked so downcast and put upon. He was in such a bad state of affairs after being locked up for several days in the Castle Prison. His dress was filthy and ripped into ribbons, him shaking inside it like a jelly, and almost a beard upon him.' This was a change of heart for my clerk. To my amazement I saw Trotter's eyes welling with tears.

'But to appear in a dress for the committal hearing.' I could not hide my disgust. 'So, what did Mr Turner decide?'

'He went on about the new legislation. Mentioned something about Hobb attempting to importune men in the Star Yard off Stonegate. Said Hobb was a risk to the public in general, men in particular. He refused to set bail until further enquiries could be made to see if he might have any previous convictions.'

'In short, our Mr Turner seemed very hostile to the Reverend.'

'In short, yes, very. It seems Mr Brown was right about the seriousness of his client's position.'

* * * * *

I walked towards one of the oldest spaces in the city, mentally rehearsing the impossible defence I was about to embark on in an hour or two. It was early morning and St Helen's Square was unusually quiet. That day I was representing William Huddleston. He was a well-known and highly successful pickpocket about the streets of York, who, however, was finally undone in very unusual circumstances. The unfortunate Huddleston was caught red handed with his hand down a tax collector's back pocket.

Bang. I jumped in my stride like a soldier responding to gunfire. *Bang.* Another explosion of noise bounced round the square and down the ancient snickets of York. A beating drum? Impossible at this hour in the city centre.

Ahead of me I saw some sort of affray was happening outside the Mansion House. A small crowd had gathered. It was to be hoped the Lord Mayor, Joseph Sykes Rymer, was not still in bed. Curious, I crossed the cobbled square to the activity. My musing over *Regina v Huddleston* would have to wait.

It looked to be a pathetic business: two burly policemen were trying to disengage a female from the railings. Her companion stood a little way off beating a drum. Sad and funny, I thought, until, on freeing the woman with some difficulty from her chains with a hacksaw, I saw one of the policemen take a swing at her with his fist knocking her back down on the pavement with a smack.

Far from being outraged the exclusively male audience jeered with derision as the woman tried to crawl back on to her feet, only to fall back in a huddle of petticoats and dress.

'How can you stand for the council, when you can't even stand on your feet, luv?' yelled a flat cap. Others screeched their approval at this piece of wisdom like hysterical baboons.

Each policeman hooked the semi-conscious woman under the armpit and tried to prop her up. Her jellied legs would not take it. She began to collapse away like an empty sack.

'Leave her alone! Leave her alone!' screamed her companion, drum sticks held aloft as she timidly began to close in. But the jeering men easily elbowed her off, forming a tight ring round the incident and preventing her going to the support of her friend. I could see nothing now. I could not see what the policemen or small crowd were doing to the woman. They were the pack and she was their prey. 'For pity's sake, can't someone do something,' appealed her companion. One blonde braided plait had broken free and dangled below her cap – a Tyrolean drummer then. A small cry, more a squeak came from the melee. That was enough for me, that was my signal. I pushed men aside with my rugby bulk. I pushed my way through those cowards easier than any scrum, carrying on my hands the coarse sensation of tweed where I had grasped their jackets.

At the centre of all the fuss now, I could not believe what I was seeing. The woman was slumped on the pavement, her nose bloodied, the bodice of her dress likewise. I could see a policeman's dark blue leg lifting and stretching.

'Don't!' I yelled, plunging myself between black boot and prone woman. 'Don't you dare kick her.'

'You,' exclaimed the open-mouthed policeman, staring into my face with bewilderment.

'Goater, I might have known.'

'She won't get up, Mr Cairn.'

'That's right, sir,' added his police colleague who was unknown to me.

'Can't you see, you fools? She won't get up because she can't. You've knocked her out cold.'

On cue the woman moaned.

'No we haven't,' said ridiculous Goater.

'Move back, move away, let the lady get some air.' His late-in-the-day colleague told the mob. No doubt he sensed some disciplinary inquiry could be brewing.

True to form, Goater could never see anything brewing.

'Yes, about your business, off to work you lot. You too, Mr Cairn, sir. You can leave this young lady to us,' he growled.

'I'm all right now,' gasped the floored woman, desperately trying to lever herself upon the railings.

'See, she's all right,' joined in Goater's colleague with enthusiasm.

'Yes, Constable Robins and I will deal with this,' affirmed Goater.

The woman clinging to the VOTES FOR WOMEN – VOTE FOR WOMEN COUNCILLORS placard began to slither down the wall again.

'No you won't. There is no way I will leave this lady in your care,' I said, beckoning to her musical companion through the dispersing men, instructing her to call a carriage at my expense. Unhooking her drum strap, she carefully placed instrument and sticks on the ground and was gone.

'But this woman is under arrest,' objected Goater.

'For what?'

'For obstruction.'

'Obstructing what?'

'She was obstructing the pavement.'

'How can she have been obstructing the pavement when she was out of the way chained to the railings?'

'That's a lawyer's argument. She is obstructing the pavement now.'

'Only because you've assaulted her.'

Constable Robins paled at this. 'Herbert, perhaps we should forget...' he began.

'The carriage is waiting over there,' interrupted the drummer.

I knelt down next to Goater's victim. 'Are you able to stand yet, my dear?' She nodded and I gently raised her up on my arm. She swooned again, forcing me to support her round the waist.

'Just let me collect my wits,' she murmured; her voice surprisingly well-modulated considering the circumstances.

'The two of you are not enough to make a viable protest,' I told her.

'No, but we will grow.'

Between us the drummer and I were able to conduct the lady to the waiting carriage. She was hatless with dancing curls the colour of winter bracken. Without her swollen and bloody nose, I think I would have been looking at an extremely lovely woman.

'About time,' complained the irritable brougham driver, until scowl turned to frown over the battered condition of his female passenger. 'She alright, guv?' he asked me.

'Just take them both home,' I told him, flinging him half a crown. 'And quickly.'

'My drum!' cried the drummer. 'I've left my drum!'

'Our placard!' groaned her injured friend.

I turned to examine the pavement behind. It was empty apart from the two irate constables. 'They've gone,' I commiserated. 'Someone in the crowd must have taken them.' Carefully balancing myself with one foot on the carriage step, I grabbed the open window frame.

'Careful, sir, or you'll spill us with your weight,' warned the driver.

Ignoring him and clinging on the carriage sill for dear life, I passed the drummer my card in case of any further repercussions from the police.

'I'm Lucy Alexander and this is Winifred Holbrook,' the drummer said, nodding across to her companion. Winifred Holbrook didn't look at all well. Her head was resting against the back of the cab, her eyes dark and closed.

'I hope she is going to be all right,' I said, truly concerned. 'You'd both better hurry on your way now.'

'You've been very kind, Mr Cairn,' said the drummer, checking my name on the card.

I stepped down and nodded up to the driver.

'Get up! Get up there!' He flicked the reins and the horse jerked forward.

Goater was waiting for me on the pavement.

'Mr Cairn, you'd no right to interfere,' he began red-faced.

'What, in your assault of that young woman?'

'Well...' blew Goater. 'I had my orders. They've been here since dawn. Both of 'em set on disrupting an important council meeting taking place down there this morning.' Goater nodded to the narrow passageway through the Mansion House arch to the Guildhall. 'You'd no right, sir, to obstruct an officer in pursuit of his duty.'

'You could be hearing from me. I have your number.'

'And I have yours,' sneered Goater, until his colleague put an arresting hand on the stripes at his cuff.

'Where are you stationed now, Goater?' I asked, beginning to walk away.

'Jubbergate,' he roared defiantly after me.

'We'll meet again, Police Constable Goater, I am sure of that.' And I was, somehow even then I was.

Chapter Three

'You don't like people very much, do you, James?' Carlton-Bingham asked me back in chambers over late afternoon tea and sultana teacakes.

'No, not very much. Do you?'

'No, I don't,' admitted my boss with a bitter laugh that wasn't a laugh at all. 'I've never seen very much to commend the human race.'

'I've just had to intervene in an altercation.'

'Really?' Carlton-Bingham's eyes lit up with interest above his teacake.

'Yes, two coppers were about to beat a young woman senseless outside the Mansion House.'

'What had she done?'

'She and her friend were hoping to waylay councillors attending a meeting in the Guildhall this morning. They want women to stand in the district elections.'

'But they do have that right, don't they? Now we have the Parish and District Councils Act.'

'All the same you know as well as I do, sir, those old bores down at the Guildhall will have none of it.'

'How can you refer to our esteemed city fathers in such a derogatory fashion?'

'They will pull any trick they can to keep women out. We allow our sisters, wives and daughters to slog away doing charitable works. It is allowable for them to sit on Poor Law and School Boards, but however intelligent they might be they are precluded from any say in government merely because of their sex.'

'Don't be irate with me, James. I share your sympathy for the women's cause. Alas, it is a pity that the press as a whole does not.'

'Journalists are men.'

'Indeed. But they sell their papers by reflecting popular public opinion.'

'Male opinion.'

'Without enlightened men aboard women's suffrage will never achieve its objective.'

'Tell me this though, sir. Whatever their beliefs how can men physically ill-treat women in the appalling fashion I have just witnessed?'

'They always have. Remember the terrible destiny of Margaret Clitherow.'

'I confess I am not familiar with that name or her destiny.'

'When Henry VIII parted from the Roman Catholic Church, he divided England, leaving his daughter Elizabeth with a terrible legacy. In 1571, a fifteen year old girl called Margaret Middleton married a wealthy York butcher John Clitherow, and bore him three children. At the age of eighteen, she converted to Roman Catholicism. Though remaining a Protestant, her husband was supportive. John's own brother was a Roman Catholic clergyman. Her son, Henry, went to Reims to train as a priest and Margaret often held secret Masses in her home in the Shambles for likeminded people. She even had a hole cut between the attic of her house and the house next door for the persecuted padre to escape if there was a raid.'

'A woman of conviction.'

'Indeed. However, in 1586, Margaret was arrested and brought before the assizes at the Guildhall for harbouring priests. She refused to contest the indictment, knowing that her children would have been tortured and made to testify against their will. On Good Friday two reluctant sergeants, who were responsible for carrying out the sentence of the court, hired four desperate beggars instead. Margaret was taken to the toll booth on Ouse Bridge, stripped naked, and a handkerchief was tied across her face. The beggars spread her out on her back across a sharp rock the size of a man's fist. A door was placed on top of her and slowly loaded with an immense weight of rocks and stones. The sharp rock beneath her eventually broke her back. She died in agony fifteen minutes later.'

'Another perfect example of man's inhumanity. Is it any wonder that women are rising up against male oppression?'

'Still don't forget, James, it was a woman on the throne of England at the time. Elizabeth I, perhaps our greatest monarch despite her paternity. However she did write to the people of York expressing her horror at the treatment of a fellow woman. Due to her sex, Margaret should never have been executed in such a manner.'

'I believe, sir, Queen Elizabeth's Catholic half-sister, Mary Tudor, was not beyond a little religious tyranny herself.'

'Ah, Bloody Mary and her Protestant torches,' acknowledged my boss. 'If you haven't heard of Margaret Clitherow then I suspect you will not know the earlier story of the evangelical Valentine Freez, son of one of the first Dutch immigrant book printers into this city. He refused to accept transubstantiation, the changing of bread and wine into the body and blood of Christ. Freez and his wife were burnt at the stake on the Knavesmire during the reign of Mary Tudor.'

'Will we ever learn?' With his usual intuitiveness, Carlton-Bingham had done well to pick up on my scepticism regarding mankind.

'God forbid, we always nearly leave it too late. Whatever our religion, our gender, we are a species, a species in need of much improvement.'

'Then you are an evolutionist rather than creationist, sir?'

'I am a great compromiser.'

After witnessing the violence against Winifred Holbrook in St Helen's Square, I was not sure I could consider myself a midway man anymore. Oppression upon oppression — York has taught me well. But this is my city, this is why I love and hate it all in one. Roman, Viking, Norman, the medieval period layered upon layer. Great acts of chivalry and cruelty have been perpetrated within its walls, its alleyways have run with both passion and blood. Stroke the summer warm, the winter cold stones of York and you can sense history oozing out of them.

'Are you all right, James?' Carlton-Bingham's steady voice again. 'You look a little peaky.'

'Fine. I'm fine.' We munched our teacakes in silence.

* * * * *

We live to fight another day, another case. The previous night had been clear and cold, the sky full of milk and tears. The air remained fresh outside the morning courthouse. In contrast, whatever the weather, the robing room was always close and fetid. There was little water for washing and only a few scattered towels on which to dry one's hands and face. I took up my horsehair wig, leaving my comb inside its tin for any post-courtroom adjustments. The communal combs that were provided for the purpose were filthy.

That morning's courtroom was peopled by characters best described as belonging to one of Mr Dickens' novels. My client, a local York landlady, waited patiently in the dock. Her plump ringed hands rested casually on the balustrade. The odd nervous tic in one cheek, the only indication of her true terror of the occasion. With her husband she ran one of the smaller public houses in York, where I was an occasional visitor. Standing behind the small taproom counter, Florrie Cary always struck me as an imposing figure, a woman who wouldn't suffer any nonsense from her drunken clientele. In the dock today however, sporting her best feather hat for luck, Florrie looked almost diminutive, insignificant.

Not so Aggie Wright, her London cousin and co-accused, dressed in a sequined plum skirt. Men could not take their eyes off her, although Aggie seemed unaware that she was the centre of attention. She rustled and writhed in the confining box only a few feet away from Florrie. Court appearances were not new to Aggie, nonetheless she always felt restless waiting her turn to come up before the beak.

'All rise!' The words of the clerk of court rang out like a gun firing for the off, and in glided his Honour Judge Samuel Thrums.

'Oh no, not Thrums,' Trotter whispered. 'You didn't tell me it was him.'

'Would it have mattered?' I snapped back under my breath. 'To hear you talk none of them are any good anyway.'

'But Thrums,' muttered the disgruntled Trotter.

My client, Florrie, clung to the balustrade as if her life depended on it. In contrast Aggie screwed up her face, regarding his honour with as much distaste as Trotter.

The gaunt figure of John Smedley rose like a crane fly to his feet for the Crown. John Smedley always struck me more as a university academic in appearance than a prosecuting counsel. Smedley did a lot of hill walking over the Yorkshire Wolds.

He called various assistants to say that items had gone missing following the visits of the defendants, Florrie Cary, Agnes Wright and her daughter to their stores. And surely there was no way that my client, Florrie, could not have been privy to the thefts standing right next to her cousin during these visits.

I had heard enough. With a flick of my gown, I swooped into my cross-examination.

'But did you yourself, Miss Green, witness Mrs Agnes Wright secreting the bangles and rings about her person before she left your shop?' I asked.

'No, no I did not.' The young jewellery assistant shook her head on its spindly neck. Her curtain of blonde hair shook too, rather fetchingly I thought.

'Had the defendant, Florrie Cary, been in your shop before?'

'Many times.'

'The defendant was well known to you then?'

'Yes, I've know Mrs Cary for years. She always buys her rings from us.'

'And in all that time have you ever suspected Mrs Cary of being a thief?'

'No, definitely not.'

'Have any jewellery items ever gone missing following these other visits of Mrs Cary?'

'No, sir,' she replied.

Resuming my seat, I watched with a smidgen of regret as the blonde hair exited the courtroom. The Crown's next witness was a less glamorous Police Sergeant Owen Howell. Howell began to deliver his testimony in an attractive Welsh accent. He said he had observed from a doorway in Market Street, a young woman with a child pressed into an alleyway between two buildings. He saw the woman, Agnes Wright, open her coat and remove jewellery pieces from a secret pocket before giving them to the child to hold.

'Exhibit Five, your honour.' Smedley pointed across to the exhibit table. 'Perhaps the jury would like to take a look at Agnes Wright's specially designed coat.'

Thrums nodded to the usher.

'This isn't Mrs Cary's coat, I hesitate to point out to the jury,' I interceded quickly.

'I think we all realise that, Mr Cairn,' said Thrums.

'Can you tell me, Sergeant Howell, was the defendant, Florrie Cary, with her cousin and the child in the alleyway?' Smedley pointed across to my forlorn client.

'No, sir,' admitted Howell. 'After visiting several shops together, they had separated at the time. I followed Agnes and her girl to Low Ouse Gate where they stopped on the bridge as if waiting for someone. I decided to apprehend the pair. Florrie Cary only arrived back when that woman over there (pointing to Aggie) and her girl were resisting arrest. I whistled for reinforcements.'

'Am I not right in thinking that you had been following Agnes Wright and her daughter for days? In fact hadn't you been following them since they'd got off the London train in York?'

'Yes, sir, we had been alerted by New Scotland Yard that Agnes Wright was on her way up to our area.'

'And hadn't you taken the trouble to forewarn the defendant, Florrie Cary, about her London cousin's shoplifting reputation?'

'Yes, sir, I told Mrs Cary to get rid of Aggie and her daughter as soon as she could. I told her Aggie was bad news.'

'So Agnes Wright was staying under the defendant's roof, was she?'

'Yes, sir, at Mrs Cary's public house.'

'The defendant was knowingly harbouring a criminal.'

'Objection, your honour!' I couldn't get to my feet quick enough. 'The defendant's co-accused, Mrs Agnes Wright, has no previous convictions for theft.'

'Only because she's never been caught,' muttered Howell.

'Your objection is upheld, Mr Cairn. The jury will disregard this unfounded allegation. In due course, I am sure we will hear Mrs Agnes Wright speak up in her own defence.'

'Thank you, Sergeant.' A frowning Smedley resumed his seat.

'Tell me, Sergeant Howell, having followed this trio on all their various shopping trips, did you ever see Mrs Cary physically steal anything?' I asked. The sergeant shook his head. 'Is that a "no", Sergeant Howell?'

'Yes, sir.'

'Did you ever see Agnes Wright steal anything?'

'Objection!' jumped up agile Smedley. 'This line of questioning is irrelevant at this point in time. It is Florrie Cary who is here to answer at present.'

'Mr Cairn?' enquired Thrums.

'I think at this juncture we have to ascertain whether a crime has been committed, your honour.'

'Please answer counsel's question, Sergeant Howell,'Thrums said wearily.

'No, Aggie is a total professional. It's like sleight-of-hand with her. I doubt that anyone could ever see her pocketing anything.'

'And that includes her own cousin, the defendant, does it not?' Lifting my tails with a flourish, I didn't wait for Howell's answer but took my seat.

'You can stand down for now,' Thrums ordered the dejected looking sergeant.

'But what about the stuff I saw Aggie give her girl, your honour?' cried Howell in disbelief.

'Nothing was found on Agnes Wright's daughter back at the police station, was it?' I asked, on my feet again. 'Nothing was found on Florrie Cary either.'

'But the shop assistants,' spluttered Howell. 'Every time those three went into a shop items went missing immediately afterwards.'

'Sergeant Howell, you are dismissed,'Thrums told him firmly.

'Call Thomas Barnet,' cried the clerk of court. 'Thomas Barnet.'The call ran down the long corridor outside.

I saw an expression of exasperation pass from red-faced sergeant to constable as they crossed in the well of the courtroom.

'I am a police constable stationed at Jubbergate Police Station in the city of York,' began Barnet.

'Yes, yes,' muttered Thrums irritably, causing Barnet to hesitate a second.

'While patrolling my beat along Fetter Lane on Saturday afternoon, the eighteenth of November last, I was summoned by Sergeant Owen Howell's whistle to an altercation between him, two women and a young girl in Bridge Street,' continued the unfazed Barnet, reading from his little black book.

'So, by the time you reached the confrontation between Sergeant Howell and the women, the struggle had moved off the bridge itself,' clarified Smedley.

'Yes, sir, members of the public had forced all parties to move off the bridge as they were causing an obstruction for both pedestrians and vehicles.'

'Sounds more like a scene from Hogarth. Pity you didn't get there earlier.' I couldn't resist making a theatrical aside from my seat. Someone in the public gallery with good hearing laughed.

'Mr Cairn,' warned Thrums.

'And how were these three females acting when you arrived? Suspiciously, would you say?' continued Smedley undaunted.

'They were all clinging to each other like a bag of screeching cats.'

'Now that is a scene from Hogarth,' whispered Trotter.

'I see,' said Smedley, quietly mulling over the policeman's vivid description.

'And the sergeant was right in the middle of it, trying to separate them in vain,' added Barnet.

'Really,' said Smedley, smiling that introverted smile of his. 'No doubt getting clawed for his efforts.'

'Indeed he was, sir.'

'Why did you arrest Mrs Cary, Constable Barnet?' I asked, re-arranging my notes.

'She would not allow us to take the girl into custody with her mother, sir.'

'So, it was merely because the defendant wanted to protect Mrs Wright's young daughter from a prison cell that you arrested her?'

'Yes, sir,' muttered the constable. 'She was resisting arrest.'

'Umm, so the defendant stands before this court not for theft but for resisting arrest, is that what you are saying, Constable?'

'No, sir, not exactly. Sergeant Howell told me later that the three of 'em had been in shops where goods had been stolen.'

'So, you arrested Florrie Cary for theft in retrospect, is that not so?'

'The sergeant saw them…'

'No, he did not,' I interrupted. 'Sergeant Howell testified that he did not see the women physically steal anything.'

The case for the prosecution was over. Thrums called a short break. I was about to present my one and only witness who I hoped would clear up this mess once and for all.

'Call Clara Wright!' A pale, thin sheepish looking child of about ten years of age was sworn in. Clara Wright's voice was little more than a squeak. She ran her small damp hands down the front of her brown dress.

'All *Wright* nothing *wrong*, eh,' whispered Trotter mischievously.

'Now tell me, Miss Wright, do you know the lady over there?' I pointed across to Florrie in the dock. Clara nodded.

'Say "yes" or "no",' Thrums instructed the child.

'Y… yes,' said Clara hesitantly, mouse-like.

'Do you like the lady over there?' I asked gently.

'Yes,' Clara said guardedly with a little more conviction.

'My good friend, counsel for the prisoner, is leading the child, your honour,' objected Smedley.

'She is only a child,' I countered.

'Please be good enough to continue, Mr Cairn,' snapped Thrums, who seemed to be approaching the point of no return himself.

'Do you like pretty things?'

'Yes,' said Clara, looking down in dismay at her plain brown dress. Obviously her mother did not lavish as much attention on her daughter's appearance as she did her own, or the dress was merely another of Aggie's clever theatrical props.

'Did Mrs Cary ever give you pretty things, bangles, rings and the like?'

Clara shook her head.

'What did Mrs Cary give you then?' I asked quickly before his honour could intervene.

'Ham and eggs,' squeaked Clara, who looked as if she could do with a few more plates of Mrs Cary's ham and eggs.

'What did the child say?' asked Thrums.

'She said "ham and eggs", your honour.' An amused chuckle could be heard in the gallery.

'Silence!' exploded Thrums.

'Does your mamma give you pretty things from time to time?' I tried to make the question sound innocuous. Clara buttoned up her lips. She was up to the trick. She looked across to her mother in the strange box for guidance. Aggie gave her daughter the hard stare before returning to the examination of her own fidgeting fingernails. Clara didn't like seeing her mother penned. She did not care for being corralled up in this box thing herself. She saw all these strange wigged men looking at her and she didn't like them either. 'Well,' I insisted.

'Does Mother say so?' articulated Clara in a strong London accent.

'Does Mother say what?' I asked in amazement. The child made no attempt to answer. 'Did your mother give you anything to look after on the bridge when the policemen came.'

'Does Mother say so?' repeated Clara.

'Did you throw anything in the water from the bridge when you saw the police sergeant coming?'

'Does Mother say so?' Clara was primed like a parrot.

'Try to answer Mr Cairn's questions, my dear,' cajoled Thrums.

'If Mother…' Clara's forehead puckered doubtfully making her look much older. Once more she glanced across at her mother for guidance. Once more caged Aggie looked down at her polished nails. She wasn't about to give her daughter the say-so, the go-ahead on anything. Aggie wanted to get out of this stinking hole of a place, get back to her adopted London. London was a big city where she could ply her skills more safely, be easily absorbed. Even the bobbies there had respect for her.

'Would your mother not say you have to tell the truth, the whole truth, at all times?' I asked desperately. Clara looked about her in bewilderment. Her previously buttoned lips began to quiver. 'Well?' I persisted. I wasn't about to let a child stand in the way of freedom for an innocent woman.

'… Mother say so,' simpered Clara, a child again.

'I think we have gone as far as we can with this, Mr Cairn,' announced Thrums. 'You can step down now, Miss Wright.'

'But, your honour,' gasped Smedley.

'Enough, Mr Smedley. Gentlemen of the jury, never be under the misapprehension that the law takes thieves lightly. Indeed it is within living memory that convicts of either sex were either hanged or, at best, transported to the Antipodes for life for stealing a yard of cloth let alone expensive jewellery. There is no legal or moral justification for stealing from businesses. It is the same as stealing from the individual. But in this case the Crown has failed to provide one shred of evidence that the defendant was engaged in or was an accomplice to theft.' His Honour Judge Thrums turned to the jury and instructed them to bring in a verdict of not guilty on Florrie Cary, while reminding them that there was another female defendant waiting to be heard in this case and the same verdict must undoubtedly apply to her. 'The defendant is in your charge,' he told them. 'Please confer among yourselves and choose a foreman.'

'Not guilty!' announced the foreman without the jury troubling to retire.

'Case dismissed,' Thrums told the sparsely peopled courtroom.

'Been on any good walks lately, John?' I shouted across to Smedley.

'Recently, when I got lost half way through one but found the right path home eventually,' he replied, giving me one of those secret smiles of his.

'A good result then.' I smiled back. I liked John Smedley.

'Yes, a good result,' he agreed.

'Do you know much about Jubbergate Police Station?' I asked Trotter the next morning in chambers.

'No more than you do, sir, I expect,' mumbled Trotter, preoccupied with rearranging a handful of documents. 'Why?'

'I know it's one of the city's main police stations, of course. But I've recently heard its name mentioned so many times in so many days.'

'I believe it was where Reverend Hobb was first taken following his arrest. Perhaps that's why it has lodged in your mind, sir.'

'Was it really?'

'Was it really what, sir?'

'The first place George Hobb was taken dressed in drag.'

'Yes, sir, I remember it coming up at the police court with Mr Turner presiding.'

'But I wasn't there, Trotter.'

'No, but that piece of information must be in the Hobb's memorandum brief somewhere.'

'That's strange, I can't find it anywhere.'

'Let me take a look,' offered Trotter, slapping his own documents onto my desk. 'Yes, see, here it is. Two pages have got slightly stuck together. The arresting officer was a Constable Gruelthorpe stationed at Jubbergate.'

'Good, good,' I said, smarting at my own incompetence. Martin Trotter's ability to find things, things I could not find, galled me at times.

'I remember now,' said Trotter, still peering down on the memorandum. 'The Reverend became very agitated about discussing his overnight confinement there.'

Chapter Four

It was ten o'clock in the morning and I stood with Brown in the dark Castle cell which had changed little in six decades, certainly no improvements had been made since the recent incarceration of my previous client, Daniel Robertshaw.

The strident trilling of a territorial robin penetrated through the high barred window – a sound made all the more sad for that. *Brripp—brripp—brripp.* I was reminded of another song, a new bird winging its way through the sky. The previous March, Guglielmo Marconi had sent the first wireless message some thirty-one miles across the English Channel and yet I was still faced with this – this medieval scene. The "it", which it was now proposed I should represent, had metamorphosed in the course of only a few days from the grotesque into something even more pitiable.

Hobb snivelled and moaned in the dirt on the floor, still in his now tattered dress. I felt sick in the pit of my stomach, not out of any abhorrence for Hobb himself but because he had been reduced to this by the questionable actions of other men.

'Pull yourself together, man. Mr Cairn, here, has come to interview you,' Brown told him. Hobb continued snivelling and moaning.

'He's been like this since the police surgeon examined him. Took three of us to hold him in position,' explained the warder. Hobb sobbed louder at the memory of this ultimate humiliation.

'Sounds more like an assault than an examination,' I said, alert to the legal possibilities. 'And they failed to notify you that this was going to take place,' I turned to Brown.

Brown nodded. 'The surgeon arrived at eleven o'clock at night.'

'But surely the police needed some solid evidence that a sexual offence had taken place?'

'Seems they felt they had it. At that stage I doubt my objection would have carried much weight anyway,' shrugged Brown.

'We'll see about that,' I muttered under my breath.

'I must say it amazes me the power the law seems to have under this new legislation.'

'But, on the other hand, Oscar Wilde would have hanged as a sodomite under Henry VIII's Buggery Act of 1533.'

'Indeed. Captain Henry Nicholl was the last man to hang for that offence in England, was he not?'

'No, no, he was hanged around 1833, I believe. Smith and Pratt were executed in '35. And the death penalty for sodomy was only actually lifted thirty-eight years ago.'

'I see you're both extremely well-informed on this base subject,' came a faltering whisper from the floor. 'But my only crime is to wear a dress.'

'I know, I know.' I rested a consoling hand on the Reverend's matted wig. 'By the way, Trotter's very much on board for this one now,' I told Brown, in an attempt to lift the occasion. 'Somehow you must have won him over, a great achievement, you have my utmost admiration.'

'Good, good,' replied Brown, before lowering a concerned look on Hobb. 'But what are we to do, Cairn?'

'Reverend, Reverend,' I knelt down beside the distressed cleric and managed to prise open his clenched fist and press my handkerchief into it. 'Try to calm yourself, sir. Now would you like me to represent you before a higher court, and see if we can overturn some of the injustices that have already been meted out to you?'

Hobb looked up to Mr Brown for direction, childlike.

'The final decision is yours, George, but what Mr Cairn is proposing makes sense. You either fight this case or you are forever condemned as a pedlar of the most gross perversion, and you will most certainly lose your living.' Brown was unequivocal.

'To be convicted of buggery is a serious matter,' I added for good measure.

'Buggery?' Hobb looked lost. 'I've told you I know nothing of such things.'

'Yes, sir, but that is what we fear they are proposing to indict you with.' I cleared my throat with embarrassment at Hobb's obvious naivety.

'They'll do their best to present a case against you with some dreamed up, mumbo-jumbo forensic evidence, and any conciliatory rent boy willing to lie in exchange for a lighter sentence. Seen it all before,' said Brown.

'So, what's it to be? Plead guilty to something of which I presume you have no knowledge? Or,' I added, trying to imbue my words with confidence, 'shall we fight?'

Hobb shook his head in disbelief. 'We fight,' he gulped.

'Where are you staying?'

'I have a room at an inn on Low Petergate,' Hobb replied.

I turned back to Brown. 'Take my advice and send a man straight round to his lodgings in Low Petergate to retrieve the Reverend's luggage. Then have him washed and out of that dress for the next magistrate's committal hearing. I want him clothed as if he were awaiting an audience with the primate of York himself.'

* * * * *

'Let there be light,' I muttered to myself, my right thumb nervously pressing the ring tab button for greater illumination.

'Amazing, the prisoner's transformation, wouldn't you say, sir?' asked the warder.

'Truly remarkable,' I agreed. My recently acquired portable light picked out the details of a seated figure at the rickety regulation table. The Reverend wore a dark jacket, black waistcoat and dog collar, with trousers bearing a distinct crease. He was clean shaven and gone was the blond wig, replaced by a neat head of short auburn curls. Though still rather effeminate in appearance, I would say George Hobb was a very good-looking man – a youthful man for his forty some years.

'What on earth have you got there?' Hobb asked me, shielding his eyes from the flashlight.

'This,' I explained, looking down on the tubular instrument now disappointingly extinguished, 'was given to me by a New York policeman on a recent visit to America.'

I noticed that Hobb's face paled. In contrast the warder asked all wide-eyed, 'You've been to America then?'

'Expect Mr Cairn's been everywhere, he's a very distinguished barrister.' Hobb still sounded subdued.

'I didn't think you'd taken in my name. You were in such a state earlier.'

'Bob reminded me, told me to expect you.'

'Bob?'

'Mr Robert Brown, my solicitor.'

'Of course, "Bob".'

'Prisoner Hobb has been allocated a new mattress for good behaviour,' announced the warder, pointing across to an undistinguishable lump against the shadowed wall.

'You mean he's finally complied with prison dress code.'

'Male prison dress code,' corrected the warder.

'What is your name?' I asked him.

'Crossman, sir.'

'Warder Crossman, would you be so good as to give me a minute or two alone with the prisoner?'

Clang! No sooner said than done, Crossman was gone.

Hobb started up from the table. 'My nerves are in tatters,' he complained.

'I'm glad to see Mr Brown has retrieved your luggage at least.'

'Bob insisted I dress in my other clothes.' He pointed dismissively to his valise on the floor.

'You look so much better in them.'

'Do I really? I'm not sure that I do.'

'I don't understand,' I said.

'I don't expect you to.'

Judging my battery rested enough I reapplied pressure on the ring tab to get a better view of my subject. 'If I am to represent you then I must have some understanding of your situation,' I explained, before the light went out again and Hobb's head sank lower onto his chest.

'Doesn't last long,' he mumbled.

'What does not last long?' I asked.

'Your light.'

'That's why it's called a flashlight. The zinc-carbon battery can only sustain the current for a short time.'

'Good thing too,' muttered Hobb, flouncing dramatically back on his newly acquired mattress.

'Why is it a "good thing"?'

'So that you can't see me dressed like this.'

'Dressed like a man, you mean?'

'Exactly. I feel more myself, more comfortable with soft satin against my skin rather than this prickly coarse serge. I hate this, hate it,' he hissed, tugging at his trouser leg in disgust.

'Are you telling me that by wearing female attire your purpose isn't to solicit or importune other men?'

'I'm not interested in any of that. I've already told you.'

'So why dress as a woman, want to be a woman, if you don't want a man?' I was struggling to make sense of it all.

'It's not about anyone else, about sexual encounters, it's about me.'

'Surely as a man you appreciate that you have greater power in our society.'

'Puh! Power. What power has the common man? I suppose you mean we have the right to vote,' scoffed Hobb. 'Don't know what Millie Fawcett and her fellow suffragists are on about. I suffer because I've the right to vote.'

'Does it not say in the bible that the woman shall not wear that which pertaineth unto a man, neither shall a man put on a woman's garment: for all that do so are abomination unto the Lord thy God?'

'Deuteronomy, chapter twenty-two, verse five. There is a lot of stoning to death as well in Deuteronomy.' Hobb smiled sadly at the personal irony of being stoned.

'You know it off by heart then.'

'By heart, chapter and verse.'

'So doesn't your behaviour go against your beliefs as an Anglican priest?'

'That was a political censure, written a long time ago, when promiscuity was rife in Canaan. And talking of priests, are we not like robed duchesses in tea-gowns anyway? And isn't Jesus himself always depicted with shoulder length hair and a dress down to the ground? Perhaps it is simply a question of fashion.' Hobb's laughter reverberated in hollow echoes round the cell.

'But not to you,' I pointed out. 'Dressing up in women's clothing is more a way of life to you than fashion. Such a need that you will risk life and limb for it, am I not right in that assumption?'

'You are right of course.' Hobb pinioned me with his eyes. 'I dress up as a woman because I am partly woman.'

How brave, I had come round to thinking, back at my desk in Bootham Chambers. How brave for a man to admit he feels himself to be partly woman. That to me, who had always led such a constrained life, was perhaps braver than the bravest soldier, more courageous than the most daring expeditionary, certainly more radical than anything that could have been dreamed up by anyone in my old school's boorish rugby fifteen.

'Trotter,' I screamed. Trotter came in at a run. 'Get me an appointment with the Archbishop of York's secretary.'

* * * * *

Tap, tap. The sound of echoing feet from an approaching robed figure beating out a greeting on the polished floor in harmony with my own expectant heart beat.

'Good to meet you. I'm the Reverend Samuel Phelps, dean and assistant to the Archbishop.'

'Oh,' I exclaimed, somewhat taken aback to be received by the Church's hierarchy. 'Very Gothic, isn't it?' I said, pointing up to the high-ceiling of the entrance in an attempt to collect my thoughts and hide my awkwardness.

'The original parts of the palace were built by Archbishop Walter de Grey in 1226.'

'That long ago?'

'But this entrance hall is certainly in the Gothic style. You are absolutely right about that. It was based on Horace Walpole's house at Strawberry Hill in Twickenham.'

'Ah! Strawberry Hill Gothic,' I laughed

'Exactly that.' Phelps' smile was temperate. 'Please be kind enough to follow me.'

Tap, tap. I followed him into a smaller room, a drawing room adorned with paintings of genial past archbishops.

'I think we will be more comfortable in here,' said Phelps. 'More private. Please be seated, Mr Cairn.' Again I looked to the ceiling before sinking into a low upholstered sofa chair. Though the weight was off my feet, I still did not feel comfortable. Indeed, I was beginning to feel profoundly uncomfortable with the dean and the clerical great and good staring down on me. 'You have an interest in ceilings, Mr Cairn, I can see that,' continued Phelps, gently lowering his willow-thin body into the chair opposite. 'This moulding was done by Guiseppe Cortese and the fireplace is Sicilian marble.' The lizard gaze remained fixed on my face.

'Wonderful,' I said with little conviction, my thoughts being back with my client in his small austere prison cell.

'The Reverend Doctor Hobb, you said in your letter that you wished to discuss his present unfortunate situation.'

'Yes, he is about to undergo a second hearing in the magistrates' court, but his sincere wish is to be represented by me in a higher court so that he can fully clear his name.'

'A higher court, you say. For us churchmen there is only one higher court and that is presided over by God alone.' The edges of Phelps' mouth lifted slightly but there was no amusement in his eyes.

'Yes, I know,' I sighed. 'But unless the Reverend is defended well, he could face a hefty prison sentence on earth.'

'So I understand. The police have already been here to interview us regarding that gentleman.'

'"That gentleman" but he is a priest, one of your own,' I pointed out, immediately seizing on Phelps' attempt to distance himself.

'The Reverend Doctor Hobb has always been considered a man of the highest intellect and we believed integrity.'

'That being the case will you vouch for him in court?'

'We are prepared to write a note for the magistrate stating that much.'

'But nobody from the Church will appear in person to testify to his good character?'

'We will write a note,' repeated Phelps.

'Hobb was only wearing a dress, God damn it.'

'Please.' Phelps raised a sanctimonious hand.

'*A dress*,' I reiterated.

'Not according to the police.'

'What do you mean?'

'According to them there is a lot more involved than a dress. You must appreciate, Mr Cairn, the Reverend Doctor Hobb was only a visitor to us here in York.'

'What business did he have with you to come all this way from the Isle of Wight to Yorkshire?'

'Wouldn't you be better asking your client that question?' pointed out Phelps, not unreasonably.

'I will, I will,' I excused myself, hands up. 'I've just not got around to it yet. We've had more important things to discuss so far, fashion accessories, that sort of thing.'

Phelps' solemn expression did not falter at my sarcasm. 'The Reverend is from away. How can we be expected to give a full character reference to someone we do not intimately know?'

'And a note regarding Hobb's intellect is as far as the Church is prepared to go.'

'That is as far as we can go.'

'I see,' I said, disappointed.

'You must appreciate our position, Mr Cairn.' Phelps unfurled on to his briefly exposed pointed toed boots. 'By the way, do you know I believe there is a Mrs Hobb somewhere?' With that Phelps turned on his heels and I was left staring up at the Cortese ceiling as if awaiting some enlightenment from heaven.

* * * * *

'You are to go before Mr Turner tomorrow.' I shook my extinguished flashlight in frustration.

'Will you be there?' asked Hobb. The chair scraped on the floor as he turned from the table.

I shook my head. 'Not at this stage but Mr Brown will be representing you and I'll send Trotter along to report back to me.'

'Trotter will be delighted about that.' Hobb was obviously a man who caught on quickly.

'Trotter will do as he is told,' I told him sharply. 'Now, are you sure you want to take your case to a higher court?'

'If found guilty by the magistrates' court, how much time can I expect to spend in gaol?'

'A couple of months with hard labour.'

'Is that all?'

'No, that isn't all. What about your reputation and vocation in the Church? I've already talked to them about you, they'll not accept a convicted felon back as a priest. And that's not the half of it,' I hesitated.

'So, what is the other half of it?' asked Hobb, more in panic than amusement.

'I fear the Crown has a choice of two pieces of uncompromising legislation on which to convict you.'

'Which are?'

'The Vagrancy Act and Labouchere Amendment.'

'I am not a vagrant and who is Labouchere?'

'Henry Du Pre Labouchere. The Liberal MP. Haven't you ever heard of him?'

'No, and I am not sure he sounds too liberal to me.'

'Well, compared to older sodomy laws that proscribe death or life imprisonment, his amendment might be regarded by some as fairly lenient.'

'But not by you?'

'It has been dubbed "the blackmailer's charter" because it was used to convict Oscar Wilde in '95.'

'"Oscar Wilde",' exclaimed Hobb horrified. 'I'm no Oscar Wilde as I have repeatedly told you. He got two years hard labour in Reading Gaol, did he not? I heard it broke the poor fellow.' I nodded. 'So, what does this Labouchere Amendment say exactly? What can I be accused of?'

'It is an offence to try and procure another man to commit an act of gross indecency with you either in private or public.'

Hobb stared at me in disbelief but not, I suspected, because he was impressed by my feat of memory.

'I've said all along, I've never tried to procure any man for sexual purposes,' he gasped.

'I know, I know,' I reassured him. 'But that is what they might try to throw at you.'

'But why?'

'To make an example of you, of course. They feel too many men of letters, theatricals, artists and the like were too sympathetic to Oscar Wilde's plight.'

'Who are *they*?'

'The Establishment of course. See, here, would you like to keep this by your side?' I offered Hobb my flashlight. He ran the instrument thoughtfully through his hand. 'The light is so bad in here. That high window offers little or no illumination, and the gaslight out in the passage less when your door is bolted and the food hatch closed.'

'Ah, but wasn't this your present from the New York police force?'

'Don't trouble yourself over that.'

'What were they like?

'What were who like?'

'The New York police.'

'Tough. Very tough and mainly Irish.'

'I see,' brooded Hobb.

'Regarding policemen, am I to understand you were apprehended by officers from the Jubbergate station?'

'Yes, why?'

'Did the officers rough you up at all?'

'A bit.' The admission was said in a whisper. I decided to leave it at that for now.

'Keep the flashlight.' I closed his finger round the cylinder. 'It will give you some brightness from time to time.'

'Thank you,' he said. 'But I am hoping to spend as little time in here as possible. Do you think the magistrate will grant me bail?'

'I would imagine so, this second time.'

'The only problem is I am not a rich man as you can see. I am not sure I'll be able to afford you, Mr Cairn.'

'Let's not worry about that for the moment. Bootham Chambers' main interest in this case is to test the law.' Hobb looked a little crestfallen at my revelation of self-interest. 'Which might be used to ensnare you,' I added

'This Labouchere sounds like someone who should be manning the guillotine.'

'We'll do our best to avoid the blade.'

'Let's hope so.'

'Tell me, Reverend, the dean seems to think you're a family man. Could not your wife, or your wife's relatives, or indeed some relative on your side of the family stand bail should the tariff be set beyond your means?'

Hobb stared back at me as if I had just stabbed him through the heart. 'My wife is long since dead,' he said, fiddling nervously with the flashlight tab. 'There is no one.'

'No one?' I asked in amazement.

'No one.'

Chapter Five

Summer moved on – tree blossom withered, browned and fell – as I moved in and out of court. I defended husbands kicking wives and wives kicking husbands. The weather had grown warmer, and I wondered if this surge in domestic violence was all due to the weather. I failed to defend Sally, the flower girl, who, as well as picking flowers from public parks and people's gardens, supplemented her income by picking a few of her gentlemen clients' pockets too. I had wondered if she was related to my previous pick-pocketing client, William Huddleston, but she wasn't.

My most interesting case by far was a soldier, Thomas Munster, who was accused of stealing women's shoes off market stalls, from ladies' shops, even off cobblers' worktops. My father wrote a letter to me just before he was killed, I still have it. He talked about something called fetishism in darkest Africa – I have heard the term used in a political sense by Karl Marx – but it seems we have it here, here in York. Sergeant Thomas Munster has it. The police found over a dozen pairs of ladies' shoes in his lodging room at Fulford Barracks. Perhaps I could have argued some logical reason for their presence, for the theft, if Munster had been married, or had a lady friend, or a sister, or daughter even. But a committed bachelor, fifty-year-old Munster had enjoyed none of these things.

'Munster has had a lifetime of service to Queen and country. That is his problem,' I explained to his Honour Judge Crispin Fox.

'In what way, Mr Cairn?' His honour sniffed the air of the packed court, sniffed like the old fox he was scenting a chicken.

'He has never been exposed to the gentle company of the fairer sex. His sole connection with ladies has been his addiction to their footwear,'

'That's right, that's right, your honour.' Munster roared his agreement from the dock.

'Silence,' hissed Fox. 'Or I'll have you taken down here and now.'

'Has the defendant not been punished enough, your honour, without a custodial sentence?' I grovelled my appeal. 'He can never return to the barracks which has served as his home for all these years.'

'That's right, your honour, I am nothing more than a laughing stock to all the boys now,' interrupted my client again.

'You should have thought of that before,' spelt out Fox in his best clipped English voice.

'I understand that Sergeant Munster is about to be dismissed from the army in light of his guilty plea, even though he might be needed in Africa,' I added a little desperately. I seemed to have Africa on the brain.

'Africa! Africa! What on earth has Africa to do with the defendant's predisposition to women's footwear, counsel?'

'The Boer, your honour, the Boer are causing trouble in Transvaal again.'

'I don't think we need a political history lesson from you, Mr Cairn.' Fox turned narrowed eyes back on Munster in the dock. 'Why did you steal these shoes in the first place. What is your foot size?' asked Fox, to the guffaws of one or two gentlemen of the press who had decided to stay out of sheer bravado for they surely had missed that night's deadline for a comic piece.

'Eleven, sir,' obliged Munster.

'Eleven? So what does a big fellow like you want with a flimsy pair of women's slippers like those over there?' Fox pointed to the exhibit table.

'It's an illness, your honour. He just likes looking at them, touching them,' I did my best to explain the justifications previously presented to me by my client. 'It's the only connection he has with ladies, the only interaction he is capable of.'

'Do you not think a more likely explanation is that your client stole them merely to sell them on?' asked the uncompromising Fox.

'No, your honour, I truly believe Sergeant Munster's urge to possess women's footwear is beyond his control.'

'Harbouring such an insane desire, do you not consider that the defendant might be a danger to womenfolk?'

'No, your honour, I believe him to be harmless.'

'Harmless? Harmless to the public in general?'

'Yes, your honour.'

'And what about those who catch him in the act of thieving? He is a strong and powerful man, a trained soldier. Could he not do harm to them?'

'Sergeant Munster has no criminal record for assault, your honour.'

'Umm!' sighed Fox with a wry smile. Adding in an undertone, 'Yes, I hear you, Mr Cairn, the defendant is "harmless" like those men who wear dresses, I don't doubt.' He turned back to the dock, increasing the volume of his voice. 'Some thirty years ago, I would have had no hesitation in having you transported for this. Three years hard labour for you, Sergeant Munster, you are a disgrace to Her Majesty's uniform.'

After sentencing, six foot moustachioed Munster, who had served in the army for the best part of his life, broke down sobbing like a girl as a warder edged him back from the dock.

'Did I hear correctly?' I whispered across to Trotter. 'Did his honour make reference to men who wear dresses?' Trotter nodded. 'How on earth does Fox know I am about to defend George Hobb? Who could have told him?'

'Plenty of people, I wouldn't wonder,' replied I-told-you so Trotter. 'I did warn you, sir, a little more discrimination regarding the cases you take on would not go amiss.'

'You did. Nevertheless, I feel the courts are dealing too harshly with men such as these, men who are not securely anchored to their sex. Look how the system has destroyed a genius like poor Oscar Wilde.'

'All the same, sir, you are going to get a reputation for defending such cases. It'll all end in tears just like Mr Wilde, mark my words,' muttered Trotter, buttoning up his overcoat against the night.

'So you keep reminding me, Trotter.'

'By the way, sir, that lady up there in the public gallery handed me a note for you.'

'What lady?' I followed the line of Trotter's pointing finger towards the end of one of the public benches. The lady smiled down at me. She was resplendent in a dark velvet feathered hat. I did not recognise her at first until I saw the colour of her curls peeping beneath the brim. Then I remembered her, remembered her name. Winifred Holbrook mouthed a "bravo" and blew me a surprising kiss with her delicate hands. Surprising? – surprising for an ardent woman of suffrage.

I resisted opening Miss Holbrook's note in front of the inquisitive Trotter but saved it for home. Written in a rounded flowing hand, it was an invitation to high tea at her parents' home a week on Sunday.

Unknowingly, Judge Crispin Fox had given me food for thought too. Was there a link in the unusual urges of Sergeant Munster and the Reverend George Hobb? It would take someone of the magnitude of this up and coming Austrian physician we keep hearing so much about – it would take a Sigmund Freud to unlock the mystery. Nevertheless, from the failure of my Munster defence, I realised I had to try to give some rationale for Hobb's behaviour or he would most certainly be destroyed by a prison sentence of hard labour, and Trotter's pessimistic prediction would certainly come to fruition.

* * * * *

'You were absolutely right, sir, in fearing they would throw the book at the Reverend.'

'So what has Mr Turner come up with against Hobb at the behest of his legal masters, Trotter?'

'He accused the Reverend of persistently soliciting and importuning other males for immoral purposes in a public place.'

'The amended Vagrancy Act,' I sighed. 'I thought so.'

'That's not all. He said that a Reverend G. Hobb had already appeared before a Nottingham magistrate for a similar offence.'

'Nobody mentioned anything about this to me. Did Brown ever speak of this to you, Trotter?'

'No. He knew nothing about it. It seems Hobb was bound over to keep the peace back in the 1880s.'

'Don't tell me, he caused a riot by wearing petticoats at the Goose Fair.'

'No, no, it was a lot more dramatic than that. The petticoated Reverend got involved in a fight with the proprietor of an ale-house when he was asked to leave. It seems the landlord threw the first punch but the Reverend threw the last. The landlord came off worst and was kept in hospital for a week with a badly broken jaw. Hobb was lucky, the magistrate found that it was he who was severely provoked by someone considered locally to be a roughneck.'

'It seems there is a lot more to George Hobb than at first meets the eye.'

'You could say that, sir.'

'For a man of the cloth he certainly seems to have a taste for the low life.'

'An habitué of such premises, one might say, sir.'

'Exactly so.'

'Now, sir, are you ready for the really bad news?'

'You mean it gets worse?'

'As instructed by his client, Mr Brown chose for the case to be heard in a higher court before a jury.'

'And?'

'Mr Turner set bail at two hundred pounds.'

'Two hundred pounds! You are joking, Trotter.'

'Alas, sir, I am not. The Reverend George Hobb has been returned to the Castle.'

* * * * *

'Mr Brown and I will have to see if we can raise bail on your behalf,' I told Hobb a few days later. 'If we can then you will be free to go once it is paid and accepted by the court.'

'Will I?' he asked, paint-less lips ajar in disbelief.

'Yes, but you must supply the court and me with a permanent address for all future hearings.'

'Oh, I will, I will. Thank you for putting your trust in me, such cynical times we live in.'

'Yes, such cynical times,' I repeated; an inkling of doubt stabbing my chest wall.

'I think I'll return to the Isle of Wight.'

'Reverend, I haven't raised your bail money yet.'

'Oh, you will, I know you will. I have perfect faith in you, Mr Cairn.'

'I don't suppose you know of any benefactor who would post bail for you. A friend say?'

Hobb shook his head slowly from side to side like a puppet. It suddenly struck me how out of touch with reality this man was.

I was glad to be outside in the air again free of Hobb's gender fixation; free of his intolerable situation; free of the prison's high confining outer wall, a dark millstone wall which now encircled the remaining keep of a once royal palace. Standing in a solitary corner of the new prison, old prison, law court complex, I stared across to Clifford's Tower atop its motte of grass and spilt blood. This tower served as a reminder of how easily the scales of justice can be bent into the service of those with power. Little consolation in this tale for mankind, here was the scene of a historic injustice. Indeed, the drama that took place within Clifford's Tower's original wooded construction takes on biblical significance – Masada significance – and is one of the most shameful periods in my adopted city's murderous history.

Back in 1190 a certain "gentleman", Richard de Malbis, was in debt to Aaron of Lincoln, an influential Jewish Banker. A fire broke out in the city of York, and de Malbis used the incident to incite a mob to attack the home of a recently deceased agent of Aaron's called Benedict of York. The mob killed Benedict's widow and children and burnt their house to the ground. The leader of the Jews in York, Josce, sought sanctuary for his people in York Castle, fearing a holocaust in this anti-Semitic time of Richard the Lionheart's third crusade. A hostile crowd soon surrounded them outside and once the warden had left the castle, he found the Jews would not readmit him fearing the entry of the mob. The warden appealed to the sheriff to reinstate him and the sheriff called out the militia. The castle keep, known as Clifford's tower, was under siege for several days until it caught fire on the Friday night, 16th March. Several Jews were burnt to death but the majority, including Josce of York and the learned rabbi Yom Tov of Joigny, committed suicide rather than renounce their faith as demanded by the mob. The few who decided to surrender were killed despite being promised clemency.

'Cairn! James Cairn!' Someone was shouting and gesticulating wildly to me from across the square. A darkly garbed figure, singularly devoid of any graceful athleticism, was approaching at high speed.

'Just looking up to the tower,' I explained self-consciously.

'Such a sad expression. Why do they hate us so much?' Was the first thing Benjamin Levi asked me.

I shook my head. I had no answer. I was stunned. To be unexpectedly confronted by a Jew opposite one of his peoples' most emotive places.

'So what brings you to York, Benjamin?' I asked instead.

'I have become too infamous in Leeds.' Levi never laughed out loud at his own jokes, only his dark eyes gleamed laughter.

'No, really, why are you over here?'

'They want me to prosecute some *faygele* who insists on wearing a dress.'

'"*Faygele*"?' I queried.

'A pathetic little bird,' he shrugged, as if the term was too low for explanation.

'What, they've brought you all the way from Leeds just for that?' I was determined to give nothing away, keep my composure. 'Wasn't there anyone available locally to take it?'

'They want the best, my boy.' Again the dark eyes gleamed, another nervous shrug. 'They say nobody in your neck of the *trees* (Levi was well-known for his malapropisms) is capable or keen enough to take it on. And for this case they want someone really keen.'

'And are you sure that you are the right man to prosecute a man in a dress?'

'No, I am not sure that I am.'

'Are you acquainted with all the evidence against this man?' I asked, again feigning ignorance.

'No, not yet. I'm on my way now to the governor's office. I can hardly contain myself.' He smirked back at me, pointing across to the old Georgian debtors' prison. 'Look, James, even the gaols back then had style.' Lightning speed change of subject was another facet of Levi's personality: a difficult man to pin down.

'That building is believed to have been designed by William Wakefield, a trained lawyer and amateur architect.'

'A clever chap like you, James, interested in both the law and architecture. See, I remember.'

'But, I have to admit, I'd never appreciated your love for English baroque, Benjamin.'

'I like English everything, apart from that monstrosity awaiting me over there. I hate going into such places, hate it. All the gaols of our age are built with the same lack of imagination. Those wings resemble spiders' legs.'

'So where is the accused man?'

'In a little side cell to keep him out of harms way, I understand. Maybe they should let some of those murderous brutes get at him, eh? That might cure him of this dressing up thing for good.'

'Without seeing all the evidence, you seem to have built up enough enmity towards this man to pursue a creditable case,' I threw in wickedly.

'Enmity,' sighed Levi. 'It's not me, old chap, it's the Crown, the country, who are determined to throw the *Bible* at this man, a religious man at that. They seem determined to *step* out all this homosexual sort of thing. I expect it has something to do with being repressed English public school gentlemen, but then you'd know more about that sort of thing than me, James.'

'I'm not sure I do.'

Levi paused. 'We miss you, you know, the Crown misses you. Such an astute young QC you were during your brief time at the bar.'

'I always had a greater partiality for defence,' I began to explain before Levi's next statement stopped me in my tracks.

'By the way, James, if it is you who are thinking of defending this *faygele*, I'd think again.'

With that the not-so-frivolous Benjamin Levi winked and waved a cheery goodbye, leaving me wondering how a member of a community who had suffered from such terrifying persecution down the ages could consider taking on such a case. Or was it simply I who, yet again, was beginning to empathise with another of society's unfortunates.

'*Neither a borrower nor a lender be,*' I sang quietly to myself across towards Clifford's Tower, sucking up the damp freshness that had once reeked of smoke and burning flesh. Hard to absorb that I was staring across at the scene of death of at least one hundred and fifty men, women and children of Benjamin Levi's race. All a long time ago, now we are supposed to be living in an age of enlightenment and justice – a justice that Levi and I choose to serve – alas, a justice I feared still too often erred towards the rich and powerful.

'Puh! The Vagrancy Act,' I muttered to myself, as my knees rubbed past the outstretched hands of ginnel beggars before I reached the more exposed, aptly named Parliament Street. An Act of Parliament, the Vagrancy Act of 1824, which was primarily introduced to celebrate our heroic Napoleonic War troops – homeless, penniless, jobless returning soldiers – by prohibiting them from bedding down on the streets for the night. And their bedfellows? – a massive influx of Irish and Scottish economic migrants usually too hungry to snore and too poor to be snoring cheap-liquor-drunk. But last year's reformed Vagrancy Act, while affording women some protection by making rogues and vagabonds of all men who live off their immoral earnings, had an additional sting (in its tail). It made it an offence for any male person to persistently solicit or importune for immoral purposes in any public place. As if Labouchere's section of the Criminal Law Amendment Act 1885 wasn't enough.

Neither rich nor powerful, merely sexually divided, would Reverend G. Hobb receive justice? Did Wilde only a few years ago? – there, I considered I had my answer.

On my return to Bootham Chambers, I told Trotter about the chance encounter with my possible legal adversary.

'Oh, no, not Mr Benjamin Levi,' was Trotter's immediate response. 'He's sharp that one.'

'I hope you don't hold anti-Semitic views along with your abhorrence of fay men.'

'No, no, I'd use the term "sharp" to describe any man with Mr Levi's intelligence. Might I ask you in return, sir, why you thought the word to be a slight because it was used in reference to a Jew?'

'You are absolutely right as always, Trotter, perhaps we are all a little too sensitive regarding religion and race,' I conceded.

'I did wonder...' Trotter hesitated. 'Are you, sir, of the same persuasion as Mr Levi?'

'No, no,' I said. 'If I have any Jewish blood it is very much diluted on my mother's side.'

'But it's your mother's side that decides matters as I understand it,' began encyclopaedic Trotter.

I shook my head in warning. My family genealogy was my business not Trotter's.

'Mr Levi is one of the smartest QC's I have ever seen perform in a courtroom anywhere,' said Trotter, clearing his throat, seemingly relieved to be back on safer ground.

'What, even better than Cuthbert Henge?'

'Oh, yes, much better than him. Mr Henge's strength is his experience and cunning, Mr Levi's his intelligence.'

'We are in full agreement over that at least.'

'But there is one QC who perhaps approaches Mr Levi's professional brilliance but who is a great deal more erudite.'

'And who might that be, Trotter?'

'Mr Eustace Frere up at Northallerton.'

'Expect they'll give it to Frere now,' said Benjamin Levi, half-an-hour later.

Trotter gawped in disbelief at our unexpected visitor.

'You're not going to prosecute the Reverend G. Hobb then?' I asked Levi in amazement.

'I cannot bring myself to persecute the *faygele*.' Was "persecute" yet another of Levi's malapropisms or a poignant slip of the tongue. 'A waste of public money, if you ask me.'

'Is that your only reason?'

'No, no, I've just seen the surgeon's report. It is sad, disgusting, such an invasion of the person on so little pretext.'

'Good man.' I walked round my desk to slap Levi's back. 'How about a coffee in the Shambles?'

'No, no, another time I've a train to catch.'

'So, to what do I owe the pleasure?' I asked, somewhat bewildered.

'I hope you will heed my warning, James, and drop any thought of defending this case.'

'I don't understand.'

'If you do take it on, it could ruin you,' said Benjamin, the gleam gone from his eye now. 'They will ruin you.'

* * * * *

Thump! *Thump!* That evening in my townhouse on Gillygate I was studying Brown's notes on the indictment made out against Hobb, when I heard a noise against the sash window. Something was knocking heavily on the glass. One, two, three times – a heart stopping moment. Then I saw him hovering before the pane, talons poised, fixing me with his predatory stare. The fierce eyes as fierce as the beak. The fanning feathered wings outstretched and horizontal, as light as air, framing the nucleus body with its delicate ethereal splashes of brown stripes. His chest was barred like a generalissimo. On the bird's brief retreats, I could see his tail feathers were barred likewise. But it was the bird's legs that were the give away: yellow like his eyes, like the cere above his beak. I realised my visitor was a sparrow hawk confused not by me but by his own sharp reflection, seeing only an adversary fighting back. If I had never known it before, I knew it then, what it felt like to be a mouse before such a raptor. The bird was gone and I was left wondering if this was an omen of all that was to follow.

Chapter Six

It was drizzling light summer rain at the appointed hour. Winifred Holbrook and her parents lived out of town in the village of Heslington. I had arranged for a friend of mine, the flamboyant Digby West, a barrister in a neighbouring chamber, to pick me up outside my Gillygate home in his racy, two-horse spider phaeton.

'Good lord!' yelled Digby from his high carriage. 'You look as if you're dressed for a regatta.'

Ignoring his sarcasm, I climbed the phaeton's ladder with glee. I felt like cutting a dash drawing up to the Holbrooks' residence, show them I was a man of substance with friends in fast eye-catching vehicles. 'Just drive, Digby,' I told him, preening myself on the powder blue seat.

The house in Belle Vue Terrace was a complete surprise to me. It was a square Georgian building with small red bricks peculiar to the East Riding of Yorkshire. A fine, flat unpretentious building with just the one bay window breaking its symmetry. In a street of uniform terrace houses with pavement doorways, it was set back, distant and imposing. A neat front garden of ripening cherry trees abutted the street, green lawns framed it on either side.

'Good lord!' gulped Digby. 'I thought you said she was an ordinary sort of gal, James. Is she working in service here or what?'

My spirits fell. Unless someone was peeping out of a bedroom window there would be no one to witness my orchestrated arrival.

Disappointed, I dismissed Digby with instructions for him to return within the hour.

'You sure? It'll not give you long here.'

'I'm sure,' I told him. 'An hour will be long enough.'

I walked down the path to the richly painted burgundy door and rapped twice. I had grasped the brass horsehead knocker for a third attempt when the door open a fraction, and then a fraction more.

'Yes?' impatiently asked a man-servant in tails as if I had chosen the wrong entrance. I couldn't believe any of this. I immediately regretted my choice of casual dress for high tea with the Holbrooks. Their man handled my boater with its sporty navy and red striped ribbon like a dead fish.

'Doctor and Mrs Holbrook are awaiting you in the drawing room, sir,' he told me stuffily, as if no one in their right senses should be "awaiting" me.

'How nice of you to come, Mr Cairn,' said seated Mrs Holbrook, too well-mannered to flinch at my blazer as I bowed and took her hand. Though past her prime, Mrs Holbrook still had a robust, red-headed beauty to her – a Gaelic look – a look she had passed on to her daughter.

'Yes, Winifred told us that you were her Good Samaritan a week or two ago,' said a tall gentleman. He had a pointed beard and moustache and rested his ringed hand casually on the mantelpiece, rather affectedly it seemed to me. Then again, who was I to talk with my missed phaeton entrance. 'Jake, will you be good enough to inform Miss Holbrook that our guest has arrived?'

'Yes, and you can tell Cook we are ready for tea, Jake,' put in Mrs Holbrook. 'Please be seated, Mr Cairn.' There was a slight lilt to her perfect English.

'Can I have a teacake now?' The plea came from a small boy playing with a wooden train on the curved bay window seat. The boy, whom I took to be another Holbrook offspring, was dressed in a sailor suit. He must have been about four or five years old.

'Soon enough, Cedric,' gently admonished Mrs Holbrook.

'But I want…' The boy pointed to the waiting tiered stand of sandwiches and cake.

'You heard your mother,' Dr Holbrook told the lad sharply

'Did you find us easily?' asked Mrs Holbrook, turning back to me.

'No trouble at all, Mrs Holbrook. I came by phaeton,' I dropped in casually; my words falling unnoticed and without comment into the deep-piled carpet.

'It must be convenient living in the city,' said Dr Holbrook. 'Handy for both your clients and the courts.'

'Indeed, but your village location is wonderful here.'

All niceties of conversation ceased at the soft approach of feet. And there she was, slippered Winifred Holbrook walking through the doorway like a vision. My mouth fell open and I was unable to stifle a gasp. This Winifred Holbrook looked nothing like the beaten-up, women's suffrage campaigner who had locked herself onto the Mansion House railings; nothing like the lady in the tailored suit applauding me from the public gallery a week ago. This woman who took my damp hand in hers had metamorphosed into someone breathtakingly magnificent.

Comparing them in the close proximity of the drawing room, I could see that mother and daughter were even more alike than I had originally realised. Although Winifred's hair was of a slightly lighter hue than her mother's, it was gathered in a chignon at the back of her head making her expression even more intense. The gown she wore was olive green with huge puffed up leg of mutton sleeves, emphasising the gold sash round her small exquisite waist.

'How you tried for Sergeant Munster's release against such an unsympathetic judge, Mr Cairn,' she said.

'James, please,' I told her.

'What's that? What are you referring to, my love?' Dr Holbrook asked his daughter, losing the thread of conversation.

'I told you about the case, Papa. I went to see James defend the man who desired women's shoes.'

'Ah, the shoe fetish.'

'You know about this sort of thing, sir?' I asked.

'Should do, young man, although I must admit I am more familiar with pure foot fetishes than their leather counterparts.'

'How is that, sir?' It was my turn for confusion.

'Papa is a physician at The Retreat,' explained Winifred.

'Of course, it is just up the road from here, is it not?'

'Do you know it well then, Mr Cairn?' asked Mrs Holbrook.

'I have never been a patient there, ma'am, if that's what you mean.'

Loud chuckles issued from the pointed beard at the fireplace.

'Mama, really,' objected Winifred.

'I only meant...' replied her mother, flustered.

'In the course of my career I have had occasion to use The Retreat library on more than one occasion.'

'For Sergeant Munster?' asked Winifred.

'Indeed, but I could find no relevant study done regarding his specific obsession.'

'That does not surprise me,' said Dr Holbrook. 'But perhaps I might be able to help you with your clergyman who likes wearing frocks. I believe Doctor Magnus Hirschfeld in Germany has done some work in that area of interest.'

'But how do you know, sir?' I asked in amazement. 'How do you know about the clerical gentleman, I might or might not be representing?'

'The whole of York, nay Yorkshire, must know about it, Mr Cairn. See, it is written up here in yesterday's *Mercury*.' Dr Holbrook handed me the newspaper.

'And didn't the judge mention something of the sort before sentencing poor Sergeant Munster?' asked Winifred. 'I must say, James, I thought His Honour Judge Fox was very much beyond the pale at times.' The leg of mutton sleeves shook with indignation.

'Ah, good,' announced Mrs Holbrook. 'Tea at last. Do you take yours with milk and sugar, Mr Cairn?' I nodded and their man-servant did the honours. I requested that insubstantial accompaniment to refined English high tea – a crustless, thin white bread cucumber sandwich – as I studied the *Leeds Mercury* report.

It stated that at the police court, the Reverend George Hobb was accused of wearing a frock to solicit and importune other males for immoral purposes in a public place. The alleged incident took place on Monday, 22nd May, during the Whitsuntide holiday. The presiding magistrate, Samuel Turner, set bail at two hundred pounds. Pending bail, the accused man was returned to the Castle Prison. The Reverend George Hobb's solicitor is believed to have contacted *Bingham, Leacock, Fawcett & Cairn* to represent the Isle of Wight clergyman in a higher court.

'This is highly irresponsible journalism,' I seethed. 'Suggesting that our chambers have already been instructed.'

'But true, no doubt, from your reaction.' Dr Holbrook's eyes glinted with amusement.

'Forgive me, sir, but there are better papers to read.'

'You really think so?'

'I am simply curious, sir, why a highly educated man like yourself should read the *Mercury*, when we have a perfectly good local paper here in York. And there is always the *Times* of course.'

'It's a long story, James, but I was a great friend of Edward Baines junior, Sir Edward Baines at his time of death. He and his father before him were the proprietors of this newspaper. The *Mercury* reflects many of our family's liberal views. Edward was very much against the slave trade. He was an abolitionist like me.'

'And like me,' said Winifred.

I smarted with embarrassment now rather than rage.

'Slavery still goes on in other parts of the world. We are part of Anti-Slavery International which opposes human subjugation in all its forms,' explained Dr Holbrook, looking more serious, older all of a sudden but losing nothing of his lean handsomeness. It struck me then that he was actually older, very much older than the rest of us. I guessed him to be at least twenty years senior to his wife.

'Yes, there are the Aboriginals in Australia,' mumbled Cedric, through a mouthful of teacake.

'I suppose you know all about the Hottentots too,' said his father.

'And the slavery of women here,' said Winifred, ignoring Dr Holbrook's less than charitable Hottentot comment to her young brother.

'I completely share all your sentiments,' I said, gaining the prize of a Winifred smile.

'Do you really?' said Dr Holbrook. 'Oh, perhaps Winifred failed to mention, we are also a Quaker household.'

Tangy and melting in my mouth, I nearly choked on the piece of lemon cake I was so enjoying. I had nothing against Quakers, indeed my association with them in the past had been more than cordial, but I had not considered for one moment that the Holbrooks might be Friends. 'And so is The Retreat,' I managed to put in smartly, trying to regain lost ground.

'Is what?' asked Dr Holbrook.

'A Quaker establishment.'

'Yes, it is,' confirmed Dr Holbrook.

'I expect that is why you choose to work there, sir.'

'Partly.'

'Hannah Mills,' sighed Winifred.

'Indeed, Hannah Mills,' agreed her father. 'Do you know the story of Hannah Mills, James?' I shook my head. 'Hannah Mills was a bereaved

Leeds widow who was suffering from melancholia. She was admitted to York Lunatic Asylum, close to your chambers at Bootham, I believe. That was on the fifteenth of March, 1790. Friends tried to visit her but were denied access because it was said she was undergoing treatment. It transpired the treatment she was receiving was that of a dog. She was being kept in the most foul conditions. Starvation and beatings were the order of the day. Hannah died just over a month after her admission. A tea merchant, William Tuke, was so horrified by the circumstances of her death that he and the Society of Friends opened The Retreat six years later. The new hospital's ethic was on moral treatment rather than punishment.'

I had stopped eating. I felt ashamed to be eating. I looked across at Winifred, her eyes were brimming with tears over the fate of poor Hannah. I looked back at her father and wondered if my position was tainted by my chambers being near the still notorious York Lunatic Asylum.

'I am sure Mr Cairn doesn't want to hear all this over tea,' Mrs Holbrook told her husband.

'Chug, chug,' yelled oblivious Cedric, pushing his little wooden train between our feet.

'Cedric!' admonished his father as the grandfather clock struck five in the hall.

'Good Lord, I must be going,' I said, making a pretence of examining my pocket watch.

'Really?' said Mrs Holbrook in surprise. 'Why, you've only just come.'

'Nevertheless…'

'Yes, stay a little longer, James.' Winifred sounded disappointed.

'Perhaps you would allow me, sir, to escort your daughter on a day trip to the minster of Kirkdale while the weather is still temperate,' I suggested. Adding, 'If of course she would like to come.' Dr Holbrook seemed a little taken aback. His daughter, however, beamed enthusiasm. 'Though the minster, I expect, will be ornate in comparison with your own meeting houses, it is of terrific historical interest.'

'Perhaps Lucy would like to accompany you,' suggested Mrs Holbrook.

'Yes, if Lucy can go, I will go too,' said Winifred.

'So, unless I hear otherwise, it is agreed then. I will send a carriage for the ladies next Saturday morning at seven o'clock and we will meet at York Railway Station.'

'Seven?' exclaimed Winifred in horror.

'Seven thirty then.' I laughed.

'Lucy lives just round the corner from the station and you've no need to send a carriage for Winifred. I'll drive her to the station myself.' Dr Holbrook made the offer with a firmness that would brook no opposition.

'Fine, fine.' I laughed again: everything was absolutely fine with me with the prospect of Winifred Holbrook and Lucy Alexander on each arm.

'You looked a little disconcerted when Papa told you we are Quakers,' whispered Winifred at the door.

'You are not dressed like any Quaker woman I have ever known.' I touched her puffed sleeve where it gave way to a slimmer line.

'I am at home.' She jerked her arm away from my touch. 'And I will dress as I choose.'

'Of course you will. You are a woman of suffrage.'

'I expect you came across many Quaker women when you saved Daniel Robertshaw from the gallows.'

'You know about that too?'

'Everyone at our meeting house knows about it, and now, I fear, you have an even greater challenge ahead.'

'I think you might be right,' I replied.

'James, you do realise you owe me nothing. It is I who owe you something. I don't want you to waste a leisure day on Lucy and me.'

'Don't spoil things. It will be a delight to escort two such vibrant companions to a place I've long wished to visit myself.'

'I merely wanted to thank you, personally, for the other day. I think you saved me from a fate worse than death at the hands of those men.'

* * * * *

'Did you impress Mater and Pater then?' chuckled Digby, as we reached the outskirts of York.

'Not very much, I fear.'

Digby was forced to slow the horses down when we reached Walmgate. The cobblestones were moist and glistening with the earlier rain. I think I saw the mother and child first. They were walking hand in hand a few yards ahead of us. From his height, the boy must have been about Cedric's age. I heard the gust of wind come out of nowhere, the rustling of leaves in the trees, and the first anxious snort of one of our horses. On the periphery of my vision, I saw the boy break loose from his mother and step off the kerb into the path of our nearside horse. Digby jerked the reins, shouted out a one syllable warning. Instantly, the boy's mother pulled him back on the pavement like a rag doll. Too late for the horses. Startled, they reared and shied in their shafts. Digby struggled to hold the pair as they began to bolt down the greasy, uneven cobbled surface.

How fragile our lives, how we want to live. The few Sunday people there were about scampered out of the way of our two runaways. The spider carriage was swinging from side to side, building up momentum. I was sure it would overturn. They say your whole life runs before your eyes in such situations – mine certainly did then.

Digby West was an extremely strong and sturdy chap. Somehow, I don't know how, he managed to regain control of his beasts.

'Good lord!' he exclaimed, squirming and straining on the French leather seat as he reined them in. We slowly and unbelievably drew to a standstill outside a public house. 'Fancy one?' He nodded across to the pub; his face redder than ever; his knuckles white on the reins. I shook my head, feeling I was about to vomit. 'That was a close shave, ay? That was one spider nearly turned on its back.'

'Thank you,' I told him.

'Reckless young blades,' someone shouted from across the street.

Digby stretched his neck like an angry ostrich. I could see he was about to dismount and take issue with the caller.

'No,' I said, grasping his arm. 'Let it be.'

'What's this I've been hearing on the legal grapevine that you might be representing some Mary Anne in court?' he asked me, as we drew outside my Gillygate townhouse.

'Not someone else.' My sigh was deep, weary and heartfelt.

'How do you mean, someone else?'

'The whole world, it seems, knows my business.'

'A word of friendly advice, James.' I had never seen Digby West looking so serious, not even when his horses were bolting. 'Defending a simple Staithes lad accused of murder is one thing...'

'Wrongly accused of murder,' I interrupted.

'But defending a sodomite in an English courtroom is another.'

'"Sodomite", I never knew you could be so biblical, Digby.'

'Withdraw from this case, James. It will do nothing for your reputation.'

'You sound like Benjamin Levi.'

'Levi is right on this one, believe me.'

Chapter Seven

I stood waiting alone outside the railway station for Winifred and Lucy to arrive, a prepared hamper at my feet. I was a quarter of an hour early. Despite his opinions on "Mary Annes", I knew Digby West had my best interests at heart and I had asked him if he would be interested in making up a four for the trip.

'Nah.' Digby's bright red face puckered in disgust. 'Dusty old churches aren't my thing at all, James. Now if you'd been talking about going to the races.'

How wrong Digby was not to have come. How infuriated he would be not to be here seeing this spectacle approaching up Station Road.

Chug, chug, it sounded like the imaginative train noises young Cedric had been making, however there was nothing imaginative about the approaching vehicle. Fleshed horses reared to one side, drivers cursed, pedestrians stared open-mouthed as the fuel-driven horseless carriage wove its course through the city.

Dr Holbrook had said he would drive his daughter to the station. I had never envisaged that he meant in one of the new internal-combustion engines that I had been recently drooling over in the *Illustrated London News.* The machine's reality was everything and more than a pen and ink drawing. For once Winifred Holbrook's beauty was just part of the scene. Dr Holbrook pulled the Benz Comfortable into the side of the pavement.

'Good job the two mile an hour town speed limited is at an end, sir,' I joked.

'And the attendant armed with a red flag to lead the way,' reciprocated Dr Holbrook, through his camouflage of leather cap and goggles 'No, at two and three quarter horsepower, this girl has a top speed of almost twenty miles an hour.' Dr Holbrook seemed reluctant to extricate himself from the automobile. I gawped on picturing myself travelling the highways and byways on those pneumatic tyres at speeds well-exceeding the new fourteen miles an hour rural restriction.

'That will never take on,' shouted a pedal cyclist. 'That machine will never replace the horse and carriage nor this.' With a good-natured grin he rang his bicycle bell like a passing ship sounding its horn in acknowledgment.

'We'll see,' replied Dr Holbrook evenly.

Chug, chug, the petrol engine kept turning like a rare species of animal. A perched Winifred gave a discreet cough, waiting for one of us to hand her down. Obviously she expected both gallantry and equality. In the open car I could see that she was wearing a simple grey fashion dress with no pockets, buttons or frills. An equally plain bonnet graced her head. I suspected her attire was a tongue-in-cheek Quaker affectation for my benefit.

Smiling, I raised my broad-brimmed hat to her – a beige wideawake specially chosen for a sunny day in the country. I felt rather rakish in this particular hat, like an artist. I liked the feeling. It's amazing what a hat can do for a man. I, too, could change my colours like a chameleon. I took her hand and drew her on to the pavement beside me. It was only then that I truly saw how her bland apparel only served to enhance rather than diminish her. My hand began to shake uncontrollably in hers and I jerked it away in embarrassment. She looked surprised, affronted.

Her father reluctantly dismounted from his automobile but left the engine running. He and I began to circle it, examining it like a work of art. I loved the sombre tasteful colours of the bodywork, the plush leather seats, the parasol that could be pulled over if it rained. Gone were the carriage lamps from the earlier models. I sensed this car was heralding a new age of speedier travel.

'German, you know. Starts by means of a crank,' explained Dr Holbrook. 'Still a bit of a devil to start.'

'Best to leave the engine running then. How do you go on for fuel, sir?'

'There's a local hardware shop along the way. You're a dandy for the hats, James, I must say,' commented Dr Holbrook, abruptly changing the subject.

'Nothing like...' Winifred stopped mid-sentence. Her father and I turned to follow her line of interest down the street.

The approaching Lucy Alexander was certainly not a Quaker, I could see that straight away. She was the epitome of what the French call *la belle époque* – the beautiful era. She wore a cerise skirt with a fussy, cream embroidered blouse.

'You look fabulous,' Winifred told her.

'Just like a Gibson Girl,' joined in her father.

I was lost for words. As pretty as a picture came to mind but it was far too cliché.

Under scrutiny, Lucy adjusted her feathered straw hat perching it at an even jauntier angle. With or without a drum, there was nothing irresolute about her.

The 8-30 a.m. train was already there at the platform. Our exuberant party scrambled aboard. Barely seen, certainly unconsidered, the shadow of a figure passed by our carriage like a brief cloud across the sun on that sunniest of days.

We arrived at Kirkby Moorside station as if by Cinderella's coach. Although the train journey had actually taken an hour and twenty-four minutes, calling at a dozen backwater stations including the market town of Helmsley, to me it seemed to have taken no time at all. I could see the envious expressions of other male passengers peering through our compartment window, not daring to interrupt our sprawled presence. I was the sole escort of the two most attractive, interesting women in northern England. And "sole" I intended to remain.

A porter helped me down with the hamper. Winifred insisted on lending a hand with it as we made our way to Market Square. Outside the George and Dragon, as arranged, the country wagonette was waiting for us. This was anything but Cinderella's coach and, in light of Winifred's stylish arrival in her father's automobile, I was a little chastened as we took our places on the facing benches.

'This is grand,' she said, as we began to trundle out of the square.

Bless her for her lack of airs, I thought.

'Look at the houses,' shrieked Lucy, pointing to the town's ironstone cottages with their red pantile roofs. 'So different from York.'

'There's the man in the bowler hat again,' said Winifred, indicating a thick-set chap climbing into a carriage. 'I noticed him staring at us on the platform in York.'

'Lots of men have been staring at you two all morning,' I teased.

'Yes, but he must be the only one who's got off with us at Kirkby Moorside.'

'She's been like this ever since she was attacked by that policeman,' explained Lucy. 'She's either felt threatened or that someone was following her.'

'Karl Ludwig Kahlbaum,' sighed Winifred.

'Sorry, Karl who?' The sun was shining directly into my eyes. I pulled the brim of my wideawake even lower to study her face.

'Kahlbaum. He died in April. He was the first doctor to use the term "paranoia".'

'I suppose it helps having a father working in the madhouse to enjoy all these obscure conditions,' jeered Lucy.

'"Enjoy" isn't the word I'd use,' retorted Winifred.

An impressionist painting – the green meadows above Kirkdale were dotted with yellow, blue, red colour – scabious, campions, harebells and oxeye daisies. We turned into a small lane, the sun occasionally splashing through a canopy of leaves above the open wagonette. Our two sturdy brown and white cobs began to increase speed down a steady incline to a dry ford.

'St Gregory's Minster ova' yonder,' announced the driver in a strong Wold dialect. Throughout the journey this was the first comment our weathered guide had made. 'I'll stay wi' horses and see 'em right.'

'It's very small for a minster,' said Lucy, jumping to the ground unaided.

'Hardly York,' said Winifred, struggling to help me unload the hamper.

'Its title of minster denotes its age,' I puffed. 'It comes, I believe, from the Anglo-Saxon and means a settlement of clergymen living a communal life.'

'It is in a rather pretty spot,' said Lucy, warming.

With the hamper safely delivered to earth, Winifred began to examine our surroundings in greater detail. 'I think it is the most ideal church and setting I have ever seen.'

'I'll take care of yon as well for a while,' said the driver, nodding to the hamper.

'Come, ladies,' I said, tipping my hat.

'Who was St Gregory?' asked Winifred as we walked down the grave-lined path.

'He was a sixth century pope, the first pope to introduce the Anglo-Saxons to the teachings of Christ through his emissary, Augustine.

'You sound more like a historian than a barrister, James,' said Lucy.

'I am primarily interested in fossils.'

'What, old fossils?' She giggled.

'I know of no other kind.'

'All these dead people.' Winifred nodded across to the graves.

'What a sublime instrument that is,' I said, eager to brighten the moment, pointing up to the ancient sundial above the south door as we huddled into the porch.

'Really,' said Winifred with little enthusiasm.

'Orm Gamalson's sundial. Arguably the best surviving example of an inscribed Saxon sundial in the world.'

'Really,' said Winifred again, still sounding unconvinced.

'Yes, really,' interrupted an unknown voice. I turned to see a tall, regrettably handsome young man standing behind us. He seemed to be regarding our party with wry amusement. I wasn't sure I needed this new ally to convince Winifred of the sundial's importance. Now four of us were pressed into the porch gazing up at the tooled tablet set vertically into the minster's fabric. The tablet looked to be about eight feet long by twenty inches wide and was divided into three panels, the central panel contained the dial.

'*Orm Gamal suna bohte Sanctus Gregorius minster ðonne hit wes æl tobrocan and tofalan...*' The young man began to read from the left facing panel in the most perfect Old English I had ever heard. Winifred and Lucy stared admiringly at the fine academic face mouthing words from another age. I fear I stared blankly.

'But what does it all mean?' Lucy asked the question I was too arrogant to ask.

'Orm Gamalson bought St Gregory's Minster when it was all quite ruined and quite collapsed...' The young man began to translate.

'That means there was an even earlier church,' I butted in.

'Indeed,' said the young man, before continuing with his translation. 'He let it be made new from the ground, for Christ and St Gregory, in the days of Edward king, in the days of Tostig the Earl.'

'Edward the king. Is that Edward the Confessor?' I asked.

'The same. Earl Tostig of Northumbria is believed to have murdered Gamal, Orm's father, while he was on a visit to his hall lair under safe conduct.'

'How treacherous,' said Winifred.

'Indeed,' agreed the young man.

'I seem to remember he got his just deserts at the Battle of Stamford Bridge.' I was glad to make some contribution to the discussion. 'Wasn't he killed by his own brother Harold?'

Our Anglo-Saxon expert nodded before pointing to the dial itself. '*Þis is dæges solmerca, æt ilcum tide.* This is the day's sun-marker, at every tide.'

I looked up at the dial's segmented pattern. For me this was a geometric nightmare. This was as much a challenge as it must have been for those early wayfarers accustomed to strategically positioned stones on hillsides to tell them the time of day. Even so as the young man spoke the Old English words, I could phonetically hear a residue of Norse.

'See there.' He pointed to the bottom central panel. '*And Haward me wrohte, and Brand, presbyter.* And Haward wrought me, and Brand, priest.'

Lucy stared up at the stranger, absorbed. Winifred's position was not as easy to read but she seemed rather taken with him as well.

'Howard Greenstock.' He reached his hand out to mine, not to the ladies, the ladies didn't warrant a hand, a bow or even a touch to a hatless head. I was pleased: women of suffrage always liked to be acknowledged.

'Are you the verger?' asked Lucy. Howard Greenstock shook his luxuriant head of dark curls.

'The curate perhaps,' offered Winifred.

'I am a postgraduate student of history, ladies.' Finally the briefest of tweaks to his head. 'And I have come all the way from Oxford to see this.' Howard Greenstock pointed to Orm Gamalson's sundial.

'It is so hot at present, perhaps we should seek some shade in the minster itself,' I suggested to Lucy and Winifred. 'And leave Mr Greenstock to his sundial.'

'No, no,' said Greenstock. 'I, too, would like to take a look inside.'

I could smell history and beeswax as soon as we passed through the doorway. In the nave ran neat rows of highly polished box pews. Between the nave and the north aisle towered an arcade of arches, magnificent arches for such a modest building. Plain, modest, understated, surly even a Quaker wouldn't feel out of place here. I lowered myself into a pew at the back of the minster. Greenstock was showing Winifred and Lucy this and that, explaining this and that, while I sat quietly absorbing the atmosphere. God – God being the potent word – how many generations had worshipped here, I wondered. Saxons, Danes, Normans even had sat on this very spot, no doubt contemplating similar troubles and joys to mine.

'Minster though.' Lucy seemed obsessed with accurate terminology.

'Perhaps it was a daughter-house of the old monastery of Lastingham,' suggested Greenstock. 'Lastingham was an extremely important part of the territory of Northumbria which Kirkdale was part of then.'

'I don't care if it is important or not,' said Winifred. 'The inside of this building is even more exquisite than its exterior. I am truly surprised that no one else is here to admire it, that we have it all to ourselves.'

'Aren't you glad though?' asked Greenstock.

'It's small but quality,' I shouted from the back of the church. *Quality, quality*... My words echoing down the aisle. 'How about lunch, Lucy and Winifred?' *Winifred, Winifred* ..

Winifred turned and gave me a radiant smile.

'Thank you for bringing us here, James,' she said.

We chose a spot on the lawn outside the minster leaving Greenstock to his sundial. At least I hoped we had left Greenstock to his sundial. The wagonette driver obligingly carried a rug and our hamper across to us. The two o'clock sun still beat down on our lightly seasoned chicken wings and tomatoes. The tomatoes were so sweet and full of flavour, they complemented the delicate tartness of the Bucelas wine perfectly. I vowed to thank my grocer for his excellent advice on my return to York. Amid a sea of flowers, close to the higgledy piggledy gravestones, I thought of George Hobb back in his dark cell and my heart grieved for him.

'Penny for them,' said Winifred.

'How did you both get into women's suffrage?' I improvised.

'Have you got all day?' Winifred laughed.

'When I was about thirteen, I went with my mother to hear Florence Balgarnie speak on the Contagious Diseases Act,' explained Lucy.

'Wasn't her father a Congregational minister over in Scarborough?' asked Winifred.

'That's right,' said Lucy. 'Anyway, James, I thought it was shocking that police officers could arrest prostitutes in certain ports and garrison towns and then subject them to compulsory checks for venereal disease. If found to be infected a woman could be detained in a locked hospital until cured. What about the infected men, I asked myself. The men who had undoubtedly seduced many of them into that profession in the first place.'

I had no answer either. I knew that the act had been repealed some thirteen years before, mostly due to women like Winifred and Lucy. According to my quick arithmetic, Lucy must be about twenty-seven years of age at least now.

'Josephine Butler nursed dying prostitutes in her own home to save them from the horrors of those awful "Lock Hospitals",' said Winifred; her colour rising not from the sun but from anger. 'She published a letter expressing the views of one of her charges' encounters with men. "It is men, only men, from the first to the last that we have to do with",' began Winifred with a fair impression of a Cockney accent. '"To please a man I did wrong at first, then I was flung about from man to man. Men police lay hands on us. By men we are examined, handled, doctored. In the hospital it is a man again who makes prayer and reads the Bible for us. We are up before magistrates who are men, and we never get out of the hands of men till we die".'

'"Men police lay hands on us",' I quoted. 'Like Constable Goater laid hands on you.'

'Goater? Is that really his name?' asked Winifred in disbelief.

'Appropriate, don't you think? His manners are little above a goat's.'

'God is in everyone, James, in everything.'

'What in that violent mob of men so full of hatred against you, in those two villainous policemen who assaulted you?'

'Yes, even in them.' Winifred gulped down her glass of white wine.

'More?' I offered her the bottle. She took it and poured – a modern woman in every sense.

'Didn't Alice Cliff Scatcherd visit your house?' Lucy asked her.

'She still does, even now, all the way from Morley. She's a good friend of Mother's.'

'A radical campaigner, Alice used to address the York Women's Liberal Association until Florence Balgarnie announced the formation of our suffrage society,' Lucy explained.

'The Church of England marriage service is "much to keep up the subjection of women in our land",' boomed Winifred in a cultured West Riding accent. She obviously enjoyed playing the mimic and studied her subjects closely. '"It lends the sanction of religion to much that is degrading and wrong in married life. I, for one, can never sanction that service with my presence".'

'Bravo Alice!' applauded Lucy.

Click! I heard a definite click in the silence that followed our laughter. Winifred and Lucy must have heard it too for they visibly pricked up their cars. *Click*! There it was again. Then the sound of scrabbling feet. I stood up to catch a glimpse of a bodiless bowler hat disappearing along the top of the stone wall.

'One of you must be famous,' shouted Howard Greenstock from the minster porch.

'What do you mean?' I shouted back.

'Well, there's been a fellow crouching on the other side of that wall for the last five minutes. Even from here I could see he had one of those wonderful new cameras, an Eastman Folding Kodet, I think they're called. I'd love to own one of those myself but they are way beyond my means. I thought he was taking distance shots of St Gregory's, until I saw him point the lens in your direction.'

'It's the man who's been watching us,' cried Winifred, bouncing to her feet in alarm. 'I told you. I said I felt I was being followed. Do you all believe me now?'

'It'll be nothing, no one,' I said, doing my best to reassure her.

'Was he a stout man wearing a bowler hat?' she asked Greenstock. He nodded. 'There you are you see, the police have set a detective on to Lucy and me.'

'Or me,' I put in lamely.

'But why would the police want to keep vigilance on two such adorable women?' asked Greenstock, his flattery coming to the fore a little late in the day. 'What I mean is… what have you done wrong?'

'Nothing,' replied Winifred, 'apart from demanding a fairer society.'

'Have you seen a gentleman in a bowler hat?' I asked the driver back at the wagonette.

'Yes,' he nodded, puffing thoughtfully on his long clay pipe. 'Fella in a brown check suit. He arrived shortly after you three went over to the church.'

'What, he's been hanging around here all this time?' asked Winifred, alarm building in her voice again.

'The gent must have some brass for he hired a carriage all day. Carriage driver told me hisself.'

'Is that him?' asked Greenstock, pointing to a cloud of rising dust up the road.

'Ay,' replied the driver.

I tried my best to distract Winifred as we made our way down the hill towards the ford and Hodge Beck. Her brow remained furrowed, worried. Lucy danced behind us with Greenstock, who had asked if he might accompany us to the Kirkdale Cave. Compared to Winifred, Lucy seemed unaffected by the thought of being stalked or, more aptly, favourably affected by Greenstock's personality.

The valley of the beck was densely forested by Kirkdale Wood. We walked a little way up a rough track on the eastern bank, and soon we saw in a clearing on the right evidence of quarrying.

'You came from Oxford to see Orm Gamalson's sundial, I would have travelled across the world to see this,' I told Greenstock, pointing up to the cave's narrow entrance set into a rock.

'To see that?' asked Lucy dubiously.

'Yes, because that cave first brought into question a rigid acceptance of the Eternal Flood, The Book of Revelations, the Creation itself.'

'How interesting,' said Winifred. 'But I doubt Lucy and I will be able to reach the spot where history was made.'

'No, but we can,' said Greenstock. 'Come on, James.'

I felt sorry for Winifred – the realisation that she was again tethered to an inferior position by her skirt, her sex – the same sort of biblical tethering Dr William Buckland must have experienced, confronted by the palaeontological evidence he found, crawling on all fours along the restrictive cave floor with his hands caked in mud.

Chapter Eight

The Second Boer War was looming on the horizon. I was reading a brave article by the Leeds socialist, Isabella Ford, condemning our government's policy in Africa. She was fiercely opposed to war in all its forms. Her name was familiar. Had she been mentioned as one of those mysterious regular visitors to the Holbrooks' home?

'This coffee is a little hot,' I complained to Trotter. After my American trip, I had taken up the American habit. 'Coffee should never be over heated, it spoils the flavour.'

'The girl's not here this morning and I've had to boil it up myself.'

'That's just it, Trotter, coffee should never be boiled.'

'I am doing my best, sir.' Trotter's bottom lip jutted forward.

'And what is wrong with Emma?' I asked out of politeness.

'A cold.'

Only a few weeks ago I knew nothing of the Holbrooks, now I suspected I was reading one of their friend's opinions in the newspaper. Never in my wildest dreams had I realised how rich and politically connected they were. Winifred had told me her father was born into a prominent family of Bradford wool merchants. On our journey back to York there had been talk between her and Lucy of a recent visit to Belle Vue Terrace by the radical Liberal couple, Ursula and Jacob Bright. Ursula was a member of the Manchester Women's Suffrage Society and interested in the abolition of the House of Lords. Jacob I knew of as an elderly retired MP. I was to learn on our train journey home that he was a peace campaigner and campaigned for women's rights too.

I had not contacted Winifred in days. I judged her to be financially out of my league and I could never conceive of her agreeing to honour and obey. In contrast, Lucy Alexander and the patriarchal Howard Greenstock had eagerly exchanged addresses on our plodding wagonette ride back to Kirkby Moorside. Greenstock had told us he intended staying another night at the King's Head, on High Market Place, before heading south.

'He's Jewish, you know,' said Lucy, waving like mad to her new amour out of the carriage window as our 5.44 p.m. train had gathered speed. 'He says even though Jews have been allowed to study at Oxford since seventy-one, there still remains a lot of prejudice.'

'What, despite Disraeli?' Winifred asked.

'Disraeli, if you recall, was a Christian convert and a Tory.' Lucy sighed.

'Come back inside,' Winifred had snapped at her. 'You are making an exhibition of yourself.'

Our return journey to York had seemed longer, more difficult, after the magic of the day.

'The post has arrived, sir.' Trotter's voice, Trotter's interruption.

'You open it,' I told him. I was enjoying my memories of my day off in the sun.

I could hear him making such a to-do with the paperknife: tearing, crackling and balling up unwanted mail. Dealing with correspondence in an otherwise quiet room can sound amazingly loud. But then I had my newspaper – I rustled it in competition.

All of a sudden there was a cessation in hostilities. I looked into my adversary's face. He was ashen.

'You had better take a look at these yourself, sir.' Trotter handed me a brown card envelope like a tray, two photographs resting on top. Both the photographs had been taken from an angle that distorted reality. With our heads thrust back in laughter, Winifred, Lucy and I seemed pressed far too close together for decency's sake on the lawn outside St Gregory's. I could even make out some of the blurred gravestones in the background. In the other photograph, Lucy and I were raising our wine glasses to Winifred in what appeared to be some debauched drunken ritual.

My immediate thought was that this would not go down well with the Friends. My second thought was Dr Holbrook.

'Is there a note?' I asked Trotter. He nodded for me to check inside the envelope.

What company you keep, Mr Cairn.
Sapphos and poofs seem to be to your taste,
anarchists too are on your menu.
You are advised to leave the Sapphos alone,

the poor without representation,
the anarchists to their anti-Christ fate.
Otherwise you will be exposed.

'This is outrageous.' I passed the note across to Trotter.

'I did warn you. Mr Levi warned you.'

'But who is behind this, this threat?' I spluttered. Trotter shrugged. Trotter no longer my adversary but a man as shocked by this unpleasantness as I was. 'Will you be kind enough to fetch Mr Carlton-Bingham here immediately?' I told him.

'Well you're a dark horse, I must say,' laughed Carlton-Bingham, examining the photographs. 'Who are your glamorous lady friends?'

'Just that, friends.'

'Wait a minute, these aren't the two suffrage demonstrators you protected against our boys in blue at the Mansion House?' he asked. I nodded somewhat embarrassed. 'But why such urgency over a couple of photographs, James?'

I passed Carlton-Bingham the note, he wasn't laughing anymore.

'Any idea who might be behind this?' he asked. I shook my head. 'Or the reasons why they want to frighten you off?'

'Frighten me off what exactly? Three possibilities are mentioned here.'

'You should have a better idea of that than I.'

'There is this case, Mr Carlton-Bingham,' interjected Trotter.

'You mean the clergyman who dresses in dresses?'

'Yes, sir, the Reverend George Hobb.'

I must say this is all rather sinister, worrying. I was right in the middle of preparing a brief myself but that can wait. If these two photographs were released to the press it would reflect badly on both the Hobb case and chambers. What do you think, James?'

I shook my head. I felt numb. I could hardly think at all. Perhaps my boss and clerk thought I had acted improperly with the two pictured women. They could be forgiven for forming that impression.

'It has brought it home to me how the click of a shutter, a frozen frame in time, can actually misinterpret reality,' I said.

'On the other hand it can reveal a facial expression, the attitude of a bodily pose, that might have been missed with the passage of time,' countered Carlton-Bingham.

'What are you implying, sir?'

'I am implying nothing. The point is how these two photographs might be perceived and what are we going to do about it? We have already had some unwelcome press coverage regarding the Hobb case, have we not?'

I nodded. Of course the *Leeds Mercury* article Dr Holbrook had shown me. I looked to Trotter and Carlton-Bingham, I could see the three of us were jumping to the same conclusion.

'Do you think these could come from the same source?' Trotter asked, lifting the photographs up by his fingertips as if they were contaminated. 'A press source perhaps?'

'Could be,' said Carlton-Bingham, examining the note more closely. 'There is one reference that has me bemused above all the rest in this text, that doesn't quite fit.'

'And what is that?' I asked.

'"Anarchists to their anti-Christ fate". A "poof" maybe but you would never describe Hobb as an "anarchist" would you, James?' I shook my head, Trotter shook his. 'Well, there is a clue perhaps.' With that Carlton-Bingham returned to his office, to the preparation of his own cases. Trotter remained hovering.

'Trotter, make an appointment for me with Doctor Holbrook at The Retreat as soon as possible.'

* * * * *

There was no Digby West phaeton for a grand arrival at Heslington this time. I had hired a modest hansom at short notice for the journey. The cab rattled on while I was preoccupied with thoughts of Sapphos, poofs and anarchists. Sappho, I knew, was an Ancient Greek lyric poet born on the island of Lesbos around 620 BC. She had the reputation of falling in love with other women. Was the implication that Winifred's and Lucy's relationship was sapphic?

'Well, what do you expect with all this rights for women stuff?' An imaginary demon Trotter voice invaded my consciousness.

Although I found this possibility troubling, Carlton-Bingham was right about the reference to "anarchists" being the odd man out.

I saw that we were approaching higher ground south of the city. Lamel Hill, I had read recently, was a Stone Age burial mound and not a hill at all. An excavation at the base of the mound, some fifty years ago, had further exposed an Anglo-Saxon burial ground. But perhaps Lamel Hill's unique claim to fame was for being the site of General Fairfax's largest gun, trained to fire on the Royalists at Walmgate Bar during the Siege of York in 1644.

The Retreat was set amid pastoral countryside. High walls protected its gardens from the curious outside while a cleverly landscaped ha-ha indulged the inquisitiveness of those confined. With open views across to Walmgate Stray, to grazing cattle and white dots of sheep, I thought I wouldn't mind being admitted here myself. How pleasant compared to the grime and slime of city asylums. I could see no bars or gratings on the building's windows. I got no sense of incarceration here.

Walking down the long corridor to Dr Holbrook's room, it was hard to discern the patients from the staff. Everyone was so neatly and cleanly dressed.

'I am the Queen, you know.' Finally, an inmate accosted me outside Dr Holbrook's name-plated office. This poor woman, although well-scrubbed, was easily identifiable as an inmate because – despite her assertion of royal lineage – her toes were poking through the frayed fabric of her slippers. I guessed she was about fifty but looked much older. Her floral dress had the same faded yellow pallor as her skin and hair colour. 'You are the King, I can tell. You are my husband.' I stared at the wall of madness between us and knew I would never be able to break it down with reason. Was she about to erupt into violence? Do me harm?

'Good to see you, James.' The door to Dr Holbrook's office swung open and there was salvation. 'Now what can I do for you, Nell?' he asked the Queen. 'I could hear you shouting a mile away.' Nell answered him by putting a possessive arm through mine. 'No, Nell, go away, go back to your room this instant,' he told her more firmly, trying to bundle her out of his doorway while she was still hooked to me.

Somehow I managed to disengage myself and along with Dr Holbrook made a bolt for it, banging the consulting room door shut behind us.

'Welcome to The Retreat, James. "Hunger will tame the fiercest animals, it will teach decency and civility, obedience and subjection to the most perverse",' laughed Holbrook.

'You don't really hold those views, do you, sir?'

'No, I certainly do not. Those were the words of the Reverend Joseph Townsend over a hundred years ago. Although I am sure there are plenty of misguided souls who still adhere to those beliefs including your Bootham asylum neighbours.'

'But surely, Doctor, things have improved a little even there in a hundred years.'

'A little? Little being an apt word – for some a little too late. From its conception this hospital has been based on our Quaker principles of self-control, compassion and respect. As I think I've already told you *traitement moral* is our quest here. Today, the majority of people queuing for our beds are not even Friends.'

'Nor enemies like me.'

'No, I am sure you come in good faith, James.'

You don't know the half of it yet, I thought, asking instead, 'But what do you do with patients who are physically unmanageable?'

'If long walks and labouring on the farm fail, we do have other methods of restraint, James.' Holbrook nodded across to what looked like the shell of a torso resting against a bookcase.

'That's the first straitjacket I've seen choosing a book.'

'I can show you a lot more than straitjackets when I am not so pressed for time.' Holbrook took out his silver fusee pocket watch. 'So, how can I help you, young man? Is this about your personating clergyman?'

'No, no, sir. In the circumstances, after all your kind hospitality, I thought it best to come clean regarding a certain matter.'

'What circumstances?' I saw a flicker of alarm in the eyes of a man used to keeping his emotions well under control. I took the two St Gregory's photographs out of my briefcase and handed them over to him without a word. 'Who took these?' he asked.

'I've no idea, sir. He has only been identified as wearing a bowler hat and being of a stocky build.'

'A journalist perhaps? Using these to extort some information from you,' suggested Holbrook, crackling the photographs in the air.

'If so he must be at the pit end of the profession, working for a penny rag say. I've never known a newspaper man worth his salt who would engage in moral blackmail.'

'Luckily, newspapers aren't able to reproduce these images on mass yet.'

'No, but I have heard printers are working on a new science.'

'It's called offset lithography,' furnished Holbrook. I was impressed. 'Dots, everything is dots these days. Let's get away from blasted dots. Density of dots in halftone printing, even some works of art are made up of dots.'

'You are not a fan of the French school then, sir.'

'I certainly am not.' Holbrook peered harder at the photographs, his expression suddenly changed. 'Is that a glass Lucy is holding? See there, Winifred has one eye closed as if she is inebriated. Did you get my daughter drunk, James?'

'No, sir…' I faltered. 'We had only one bottle of wine between us, I assure you, Doctor Holbrook, and I drank most of it myself. Winifred merely had one eye closed against the fierce sunlight.' It intrigued me that the good doctor seemed more concerned that his daughter would be perceived as being drunk rather than at the two ladies' indecent proximity to me.

'Our faith does not encourage drinking, especially among our daughters. We believe in temperance. How could you compromise Winifred and Lucy in this way?'

'It was never my intention…' I began to waffle.

'But who could be responsible for taking this?' interrupted Holbrook. 'What do they want?'

'I wondered that too.'

'Could this have something to do with that Hobb business? Are the powers that be trying to dissuade you from taking on his case?' Holbrook handed me back the photographs.

'That might be so. However, Winifred told me she had the feeling she was being followed prior to our visit to the minster.'

'She made no mention of that to me or her mother.'

'I expect she didn't want to worry you.' (Or for you to think she was being paranoid, I thought to myself.) 'Excuse me for asking, Doctor Holbrook, could you and your family have any political enemies?'

At first Holbrook shook his head before eventually muttering, 'Well, as you know, Winifred is heavily involved with the YWSS.'

'YWSS?'

'York Women's Suffrage Society.'

'I believe Lucy did mentioned such an organisation during our day out.'

'Oh, yes, I wouldn't be surprised if they are soon affiliated to the National Union of Women's Suffrage Society. I suppose it is just possible that someone who is opposed to women's suffrage could be involved.' Holbrook sounded doubtful.

'You told me that you are a liberal family.'

'We are.'

'But would you not agree that some of your opinions could be seen as radical?'

'Some people might consider them to be so.'

'Winifred mentioned that you had some eminent visitors to your home, such as the Brights.'

'Yes, Jacob and Ursula are old friends of ours.' Holbrook looked puzzled. 'You can throw Philip Snowden and James Keir Hardie into the mix for that matter.'

'But Hardie and Snowden aren't liberals. They belong to the Independent Labour Party, do they not? Indeed, Keir Hardie was the founder member of that party.'

'Yes, but they were Liberal Party members before joining the ILP. Winifred's friend, Lucy Alexander, has done the same thing but we don't hold it against her.'

'What, Lucy is a socialist?'

'You have us all politically pigeonholed now, James.' Holbrook looked at his watch again. 'Well, if there is nothing else?'

I took hold of the door handle before turning back to Holbrook. 'Tell me, sir, what is the one thing you have in common with all these people?'

'We are all against war,' replied Holbrook without hesitation. 'Some like Hardie and Snowden are Christian Socialists, I am a Quaker and a pacifist. Ever heard of the Peace Society? There's a branch in Leeds.'

'The Peace Society. Have I got this right, you are saying that you and your friends are against a second war in Africa?'

'We most certainly are. You should come and listen to one of our meetings sometime.'

'I might do that, sir.' Obviously, Dr Holbrook was a true liberal in every sense. I was glad, however, that I had decided not to show him the shocking message accusing his daughter of sapphism. This, I felt, would have sent him into a state of apoplexy.

'James, I will do all I can to help you with the psychiatric evidence in the Hobb case. But I feel, in the present circumstances, it is better that you do not contact my daughter.'

My spirits fell. There it was – my expected rejection was official.

* * * * *

'Someone is out to get someone,' I told Trotter back in chambers. 'I don't know who yet or why exactly, but I feel it in my bones.'

'What are you going to do about those photographs, sir?'

'Nothing for the moment.'

'If you do decide to take the initiative, I know just the man,' said Trotter.

That is how Mortimer Blakely came to be standing in front of my desk that afternoon. Blakely's bald head looked as if it had been polished with beeswax. He held his bowler hat before him with the same awkwardness of a man holding out his chamber pot for cleaning. I did a double-take: he was dressed in a brown check suit like our blackmailing photographer at the minster, and he was of exactly the same burly build as the man I saw getting into a carriage at Kirkby Moorside, as it turned out, in pursuit of our wagonette.

'Ever been to Kirkdale?' I felt obliged to ask.

'Kirk what?'

'Never mind it must be a uniform.'

'I don't understand, sir.

'Do all private detectives dress in the same manner? You look very similar to the man I am asking you to find, a man in a check suit.'

'You think the subject might be a detective then?'

'That is for you to tell me.'

'I cannot do that yet, sir, but I can explain the detectives' mode of dress. You see we are like grouse shooters out on the open moor side, we are camouflaged to blend in with our surroundings as best we can. Many of us are ex-bobbies.'

'I am not sure checks blend in, even quiet autumnal checks. I expect Mr Trotter has already briefed you on some of the more unsavoury details of this case.'

'He has, sir. Here is my card should you ever need me urgently.' Blakely casually slid his card onto my desk.

'So, what do you, an ex-bobby, make of it all?'

'I find it interesting, curious I might add.'

'How is that?'

'Well,' pondered Blakely. 'Matters seem to have escalated since your involvement with Miss Holbrook and Miss Alexander, am I not right in thinking?'

'Did Mr Trotter tell you they are women of suffrage and that Miss Holbrook has felt she has been under surveillance for a while?'

'He did and, yes, the suffrage question has certainly begun to upset certain politicians.'

'Even Salisbury.'

'Indeed, especially the Marquis of Salisbury but who knows what he really thinks.'

'So you think that an anti-suffrage movement might be at the bottom of this?'

'Could be. But it is you who have received the menaces, Mr Cairn, not the two ladies. You were the one sent the hate mail and the photographs.'

'But why?'

'Might I ask you a personal question, Mr Cairn?' Blakely cleared his throat and began swirling his hat round and round nervously.

'Go ahead.'

'Do either of these two ladies hold some special interest for you? Might we say some romantic interest?'

'No, no,' I denied, my cheeks aflame.

'No?'

'Well, I do think Miss Holbrook is a wonderful person though she is very socially above stairs and of the Quaker persuasion.'

'Does the father know you are taken with his daughter?'

'Doctor Holbrook?' I stared at Blakely in astonishment. 'You don't think he could be behind all this?'

'I tend, Mr Cairn, to go for the simplest explanations first and once they are eliminated we can look for more complicated explanations.'

'But to have your own daughter followed and compromised,' I was staggered at the suggestion.

'You would be amazed the lengths anxious parents will go to bring their daughters to book.'

'But surely…'

'Another possibility could be that one of the two ladies has an admirer, a spurned suitor, and you are perceived as a threat. A very real threat I hasten to add for you are an extremely eligible man, if I might be allowed to say so, Mr Cairn, sir. And I must say you look equally relaxed with both young ladies.' Blakely pointed to the two photographs on my desk.

'It was the clever angle they were taken at. They make our proximity to one another on the rug look far more intimate than it was.'

'I believe you, sir.'

'It's the truth.' I snorted once more.

'So, we know that our man is an accomplished photographer, a professional perhaps.'

'What about the Hobb case? Has Trotter told you about that? Colleagues have warned me of the risks to my reputation if I defend the Reverend, and the press have already suggested that my chambers might be representing him.'

'That is another distinct possibility. Have you ever heard the term "the Common Bounce"?'

I nodded my head. 'It is an urban nightmare,'

'It is the extortion of money by accusing a man of sodomy. It is perhaps more rife in our society than the act itself.'

'But no one has ever attempted to make that slur against me. I have never been subjected to that.'

'Not yet.' Blakely wafted the offensive note under his nose as if sniffing for a scent. 'Although, according to this, they are accusing the two young ladies of a similar abomination, are they not? This text is tainted with innuendo.'

'Sapphism isn't against the law.'

'Not the law of man but such an accusation will hardly serve to cement Miss Holbrook's or Miss Alexander's reputation in society.'

'That is why I cannot believe Doctor Holbrook is involved.'

'On reflection, I think perhaps you are right.'

'Who else knew you were going to Kirkdale that day?'

'Well, not too many people. My friend Digby West knew, my grocer on Goodramgate knew ...'

'The grocer, the butcher, the baker, even the candlestick maker,' interrupted Blakely. 'Draw up a careful list, Mr Cairn, and send Mr Trotter round with it to my office before nightfall.'

Chapter Nine

Those last days of summer were warm. They felt precious before inclement seasons set in and I wanted to be out and enjoy them. I was tired of my stuffy office and paperwork. Offices are autumn and winter places.

'Trotter, how about a lunchtime picnic in the Botanic Garden, now Mr Brown and I have settled the Reverend's bail and he's scuttled safely back to the Isle of Wight?'

My clerk nodded vigorously, he is a man for the outdoors. 'I'll go to that grocer you've been recommending to high heaven. He's on Goodramgate, is he not? I'll go there straight away and buy fruit and English cheeses. There's a marvellous bakery nearby too,' he tells me; a glint to his eye.

The smell of freshly baked bread wells up in my imagination. 'I will supply the wine,' I tell him with matching enthusiasm.

We sat sprawled and beaming on my office sofa's throw-rug, thrown over the green grass. The Ouse oozed slowly past at the bottom of the gardens, the romantic Gothic ruins of St Mary's Abbey our more immediate backdrop. In modern contradiction, the voices, the splashing of ecstatic children rang out from the open air swimming pool nearby. We were like newly enfranchised citizens of the French Republic taking our joy in a royal park for the first time.

'So, he's really gone,' said Trotter.

'Gone for the time being, I hope.'

'Pity. I had almost grown fond of the Reverend.'

'I never thought I'd hear you say that, Trotter.'

'Well, the chap wasn't so bad.'

'I suppose he isn't bad at all. He just has this plight...' I hesitated, struggling for the best description. 'His personal peccadillo.'

'"Peccadillo", I like that,' sniffed Trotter. 'I must say I was surprised that you and Mr Brown took it upon yourselves to act as guarantors for his bail. Never known you do that for a client before, sir.'

'We didn't.'

'But you said...'

'I know what I said but this is in the strictest confidence, Trotter.'

'Of course, as always.' Trotter looked offended.

'We put a discreet notice in the local Isle of Wight paper and a church donor, hearing of the Reverend's present predicament, came forward to stand as bondsman for his bail. The donor wishes to remain anonymous to everyone apart from the magistrate, myself and Mr Brown of course.'

'Golly, how mysterious. I expect this donor is bona fide, has proved to be credible.'

'Oh, very much so. Mr Brown checked the guarantor out thoroughly. This person is of considerable standing and substance on the island.'

'We should do this more often,' said Trotter, leaning back on his elbows to enjoy the full warmth of the sun on his face.

'Indeed, we must,' I laughed, taking up my glass of red wine in a toast.

'This spot is truly magical,' said Trotter, looking about him in awe. 'It has a presence all of its own.'

'You mean an aura,' I offered.

'Yes, that's it,' agreed Trotter, 'an aura.'

'It has a history too.'

'We are surrounded by, spoilt for history in York, aren't we, sir?'

'Why do you think I chose to live and work here?'

'But your real speciality is prehistory, is it not? Beasts and sea serpents and suchlike.'

'You are right, Trotter, indeed I do have a passion for palaeontology. Then again, all history interests me. Look around you, York's walls, the buildings, the names – the Romans, Angles, Vikings, the Normans have all left their mark. See St Olave's over there, founded by Earl Siward, a Danish warrior, whose defeat of Macbeth was recorded by the Bard himself.'

'S i w a r d.' Trotter struggled to get his tongue round the Viking name.

'Yes, it was Siward who, when he felt himself to be dying of dysentery, urged his retainers to gird him in his armour. So, fully equipped with sword, shield and battleaxe, he awaited his final enemy, death. He is thought to be buried somewhere over there.' Again I pointed across to the classical outline of St Olave's church.

'What a warrior he must have been,' spluttered Trotter; his mouth full of bread and cheese. 'A warrior to the end.'

'Yes, quite the man. I wouldn't mind dying like that myself, in harness.' I shivered: not at the thought of dying but because we were suddenly cast in shadow.

'Oh, no.' Trotter's mouth gaped. 'Speaking of men.'

'Mr Cairn, Mr Trotter, I am so glad I've found you. Your chambers told me I might find you both here.' George Hobb stood over us blocking out the rays of the sun.

'But...' Trotter's mouth gaped more, now thankfully empty of contents.

Somewhat exasperated by this unexpected intrusion, it fell to me to find a response. 'I thought you would be well on your way back to the Isle of Wight by now, Reverend.'

'I couldn't bear to leave without thanking you. Both of you,' he emphasised smiling.

'Will you join us in a glass?' I asked, forced into politeness.

'I will gladly,' he replied, rubbing his hands down the front of his serge trousers in glee as he flopped down onto our rug.

My heart fell. Trotter's face bore the fierce expression of one of St Olave's snarling gargoyle beasts across the way. He would not be so easily won over this time by George Hobb.

I handed the Reverend a glass of wine, and scowling Trotter indicated that he would like another piece of the quartern loaf to accompany his speared blue stilton.

'Cheese, Reverend?' I asked Hobb first.

'Yes, yes, I'd love a piece of that Wensleydale. It looks really creamy.'

'It is creamy,' I assured him. Trotter's scowl deepened.

'Nothing like English cheeses and a good claret,' said Hobb.

'Nothing,' I agreed.

'Did you know this particular cheese was first produced by Cistercian brothers at Jervaulx Abbey in the twelfth century?' asked Hobb, the ecclesiastical gourmet. I shook my head. I was ignorant about so many things.

'Did you know this bread is entirely made of wheat?' asked Trotter sarcastically, reaching over to help himself to a piece of the quartern loaf.

'Well, we are blessed then for your neighbours in the West Riding of this great county of yours eat nothing but oaten bread. Some years past, I myself had occasion to bicycle through the town of Otley, a derivation of Oatley or Oat-field, I believe, where they grew no other grain.'

'A vulgar misconception,' muttered Trotter under his breath. Trotter who knew. Trotter who originated from lands along the lively Wharfe rather than the mudflats of our somnambulant Ouse. 'In Doomsday it was referred to as Othelai or the field or clearing of Othe or Otho,' he instructed us more forcefully.

'I am sure you are right,' laughed Hobb without taking offence. Indeed I began to wonder how far one would have to go to cause George Hobb offence.

'Wheat or oats, I am sure we should be thankful for small mercies,' I said.

'How do you mean, sir?' asked Trotter.

'Well, if it wasn't for the microscopist, Doctor Arthur Hill Hassall, and the Sale of Food and Drugs Act 1875, this staff of life might still be adulterated with alum for whiteness, copper for colour and sawdust for bulk.'

'And this wine might be poisoned with lead,' added Hobb, lifting crystal and wine to the sunlight.

'All the same you were wrong about the origins of the place name Otley,' badgered Trotter.

'But am I not right in thinking that Otley was the birthplace of the furniture-maker Thomas Chippendale?'

'You must have an interest in social history,' I suggested flatteringly, trying to make amends for Trotter's rudeness.

'Well, I wouldn't go so far...'

'Were you wearing a dress?' cut in Trotter.

'Sorry?' asked the Reverend.

'Were you wearing a dress when you bicycled through Otley?'

'Trotter,' I warned between gritted teeth.

'Because if you were you risked having your brains beaten out.' Some reconstituted matter sputtered out of Trotter's mouth narrowly missing the Reverend. 'The lads over there don't mess about.'

'That's enough,' I snarled.

Hobb lifted up his hand to placate me. 'It doesn't matter, Mr Cairn, I am used to this. And the answer is "no", Mr Trotter, I wasn't wearing a dress at the time. What is that imposing building over there?' asked Hobb, changing the subject.

'Oh, that,' I sighed. 'That is the Museum of Antiquities and belongs to the Yorkshire Philosophical Society. In there is housed my true passion.'

'So what is this true passion of yours?' asked Hobb.

'It's Mr Cairn's secret,' again rudely interrupted Trotter.

'No it's not,' I objected. Trotter's possessiveness was beginning to irk me. 'Plesiosaurs, ichthyosaurs, you name it. I am a student of the natural sciences.'

'How wonderful.' Hobb clapped his hands together in delight. 'I would love to see some of those specimens for myself one day.'

'Did you know, Trotter, they had a small menagerie in these gardens at one time?' I asked, attempting to humour my clerk back into party mood. Trotter's expression remained sulky. 'Well, it's true, the present curator told me himself. They had a stoat, a swan, a heron, a porpoise and a python, would you believe? As well as a golden eagle, several monkeys and a bear. But according to the curator it was the bear that became difficult and expensive to house. Finally, it escaped from its cage one day and chased John Phillips, the first Keeper of the Museum, along with another gentleman, a Mr Harcourt, into an outbuilding. The two men never forgave the bear and it was soon expelled to London Zoo on the York coach as an outside passenger.'

'I don't believe you,' said Trotter 'How would the other passengers feel having a bear on board?'

'Well, I understand the journey took place during the winter months...'

'I know, I know what you are going to say,' screamed Hobb, rolling around in a fit of hysterics. 'The bear's fellow passengers wrapped him round themselves like a rug.'

'Now you're both pulling my leg,' objected the sullen Trotter.

'No, we're not,' I assured him.

'Anyway, I have work to do.' Trotter struggled to his feet.

'Stay a while longer,' said Hobb, pinching the hem of Trotter's trousers. 'My train doesn't go till this evening.'

'As I said, I have work to do.' Trotter shook his trouser leg offhandedly

'And you?' Hobb's dark eyes beseeched me like a woman's – a woman it was hard to refuse.

'Let me tell you more about the museum over there.' I pointed across the garden to the museum's classical pillared architecture. The Yorkshire Philosophical Society was first established as a gentlemen's science club…'

'"Gentleman's", that rules the Reverend out straight away,' hissed hovering Trotter. I heard him but I was not sure Hobb had. I wished Trotter would just go away now.

'To study the area's vast repository of antiquities and geological specimens,' I continued undeterred, giving no credence to Trotter's spite.

'We've nothing so grand in the Isle of Wight,' sighed Hobb.

'No, but you had the late Reverend William D. Fox. Fox must have had more dinosaurs named after him than any other man in England.'

'Indeed, I suppose you're right,' replied Hobb thoughtfully.

'Trotter, see to our picnic things,' I commanded rather than asked. 'I am going to escort the Reverend round the museum. I'll be back in chambers in an hour or two.' What harm could there be to it? I never tired, was addicted to viewing the bones of those monsters that roamed a very different landscape to ours.

'As you please, Mr Cairn.' Trotter snatched up our bottle and brown cheese wrappers, swung the throw-rug across his arm and left in disgust.

'He still doesn't like me very much, does he?' asked Hobb.

'It's not that he doesn't like you, George,' I replied. 'He doesn't like you in dresses.'

'Then he doesn't like me.'

I loved the museum and had already spent many hours viewing its comprehensive fossil collection. The building was designed by metropolitan architect William Wilkins in the Greek Revival style and was opened in 1830. It was one of the first purpose-built museums to be opened in the country, when the construction of the British Museum was only just getting underway. There were four exhibit rooms, a lecture room and a room for the curator. Some of the galleries were top-lit to increase the available space for display. High-ceilinged and echoing, it reminded me of the new tiled indoor swimming pools popping up here and there in many of our industrial cities. Then again, it wasn't unlike a library with its restrained silence where the slightest noise – a cough, the scraping of a boot – assaulted the senses like a gun shot.

'Welcome to one of my favourite temples of learning.' I was feeling flamboyant, free of Trotter.

We made our way with difficulty round elephant skulls and jutting tusks, skeletons of horned giant elk and a massive horse.

'What on earth is that?' asked Hobb, pointing to the pinned bones of a giant bird.

'That, my friend, is an extinct moa bird from New Zealand,' announced an amused voice behind us. I swung round to find the museum's curator. 'James, how are you?' We shook hands, Hobb shook hands, smiles all around. 'Come, James, bring your friend, I've something to show you both in my stock room.'

I blinked in the dim light. Hobb gasped. An enormous fossilised skull and skeletal body lay on the curator's floor.

'But its head is as big as a card table,' I exclaimed.

'Quite so. We believe this to be the biggest ichthyosaur ever found,' said the curator.

I knelt down next to the creature and placed a fist in one of its eye sockets. My fist was completely absorbed.

'Amazing,' I said.

'And guess where it was found, James? Kettleness, not a stone's throw from where you found yours at Staithes.'

'"Yours"?' repeated Hobb.

'Yes, didn't James tell you about his ichthyosaur find?' asked the curator. Adding with feigned hurt, 'The one he saw fit to sell to Whitby museum rather than to us.'

'But mine was only a baby.'

'Yes, and this might have been its mama.'

'Nevertheless, this one puts my ichthyosaur very much in perspective.'

'He's too modest, is he not?' The curator asked Hobb.

'He certainly is that,' replied the Reverend.

'You must get him to tell you how he found the baby ichthyosaur,' suggested the curator.

'Well?' responded Hobb, his eyes riveted on mine.

'Some other time,' I prevaricated. 'There's already so much to see in here.'

With that, and our thanks, we took our leave of the curator to stand side by side peering down into glass upon glass of display cabinets housing the assorted teeth and bones of long extinct animals. We regarded them with as much wide-eyed awe as if they were relics of the gods.

All of a sudden I began to feel uncomfortable as I looked to see if anyone else was observing us. Although Hobb was dressed conventionally, there was still an air about him, a femininity. But the fear of been seen by anyone else who knew me with this rather unusual client proved to be groundless. Because the weather was so fine outside we appeared to be the only two visitors in the museum that afternoon.

'Some of these marine reptilians must have been enormous,' said Hobb, leaning agog over another cabinet.

'That's the head of a fossilized crocodile, teleosaurus chapmani, it could grow to thirteen feet long. But some of the land roaming animals had a size and power almost beyond our imagination.'

'Is that what attracts you to these prehistoric beasts, their power? Do you find power attractive, Mr Cairn?' Sometimes Hobb had a way of making the most innocuous sentences sound erotic.

I shook my head and smiled. 'No, I am drawn to fossilised shells and bones because of their rarity, their mystery. I enjoy being the first man to see them in the place they fell, the science of extricating them perfectly.'

'You are a perfectionist then?'

'No, George, not just that. Even dead creatures have a tale to tell. I am a disciple of the new science.'

'Ah, the science that excludes God.'

'Not necessarily.'

'But you are a Darwin man?'

'I am a Darwin man.'

Hobb fell silent as we began to re-examine each cabinet proudly displaying the names of the finds' donators.

HEAD AND PART OF A SKELETON OF THE ICHTHYOSAURUS FROM THE WHITBY
ALUM SHALE; 480 OTHER FOSSILS FROM THE STRATA OF YORKSHIRE AND
OTHER PARTS OF ENGLAND; AND 57 SWEDISH, ALPINE, AND OTHER MINERALS

REVEREND W.V. VERNON

SKELETON OF AN ICHTHYOSAURUS, WITH OTHER PORTIONS OF ICHTHYOSAURUS,
AND OTHER FOSSILS, FROM WHITBY ALUM SHALE

MR BIRD

'See here, the Reverend J. Graham, the Reverend W.D. Conybeare, they can't all be Darwinists like you.'

'I am not sure what they are.'

'And see here the Reverend W.V. Vernon mentioned again.'

'So, palaeontology is predominated by clerics and doctors. What's your point, George?'

'Well, they can't all be disbelievers.'

'Come,' I beckoned him over to a cabinet we had not yet examined. 'I have a story to tell you and the story is here.'

The inscription on the cabinet read:

SPECIMENS OF FOSSIL BONES AND TEETH FROM THE CAVE OF KIRKDALE, OF THE
ELEPHANT, HIPPOPOTAMUS, RHINOCEROS, OX, STAG, HYENA, FOX, WATER-RAT
AND WIDGEON: THE BONES AND TEETH OF THE HYENA AMOUNTING TO 122.

MR JAS. ATKINSON. MR SALMOND MR THORILE.
H.A. ATCHESON. MB. REVEREND W. EASTMEAD.
REVEREND W.V.VERNON

'Kirkdale Cave, where is that?' asked Hobb.

'Just over twenty miles from where we are standing.'

'But some of these bones are from African animals, are they not?'

'This was one of the greatest mysteries of our age. How did they get here? How did African elephants finish up in a Yorkshire cave? And it took another of your fellow clergymen, Dr William Buckland, to solve it.'

'I've heard of him of course but how did Buckland come to discover a cave in Yorkshire?'

'He didn't. It was quarrymen working near Kirkby Moorside in the first half of our century who first exposed it. Unusual bones and teeth had been found in the area for sometime. John Gibson, a visiting fossil collector, traced them back to the cave. In the summer of twenty-one, a small number of local geologists set about excavating the site, these same named men here I shouldn't wonder,' I pointed to the cabinet's inscription. 'It wasn't until the following year that Buckland himself became involved.'

'I fancy the good Oxford lecturer wasn't overjoyed with the likes of Jas. Atkinson and Co. taking bones from the site before he was able to examine them in situ.' Hobb seemed to know more about palaeontological exploration than I had given him credit for.

'Knowing the reputation for professionalism of Dr Buckland you may well be right, George. Although in defence of these local men, they might have feared many of the fossils would be destroyed by quarrying.'

'What a puzzle.' Hobb inhaled a gasp of air.

'What a puzzle indeed, George. At the time it was a widely held belief that these animals had perished in the Universal Flood and that their remains had been washed into the cave.'

'All the way from Africa?'

'That isn't the end of the story, as with Darwin, so with the more politic Buckland, it was the beginning.'

'Please go on,' said Hobb, looking as if he wasn't sure he wanted me to.

'I can tell you verbatim Buckland's findings, or as near as dammit, if you would like me to.'

'How can you do that, the fellow must have been dead half a century?'

'He died on the fourteenth of August, 1856.'

'I have already been impressed by your knowledge of dates, but how can you remember his exact analysis of the bones?'

'A gift of memory I was born with. I see both letters and mathematical figures in pictures.' I felt my face flush up. I always found this unusual facility of mine embarrassing to talk about. Sometimes I felt it less an asset and more a burden, a peculiarity marking me out from other men.

'Amazing. So tell me about the Reverend William Buckland's findings.'

'"Scarcely a single bone has escaped fracture…"' I lowered my voice an octave or two for the big man and decided to pronounce only his most salient findings.

'I feel as if I am at a seance,' said Hobb enthralled.

'You are. "Some of the bones' marks appear to fit the form of the canine teeth of the hyena that occur in the cave. The hyena's bones have been broken, and apparently gnawed equally with those of other animals. Not one skull is to be found entire; and it is so rare to find a large bone of any kind that has not been more or less broken and there is no hope of obtaining materials for the construction of a single limb, and still less of an entire skeleton". Buckland calculated that the greatest number of teeth were those of hyenas and many of them had died before the first set of milk teeth had been shed.'

Hobb looked even more intrigued. 'Roughly, how many hyenas are we talking about?' he asked.

'Buckland believed there could have been two to three hundred of them.'

'But how big was the cave entrance?'

'Too small for a hippopotamus to have been washed into. Something in the region of three feet high by five feet broad, and in the interior of the cave Buckland could not find a single pebble that bore the mark of having been rolled by water.'

Following this information, Hobb peered deeper into the display case. 'Look, see there on that bigger bone, hundreds of marks the size of pepper corns. What are they?' he asked. 'Are you saying those are teeth marks? I've never seen anything like them before.'

'Indeed,' I agreed. 'What is more Buckland took a party of gentlemen to Wombwell's travelling show for a unique demonstration, a demonstration to explain your pepper corns. He threw the shin bone of an ox into a Cape hyena's cage. After several minutes, Mr Wombwell's assistant distracted the animal with a plank of wood, while the showman retrieved the gnawed bone. Buckland's party could clearly see that the hyena's teeth imprints matched the mystery marks on the Kirkdale bones exactly. If you will forgive the pun, Buckland had made his mark and his name.'

'Good gracious,' gasped Hobb. 'So what conclusions are we to draw from all this?' I almost felt sorry for Hobb, he looked so bewildered,

'That Kirkdale was inhabited by hyenas in antediluvian times, scavenging and butchering the dead animals around them before dragging their remnants inside the cave to devour at leisure. Although, unlike Darwin, Buckland did concede that the Flood might have arrived later to cover their bones in a layer of mud.'

'A small concession.'

'A small concession to Genesis, I grant you.'

'I take it you have visited this cave yourself?'

'Of course. It is located on the side of a quarry surrounded by the most beautiful and tranquil countryside to be seen in England. You know, George, I am beginning to suspect you have as much passion for palaeontology as I do.'

'I don't know what gives you that impression. But these men – Darwin, Buckland and the like – are changing our religious values, our entire way of thinking.'

'And as a clergyman that makes you feel uncomfortable.'

'I have read Darwin.'

'And how he contradicts much of the teachings of the Bible, The Book of Revelation for instance.'

'If there is a God, then I believe that God is above everything.'

'Do you know, the really odd thing about Kirkdale Cave is its location.'

'In what way?'

'Because only a few yards across the ford from the cave is an Anglo-Saxon church, St Gregory's Minster. I have visited there quite recently, and think it is the most sublime place of worship in the most exquisite setting I have ever seen.'

'A monastic house then.'

'I believe a community of Augustinian canons held the living there at one time.'

'I would have loved to visit your Kirkdale.'

'But you've run out of time,' I told him kindly.

'Yes, yes, just so. But tell me about your baby ichthyosaur find, how did that affect you? When you held it in your hands, did your Christian faith dissolve in a moment?'

'That is another story, and to put the record straight I did not find it entirely on my own. A dear friend of mine, later to become a client, led me to the site.'

'How interesting. Is it not more usual for a client relationship to develop into a friendship rather than vice versa?' asked Hobb.

'George, George, how lovely to see you.' I had thought we were alone in the museum until a foppish young man sidled up to us over the Kirkdale cabinet. 'And who's this? Pardon me but I couldn't help sneaking a listen. So knowledgeable, such a handsome fellow, such an interesting conversationalist. You've certainly kept this erudite young gentleman to yourself, eh George?'

'James Cairn, Kenneth Bright.' Hobb reluctantly introduced us, freeing his arm from Bright's clutch.

'I never associated you, George, with a lot of old bones,' tittered Bright.

'I could say the same about you, Kenneth,' replied Hobb.

'I cannot tell a lie. I saw you both through the window.' Bright pointed towards a trickle of afternoon sunlight illuminating the room. Endless rising dust particles floated round our heads as we eyed one another.

'I've a train to catch,' said Hobb abruptly, pulling out his pocket watch.

'Going so soon,' swooned Bright as Hobb made a rush for the door.

'Who the hell was that?' I asked, eventually catching up with the Reverend halfway across the garden. 'He's not related to Jacob Bright the politician, is he?'

'He's no one,' sighed Hobb. 'No one for you to worry about.'

'Being seen with a "no one" like that in your present situation could put you in prison for ten years.' We had reached Museum Street and Hobb began trying to hail a carriage. It was the end of a working day and most of the carriages were taken. 'Tell me, George, I've been dying to ask you this, why did you come all the way to Yorkshire in the first place? Surely Yorkshire isn't the most sympathetic place in the world for a man to be seen in a dress?'

'I had arranged to meet someone.'

'Not that awful fellow, Bright,' I nodded back to the museum.

'No.' Hobb smiled. 'I had arranged an audience with the archbishop. The Archbishop of York is as far away from the Isle of Wight as you can get in the Church of England hierarchy.'

'Yes, the archbishop, Mr Brown did mention something of the sort to me.' I decided to be economical with the truth about my own visit to the Bishopthorpe Palace.

'I had…' Hobb paused, 'I had a serious crisis of conscience.'

'Why am I not surprised when you mix with the likes of Bright?'

'Kenneth Bright is harmless enough. He just likes dressing up like me.'

'If you say so.' The old pervasive doubt washed over me in a way the Universal Deluge had failed to do over Buckland's cave. Were Hobb and his friends satisfied with merely wearing dresses or was there more to it? 'How many of you are there out there who like dressing up?' I asked him.

'Not enough for you to worry about. And for your information my conscience is untroubled by the dresses I wear. I am more troubled by the doubts in my head.'

'By the way, George, where is your luggage at present?' I could see a hansom cab flying towards us down St Duncombe Place.

'My valise is already waiting for me at the station,' said Hobb, raising his arm towards the cab like a conductor.

'I think you might be in luck with this one.' The approaching cab appeared to slow a fraction.

'And you won't be able to resist telling me that the hansom cab was invented by a York architect, will you?' grinned Hobb; as the vehicle slewed into the side, stopped and rocked.

'Joseph Aloysius Hansom, 1834.'

'Umm,' said Hobb. 'But then, the Reverend Samuel Phelps told me you had a detailed knowledge of architecture.'

'The dean of Bishopthorpe Palace has been in touch with you?' I asked in surprise.

'Don't be fooled, Mr Cairn, the Church is one of the most intimate clubs in the world.'

With that Hobb swung into the waiting hansom. 'By the way, you know you mentioned Fox?' he shrilled though the hansom's open front.

Did he mean Crispin Fox, the judge, I wondered, disconcerted for a second.

'William Fox, the palaeontologist, remember? The man who had more dinosaurs named after him than any other living person. I have a confession to make. When I was a newly arrived young curate on the Isle of Wight, William Fox worked in the neighbouring parish. He became a good friend of mine.'

'Why didn't you say?'

'When you begin preparing my case, you must come and stay with me at the Rectory.' With that Hobb knocked for the driver to be off. 'The Isle of Wight is full of fossils,' he shouted back to me.

And a few more skeletons hidden away in the cupboard, I don't doubt, I thought to myself as Hobb's cab disappeared down Museum Street. Nevertheless, despite my suspicions, despite my better judgement, I had grown to like George Hobb very much.

My mouth suddenly felt dry with too much lunchtime wine. I took the cup at the Museum Road fountain and drank, staring at the five lion crest of York as I did so. I loved this city. I could never bear to leave it for any length of time but on that I was wrong.

Chapter Ten

'Had a good time in the museum, did we, sir?' Trotter still looked sulky the next morning.

'Yes, so much so by the time I got back here to Bootham Chambers you had all gone home.'

'Must have been a long session with the Reverend then.'

I chose not to respond to the taunt. I didn't think Trotter was in any mood to appreciate my having enjoyed my afternoon with the enigmatic George Hobb.

'I hope you don't mind me saying this, sir, but you risk your reputation being seen out and about in the city with a...' Trotter took a deep breath, 'with a man like Hobb.'

'Oh, but I do mind, Trotter.'

'But a man in your social position,' persisted Trotter.

'I don't think I need you to tell me how to conduct myself in society.'

'I was only...'

'Out!' I screamed, jabbing an angry finger towards the door.

Trotter hesitated: for once he had failed to read the signs.

'But, sir,' he objected.

'But nothing, sir. You were extremely rude to our client yesterday afternoon. If there is one thing I will not tolerate in chambers it is bigotry.'

Just as he was exiting my room in a dither, Thomas Leacock tried to edge in past him.

'What's wrong with Trotter?' asked Leacock.

'He must have got out of bed with his left leg foremost,' I muttered.

'What?' Our chambers' veteran partner looked more confused.

'He's in a foul mood,' I explained.

'I see,' said Leacock, not seeing at all.

'And come to think of it so am I,' I added angrily.

'Perhaps now is not the right time then,' fluttered Leacock about to make his exit too.

Leacock was a few years older than Andrew Carlton-Bingham but, having joined the partnership later, Carlton-Bingham remained senior partner. The two men were very different in personality and appearance: Leacock was a quiet serious man, thin and studious looking. He was subject to stomach ulcers and not as robust as Carlton-Bingham. Our other partner, Gerald Fawcett, felt Leacock should retire and was doing his best to encourage him in that pursuit. I watched Leacock nervously brush his fringe of still amazingly black hair from his eyes. I liked Leacock and I thought he liked me.

'No, stay. How can I help you?'

'Andrew told me about this brief you've got with the skirted priest. When I was out in India I was involved in setting up the legislation for Stephens' Criminal Tribes Act, for my sins. Thought these might be of interest to you.' He thrust a wad of papers on my desk just as Carlton-Bingham had done with the legal papers and newspaper reports on *Regina v Boulton, Park and others*. 'You'll also find in there the up-to-date amendment of the act. Penalties on registered eunuchs appearing in female clothes, that sort of thing.'

'Why for your sins? Did you not like India?'

'Loved it, old boy, I just wasn't too sure about the right of our presence there or the Stephens' legislation. The heat, the smells of spices and shit, the people, the religion, everything about India is alien to us and we to it. Their civilisation is far older than ours. They know far better than us how to manage their blistering climate, their society, their water. What right do we have to thrust our laws and manners onto them? What right, tell me that?'

I looked into the gaunt face of Thomas Leacock and knew I could tell him nothing. I had not been there. I had never felt the penetrating rays of their sun, experienced the men and women of India. Glancing down on Leacock's papers on my desk, I somehow desperately hoped I might find some justification for us being there other than cotton and tea.

'Do you know we even had servants, punkah-wallahs they were called, pulling on ropes all day long to work the fans.'

'"Remember Cawnpore!"' I cried, lifting up an arm, trying to instil a little theatrical humour into the discussion. Leacock remained resolutely unsmiling. 'At least you weren't there, Thomas, for the sepoys' mutiny against the British East Indian Company's army,' I offered provocatively.

'Puh! That company had a lot to answer for. The Indian Mutiny of Fifty-seven. Thank goodness, the horrors of it were some thirteen or fourteen years before my time. India's cruellest time.'

'To think it all started over the introduction of the new Enfield rifles and the native soldiers' refusal to bite the greased cartridges to load their weapons. Rather a petty reason for a murderous rebellion, wasn't it?'

'They believed the cartridges to be contaminated by animal fats and contrary to their religious beliefs,' said Leacock in vindication; Leacock who sounded as if he had not only gone native but remained native. 'And I think that is a gross oversimplification of the true reasons for the rebellion, James, if I might say so. That story was something given out by our government and journalists.'

'But didn't the sepoys massacre women and children? They threw British children down wells alive to suffocate amid the putrefying bodies of their mothers and siblings.'

'Unfortunately, as in all wars, savagery wasn't confined to one side,' explained Leacock quietly, deathly quietly. 'In retribution for one house massacre our soldiers made the Indian rebels lick the blood off the walls and floors.'

'But what about the deflowering of General Wheeler's youngest daughter? Wasn't that true?'

'There were two young girls involved in that incident. But the British press chose to dwell on the higher status girl of course.'

'Just like the caste system of India,' I mischievously pointed out. 'But please go on, I am all ears.'

'A seventeen-year-old Eurasian girl, Amy Horne, miraculously survived the Satichaura Ghat massacre on the banks of the Ganges. But she fell from a boat while making her escape and was swept downstream. Soon after scrambling ashore she met up with Wheeler's youngest daughter, Margaret she was called. Fearing for their lives, the two girls hid in the undergrowth for a number of hours until they were discovered by a group of rebels. Margaret was taken away on horseback, never to be seen again, and Amy was led to a nearby village where she was placed under the protection of a Muslim rebel leader in exchange for converting to Islam.'

'A fate worse than death.' I swooned in Gothic fashion, remembering Winifred's words.

'James, if you are not going to be serious about this.'

'Sorry, I apologise. I cannot break the habit of treating horror and humour as one. It is my adolescent way of dealing with unpleasant things.'

'You are an extremely complex man, James.'

'Am I?'

'Yes, and you are too bloody attractive for your own good. You don't have to try. Both men and women fall over themselves to please you.'

'Is that how you really see me?' I asked in amazement.

'It is. And no, it wasn't quite a fate worse than death, because six months later Amy was rescued by Highlanders from Sir Colin Campbell's column on their way to relieve Lucknow. It was rumoured that Margaret had been killed by her captors, although many in India believe she survived the massacre and was forced to marry a Muslim soldier. Indeed, I had a bearer who swore he knew her husband.'

'I do hope you have forgiven me my levity, Thomas, I was merely conjuring up the reaction in the society salons back here.'

'I'm sure that is not far from the truth. Better to be killed than lose your virginity to a Dalit, eh?'

'It must have been a terrifying ordeal for both young girls to endure. Did I hear you correctly when you said Margaret was regarded by the British press as being of higher status?'

'You did.'

'But I understood that General Wheeler was married to an Indian woman, making Margaret an Anglo-Indian.'

'That's right but she was a general's daughter. You see, at first the East India Company encouraged their employees to marry Indian women, although by the time I got there such marital arrangements were beginning to be frowned upon. Puh! The Raj. What arrogant fools we are, James, and India is our tragic comedy.'

'Like Africa?'

'A mess,' he agreed. 'Bharat is like the Bengal tiger never to be tamed.'

'But what about the town of Simla? I heard Simla is civilised and very agreeable.'

'Ah, Simla, now you are talking, James. Simla "the Queen of the Hills".'

'I've heard it acts as a retreat for soldiers, merchants and civil servants from the summer heat of the Great Plains.'

'And ladies, James, many ladies.'

'Do you mean native women?'

'No. In Simla the great temptation was English women.'

'And you were tempted?' I asked. Leacock nodded. 'How many English women?'

'Half-a-dozen or so,' boasted Leacock.

'And was Mrs Leacock with you during your Indian posting?' I could not help asking; a little taken aback because I knew Leacock to be a happily married family man of many years.

'You have to understand, James, I was an impressionable young man then and I was far away from home.' The usually serious and intense Leacock gave me a frivolous wink. I had never seen this side of him before.

'So, you were married at the time?'

'No, no,' laughed Leacock. 'I was exposed to the intrigues and dalliances of Simla society long before I met my good lady.'

'And who were these half-a-dozen or so women of yours?'

'Most of them were married,' admitted Leacock. 'I remember one in particular, Adelaide she was called, Addie for short. She was beautiful and blonde, slim and vivacious. Her husband, I seem to remember, was an army lieutenant and had been away for a year or two trying to root out the Thuggees from the jungles of West Bengal. What a girl Addie was. She could dance the pants off any man.'

'It certainly sounds as if she danced yours off.'

'Never thought she would give me a second look, James. Shows you how wrong we men can be about these things.'

'And how long did this affair last with Addie?'

'Only a couple of weeks. But the strange thing is, I've never forgotten her. Then there were the Anglo-Indian girls like Margaret Wheeler. I can't begin to tell you how gorgeous some of them were back in Delhi, talk about temptation.'

'And again you found you had no willpower against such temptations.' Another jibe, another twinge of jealousy on my part. It had been a long time since temptation had been put my way.

Leacock reddened, finally realising I was teasing him. 'India changes everyone. If you've never been there, you can never hope to understand. The clean delicate fragrance of the yellow flowering mimosa, even the smell of dust on the streets, the heat, the gardens of entwining Hindu statues, all these things lend themselves to heightened sensuality.'

'And then there's the fishing fleets.'

'The what?' asked Leacock.

'Have you really never heard of the fishing fleets? Salon talk is unremitting about them. The Miss Smiths, the Miss Browns, the Miss Jones, all seaworthy and bound for Calcutta to seek out Britain's finest sons.'

'I'm not familiar with that term, must be after my time, old boy. I've never heard of English ladies referred to in that way. Although, no doubt, I've shared a sheet with one or two of them.'

'Despite the nautical theme, I take it we are not speaking of ropes and sails here.'

'No, but there was a Miss Harding who arrived on HMS...'

'Isn't there a Hanuman temple in Simla where monkeys attack you?' I asked, tiring of hearing about Leacock's premarital exploits.

'Yes, yes, Sankat Mochan is famous for its monkeys.' Leacock's eyes bulged with pleasure. 'It's about six miles out of Simla proper.'

'I've heard the monkeys will steal bread out of your hands.'

'Yes, they'll pinch it out of your mouth if you don't watch out.'

'They sound like the herring gulls at Staithes.'

'Indeed, although India is far removed from Staithes. By the way, have you had any word from your old client Robertshaw?'

'No, not recently, though I believe Daniel fares well. He and his mother eventually inherited money from her sister's estate and they are running a small lodging house in the village.'

'What a case that was. To defend a Down's syndrome man accused of murdering a young girl in front of his entire village. You pulled that one off against all the odds.'

'Yes,' I agreed wearily, 'and now I have another difficult defence. You'd better let me get started on these papers of yours or I'll not have them finished by home time.'

'No hurry, James, you're welcome to keep them for a few days.' With that Leacock was gone and right on cue entered Trotter. My office was beginning to feel like a scene from a Punch and Judy show. But who was Mr Punch and who was Judy? Who would get their head battered in? Who would steal the show? Perhaps one of us ought to be wearing a reinforced turban.'

'I didn't mean to upset you earlier,' said Trotter, clearing his throat. 'I only have your best interests at heart, sir.'

'I know you do, Trotter.'

'And, believe me, I do have some experience of unfortunate misinterpretations. In this life it often matters more how things are perceived than how they actually are,' he continued, with an irksome hint of indulgence.

I started to rummage through Leacock's papers on The Criminal Tribes' Act. Trotter remained hovering over me, definitely exposing himself as my imaginary Beadle.

'Yes?' I acted as if I was surprised he was still there.

'Still friends, sir?' he asked, shoving out his bony hand.

'Yes, still friends,' I replied, the hand hard and damp in mine. 'Now let me take a look at these papers before Mr Leacock wants them back. How do you fancy discussing the Hobb case with me, Trotter, over a light lunch at the Coffee Tavern in Colliergate?'

'That would be perfect, sir, just perfect.'

'A plate of toasted crumpets for me,' ordered Trotter, amid the ferns and potted plants of the Coffee Tavern. His attention remained fixed on the manageress's, Mrs Hubie's menu, studiously avoiding making any eye contact with the waitress serving us. I had noticed this deviant attitude towards women before in my clerk. Was it shyness regarding the fairer sex or did he just not like them? 'With plenty of butter,' he added, eyes still cast down.

'It'll be the bachelor's omelette for me today, please,' I ordered.

'Puh! An omelette for a bachelor, that's a good one,' chirped Trotter.

'With plenty of eggs,' I added, winking at the sea blue, slightly prominent eyes smiling down on me. Our petite waitress was extremely attractive. Her waist was almost as narrow as Winifred's. How could Trotter fail to give such a creature a second glance? – the man was a mystery to me.

'And I'd like to finish with curd tart, if you please,' he requested, only now relinquishing the menu.

'With a high percentage of rose water in the ingredients, no doubt,' I couldn't resist saying. For most men this would have been a joke too far but, as he had done with the girl, Trotter chose to ignore me.

'Would, sir, like cream or special Italian ice cream with the tart?' the waitress asked him.

'Ice cream,' he responded, finally with an enthusiastic upwards glance.

'All with a pot of tea for two,' I interjected.

With a shrug of narrow shoulders, and dismissive toss of the head, she was gone.

'She's a bit of a haughty miss,' commented Trotter.

'A bit.'

'Anything interesting in Mr Leacock's papers?'

'I've only glanced through them as yet but, yes, there was something I found rather interesting.'

'And what would that be, sir?'

'The determination of the British government to impose its social values on a Crown colony.'

'As it does on us, its own people.'

'Indeed it does. That's what bothers me.'

'How does it bother you, sir? We have to have some form of government.'

'Yes, but we have the chance to vote into power a government of our own choosing. Her Majesty's Indian subjects do not have a vote. They are the disenfranchised, they have been colonised by stealth.'

'Are you saying foreigners, black and brown men, should have a say in who runs this country, the Empire? Why, our own womenfolk don't even have that right.'

'Quite so, Trotter.'

'I do believe, sir, you've been giving too much credence to the opinions of the likes of Mr Hardie and that Mrs Pankhurst.'

'I can think of far worse human beings to be allied to than Kier Hardie and "that" Emmeline Pankhurst.'

'But they're troublemakers.'

'Toasted crumpets, one bachelor omelette and a pot of tea.' Perhaps it was a blessing, just when our conversation was becoming opposed and difficult the petite waitress reappeared, tray in hand.

The way lean Trotter set about clearing his plate, butter dripping down his jowl, I began to question how well he ate at home. The term "wolfing it down" took on new significance.

'Hungry?' I asked, pouring the tea.

'I'm always hungry,' was his stuffed cheek response. 'And these crumpets are excellent with just the right amount of yeast to flour. How about your omelette, sir?'

'Excellent too. I love this topping of herbs and onions.'

'We're both happy then, sir.'

'I doubt I'll get through dinner tonight though.'

'Me neither,' he agreed, suddenly sitting bolt upright and straining his neck like a goose round a potted aspidistra. 'Who's that staring at us through the window?'

My back was to the window. 'Where? Where?' I asked, attempting to swivel round in the bentwood chair.

'Gone, he's gone.'

'What did he look like?'

'Just a chap, an average sort of chap.'

'Can't you give me a better description than that?'

'I only got a glimpse,' he objected, beginning to twitch. Trotter was extremely sensitive to criticism.

'Was he wearing a hat?'

'No, I don't think so.'

'Perhaps he was someone simply wondering what the food is like in here. Let's forget about it or it will spoil our lunch. More tea?' I offered.

'Please. What sort of tea is this? It's very fine, pure tasting.'

I took a delicate sip. 'A quality black Darjeeling,' I pronounced.

'I would have been impressed,' Trotter smirked, 'but I see it here on the menu.'

'As always, Trotter, you are one step ahead of me. But did you know David Crole estimated in his book, *Tea: A Text Book of Tea Planting and*

Manufacture, published only a couple of years ago, that eighty million cups of tea are imbibed in England daily?'

'Really? Speaking of tea, Darjeeling, India, have you found anything in Mr Leacock's papers that might be useful to the Hobb case?' asked Trotter; a man who lived for the job.

'As I've already said, I've not had enough time to fully examine them. Although men dressing as women isn't something restricted to these isles, I can tell you that. It certainly happens in India, perhaps it happens all over the world, who knows.'

'This Italian ice cream's good, goes perfectly with the tart. But how do they make it, keep it so cool even in the warm weather we've been having lately?' Trotter asked, tucking into his newly arrived dessert.

'Deep ice wells, ice houses, then they contain it in pails of salt and ice.' Tempted, I watched Trotter down his final spoonful of creamy vanilla ice cream.

'All the same, it's a miracle to me. You were saying, sir, about these lady boys?' Writhing from side to side on the cane seat, Trotter drew it closer to the table.

'Yes, for centuries in India it's been an accepted part of their culture, a culture within a culture as it were.'

'Really?' I could see from his expression that India was living up to all his worst expectations.

'A couple of years ago we British made an amendment to the Criminal Tribes Act 1871, which Mr Leacock originally helped to draw up.' I took a deep breath, Trotter was all ears now. 'This amendment was entitled An Act for the Registration of Criminal Tribes and Eunuchs.'

'"Eunuchs"?'

'Yes, a eunuch is deemed to include all members of the male sex who, on medical inspection, clearly appear to be impotent or admit that they are themselves.'

'But what man would admit to that?'

'There is a large community of them in India called the hijras who dress and act as women. They perform religious ceremonies at marriages and the birth of male babies which involve music, singing and sexually suggestive dancing, I believe.'

'I'm not sure I like the sound of them.' said Trotter, dismally regarding his empty tart dish.

'For the Hindus the hijras belong to a special caste and are devotees of the mother goddess Bahuchara Mata. For Muslims the hijras are regarded as a third gender which is believed to be the result of Allah's will. But, in accordance with Islamic practice, all hijras bury their dead instead of cremating them. While alive they live in close-knit families. A young boy will become a chela, a student of a guru. The guru will be responsible for usually five chelas, each chela assumes her surname and lineage. To complete the chelas' feminisation some will undergo nirvan, rebirth, which involves the removal of the penis and scrotum with a knife without anaesthetic.'

At this, Trotter turned as white as our tablecloth. 'You are not serious?' he spluttered tea.

'Oh, yes, I'm afraid I am. The British government attempted to counter this behaviour under Section Twenty-seven of the Act. If a eunuch, so registered, had in his charge a boy under the age of sixteen within his control or residing in his house, he could be punished with imprisonment of up to two years or fined or both. Under Section Twenty-nine, a eunuch was considered incapable of acting as a guardian, making a gift, drawing up a will or adopting a son.'

'Forgive me, but I can see some moral justification in that,' said Trotter.

'You mean in respect of a minor?'

'Yes.'

'I can too. But allow me to quote from Section Twenty-six of the Act, this is where it gets interesting for us. "Any eunuch so registered who appears dressed or ornamented like a woman in a public street or place, or in any other place, with the intention of being seen from a public street or place, or who dances or plays music, or takes part in any public exhibition, in a public street or place or for hire in a private house, may be arrested without warrant, and shall be punished with imprisonment of either description for a term which may extend to two years, or with fine, or with both".'

'That be as it may, how can a law made in India help our case?'

'I'm not sure yet. I'll think of something,' I laughed. 'But if there is one thing I'm sure of, it is that George Hobb is no eunuch.'

'How? How do you know that?'

'He has a daughter.'

'The Reverend never mentioned having a daughter to me.'

'Nor to me. He admitted to having a deceased wife, but never a living daughter. Nevertheless he has one.'

'But why did he never mention her?'

'The man's reasoning is beyond me.'

'How did you find out?'

'During some correspondence I've been having with his solicitor on the Isle of Wight, a Mr Bernard. It was he who informed me about Hobb's daughter.'

'Mr Cairn, how lovely to see you again.' Kenneth Bright slunk from the ferns like a lynx from the forest ready to bite.

'George not with you then,' squeaked Bright, looking round the ferns as if the unfortunate Reverend might be hidden there.

'No, he's gone back to the Isle of Wight,' I explained.

'I'm not surprised. We are not surprised are we, Marcus?' He turned to address his expressionless younger companion, whose face was unfortunately blighted with the acne bacillus. 'Don't expect we'll see Deirdre again.'

'Deirdre?' I enquired.

'George, I mean.' Bright gave out a short girlish giggle. I didn't dare look Trotter's way.

'He'll have to return to answer the charges made against him. He's only out on bail,' I explained.

'And you're defending him. I heard on the grapevine.'

'Perhaps,' I replied cautiously.

'Lovely man, lovely,' enthused Bright. 'George wouldn't hurt a fly, would he, Marcus? Terrible business, terrible. And all made up lies, you know.'

'How do you know that?' I asked, my interested suddenly piqued. 'You weren't there with him were you? You weren't at the Star in Stonegate the night that rabble gathered outside?'

'No, no.' Bright lifted his hands, palms outstretched defensively. 'No, not me, not us, were we, Marcus? We'd love to be in the company of Deirdre again though, wouldn't we, Marcus? Should she wish to return of course. She was such fun,' he added disconcertingly. With that, and a couple of swings of their hips, they disappeared back behind the pots and ferns.

111

'Deirdre? What a pantomime,' said Trotter appalled.

'Appropriate, don't you think though? Deirdre, an Irish name meaning doubtful. Hobb must use it when he's out and about in female attire.'

'Did you believe him when he said he and his companion weren't with the Reverend at the Star?'

'I am not really sure,' I admitted. 'Could it have been one of those two men you saw staring at us through the window earlier?'

'No, I think he was of a much heavier build, and it was you he was staring at.'

'How can you be so certain of that?'

'He couldn't see me. I was behind the plant.'

'Of course, the aspidistra.'

'Sir, you are getting too involved in this case,' warned Trotter, not for the first time nor for the last.

Chapter Eleven

Already the first day of September and a new century was almost upon us. I had not heard from Mortimer Blakely yet, not one word. I was glad I was not paying for his services on my own. Carlton-Bingham said our chambers as a whole would pay. He had come to the conclusion that we were under attack from dark forces set against our participation in the Hobb case. Speaking of dark forces, I read in my *Times* that Paul Kruger has given the British government an ultimatum that it has to withdraw all our troops from the border of Transvaal, otherwise the Transvaal, allied with the Orange Free State, will declare war on us. The *Times* denounced Kruger's ultimatum as an "extravagant farce".

Not another war in Africa – I had already lost my own father to a Zulu spear – in this respect alone I could identify with the sentiments of Dr Holbrook and his friends. But what say do any of us have against an elected government? What legal opposition can we bring to bear? Perhaps it would be a better world if women were allowed to vote. Things look ominous. We are about to embark on a second war against a bunch of Dutch farmers over territory and, more specifically, over gold.

For me the Dark Continent of Africa was a long way away but the memory of my client's pitiful state in York Castle Goal was much nearer to hand. I could not get my mind off the androgynous Reverend. A man locked up in his own misunderstood darkness. Perhaps they were not as dissimilar as I first supposed. much of Africa remains unexplored and so, too, androgynies remain unexplored and shrouded in contempt and mystery in our society.

How much courage does it really take to acknowledge your androgynous state? How male am I? Is there a feminine side to me too? – to most men? – that makes us so uncomfortable, so aggressive when confronted with the effeminate.

Yes, I sensed autumn and winter were on their way. I sat at my office window watching a watery sun flickering through wet clouds as if seeking approval for its poor performance. It was as if all the life, all the warmth had been sucked out of it. It was as if the world – my life – was on hold. I was filled with melancholy, overwhelmed with it, I got these low mood swings from time to time. Maybe I should consult Dr Holbrook over them.

Speak of the angel not the devil…

'Miss Holbrook,' announced Trotter, half an hour later, after one abrupt knock on the door. Without waiting for my say-so, he guided Winifred into my room with a magisterial outstretched arm. But then, he knew I would not object; he knew me better than any other man. Leaving us together, he shut the door quietly behind him.

'I don't believe this, I was just thinking about your father,' I told her.

'Why?' Winifred was always direct while managing to retain her own opinions.

'I was feeling a little dispirited that's all.'

'I am not surprised. You know the proverb, "All work and no play makes Jack a dull boy".'

'I do indeed.'

'Well some writers, such as the Irish novelist Maria Edgeworth, added a second part.'

'Go on.'

'"All play and no work makes Jack a mere toy".'

'A toy for whom?'

'A toy for those whom you allow to manipulate you.'

'And is someone trying to do that?' I asked. Winifred shrugged.

'I'm surprised I haven't seen you after our lovely trip to Kirkby Moorside. Are you avoiding me, James?'

'No, I certainly am not. Your father suggested…' I began.

'Doctor Holbrook is not my father. He's my legal guardian that's all.'

'Oh?' I was staggered.

'My real father was a wild, hot-tempered Irish poet, according to my mother. He was a Protestant who, after the horrors of the famine, became a fierce supporter of the Republic.'

'The monsoon rains have failed in India.'

'Sorry? Are you all right, James, you seem a little preoccupied?'

'When the monsoon rains fail in India, the crops fail. It causes great famine.'

'I see. How dreadful.'

'It must have been a difficult position for your natural father to be in, a Protestant and a Republican.'

'Yes, but what people forget is that Wolfe Tone, the father of Irish Republicanism, was a Protestant himself.'

'Nevertheless, your father must have been a man of extreme courage, a man of conviction, not to fall into the easy option of siding with his tribe.'

'I can hardly remember him. He was considerably older than my mother. After he was killed she left Ireland with me, little more than a babe in arms.'

'Killed?'

'Yes, my mother is very cagey about it all. But from what I've been able to gather he was involved in a pub brawl, no doubt over Home Rule for Ireland.'

'Related or not, living or dead, all the members of your family seem to be politically active in one way or another.'

Winifred gave one of her wonderful smiles. 'It certainly seems that way, doesn't it?'

'And Cedric, how does Cedric fit into the picture?'

'My little half-brother. My mother took employment as a housekeeper when we arrived over here. That's how she first met Doctor Holbrook.'

'So, to what do I owe the pleasure of your company here today, Winifred?' Part of me didn't really want to know. I was hoping she had just come to see me.

'It's Lucy, Lucy and this Howard Greenstock fellow. We know nothing about him and I am not sure I like him very much.'

'What, because he's Jewish?'

'I thought you knew me better than that, James. No, it's because she keeps going off to these clandestine meetings with him, in locations I've never heard of, somewhere between Oxford and York. She's become very secretive.'

'She is a grown woman.'

'I know but I am worried about her. I am her friend. Can't you have a word with her, James, make her see sense, make her proceed with caution? She'll listen to you.'

'Whenever anyone tells me that, usually the subject involved won't listen to me at all.'

'You could try though.'

'I don't think I can interfere directly. Indeed if I did it would only drive Lucy further into Greenstock's arms. However, I do know someone who might help.'

'I'd be very grateful.' With that Winifred brushed my cheek with her lips and was gone. The sun that had come into my room with her was gone too.

Through my window I could see a steady drizzle was falling. It was the first rain I had seen in one of the sunniest summers on record. I began to ponder over Winifred's visit. Could I refuse those appealing Irish eyes anything? But why was she so agitated over Lucy's relationship with Howard Greenstock? Perhaps I had got this gender confusion business on the brain, but could there be some element of sapphism in her relationship with Lucy? I have read there is another name for the sexual love between women, it is a rather rounded word called lesbianism. As I discussed with Mortimer Blakely, unlike the activities of Mr Wilde, lesbianism is not against the law. Indeed, I am quite sure Queen Victoria is unaware that such relationships could possibly exist. Nonetheless, is that why Dr Holbrook warned me off? – Dr Holbrook who isn't Winifred's father. Could the lack of a blood tie free him from the emotional constraints of having his daughter followed? Followed here?

"Does the father know you are taken with his daughter?" Mortimer Blakely's words rang in my ears, not like music.

* * * * *

Despite Trotter sending a boy round several times to Blakely's office, the detective failed to materialise during the next few weeks. I decided to take the initiative and visit him myself one free lunch hour.

According to Mortimer Blakely's card the office of *Blakely & Shore* was in Low Petergate. As I made my way through the busy traffic of the city, my head was filled with thoughts of Winifred. We shared the same fate of being fatherless from an early age, and both our fathers had been killed in unusual circumstances. How taken with her was I? There was no doubting that she was both beautiful and intelligent, but did she like me at all? Was I merely useful to her? What was her true sexual proclivity? Her family appeared to be infiltrated with associates and causes on the fringes of society. Could some of these associates be politically dangerous, especially dangerous to my legal career?

64A Low Petergate was above a bakery shop. I had to go through the actual shop to ascend a creaking staircase to the upper floor. I sniffed in long and hard as I mounted each deep step, the building was permeated with the smell of freshly baked bread. I loved that smell. I was reminded of my recent picnic with Trotter and George Hobb in the Botanic Garden of the museum. Poor George, I had almost forgotten him. I must not forget him. First deal with this – then I had work to do back at Bootham Chambers researching any past judgements that might be useful in his defence.

I had almost reached the top landing when a young woman rushed past, forcing me against the wall.

'Excuse me,' I uttered in annoyance.

'Sorry,' she snuffled, dabbing at her eyes with a handkerchief.

'No, it is I who am sorry,' I said, acknowledging her distress.

I knocked on the unpromising, brown peeling door of *Blakely & Shore*.

'Enter,' shouted an imperious voice. I passed the secretary my card. She had a frizzy mass of greying hair framing delicately balanced spectacles on a sharp nose. 'What can we do for you, Mr Cairn?' She peered down at my card, turning it in her hand.

'I nearly collided with that poor woman on the stairs.'

'She's upset because Mr Shore has told her that her husband is a cheat, a womaniser,' said the spinster (educated guess) secretary.

'But she now has the freedom to leave her husband,' I pointed out, wondering how ethical it was for us to be discussing this woman's affairs.

'She still cannot divorce him for adultery alone without additional proof of incest, bigamy, cruelty or desertion,' replied the married-to-her-job secretary sourly. 'Surely this isn't news to you, Mr Cairn, a man au fait with the law.'

'No, no, unfortunately it isn't. I agree with you. The law regarding adultery is totally weighted in favour of the male, the male who only has to prove one occasion of adultery on the part of his wife to divorce her. It is both biased and unfair.'

'Biased and unfair like blackmail and extortion, Mr Cairn.' The eyes above the spectacles speared me with disapproval.

'Tell me, madam, how do you know so much about me?' As soon as the question was out of my mouth, I remembered Mortimer Blakely had taken the offensive note and photographs away with him for further examination: obviously for further examination by his entire staff. I realised now why this woman was viewing me with such contempt after seeing me snuggled up with two women on a rug before a house of God. No doubt I was on a par with the adulterous husband, if not worse.

'I know everything that goes on in this office.' Her riposte was cool, condescending, as she readjusted the position of her spectacles. 'So, Mr Cairn, how can we at *Blakely & Shore* help you?'

'Is Mortimer Blakely available?'

'No, he has been away for almost a week.'

'Away, where?'

'He took the packet for Rotterdam last Saturday.' The eyelids became hoods behind the spectacles.

'Rotterdam? Why Rotterdam?'

'Business.'

'I see,' I said, but I didn't. We were paying Blakely enough not to be tearing around Rotterdam on other people's business.

The secretary's office was cluttered with books, some heavily bound and legal which I recognised. Maps, bulging files, filled every shelf and there were a lot of shelves. Directories of every description were piled high over most of the floor space. I found it oppressive like an indiscriminate second-hand bookshop. I could never have worked amid such chaos.

'He's not sent word yet when he'll be back,' she was saying.

'Perhaps I could see Mr Shore then?'

'Out, he's out.'

'But that previous client has only just left him, has she not? And unless there is another staircase no one else has passed by me.'

'He'll tell you no different.'

I stared in disbelief at this dragon at the door. She obviously held considerable sway.

'And might I ask your name?' I enquired.

'Amelia Blakely,' said without hesitation. 'Mortimer is my brother.'

'And is he in Rotterdam on my behalf?' I asked hesitantly. She nodded. 'Then he must be running up quite a bill for expenses.'

'Your case is far more complicated than anyone could have anticipated. But do not underestimate my brother, Mr Cairn. He is a man of the most astonishing instincts and possesses a profound mind.'

'Would you be good enough to have him contact me at Bootham Chambers on his return?'

'Be assured, Mr Cairn, Mortimer will go to the ends of the earth to ferret out the truth for you.'

'That is just what I am afraid of, madam.'

I needed a drink badly after my meeting with Amelia Blakely. Carlton-Bingham was a generous man but he hated any unnecessary expense. Why the hell had Mortimer Blakely gone all the way to Rotterdam? Florrie Cary's timber-framed pub, the Fox, stood end on across the road from *Blakely & Shore*. I had not seen Florrie since the successful outcome of her trial.

'Florrie!'

'Mr Cairn!'

'I had some business in your part of town so I thought I would pay you a visit.'

'On the house, Mr Cairn, sir. Anything.' Florrie beamed down on me from her platform behind the counter.

'A pint of the house brew will be excellent.'

'I packed their bags, you know, as soon as we got back here,' said Florrie, pulling slowly down on the pump handle. I watched in mouth-watering anticipation as the golden ale tumbled into the glass. 'Should have listened to Sergeant Howell's warning from the beginning. But you know how it is when it's your own flesh and blood, Mr Cairn, you'll not see them without a roof over their heads.'

'Cousin Aggie wasn't in your class,' I told Florrie as she handed me my drink. 'Not in your class at all.'

'Kind of you to say so, Mr Cairn. Now how about a nice cheese sandwich to go with that pint of yours?' she asked. I nodded, sliding a thrupenny bit across the counter to her. Shaking her head, Florrie pushed the small silver coin back to me in disgust. 'I'll not take any of your money after all you've done for me.'

This visit could prove embarrassing, I thought, carrying my pint across to a corner table.

Plonk! What seemed to be only seconds later a plate and freshly cut sandwich rested on the small round table next to my pint.

'With pickle,' announced Florrie. The beam back on her face, proud this time. Her full bosom remained hanging protectively over me as I ate. Her torso blocking the view of an otherwise busy taproom. 'Arthur's looking on,' she explained.

With a nod of my head I acknowledged Arthur behind the bar. He was a small lithe man. Florrie told me her husband had once been a professional runner, a star of the hundred yards dash.

'This sandwich is just superb,' I mouthed at her. 'Where did you get the cheese filling from?'

'Locally.' Florrie obviously was not prepared to divulge her supplier. I looked hurt out of devilment. 'A local farm,' she compromised.

'Mr Cairn! Mr James Cairn!' shouted a fellow at the bar above the general hubbub. I saw Arthur nod his head in my direction. 'Mr Cairn, I am so glad I've caught you. Ignatius Shore from *Blakely & Shore* across the road.' The forty something Shore introduced himself to Florrie and me with a little bow. He was wearing an extremely dapper lounge suit and looked nothing like his absent partner, Blakely. 'Amelia saw you come in here from her window.' I smiled. Why wasn't I surprised? 'This is addressed to you and came in the second post.' Shore handed me a letter with a Rotterdam postmark.

'Thank you. From Mr Blakely, I presume.'

'Indeed,' nodded Shore politely. His expression was intense as he waited there in his dapper little suit for me to open the correspondence. Florrie, ever the diplomat, disappeared into the background.

Saturday, 23ʳᵈ September, 1899

My Dear Mr Cairn,

I hope this letter reaches you safely as it is of the utmost importance. I felt it in my bones that something extremely complex and bad was afoot. I have been proved correct in that assumption.

My advice to you is that you keep a low profile regarding the Reverend George Hobb case. Do not court publicity. I caution you against having any further contact with the Holbrooks, or Lucy Alexander, until I am able to advise you further on my return. There are intrigues afoot that could do you great harm.

Watch your step and how you tread.

Yours faithfully,
Mortimer Blakely

'What do you make of this, sir?' I could see no harm in passing Ignatius Shore a note written by his partner. My hand was shaking as I did so. 'Everyone seems determined that I have nothing more to do with Miss Holbrook, even her own step-father.'

'Umm, Umm,' muttered Shore, as if he were carefully weighing each word. 'You must comply, Mr Cairn, fully comply. Mortimer would never write a note like this without good reason. In point of fact, I have never read such firm instructions expressed by him to a client before. Believe me he is a good and courageous man, Mr Cairn. You must follow his instruction to the letter.'

'"To the letter"?' I attempted a smile to relieve the gravity of the situation. Shore remained frowning, Blakely's letter wafting in his hand like a lure. That is when I heard the scraping of chairs in the opposite alcove. Two bullish figures appeared to jostle Shore between them as they passed by. They both bore numerous facial scars of seasoned pugilists.

My initial impression was that they meant him harm. Bruisers that wanted to start a fight. Shore appeared to gag open-mouthed. He was staring at me in shock as if he had been stabbed. I half got to my feet when he found his voice.

'The letter, they've snatched the letter!' he screamed.

'They must have thought it was a banknote.'

Ignatius Shore's look was scathing. Then we ran. We rushed out after the two men through the saloon doors, only to see them disappearing at high speed into the flowing crowds of afternoon shoppers.

'Are you all right?' Arthur must have seen them jostling Shore and had leaped over his counter. Florrie was close behind.

'Those two men, who were sitting in the alcove opposite Mr Cairn and me, have they ever been in here before?' Shore asked them. Arthur and Florrie shook their heads.

'No, nor will they be allowed in here again.' Florrie's keen blue eyes glinted certainty. The Minster clock bell struck the hour.

'I'd better be going,' I said.

'I must too,' agreed Shore, still shocked and fidgeting to open his enamelled fob. 'Amelia will wonder where I am.'

'By the way, Mr Cairn, I meant to say before your friend here came along, all the best with that big case you've got coming up,' said Florrie.

'Which case is that, Florrie?'

'The vicar that likes to dress up like a tart of course. Every ale-house keeper in York knows him. When George is in York, he always takes an attic room with us.'

'You mean George Hobb was staying in one of your rooms when he was arrested?' I asked in amazement.

'Of course. I thought you knew. If you'll forgive the contradiction, I always found the Reverend to be such a gentleman.'

'We have another regular Bertie All-tie sometimes stays with us too, don't we, Florrie?' said Arthur.

'"Bertie All-tie"?' I queried.

'Yes, this girlie-lad who wears huge silk mufflers at his neck. Greens, blues, reds, all manner of colours,' explained Florrie, with raucous, hands-on-hips laughter.

'So you, personally, have never had any trouble with George Hobb? You have never seen him trying to solicit other men on or around your premises?'

Florrie and Arthur solemnly shook their heads.

'It's not the margeries you have to watch out for. It's them who don't look the part that cause most trouble. He's harmless, luv. They're all harmless,' said Florrie.

'Would you be willing to say that in court, Florrie?'

'For you, Mr Cairn, anything.'

Chapter Twelve

11th October, 1899, said the date on my boss's *Times*.

'Deep in thought again, James? See, here is something else for you to frown over,' muttered Carlton-Bingham, cigar between teeth, rustling pages.

'Sorry?'

He passed across his paper. 'From today we are officially at war with the Boer again,' he stated flatly, before I had chance to find the leading article. 'Wasn't it your father who was involved in our first campaign against them?'

'No, sir, it was a spear not a Boer hunting rifle that killed my father, a short stabbing spear known as an *iklwa*, and it was held in a native African hand.'

'Silly of me, I remember you telling me now. He was killed by a Zulu warrior, was he not? What a terrible death so far from home.'

'Although the spear that penetrated my father's lung was certainly not made in Holland, Mortimer Blakely has gone to Rotterdam. Holland, the Dutch, the Boer, do you think there could be a connection?' I asked my boss.

He opened his arms askance, shrugged his shoulders. 'How can I possibly venture an opinion given so little information?'

An hour or two later I was kicking through the golden carpet of leaves along Bootham with that melancholy pleasure that comes with the approach of winter. Trotter once told me that Bootham means 'at the booths' and probably refers to the booths erected near Bootham Bar for a weekly market held by the monks of St Mary's Abbey. Bootham is a continuation of High and Low Petergate outside the city walls. A wall of St Mary's runs along the south side of the street. At the corner of the wall, at the junction with Bootham and Marygate, is St Mary's Tower which was heavily bombarded by the Parliamentarians during the Civil War.

Scrunch! – the summer had been dry and we were well into autumn now. The avenues and parks of York had embraced it. I believe the word "autumn" comes from the Old French word "automne". My personal preference is for the North American expression "the fall". This was originally an English term taken from the Germanic and Norse languages, taken over by the founding fathers and now unequivocally adopted by America only to be dropped or *fallen* from common use here. I was reminded of New York and enjoying there this same satisfying sensation beneath my feet. Gold leaf had fluttered above my head waiting to fall – streets paved with gold and opportunity – a young man's country. There and then I promised myself to make that journey across the great pond again soon. I loved America, the strident vibrancy of the place.

And there she was striding towards me over Lendal Bridge. It had to be her, no other woman I knew had the same assured energetic walk. She could have been American.

'Hello,' she said.

'I…' I was shaken, literally shaken off my stride, she always had that effect on me. She was hatless and wore a tailor-made suit in light tweed. Some men found this fashion threatening, unladylike, masculine even – I thought Winifred Holbrook looked magnificent standing there in the golden afternoon light on the bridge. But as always it was those green eyes of hers that held me fast.

'Have you made contact with Lucy yet? She's still not herself, acting very peculiarly.'

'How about tea in the Royal Station Hotel down the road and I'll explain everything?'

'I thought my stepfather had forbidden us to be seen together.' She tossed back her mane of sorrel hair.

'Never mind all that now,' I said; my conscience suddenly pricked by the memory of Mortimer Blakely's warning letter, Mortimer Blakely's stolen letter, Mortimer Blakely who still had not returned from Rotterdam.

'I have a meeting to attend in half-an-hour.'

'Half-an-hour then,' I said, taking her arm.

Luckily the hotel was quiet that late Wednesday afternoon. This was York's second Royal Station Hotel, built in 1878, to complement the new railway station. It was an impressive five-storey building clad in yellow Scarborough stone. We waited in one of the high-ceilinged banqueting rooms for our ordered high tea to arrive. I fidgeted rather anxiously as Winifred repeated that she only had half-an-hour. She, as usual, appeared relaxed.

'Do you know this place has a hundred bedrooms?' I told her.

'Really?' she said.

'Yes, and the twenty-seven roomed west wing was only added three years ago.'

'Interesting.'

'Do you know what it is called?'

'No idea.'

'The Klondike, after the American gold rush.'

'Appropriate.'

'Yes, I believe it costs over fourteen shillings a night to stay here.'

'Expect it does,' said with total disinterest. Perhaps she thought I was making an improper suggestion.

'But then you could easily afford to stay here,' I said; her monosyllabic answers were beginning to jar on my already frayed nervous system.

'It is my stepfather who has all the money.'

'And you're not interested in money at all.'

'That's right. As far as I am concerned my half-brother can inherit it all, I expect he will anyway.'

Thankfully the tea arrived with a stand of sandwiches and delicacies, almost identical to those I enjoyed at the Holbrooks' but this time I was paying for them.

'I don't feel very hungry,' she said.

I ignored this, hoping she was joking, and asked her about Lucy instead.

'She mopes about and then she'll vanish for days on end. She's missed all our recent YWSS rallies and meetings. Lucy's just lost interest in the cause. It all seems down to this Howard Greenstock character,' said with apparent disgust. 'She's never been herself since the day she met him at Kirkdale with us. She's bewitched by him.'

'I do hope he's not taking advantage of Lucy. She seems to me to be a rather naive, innocent sort of woman.'

'Lucy? Innocent, naive?' Winifred fine-sprayed me with tea.

'She's a little older than you though, is she not?'

'Normally, James, she is a lot more sensible than me too.'

'I have to apologise for not mentioning the problems you are having with her to my friend yet. Unfortunately, he is still away.'

'I see,' said Winifred, looking somewhat puzzled. 'I did hope you might reconsider having a word with her yourself, James. Lucy isn't stupid.'

'I never said she was.'

'You don't know this, Lucy hates it to be mentioned, but she is a woman of great intellect. She read philosophy at Lady Margaret Hall, Oxford. Though of course, being a woman, Oxford wouldn't grant her a degree.'

'I know, Cambridge is the same. Women can take the same courses as us, pass the same exams but never be admitted as members of the university. A situation I always found appalling when I was a student there.'

'It made Lucy very bitter indeed.'

'I sympathise with her over that. It must have been very frustrating. Made her beat that drum of hers even louder.'

'She's bought a new bigger one by the way.' Winifred finally gave me one of her wonderful smiles. 'We are all waiting to see if she turns up to use it at our next rally.'

'Lady Margaret Hall, eh?'

'Yes,' pondered Winifred.

'Do you think it was because of her disillusionment with Oxford that she failed to mention to Greenstock she had been there too?'

'You could be right about that,' replied Winifred, looking towards the banqueting room clock. 'And now I must go.'

* * * * *

'I would stop this war if I could,' I told Robert Brown by the roaring open fire in the Black Swan that evening. Brown looked uncomfortable and made a quick reconnoitre of the room. Seated in this medieval timber framed house with its creaking oak floors and pipe smoke, talk of raising the white flag seemed out of place. Raising the flagon was more the order of the day for customers as they ducked and dived in and out of their frothing ale pots. I could have said I would stop all wars – I could have said I would have stopped the Anglo-Zulu war that killed my father – but in this heavy masculine atmosphere I was too much of a coward to do so.

'Be careful, Cairn, the walls have ears,' warned Brown; warned good old Bob Brown; his abbreviated name an unfortunate combination of consonants.

'You don't have to tell me that (and he didn't, not after my recent experience at the Fox). Do you know where that saying originated?' I asked him, only too happy to get away from thoughts of war and public house thugs.

'No idea, Cairn.' Brown still looked uncomfortable.

'It is thought to have come from a story about Dionysius of Syracuse. He had an ear-shaped cave cut in his palace to hear what was being said in connecting rooms. The Louvre in Paris has a similar arrangement.'

'Trust the French.'

Our seasonal dish of grouse pie arrived. I noticed Brown eyed the waitress with the same intensity that he had eyed our servant-girl, Emma, back in chambers. The crown of pie, with its pastry leafed sculptures, looked appetising. It deserved full concentration as we spooned it out before hesitating over our plates with gleeful anticipation.

I speared my piece of topping with a fork before sniffing at the rising meaty steam. We both tucked in, in silence, for several minutes.

'It's the cayenne pepper that makes it,' Brown eventually mouthed through a coating of disassembled crust.

I nodded, recharging his glass with claret. 'Grouse always has a hint of cheese to it, don't you think?'

Brown did not reply. He seemed preoccupied either with his own thoughts or the dish. I did not press him further. Indeed, nothing more was said between us until the arrival of the Bakewell pudding and a decanter of port.

'Do you know a York brickmaker sold his wife in here, over a glass of ale, for one shilling and six pence?'

'How long ago was that?' I laughed.

'Less than sixteen years ago.'

'Tell me, are you married?' I asked.

'Widowed,' sighed Brown. 'She was taken from me, never sold. There is not a day passes that I don't miss her terribly.'

'Sorry.' How hollow "sorry" can sound sometimes.

'And call me Bob, James. I now live alone with my old father who is crippled with arthritis though he is still of sound mind. It's awful to see, a man of great intellect whose body is breaking down around him.'

'How sad.'

'No, no, James, it's just the way things are. He still has his books,' said Brown protectively.

'What was your father's profession?'

'He studied Classics at Trinity College, Dublin, before becoming a headmaster here in York. Speaking of academia, I received a letter from George the other day.'

'George?' I had a momentary lapse.

'Yes, George Hobb. He was really taken with your visit to the museum. Says he would like to return the favour. I expect he will be inviting you to stay with him on the Isle of Wight in the near future.'

'Well, we will have to be in contact sooner or later to prepare his case. Either he comes back to York early, before the trial, or I go over to him.'

'I must tell you, however, George is a little preoccupied with other matters at present.'

'Oh. What could be more important than his trial? The man's whole living is at stake.' I wrapped my lips round the small port glass, knocking back its entire contents in one gulp.

'George's daughter, Helena, has gone missing,' announced Call Me Bob, casually taking a nip out of his own port glass.

* * * * *

'I have come to say goodbye, Dolly Gray. It's no use to ask me why, Dolly Gray".' William D. Cobb's lyrics from the previous year's Spanish-American War rang out of every tavern door, as I began to wend my way back across the city from Peasholme Green after Bob and I had made our slurred farewells.

'"'Tis the tramp of soldiers' feet in their uniforms so neat. So goodbye until we meet, Dolly Gray".' We, the British, had changed a line or two, adapted and adopted, and now it had become ours – a recruitment song for the Anglo-Boer War.

'"Goodbye Dolly I must leave you, though it breaks my heart to go",' punctuated my every step.

'"Hark, I hear the bugle calling",' echoed eerily from male and female voices along the alleyways of York. '"Goodbye…",' the voice ghost of my father.

With my thoughts awash with war, I walked on. Preoccupied, I floated across the dark Minster Yard. It was here that I collided with two approaching ladies. The impact was so great, I was forced to wrap one lady in my arms to steady her and me from toppling over. As I swayed to regain balance, she let out an embarrassed giggle, a coarse giggle. In a cloud of cheap cologne, I struggled to extricate myself from her voluminous skirt like a fish caught in a net. There was something disreputable about the pair. Although, even in the bad light, I could see that one of them – the one I was not entangled with – was extremely good looking.

Drawing back a step or two, I finally realised there was something strange about both of them. Curious, I gently ushered them towards the nearby gas light under the pretext of restoring calm.

'What do you think you're doing, sir?' asked the plainer one flirtatiously. Her thickly applied make-up of zinc oxide failed to conceal a black eye.

Judging them to be *filles de joie* used to rough trade, I waited for the obligatory "interested in business tonight, sir?" But the phrase never materialised.

'You!' shrilled out instead. 'You! You!' shrilled in a sudden and surprising baritone off the Minster wall.

I peered closer from one woman to the other and back as if I was about to cross a dangerous street. And I was, I was about to cross into another world.

'Mr Cairn.'

'Do I know you?' My voice faltered with embarrassment. There was something familiar about them but I could not quite place the pair.

'You don't recognise us, do you?' giggled the plainer one. 'In the night we are Kathleen and Marina. In the morning we will regrettably be back to Kenneth and Marcus.'

'Kenneth Bright, I didn't recognise you at all.' I gazed in astonishment at Kathleen and her more fetching companion, the delicate Marina.

'Isn't it a wonderful time to be in York, Mr Cairn? The bands, the call to war, the boys marching off so smart and handsome in their uniforms,' gushed Kathleen, her bodice rising with emotion.

'I'm not sure about that,' I could not help replying.

'But you must have heard the tavern songs. Everyone in town is so together and enjoying themselves.'

'Soldiers die in war,' I pointed out. Kathleen's face fell as if she had never considered this reality. I felt guilty, like someone spoiling the fun at a party.

'That's what I keep telling her,' lisped Marina. 'She's so excited by it all, she won't listen.'

'I will,' objected Kathleen petulantly.

'Who did that to you?' I pointed to her eye.

'Oh, it's nothing.' Kathleen waved nervous jewelled fingers across her swollen black eye in an attempt to make light of it.

'No, tell me, who did that to you on this wonderful evening when everyone "is so together and enjoying themselves"?'

'I tell you it is of no consequence.'

'Two constables at Jubbergate Police Station,' blurted out Marina. 'They threw us into a cell the night before last saying they would throw away the key.'

'It was so frightening,' finally admitted Kathleen. 'I've never been locked up before.'

'Then they visited us,' added Marina, casting her eyes to the ground.

'What do you mean, visited you?'

'They beat up Kathleen and humiliated me,' mumbled Marina. Marina whose acne spots had disappeared under her exquisitely applied makeup.

'How did they humiliate you?'

'Don't, Mr Cairn. Don't ask her that.' This time there was a helplessness about Kathleen's waving jewelled hand.

Chapter Thirteen

Over my breakfast eggs the morning paper informed me that the Boers had invaded Natal and occupied the railway station at Elandslaagte on the 21st October, cutting communications between the main British force at Ladysmith and a detachment at Dundee. The Boer forces were enhanced by German, French, Dutch, American and Irish volunteers – I see we are as popular as all great nations are.

The African sky was reported to grow dark with thunderclouds, and as we made our assault the storm burst. In poor light and pouring rain our soldiers had to face a barbed wire farm fence in which several men got entangled and shot. Nonetheless, the majority safely cut through the wire to overwhelm the Boer position. The Boer leader, General Kock, led a counter-attack dressed in his top hat and Sunday best. This impressive, if eccentric figure, was successful in driving back our infantry until Colonel Ian Hamilton retaliated. Kock and his companions were killed. I felt an inexplicable stab of sadness at the death of this idiosyncratic Boer leader who sounded more British than the British. According to my paper this battle was a comprehensive success for us.

'Seen this? Seen this?' shouted Gerald Fawcett, his voice quavering, shaking his copy of the *Herald* round chambers later that morning. 'We'll teach those Dutch farm hands a thing or two. We'll teach them not to take on the might of the British Empire. Eh, Cairn, what do you think?' My fellow barrister and bête noire's face was flushed with victory.

'Well, unless you have another edition of the *York Herald* to mine, it makes no mention of other casualties apart from Kock and Co. of course.'

'Casualties! Casualties! Who wants to hear about casualties for God's sake? We are at war, man.' If anything, Fawcett's face flushed a deeper red. 'And as you well know, it's called the *Yorkshire Herald* now,' he jeered sarcastically.

'I do know,' I agreed wearily. 'I just can't get the new name into my head.'

'But it changed years ago.'

'I know, I know, I still prefer its original title.'

'That's you all over, Cairn, if you don't like something you simply change it.'

'Or, as in this case, retain it,' I laughed.

Fawcett did not laugh. He was a man without humour. I mentally and physically stepped back. I could see this was one of those ridiculous arguments over nothing that was going nowhere. All the same, it exposed a deep seam of hostility that ran between us; a seam that familiarity had failed to eradicate. Pedantic though he was, perhaps he had a point on this occasion, I do change things that I don't like – even if only in my head – but I had singularly failed to change Gerald Fawcett.

I could feel that I was becoming obsessed: with the plight of Kathleen and Marina; the whereabouts of the Reverend's missing daughter, who had perhaps discovered her father's taste in fashion and fled screaming, though Bob Brown affirmed not; then there was the Reverend's forthcoming trial itself to consider; Mortimer Blakely still had not made an appearance; finally, on a more personal note, there was Winifred Holbrook. Apart from these substantial and insubstantial concerns, I began to mull over Gerald Fawcett's stinging accusation that I changed everything in my head. The realisation slowly began to dawn on me that if everyone did the same, thought through the unpalatable before they acted upon it, then perhaps the world would be a better place. But people did not, I earned my daily crust because they did not.

A fascinating document arrived at Bootham Chambers out of the blue, not so much for its content as for its source. It was hand delivered by Dr Holbrook's man, Jake, with an accompanying verbal message that I should read it and could keep it. *Conscription and the Working Man* had been written by Philip Snowden within the last few years: the same Christian Socialist, Philip Snowden, who was a friend of the Holbrooks. In his essay Snowden clearly expressed his opposition to the National Service League, a movement created by the great and the good of this country to enforce conscription on the working man. I had already heard that the suggestion was to call this obligatory conscription "National Service", hence dignifying military service as our Continental neighbours did. Snowden argued that this would take wage-earning lads away from industries that badly needed them for the social betterment of the nation in general. He suggested that our universities were being turned into training schools for officers for this proposed conscript army. In short, our class system was up and running as always when it came to warfare: "After you, boys, after you". Barracked working men would be subjected to military law, punishable by court-martial (and firing squad), without the right of appeal to a civil court.

'What do you make of this?' I asked Leacock, sipping at his morning cup of Earl Grey.' He began examining my printed copy of the Snowden pamphlet with a quizzical expression.

'How did such left-wing propaganda come into your possession, James?'

'Doctor Holbrook has just sent it to me. Though he requested I have no more contact with his daughter, he seems determined to recruit me into the Peace Society.'

'Holbrook? Holbrook? Is this Holbrook part of the family that detective fellow warned you to steer clear of?'

'How do you know about that?'

'Andrew had to obtain the partners' agreement that chambers would foot the detective's costs in light of your possible blackmail. Gerald Fawcett was difficult to convince of course. Have you heard anymore from those rogues by the way?'

'Not a word. Not even a word from the man employed to investigate them.'

'We are of course assuming there is more than one individual involved.'

'You only have to read the popular press to see how many extortion gangs are roaming our streets, and more particularly our London streets.'

'Never took you for a Labour man though, James.' Smiling, Leacock shook the Snowden pamphlet in front of my face.

'I am an independent observer.'

'Standing on the fence, Fawcett would call it.'

'Is that what he says I do?' I asked. Leacock was too tactful to reply. 'Gerald seems to have many set views about me, most of them wrong.'

'Wouldn't give it a moment's thought, old boy.'

'I don't.'

'He's jealous of you.'

'I know.'

'This Snowden fellow,' Leacock lifted the pamphlet up in his lean hand again. 'I remember hearing him speak once, he speaks all over the country. He's a bit of a firebrand but a great platform orator. Comes from the

Keighley area, I believe. Father a weaver, hard woollen, Temperance Society, that sort of thing. Nevertheless, Philip Snowden is one of the Independent Labour Party's brightest sons.'

'I never took you for a Labour man either, Thomas.'

'That's what a few years out in India with the Raj does for you.'

'Nonetheless, I can see the other side of this argument too. Apart from having conscription already, France and Germany are rearming like mad. Surely that could leave us vulnerable.'

'Then again, taken from a more positive stance, we would not be seen as glorifying war, fostering and increasing international ill will as Snowden points out here.'

'So, how do you respond to his suggestion that the National Service League is financed and supported by armament manufacturers?'

'I'd say he is right about that too.'

'And brave to say it.'

'Perhaps brave and foolish to say it.'

'Foolish, why?'

'Dark forces are abroad, my friend.'

'"Dark forces"? Carlton-Bingham used exactly the same expression to me only the other day.'

'Particularly during this present atmosphere of nationalistic fervour – "Dolly Gray I must leave you".'

'But I've nothing to do with war or politics.'

'Not knowingly, you haven't.'

'All I am about to do is defend a clergyman who likes dressing up in frocks.'

'Nevertheless, Andrew did not like that blackmail threat made against you at all. He always has your personal well-being foremost in his mind, James. I hope you realise that and do nothing to put yourself in further jeopardy. And this,' said Leacock, pushing Snowden's pamphlet across my leather table top, 'is best kept locked up in a drawer.'

* * * * *

It seems Dolly Gray was not the only one left in the lurch. Ignatius Shore arrived at Bootham Chambers in an anxious state mid-week. His partner still seemed disinclined to return from Rotterdam.

'We have not had a bill from you yet, Mr Shore,' I complained.

'How can I give you a bill, Mr Cairn, when I've no idea what sort of expenses Mortimer is incurring over there in Holland?'

'That's what worries us too. Surely this prolonged stay of his isn't entirely on behalf of Bootham Chambers. The apparent blackmail attempt was made against me in this country, I cannot for the life of me see the Dutch connection.'

'Perhaps this will explain all.' Shore passed me an unopened letter addressed to me and written in Blakely's unmistakable hand.

My Dear Mr Cairn,

My business interests over here have extended far beyond those of Bingham, Leacock, Fawcett & Cairn. I am safe and well and you are not to worry about me. Any further reassurance you can give to my partner, Mr Ignatius Shore, and my dear sister, Amelia, would be much appreciated.
Yours in faith,
Mortimer Blakely

'Is this all?' I asked Blakely's hovering partner in disbelief, opening out the envelope to examine it further.

'The office merely got an additional line or two under separate cover expressing that he was well and still taken up with matters in Holland.'

'This is not dated and see how he signs it, "Yours in faith".'

'Our letter was undated and signed the same. Not Mortimer's usual style at all.'

'And there is nowhere to address a reply.'

'I know. Ours was the same.'

'I seem to recall there was a hotel mentioned at the Port of Leuve, Rotterdam, in the letter stolen from us in the Fox.'

'I don't expect you can remember what it was called, can you?'

I shook my head. I had not had time to register the headed note paper before the letter was snatched. My memory was not impeccable after all.

'Some unintelligible Dutch name, I shouldn't wonder. But, see here, this one is stamped with an Amsterdam postmark.'

'Indeed,' sighed Shore.

'Mr Blakely's whereabouts is becoming a greater mystery than the one he was commissioned to resolve.'

'Indeed,' sighed Shore once more. 'I am really sorry about this, Mr Cairn.'

'So what is to be done?'

'Wait. Wait for Mortimer to make contact,' said a miserable Ignatius Shore.

* * * * *

'You are to come with me to Belle Vue Terrace straight away, Mr Cairn. There has been a disaster.' Sitting next to Jake in the hansom, he refused to enlighten me further.

I watched in confusion as the suburbs of York flashed past. First Dr Holbrook ostracises me from his family circle, forbidding me to see his daughter, then he sends me the Philip Snowden pamphlet, now I am summoned from my Gillygate home on a Saturday afternoon without any proper explanation.

"Tell me, Jake, what would you have done if I had refused to accompany you?' I asked half-jokingly. He drew a pistol from his greatcoat pocket and continued to sit with his massive paw covering the weapon in his lap. 'Wow!' I exclaimed, my hands lifting in a deferential pose. 'That thing isn't loaded is it?' Jake did not reply, 'You wouldn't dream of using it, would you?' The question was intended to reassure myself as much as cajole Holbrook's butler. Butler? – perhaps henchman was closer to the truth.

Jake's stare was hard and insolent. Without a word he turned back to the window, back to the fields, back to the weekend cows chewing the cud. He was contemptuous of the possibility that I would be silly enough to make a move for his pistol.

The scene that greeted me at Belle Vue Terrace was unbelievable. Shattered glass and stones everywhere, every window pane in the house had gone.

'You didn't do much to prevent this,' I sneered at Jake, 'despite bearing arms.'

'My morning off,' he snarled.

'Who would have known that?'

'They must have done.'

'"They"? Who are they?'

'Wish I knew,' he replied between clenched teeth.

'James! James is here!' Cedric skipped ahead of me into the Holbrooks' drawing room, immune to the spectacle of devastation. Everything would be alright – James was here.

'Watch the glass, boy,' yelled his father.

I gaped. Cool air blasted through the once magnificent bay window. The window seat on which Cedric had played during my previous visit was strewn with glass particles. The floor likewise was carpeted with the stuff. It was as if a bomb had gone off.

'James,' acknowledged Dr Holbrook somewhat curtly. He did not hesitate in his stride as he paced the room, indifferent to the glass beneath his own boot soles. He seemed to be eking out his own track through the crushed fragments.

Winifred was applying smelling salts beneath her mother's nose on the chaise longue. Mrs Holbrook was in a swoon.

'Caitlin, pull yourself together for the children's sake,' admonished Holbrook.

Hardly the best approach for a physician dealing with mental disorders, I thought.

'Papa, she cannot help it. The shock,' objected Winifred, mimicking my own assessment of the situation. She looked up, giving me the briefest of nods, before attending to her mother again.

'Sorry, sorry,' apologised her father. 'See, what we have come to, James.'

Jake, brush and pan in hand (pistol locked safely away in a drawer somewhere, I hoped), began to sweep away at the millions of shards clinging like limpets to the deep piled carpet.

'Have you called the police?' I asked Holbrook.

'Called and gone,' he muttered.

'What did they say about this?'

'They said what did we expect with our political associations. They meant that with our radical form of liberalism a few bricks through the windows was justifiable, and they weren't going to do a damn thing about it.'

'That's ridiculous. This is an unlawful act. Someone could have been seriously hurt, killed even.' Mrs Holbrook swooned at my words. Winifred shook her head, reproving my insensitivity.

'I agree,' said Holbrook. 'This is an unlawful act and you, James, are a man of the law, that is why we sent for you. That is why Winifred suggested we send for you,' he added generously.

'I'll have a word with the police.'

'Is that wise?'

'Which station is dealing with this case?'

'Our local bobby from Alma Terrace said it was a matter for the station in Jubbergate.'

'Oh no, not there.'

'Why, not there?'

'The two officers who tried to arrest your daughter came from Jubbergate Police Station.'

'See what trouble there has been since then. Everything was running smoothly until you intervened between Winifred and the police,' said Holbrook, suddenly hostile and changing tack.

'Papa!' gasped Winifred. 'The police were assaulting me.'

'Now wait a minute, Doctor Holbrook, that's most unfair,' I pealed in.

'Yes, James was helping me,' added Winifred.

'I expressly warned you not to see Winifred until this threat was over,' said Holbrook, sticking to his guns. 'Only days ago you were seen together in York.'

'What "threat" exactly and who saw us?' I asked.

'The blackmail photographs of course. But still you've gone out of your way to seek her out.'

'He hasn't,' objected Winifred. 'If anything it is I who have sought James' advice and company.'

'And we met the other day by pure chance,' I added.

'This is all too much,' announced her mother, rallying a second before swooning back again.

'What is that under there?' I asked, pointing to the chaise. We all peered forward. Jake was first to plunge under the insensible Mrs Holbrook. With his long reach he was able to locate and withdraw a half-brick wrapped and tied in a white sheet of writing.

'An early Christmas present,' I scoffed. No one ever appreciates my sense of humour. 'What does it say?' I asked Jake. Without a word, the massive paw delivered the brick into my much smaller version.

Leave scum. If you are not prepared to conform to the laws of this great land of ours.

Chapter Fourteen

I stayed a couple more hours to help clear up the mess. The hardware shop, where Dr Holbrook bought his motor oil, sent a man to board up the windows until the glazier came. Before I left, Holbrook had a tirade against a society in which this could have happened.

'We are living in a time of Freud and Marx,' he raged, the cool exterior gone. 'Our literature is decadent. Bishops, statesmen and educational reformers are viewed with irreverence. Anarchism is the order of the day.'

'You are not a follower of the Austrian neurologist Herr Freud's new theories then, sir?' I asked, surprised.

'Of course I have read some of his papers on what he calls psychoanalysis. *Studien über Hysterie* and suchlike. But where is God in all of this, James?' Holbrook pointed helplessly around at his darkened room.

Winifred showed me out.

'I have applied for Girton college,' she told me; her parting shot across my bow. 'There I will mix with like-minded women.'

'Cambridge will certainly broaden your horizons,' I replied; my own future hopes disintegrating.

'Broader than this,' she said, pointing to one of the boarded windows.

Back in my high town house, I began to mull over recent events. There had to be some sort of connection. It was strange how Dr Holbrook had suddenly become so accusatory. He had said that everything was running smoothly until I had intervened between Winifred and the police. But that applied to me too, didn't it? Would he have expected me to leave Winifred and Lucy to the mercy of bullies like Goater and his colleague? Would he have expected me to leave them defenceless against the mob? What would he have done under the same circumstances?

'Just suppose there are two opposing forces involved here,' I suggested to my clerk first thing Monday morning, 'and I have been caught in the middle.'

'Why do you say that, sir?'

'Because that is what it feels like.'

'Then perhaps you should go to Jubbergate and see if you can find anything out. See if the police have any idea why Miss Holbrook's house should have been attacked.'

'Get me my coat forthwith, Trotter.'

Jubbergate – yet another Jewish link with medieval York. The name implies that Jews once held properties or business along this tight thoroughfare between the Shambles and Parliament Street. I sniffed, I could smell the warm sickly smell of blood from the twenty or so butchers' shops along the nearby Shambles. Locally known as the Flesh Shambles many of the shops display hanging carcases outside. At night the two gutters on either side of the street run with blood and offal as the shop owners swill down. Blood, bloodshed, perhaps some of the Jews who were massacred in Clifford's Tower inhabited this street. Perhaps in more peaceful times they would walk from here to their nearby synagogue in Coney Street dressed in their mid-calf robes, cloth hoods or well-to-do knob pointed hats. Perhaps even then they were forced to wear their white tabula breast badges depicting their difference. Benjamin Levi once told me the origins of Joubrettegat were neither simple nor romantic for Jew or Gentile. This little street's chequered history is palpable. Its original name was Bretgate or Street of the Britons. Many British Celts, forced to live on the margins of our island, had the misfortune to be taken into slavery at this time and forced to labour at the behest of their Irish Viking masters in the city.

The police station, not the mythical Valhalla, was the only institution in the business of control now. Most of the rectangular building sprawled down Silver Street, next to the Fish Market, but a short frontage shared a corner of Jubbergate. The inelegant brick building with its slated roof was more daunting than reassuring, I found its interior equally depressing. The overall impression was brown and functional, apart from the desk sergeant's delicate pink cheeks reminiscent of the famous York ham.

'What can I do for you, sir?' he asked, leaning forward on his elbows. His full chest stretching the silver buttons of his uniform like a buxom woman.

'I wondered if you have made any headway regarding the attack last Saturday afternoon against the property of a Doctor Holbrook of Heslington.'

'And might I enquire what your interest is in this incident?'

'I was called to the house shortly after it happened.'

'I see.' There followed a few minutes of silence apart from the flick, flick, of turning pages as the sergeant tried to access a report on the Belle Vue attack. This gave me time to absorb my surroundings in greater detail. It was a relief that neither Goater nor his colleague were anywhere to be seen.

'No, I can find nothing here, sir. Alma Terrace Station must be dealing with it themselves.'

'But Doctor Holbrook's local constable said the matter would be referred to you.'

'What was the constable's name, sir?' he asked. I shook my head, I did not have the name. 'Well,' continued the sergeant, 'you can see for yourself there was no incident reported for Saturday afternoon anywhere in York.' He pushed the open book before me in mitigation. 'Now Saturday night, Saturday night in York is an entirely different matter.'

'Mr Cairn, to what do we owe the pleasure?' boomed another voice. My heart sank as I turned to see from whom it had come. Not Goater, nor his colleague. This proved to be cold comfort when I realised who it was – Sergeant Owen Howell – the same officer whom I had outsmarted in Florrie Cary's trial.

'Come through, Mr Cairn. Come through and we can talk. It is much quieter in here.' Howell sounded friendly enough.

There was a half eaten pie on his desk. I apologised for interrupting his lunch before telling him about my dilemma. How it appeared that the attack on the Holbrooks' house had somehow been overlooked.

'You must regard what I am about to say to you in the strictest confidence, Mr Cairn, as I am sure you will. Though it has not been officially recorded in the incident book, some commotion at the Holbrook house was reported by a concerned neighbour of theirs in Belle Vue Terrace.' There it was again, the attractive Welsh lilt particularly on the word "officially". 'The neighbour wasn't making a complaint, you understand, just drawing our attention to the fact.'

'But why? Why hasn't it been recorded,' I asked in bewilderment.

'I'll get to that shortly. First, tell me how you got wind of this?'

'I was called to the house shortly after it was stoned.'

'You were?'

'I am a friend of the family.' Was I? Was I really a friend of the family? It seemed to me then that Winifred and her family only wanted to know me in times of trouble.

'I see,' said Howell.

'We discovered a half-brick under the Holbrooks' chaise longue. It was wrapped up in a white cloth with a threat written on it.'

'Was it really,' said Howell. 'And did you read it?'

'Yes, of course I did.'

'So what did it say?'

'Leave scum. If you are not prepared to conform to the laws of this great land of ours.'

'Why would the perpetrators have chosen those exact words, Mr Cairn? Can you tell me that?'

'I have no idea.'

'How well do you know Doctor Holbrook and his family?'

'I have not been acquainted with them long,' I admitted, beginning to feel like Judas before the cock crowed.

'No, you haven't, have you?'

'Sorry?'

'I guessed that you can't have known them long from information given to me by a fellow officer. You first met the Holbrooks' daughter when she tied herself to the Mansion House railings a few months back, is that not so?' Howell smiled sardonically at the thought of the scene.

'Goater,' I moaned.

'No, as a matter of fact it wasn't Constable Goater but his colleague Constable Robins who informed me of the incident.'

'Robins and Goater, it sounds like something from the varieties.'

'Except they aren't very funny.'

'No, they aren't,' I readily agreed.

'I must warn you that we are living in dangerous times and we are surrounded by faceless dangerous people.' Howell lowered his voice to a whisper.

'Faceless?' I queried.

'Yes, faceless, because we don't know who they are exactly. They might be colleagues, friends, a brother even. They are all around us.'

'Are you trying to frighten me, Sergeant Howell?'

'Not at all. But what does this incident at the Holbrooks' house tell you?'

'It is a warning to the Holbrooks not to dabble in women's suffrage,' I suggested.

'Puh! Women's suffrage,' snorted Howell. 'I think it might be warning them off much more than that.'

'What more?' I asked, that old inkling of unease resurfacing.

'I think a man in your profession, Mr Cairn, should avoid rubbing shoulders with radicals and the like. I repeat, there are violent men on both sides of the political divide bent on upsetting the status quo in this country.'

'Yes, I know, I have already come to the same conclusion myself,' I sighed.

'Sorry, Mr Cairn, we haven't received any official complaints about this incident at the Holbrook house and therefore cannot act. You'd best take heed of my advice, sir, leave things well alone that don't concern you.'

✴ ✴ ✴ ✴ ✴

Winter was truly upon us. The river Ouse was frozen in places. Sheets of ice, like glass, were being blown onto the stone bank walls in a loud tinkling orgy. Some of the sheets were a yard square, some less. They would ride up the wall, mounting one another as they went, only to slide back down other approaching river riders powered by the strong cold northerly wind. I had never heard or seen anything like this before in my life. I was reminded of the broken window panes at the Holbrooks' house. This was an analogy of my present situation; I was being bombarded with facts from all directions and just as I felt I had made some sense of them, landed them, they would slide back into a watery murkiness.

I needed time off, time to myself, time to see things more clearly from a distance. When Winifred had said she thought she was being followed, Lucy Alexander had accused her of being "paranoid". Perhaps we were both suffering from Karl Ludwig Kahlbaum's delusional condition.

The Michaelmas sittings were well underway, once referred to as "terms" until the Supreme Court of Judicature Act 1875 decided to modernise like the Authorized King James Version of the Bible. I liked the Michaelmas sittings, they meant Christmas, and Christmas this year would mean a well-deserved escape to sort myself out. If only things turned out as one envisaged they would.

'How about a pre-Christmas drink tonight,' offered Robert Brown. 'Father would love to meet you.' George Hobb's solicitor apparently bumped into me by accident as I crossed the yard to the courthouse early one morning. I say "apparently" because everything seemed apparent and nothing seemed certain lately.

Shake me up, Judy – the old Classics scholar was seated in his invalid chair, rug covering his lap, like Grandfather Smallweed in Bleak House. Bleak it was, too, the Brown's substantial terrace house in Coppergate. Dark, bleak and masculine – any light feminine touch obviously long absent from its serviceable rooms. There seemed something sad, almost incestuous, about the relationship between Brown senior and junior. There was no third party to lessen the intensity of the men's relationship. I really did expect the old man to demand 'shake me up, son' at any moment.

What was I doing here with all that was going on in my own life at present? I was a soft fool to have accepted.

'A glass of port, sherry perhaps,' suggested Bob Brown.

The heaviness in the room was suddenly broken by old Mr Brown's gappy smile. 'Puh! Port, sherry, can't you see, son, Mr Cairn would like a brandy,' he cackled.

'Well, I wouldn't…,' I hesitated.

'You drank plenty of port when you were out with me the other night at the Black Swan, James,' pouted Bob; childishly, I thought.

'No, no, Mr Cairn here is a good cognac man, anyone can see that, it's obvious,' interrupted his father.

'I wouldn't say no,' I finally admitted. 'Although I am not sure what being a good cognac man entails.'

Old Mr Brown continued to roar with laughter as his son disappeared down into the cellar. He was still laughing when Bob returned and handed him a bottle of the finest Napoleon Courvoisier. The old man blew dust lovingly from the bottle before charging our glasses. I must confess I was surprised: crystal brandy glasses and glugging pure brandy was not a ritual I would have expected to be enjoying in these surroundings.

'By the way, James, I nearly forgot to give you this.' Bob lifted an envelope from the mantelpiece and handed it across to me. 'I said you would be getting an invitation from George.'

'Now how do you feel about that?' roared Mr Brown senior. 'I've heard of Scottish men in kilts. When I was in Dublin I saw one or two Nationalists wearing them too at political meetings. But a clergyman in a dress, how the mind boggles.'

'Have you met George Hobb?' I asked him, pocketing my unopened letter. Obviously old Mr Brown had been thoroughly briefed by his son regarding the Reverend's present predicament, so I could hardly be accused of breaching confidentiality.

'No, but my son used to bring us back tales about him when they were at university together in London. A clever chap by all accounts. He didn't wear dresses then, did he, Robert?'

'Not that I know of.' Bob smouldered. I suspect he was embarrassed that his father was in such good form, too good form for the solicitor's sombre taste.

'Bob told me that you studied Classics at Trinity College, Dublin,' I ventured.

'Yes.' The old man sounded suddenly weary. 'I am more familiar with Ancient Greece and Rome during classical antiquity than I am with my own country. Homer is my god.'

'Not Plutarch then.'

'"The noble lover of beauty engages in love wherever he sees excellence and splendid natural endowment without regard for any difference in physiological detail."'

'Said by one of Plutarch's characters in *Erotikos*.'

'I see I have found a fellow classicist. You are a fan of Plutarch, James?'

'He was a man who examined opposing arguments in parallel.'

'Ah, and his great work was *Parallel Lives*.' The parchment skin cracked open with pleasure again.

'I might add that Plutarch also possessed the wit and wisdom of Wilde.'

'Wilde would be flattered. Speaking of Wilde, speaking of parallel lives, James, have you ever heard of the notorious case of the Bishop of Cloghor?'

I shook my head. 'Well, I am not surprised, the Honourable Percy Jocelyn

147

graduated without distinction from Trinity College, Dublin, more than a century before Wilde and myself.'

'You knew Wilde, sir?'

'I stayed on to teach at Trinity for a while. Wilde was only a lad of about sixteen when I taught there. John Mahaffy was Wilde's tutor for a while, I believe, before Wilde went up to Oxford. Trinity has enjoyed her fair share of notorious students.' The cackle again. 'Now, where was I? Yes, that was it. We were talking about the strange case of the Bishop of Clogher which might be relevant to the plight of your George Hobb.'

Chapter Fifteen

They say London streets are paved with gold. For some they may be, for others they most certainly are not, for the majority they are ankle deep in cohesive horse muck. It was a Saturday – the day before Christmas Eve – on the streets. Commerce rather than religion was the engine here. Horse drawn omnibuses vied with the occasional new motorised ones. Hansom cabs dodged at breakneck speed between and around anything else that moved, be it of flesh or metal. If there was something to sell, it was sold here, sold now. If there was something to be smelt it was smelt here: cooked chickens, rotting cabbage, horse sweat, human sweat, scented flowers, Thames pollution.

After swimming off on my own for a long time, I was a young male dolphin returning to the pod, returning to the frolicking grounds of my youth. And somehow I found I was pleased, comforted with the familiarity of it all. London is a city of villages or manors, all separate with their own distinct characters, each peopled by its own peculiar brand of folk. Though in essence London is much bigger than York for me it seemed smaller, smaller walking down Petersham Place, smaller in reality than it had been in my imagination during my years of absence. Perhaps the adolescent vices I had indulged in then were in reality smaller too. Sins reserved for the Haymarket, off the Strand, never near home, never close to here in South Kensington. The fine red brick and cream sculptured houses here always seemed to me to be above vice, above all human frailties, above indiscretions youthful or otherwise. South Kensington was where my mother and sister still lived. It was hard to realise I was back.

The small, neat front garden looked the same despite being licked by blowing curled winter leaves. I seem to remember the last time I had been home in Petersham Place it had been summertime. The house itself had not changed. The potted plants in the window had not changed. It was one of those roomy Georgian houses with a lived-in comfortable feel to it.

'James.' My mother looked older and even smaller than her location. Struggling to her feet, she reached up to embrace me.

My younger sister, Marie, had grown taller and more handsome – and handsome rather than beautiful was the truth of it. Her kiss on my cheek was cool. She resented my long absence.

'We have read all about you in the paper, James,' said my mother enthusiastically. 'Haven't we, Marie?'

'That must have been all of two years ago, Mother,' pointed out my sister.

'Ah, the Robertshaw case,' I responded hesitantly to the ice in my sister's voice. I searched her face to see if there was any chance of regaining her previous affection for me, or had I driven it too far into the ground like a corpse never to be retrieved.

'Yes,' said my mother. 'You were in the *Times*.'

'You can't get much better than that, James, to be in the *Times*,' pealed in my sister.

'We had a murder once in South Kensington,' announced my mother proudly.

'Just the one,' added my sister.

'Do be quiet, dear, you know nothing about it. James was a baby when it happened and you weren't even born.'

'I stand corrected.' My sister smirked.

'So, who was murdered?' I asked.

'I do remember there was a lot of building work going on in our area at the time. A crippled potman from the Drayton Arms public house had allowed some of the workmen both beer and money on credit. He would collect what they owed him on Saturdays. These transactions had gone on successfully for a while, until one Saturday the potman never returned to the public house. He was found dead a few days later with head injuries in an unfinished house in Glennow Gardens. It was the plasterers who came under suspicion as they were completing the building at the time.'

'And I suppose all the deceased's money had gone.'

'Walter, I think he was called Walter Lee. The poor man's pockets had been rifled, he had not as much as a farthing left on him, James.'

'Was anyone ever arrested for the crime?'

'I can't remember, dear.'

'Phew!' blew my sister. 'This is a light conversation to start with after years of abandonment.'

'Marie!' exclaimed my mother.

'It's all right.' I placed a consoling hand on her arm before turning to my sister. 'I haven't exactly abandoned you, Marie, I write to you both regularly.' My justification was lame and I knew it. I looked to the Christmas tree in an attempt to escape the consequences of my failure. I could have cried, such effort had gone into dressing it. The Norway fir was bedecked with homemade decorations, sugared almonds and fruits, candles, wire and glass ornaments and an array of more professional Woolworth baubles. Fine silver German tinsel clung to pine needles, festooned every branch. The prodigal had returned – my sister was right – I was unworthy of all this. '*O Tannenbaum, O Tannenbaum, wie treu sind deine Blätter. Du grünst nicht nur zur Sommerzeit, nein auch im Winter, wenn es schneit.*'

'What's that? What are you saying, dear?' asked my mother.

'He's singing a traditional German carol in praise of the tree,' explained my clever sister.

'Yes, Prince Albert had a lot to answer for,' I laughed.

'And so have you,' said my sister, but this time the flicker of a smile lifted the edges of her firm mouth.

Then we all laughed, we hugged, we laughed more over the next evening's Christmas Eve ham and even more over the following day's festive goose, over old family stories often told. Then my mother cried because my father was no longer with us to hear them.

* * * * *

The full moon of Christmas Day was on the wane. A dank mist clung to the Thames day and night. I always find the week between Christmas and the New Year to be a flat dreary affair. A few days after New Year's Eve, I would be making the crossing from Portsmouth to the Isle of Wight. I loved my mother and sister but I was waiting, waiting to move on. However, and I don't know why it should be so, I've often found remarkable things can happen in this time of suspension – the unexpected can rise from the blur of mulled wine and bite you in the face.

'Why don't you take yourself off to the British Museum of Natural History instead of moping about the house?' suggested my mother. 'You spent hours there as a boy.'

So I did as I was told and walked round the corner into Exhibition Road. It is true this was where I would come day after day to worship, this was the catalyst for my passion, this cavernous building with its terracotta facade was my temple as a boy. The Gibbs and Canning terracotta tiles were an attempt to resist the sooty London air. The building is decorated with sculptures of flora and fauna. Living and extinct species are displayed separately in the west and east wings at the explicit request of the museum's first superintendent, Richard Owen, as a rebuttal to his adversary Charles Darwin and Darwin's theory of a link between present and past species through natural selection.

Apart from reliving my youth, I had a further imperative for this visit. If I was going to spend time with George Hobb on the Isle of Wight preparing his defence, I was determined to spend any leisure time left to me examining the locations of the many famous Cretaceous finds on display here in the museum. Unlike the earlier Jurassic coast of Yorkshire where marine reptiles occasionally waddled ashore, the hooves of many giant dinosaurs would have been heard regularly lolloping across the Cretaceous mud plains of the Isle of Wight. Here too were the hunting grounds of naturalists such as Gideon Mantell, Richard Owen and William Buckland, here was the home of William Fox. As a lad, in the British Museum, I don't know how many times I had stood staring in wonder at Fox's Aristosuchus, Calamospondylus and Polacanthus. The curate of St Mary the Virgin in Brighstone was the first man to realise that Hypsilophodon was a dinosaur species in its own right, and not a juvenile Iguanodon. On his death he donated five hundred specimens to the museum. But what had the man written down? – that was my main objective for today. I made my way to the cool silence of the library. Outside in the street, the gas lamps had only just flickered off as inside the dim room I flicked from one page to another. 1866a Another Wealden reptile – Athenaeum, 2014, 740 1; 1866b Another *new* Wealden reptile – Geological Magazine, 3, 383; the Reverend Fox was obviously more a man for the bones than the pen. I scratched my head.

Pencil poised, a current of air, a slip of marker paper flew out of a book left on my table by someone else. I caught the marker and reached for the book. That dark miserable winter's day was about to light up for me.

Vestiges of the Natural History of Creation was written by Robert Chambers, a Scottish journalist, and pre-dated *On the Origin of Species by Means of Natural Selection* by a decade and more. For years Chambers published the work anonymously and not until after his death was his authorship exposed. I had heard of this popular work which, by many in the backbiting world of naturalists and religious scientists, had been judged to be non-scientific in its progressive transmutation of species theory. Although scathingly critical of Chambers' lack of sound scientific justifications, Darwin did eventually admit that it paved the way for his own work. Another of my great evolutionary heroes, the beetle collecting Alfred Russel Wallace, was a little kinder and wrote to a friend: "I have a rather more favourable opinion of the *Vestiges* than you appear to have. I do not consider it a hasty generalization, but rather as an ingenious hypothesis strongly supported by some striking facts and analogies, but which remains to be proved by more facts and the additional light which more research may throw upon the problem".

I lifted *Vestiges* up to my nose and smelt paper and leather. I loved the smell of books, the feel of them. I opened up the pages on another man's ideas. Chambers suggested that everything currently in existence had developed from earlier forms: solar system, Earth, rocks, plants and corals, fish, reptiles, birds, mammals and ultimately man. He did not deny that God was the mastermind behind these countless worlds but said it was ridiculous to suppose that he interfered with every shellfish or reptile ushered into existence.

'You are really enjoying that, aren't you?' I glanced up. Had someone spoken to me or was I imagining it? 'The book,' emphasised the voice.

'Yes, I am,' I conceded, flustered now, attempting to focus on the figure across the table from me. 'I've read and re-read this piece and still find something more in it.'

'It was considered a work of originality for its time.'

'You know it then, sir.'

'Indeed, I do.' A broad grin cracked through the old man's grey bushy whiskers. He had a kind accommodating face.

'The man was a genius.'

'Just to hear that said once in your life.' Amusement danced across the intelligent face. But it was the old man's hands that caught my eye, capable and graceful yet male in every respect. 'Of course Jean-Baptiste Lamarck's theory pre-dates even *Vestiges*.'

'How is that, sir?'

'Lamarck was the first to suggest that life forms develop and adapt to meet the demands of their surroundings. His most succinct example was the giraffe. Each generation of giraffe grew a longer neck to reach the higher leaves on the acacia tree.'

'The giraffe, that's wonderful.'

'You could say the same process took place in the evolutionary theory itself. Men such as Lamarck, Chambers and eventually Darwin took the theory a stage further.'

'You've not mentioned Wallace, sir.'

'No, I haven't, have I?' He pondered for a second or two before asking, 'Are you an evolutionist yourself, young man?'

'I certainly am.'

'It is not an easy thing to be, even in this age of enlightenment, this time of industrial progression.'

'There are sensitivities and prejudices to be lived through in every age.'

'Indeed, you are right. *Fors Clavigera*, fortune the club-bearer,' muttered the old man thoughtfully to himself once more.

'The name for John Ruskin's collective letters to the working man.'

'Some of his most perceptive work,' he acknowledged. 'Ruskin, Darwin, we all suffer in the name of advanced thought. I can hear the news vendors now baying for blood outside this very building. "Darwin is a monkey. Monkeys, monkeys".'

'Have you noticed that gentleman at the next desk with a monocle has never taken his eyes, or should I say, eye off us?'

'Oh, I am used to that in here,' laughed my companion.

'Hush!' complained a female reader.

'The director, William Flower, has done a wonderful job with this place, don't you think?' I whispered.

'Haven't you heard, he's gone?' frowned the old man.

'Gone? Gone where?'

'He died on the first of July.'

'I knew Mr Flower well. I have lived away for many years,' I explained, looking sadly back down on Robert Chambers' *Vestiges*. 'There is always change,'

'Yes, there is, and we are about to undergo huge social changes, just you see,' said the old man, frothing with enthusiasm.

'Do you mean with the rise of the Independent Labour Party?'

'Just so.'

'It will polarise politics.'

'Just so,' repeated the old man, grinning from ear to ear. 'The liberal elite will move to the right. It will destroy liberalism for centuries to come.'

'You are a socialist I take it, sir.'

'The working class of this country needs representation.'

'As do women?' I ventured.

'Quite.'

'But you are not working class, sir.'

'I have worked all my life, young man.'

'Might I be so bold as to ask your occupation?'

'I am an explorer of truth,' said the old man, huddling back into his book.

Chapter Sixteen

I decided to take the air and do some exploring myself. I needed a long walk, time to absorb what I had just read in *Vestiges* and my conversation with the man in the library. I strode away from the museum without any actual destination in mind, complex ideas of transmutation and socialism refusing to walk easily with me. What did I know? – I was just a simple lawyer. I took a turn towards the Thames. I loved to be by rivers. Strange this primitive attraction for water in a man who is a non-swimmer. It was not until I reached the Victoria Embankment beyond Westminster Bridge that I sensed I was being watched. I turned round but could see no one I recognised, no one obviously interested in me. Perhaps it was all those buzzing ideas haunting me, stubbornly remaining elusive, intellectually beyond my reach.

On a whim I took a short cut down the intriguingly named Cockspur Street. I was being drawn to the stomping grounds of my youth just as surely as if I were a pin to a magnet.

Not quite vice-ridden Whitechapel, or the opium dens of Limehouse, or the abject poverty and prostitution of the Old Nichol Rookery, nonetheless the streets, taverns and alleyways off the Haymarket have a certain notoriety once the theatres close.

'James, James Cairn, is that you?' I felt a tug on the sleeve of my frock coat.

'Mrs Milner, how amazing to bump into you like this.' I raised my silk hat. Of course I recognised her straight away.

'Not so amazing. You're staring right up at my house, James.'

'I did not expect to find you still living here.'

'Things are slow to change in London.'

'How is Mr Milner? Is he still taking the odd tutorial for Merchant Taylors'?'

'Away, always away pursuing his first love – education. A year ago he finally secured a position at Cambridge.'

'Bright man. Good teacher, although mathematics was never my strongest subject.'

'But not so bright that he married a theatre girl, eh?' Her arms were laden with parcels.

'Here let me take some of those for you, Mrs Milner,' I offered.

'So, I am merely Mrs Milner to you now.'

I smiled, lightening her burden. She checked up and down the street to see if we were being observed before turning the key in the lock.

'Tea?' she asked, as I placed her shopping on the kitchen table. 'I'm afraid I'll have to make it for you myself.'

'Don't tell me it's the maid's day off,' I winked; immediately ashamed of my crude flirtation. Mrs Milner deserved better than that.

'No, we had to let Mattie go. Until his Cambridge appointment, Randolph's teaching posts have been inconsistent and theatre jobs on offer for an older woman have all but dried up. But let me take a proper look at you, James.' She pushed me back a pace. 'See how you have filled out. What a fine man you have become. A barrister, I hear. It must be all of ten years since last…'

'Sixteen, sixteen years.' The kettle began to boil. I stepped towards her, took a lock of her hair in my hand, a memory of hair, *Beata Beatrix* hair. I ran those fine silk threads through my fingers before I kissed them.

'No,' she said, spinning away. 'All this time… not one… you hurt me. I knew I had to let you go. You had so much growing up to do.'

'True, but the man stands before you now.'

'And a married woman, a washed up actress grown older, stands before you. God willing, perhaps with a little more commonsense.'

'Sense was never your problem Tilly.'

'Not once did you write, attempt to make contact, James,' she complained; holding the steaming kettle in suspension over the pot. 'You can leave your coat and hat down here on the chair. We'll take tea in the drawing room upstairs, if you don't mind.'

As always she had taken control. I took the tray. Without further mishap or conflict we arrived in the drawing room full of theatre memorabilia and little maths. It was exactly how I remembered it all those years ago. I loved this room overlooking the aptly named James Street and the building where the old tennis court had once been. She took the sofa and I took one of the worn velvet chairs where her husband had spent hours trying to instill in me unfathomable equations. She poured the tea into faded china cups that had seen better days. If the inanimate can become tired and worn, what then of the animate? They say never go back. Had I made a mistake?

'Are there still problems between you and Mr Milner?' I asked, clearing my throat.

'He still insists on calling me Millicent, if that's what you mean,' she laughed. 'But we rub along well enough together.'

'Do you remember when he first brought me here for those extra lessons? I thought I had arrived in heaven getting away from that place.'

'Randolph always felt some of the older masters were too free with the cane at Merchant Taylors', despite William Baker being such an excellent headmaster.'

'Old masters, old habits. Mr Milner should have been at the first school. Matters improved when we moved from Suffolk Lane to Goswell Street. In Goswell Street we had playing fields, games, grounds in which the soul could expand.'

'Randolph felt sorry for you, you know.'

'Really.' Should I have felt sorry for the husband who felt sorry for me, I wondered. Should I have felt guilt? But who, coming from a world of men served meals by only the safest of old crones, could have resisted the warmth of Mrs Milner?

'He thought you were a sensitive, highly-gifted boy. A boy who had been damaged in some way. A boy who was doing his best to conceal that damage.'

'And what did his wife think?'

'The same.' She sipped thoughtfully at her cup. Her eyes never lifting from mine. They were neither teasing nor testing just focused. 'You don't have to sit over there,' she said.

Layers of stage makeup had taken their toll. Her face was a little more lined and dry as she lay with me on the attic bed. The harsh winter light penetrated through the dormitory window remorselessly, the sun a spotlight on our historical sin. She had always insisted we use this room, never their bedroom. I rolled over, my shadow casting her more favourably. Our positions had changed, the initiator awaiting initiation. The experienced woman – the teacher's wife teaching – waiting to be taught.

'I could look at you all day like this,' I said, and I could.

With all the time in the world, I etched out her pale naked body with my finger; an artist without brush, palette or paints; an artist to match Rossetti nevertheless; an artist of the flesh. I drew rings round the pinkness of her nipples. Her breasts had remained boyish but no less desirable for that, the stomach still flat running down to the girlish pelvis with its luxuriant growth. All those unflattering years had done nothing to diminish the beauty of her body.

'You are driving me out of my mind.' Her voice was a hoarse whisper.

'I will never tire of this,' I told her. The face I looked down on had become trusting and dependent, almost childlike in expectation.

What was I doing? Winifred, I loved Winifred Holbrook, didn't I? Doubt ran in rivulets of cold sweat down my chest, my back. I feared I was incapable of meeting the need beneath. But I wasn't really fooled, this wasn't because of Winifred Holbrook, this wasn't even guilt over an absent unknowing husband, this was because of me.

Mrs Milner's always elegant hand reached for my hardness – encouraging – discouraging. Revulsion overwhelmed me at the thought of taking that final violent step into total intimacy. I plunged my grooming finger into warm stickiness instead, a cook trying the mix.

'What about you?' she asked.

'Forget about me.'

'Nothing has changed,' moaned Mrs Milner.

'I am sorry,' I said.

While I remained awake hugging my disappointment, she fell comfortably asleep over here.

They say never go back.

By way of compensation I took her to Simpson's at the far end of the Strand. Surely nothing wicked could be construed from Mr Milner's old pupil escorting his wife to a late lunch. Well, just look at the age difference.

Simpson's was originally opened earlier in the century as The Grand Cigar Divan, a smoking house, then a coffee house and chess club. So as not to disturb the chess games, cooks would wheel large joints of meat on silver-domed trolleys to guests' tables. They still did.

There in the panelled room, under a sculptured ceiling and chandeliers, we watched in mouth-watering anticipation as our silver dome was lifted and the chef began the traditional carve. We both had chosen the specialty of the house of course – what else when at Simpson's? – Scottish beef on the bone.

'Disraeli and Gladstone used to eat here,' I told her. She appeared hungry and tired of ritual and was tucking into her beef with relish.

'Not together,' she laughed.

'I heard Richard D'Oyly Carte owns it now.'

'Perhaps he'll come in and offer me a job.'

'I'm sorry things are so difficult for you.'

'Things are always difficult in the theatre if you are female and over forty.' She dabbed the gravy running down her chin with a napkin before renewing her assault. She was devouring not eating. How wonderfully simple and animal she was. How different we were.

'My father brought me here one Christmas vacation just before he sailed for Africa.'

'Like today.'

'Yes, almost to the day.'

'I remember. He was killed out in Africa, wasn't he?'

'In the name of British imperial expansion. Disraeli was in office at the time.'

'You sound bitter.'

'I am. My father was skewered in the afternoon by a Zulu spear on the battlefield of Isandlwana during a period of absolute darkness – a total eclipse of the sun – what luck is that?'

'None at all. You must have missed him very much.'

'I expect you despise me?'

'No, I don't.'

'But you think I'm damaged?'

'I think someone mistreated you at school. I suspect it happened around the time you lost your father.'

'And you pity me?' I had suddenly lost my appetite.

'No, I care that you have been hurt.'

'I can't talk about it.'

'I know. You have buried it too deeply.'

'And you have always felt sorry for me?'

'No, I have and will always love you, James.'

'And Mr Milner?'

'Love is not exclusive.'

Day had moved into night when I escorted Mrs Milner back to James Street. I promised her that I would write this time. I hailed a hansom outside the Theatre Royal. Some mechanism was driving me to examine the past. I was a man who had lost something invaluable. I had to confront it to get it back.

I paid the driver off a street away from my destination. Going down the hollowed basement steps, my senses were immediately bombarded by the rising smells of joss sticks, tobacco from hubble-bubbles and the heady sweet smell of opium. I struggled to remind myself this was Whitechapel not Shanghai. From a cave mouth to match Kirkdale's smoke billowed.

Yes, my old haunt did not only exist in nightmares, the oil lamp burned as it always had done above the open door. Mr Yao's was still there, although many businesses had moved east to the London Docklands along with Chinese sailors and Lascars addicted to *ah-pen-yen*.

I peered in. Balls of opium glowed and dimmed in the bowls of long brass pipes like so many moons in a dense sky. The same bodies as before bowed, twisted, contorted, played out private fantasies on terraced berths. The same mouths muttered personal stories to no one listening. To an abstainer looking in it was a vision of Hell, my own remembered Hell.

'Four pennies a pill, sir.' Without recognition a grinning Mr Yao beckoned me forward. His head and neck stuck out horizontally from his body. The spine was gravitating to the cobbled floor. 'Only four pennies.'

I ran back up the hollowed steps. The answer was no longer to be found there.

Chapter Seventeen

My mother was disappointed that I had missed dinner. Following numerous reassurances that I had already eaten, I lifted my feet onto her favourite pouf and contemplated my day. Another glass of mulled wine lay ahead of me, another roaring hearth, another evening of cloying family life. Perhaps I had lived on my own too long.

'James, will you take me on one of these new electric trains that operate underground?' Marie asked.

'I would have thought an independent young woman such as you had already ridden the Stockwell line.'

'It wouldn't be safe, a woman on her own going through all those dark tunnels,' said my mother, head shaking disapprovingly. 'I would never let Marie go unescorted.'

'We'll see,' I said. My sister smiled back at me. I could tell she had set her heart on the matter. 'Do you know, I think I spent this morning in the company of Alfred Russel Wallace,' I told them. It was only after my return to Petersham Place that the realisation had finally kicked in.

'Russel who?' asked my mother.

'Alfred Russel Wallace, Mother. Friend and collaborator of Darwin,' helped out my sister.

'Oh, him,' said my mother. 'The man who doesn't believe in God.'

I was true to my half-word, my half-promise, and eight thirty the following morning saw Marie and I pay our pennies at the turnstile before waiting on the King William Street platform for the electric train to arrive for Stockwell. The City and South London Railway was almost ten years old. It was the first deep-level electrically operated railway in the world and I had not been on it myself before. Like my mother, I had never trusted it either: creeping under tons of London earth like a mole.

Creeping, now there I was wrong. A suck of air – a lurch in the right direction – whizz and we were off in our windowless third carriage at a dignified speed.

'Padded cells, I've heard them called. They don't feel very padded to me,' said my sister; said my sister loudly to the dismay of the twenty or so other passengers shuffling their buttocks on the hard longitudinal bench seats, made more uncomfortable with the thought that we must be under the Thames by now.

Kennington – The Oval – Stockwell, 3⅕ miles in all.

'This line was never meant for a system of electric traction,' our gateman told us *reassuringly* as we waited for returning City of London passengers. 'It is an experiment.'

'Oh dear.' Marie rubbed a nervous gloved finger across her eye.

The gateman rode on an open platform at the back of the carriage. He was responsible for letting people off and on at each station.

'Because of the narrowness of the tunnels this railway was originally intended for cable haulage only,' he continued, proud of his knowledge.

'So what happened?' asked my sister.

'Unfortunately, young lady,' the gateman sucked deeply on the sooty air, 'the cable contractor fell into bankruptcy during construction.'

'How awful and all too common these days,' commiserated my sister.

Stockwell – The Oval – Kennington – Elephant & Castle – Borough – King William Street, back we came.

For the life of me, I do not know what the gateman and our fellow passengers made of us as we rode up and down under the streets of the capital. Journeys are usually taken to go from somewhere to get to somewhere rather than simply for the ride. And what a ride it proved to be. Marie and I had never encountered anything like it, I was used to the jarring effects of horse-drawn cabs, the rumble of steam engines across sleepers. But this electric train was the smoothest ride I had ever experienced. Experiment or no, this had to be the future. It both frightened and thrilled us. Knowing you were travelling in a tube underground at speed was truly exhilarating. As the gateman opened the lattice gate at the back of our carriage a final time, allowing us access on to the platform, my legs wobbled with excitement.

'Amazing,' said my sister. 'Wasn't that quite amazing?'

'I almost expected ghouls and headless bodies to appear like in ghost shows at the fun fair,' I laughed.

'Look out!' screamed my sister. I felt a thump in my back, the sort of thump you get at rugby from an unexpected tackle. I teetered towards the drop and the line.

Whoosh! The suck of air. Another train into the station. My sister's hand was clamped on my arm.

'Why don't you damn well watch where you're going?' She shouted after a rapidly disappearing figure in a black Ulster coat. 'That man nearly pushed you under the train.'

She was right. My legs were now wobbling with shock, quivering so much I feared they would no longer hold me up. I leaned back against the platform wall to regain my composure. Marie still clung to my arm.

The station master approached. 'You all right, sir?'

'That man nearly pushed my brother under a train,' complained Marie. We all looked up the platform towards the exit; the man had gone.

'He jostled me by accident,' I explained, making light of it, hating being the centre of so much commiseration.

'Thankfully you're a sturdy chap with a good sense of balance,' said the station master.

'I played rugby,' I said.

After the Tube, after the incident, London street air never smelt so good. I told Marie I had forgotten how many people lived and worked in the city centre.

'You've forgotten because you've hardly been here since university. London grows bigger everyday.'

'Do you still like it here?' I asked, ignoring the reprimand.

'Isn't London supposed to be the capital of the world? You have everything on hand as soon as you cross your doorstep, libraries, museums, theatres. I've never known anything else,' she shrugged.

'Do I detect some regret in that final sentence?'

'An accident of birth gave you so much more freedom of choice than me, James.'

Marie suddenly put me in mind of Winifred and I fell silent.

'Your original old grammar school isn't far from here, is it?' She piped up again. 'Shall we take a look?'

'I'm not sure...'

'Do let's go. It will be fun.' She took my arm again and guided me like a sleepwalker down Laurence Pountney Hill towards Suffolk Lane. The 17th century Manor of the Rose was just as austere as my memory of it. The monastic arches and arched windows just as claustrophobic and forbidding. I shuddered at the memory of long shadows – real or imaginary – waiting to waylay me from many cloistered niches, knarled branches of arms and twig fingers waiting to grab me as I passed.

'You think you lack freedom, independence, Marie. We had no life in that building, it was like a prison. Can you imagine all that youthful male energy locked and cramped up in one place without outlet?'

Marie stared at me in horror. 'Forgive me, I had no idea you hated it so much, James.'

'It wasn't any fun at all. It was the beginning of all my sorrows.' The accusatory finger shook. I could feel the blood draining from my face.

'Come, come away now,' she said. 'Our time together is too precious to be spoilt by bad memories'

'You knew, didn't you?'

'No, no I didn't. Mother suspected you were being bullied but you would never say. It was such a long time ago.'

Feral pigeons soared above our heads as we walked briskly back along Cannon Street towards St. Paul's Cathedral. I was reminded of the mobbing coastal sea gulls of Staithes, although these city birds were a lot less aggressive, a lot more sophisticated in their hunting techniques. Descended from rock doves, London pigeons roost under nearly every roof and on the side of nearly every building.

'I am always afraid they will splash a little message on my hat,' said my sister, noticing my focus of interest. She was wearing a fashionable trilby, masculine but fetching for all that.

'That would be a shame, it suits you,' I told her.

'You are actually flattering me now, James.'

'Don't I usually?'

'It has been occasionally known.'

'Oh dear,' I said, watching the low flight of another pigeon dodging the omnibus roofs. 'Tell me, Marie, would you go to university if you could?'

'Like a shot,' said my sister. 'But there's Mother.'

I suddenly stopped in my tracks, blinked, thought I was imagining it. Lucy Alexander caught my attention first. She was strolling arm in arm with a bereted Howard Greenstock on the pavement across the street. I waved my arms madly and shouted trying to alert them. But the Cannon Street traffic noise was too great, and they continued to walk on unaware.

'What's wrong?' asked my sister.

'That couple walking down the opposite side of the street, I think I know them.'

'Where? Where?' asked my sister, demanding a better description.

'Over there, see, the man's wearing a beret.'

'But I know them too,' said an astonished Marie. 'Lucy Alexander and Arnon van Grunsven.'

'Arnon who?'

'Arnon van Grunsven. He's from a wealthy Jewish family. He's a really big name in the Peace Society. Just as Lucy Alexander is important in our movement.'

'What movement?'

'The National Union of Women's Suffrage Societies. Don't you know, James, women's suffrage began in Kensington with the Kensington Society?'

'And are you a member of that society also?'

'No, no,' laughed my sister. 'The Kensington Society has been defunct well before my time.'

'I see,' I said.

'But I am a committed member of the NUWSS. Do I detect a note of disapproval, big brother?'

'No, not at all. In fact I am proud of you.' Another similarity between the two women I most adored in the world. Perhaps my attraction to Winifred Holbrook was simply based on the same comfortable fraternal love I had for my sister.

'Don't tell our mother,' she begged.

'And what more do you know about Lucy Alexander and Howard… this Arnon van Grunsven?'

'I don't know them very well. I've just heard talk about them. They are both considered to be brilliant. They were students at Oxford together, I believe.'

'Were they?'

'Yes, but why all this curiosity about Arnon and Lucy, James?' Marie's interest was now truly piqued.

'Because I knew Arnon van Grunsven as Howard Greenstock in another life,' I said casually; feeling it was only fair to trust Marie with this small piece of the puzzle.

'Howard Greenstock?' Marie wrinkled her nose in bemusement. 'I've never known him as that.'

'Howard Greenstock is how he first introduced himself to me up in Yorkshire. He said he was a postgraduate history student.'

'He might well be that and much more.'

'The strange thing is Lucy didn't give any indication to the rest of our party that she already knew him, not even to her best friend.'

'When did all this take place?'

'Only a few months ago.'

'Well, Arnon van Grunsven and Lucy Alexander have been walking out together for well over a year now, I can personally vouch for that.' Marie hesitated before adding, 'James, I'd better warn you, Arnon and Lucy are both very politically active and motivated. They are regarded in some quarters as being rather extreme, dangerous even.'

'But not by you?'

'Yes, certainly by me too,' sighed my sister.

Chapter Eighteen

'What are you reading about, dear?' asked my polite, always polite mother. 'You are frowning.'

'It says here,' I said, shaking the *Times*, 'we have lost another battle at Colenso in Natal. It seems the days between the eleventh and fifteenth of December have been dubbed "the black week" for us. Lieutenant the Honourable Freddy Roberts, only son of Field Marshal Lord Roberts, died during action to retrieve a couple of guns. He has been posthumously awarded the Victoria Cross. A coin sized piece of bronze, made from a captured Chinese-made Russian cannon, awarded for the recovery of two other lumps of tooled metal – the price of a young man's life.' I suddenly felt sick over my boiled eggs. 'Poor old Baden-Powell and his men are still under siege at Mafeking. Buller, the commander of operations in Natal is having a thin time of it too. He has fallen off his horse. Literally reading between the lines, our resources are stretched over a huge area and, I've heard tell, Buller hasn't even got a decent map with him. No wonder he is losing battles. I can hear the hunting dogs barking louder in Westminster than Africa, Buller's days are numbered.'

'Your father died in Africa, dear. I hate Africa,' said my mother.

Scraping my chair on the floor I moved back from the table. I went to look out of the window, take my own thoughts of loss away from the intensity of my mother's loss. Her urban garden was inches thick with hoarfrost. The branches of the apple trees stretched out like the spangled arms of circus bareback riders. I wondered if it was cold enough to freeze the Thames as the Ouse had frozen in York before I left. York, iconic Clifford's Tower, Benjamin Levi – I was suddenly struck with the idea of a fresh approach to matters that had been both perplexing and hounding me ever since that beautiful sunny day in Kirkdale. I remembered a York rabbi once telling me that "the problem for Jews is we are a nation living within a nation".

'Like the Boer and British whites in black Africa,' I muttered.

'What's that, dear?' asked my mother.

'Nothing, Mother. I have just had an idea, for once a good idea, that's all.'

'I hope you are not considering joining up and going to Africa like your father, dear.'

'No, not any time yet, Mother,' I reassured her.

Surely, what was a Jewish problem could be turned to my advantage. That morning I penned a letter to catch the first post for Benjamin Levi's Park Lane chambers in Leeds. Benjamin, I remembered, originated from London as I did. The Jewish community was an especially tight one in London and with good reason. In the East End they were still living down the allegation that it had been a Jew who had committed those horrific Whitechapel murders which began a decade ago, and increasingly anti-immigration and anti-Semitic rhetoric could be heard from the likes of Major William Evans-Gordon and his followers.

I was moving my bags out into the hall the next day, under the watchful rather resentful gazes of my mother and sister, when *click* – the postman pushed his delivery of letters through their box. Two of the letters were addressed to me. This I could see was adding insult to injury for my mother in particular: more demands from other people for her son's attention even at a time of fond farewell.

'I'll open them on the train to Portsmouth,' I told her.

Poor Marie, she was struggling to hold back the tears as we embraced. As mature adults we really had bonded this time.

Bags in hand, I stood with one foot through the open doorway before turning back to her.

'By the way, Marie, I forgot to ask, have you ever heard of Winifred Holbrook?' I whispered close to her ear, my hand briefly brushing her crumpled face trying so hard to be stoical.

'Not yet,' she said, forcing a smile.

⁘

Waterloo Station was thankfully not its usual busy self. I loved railway stations. I particularly loved Waterloo with its high girder roof. Normally, I loved the bustle of the place, the energy of going places, but after my holiday with my mother and sister I wanted time to myself again, time to breathe.

I was in luck, there were plenty of empty compartments on the Portsmouth train. Passengers were obviously reluctant to travel to the coast in these first inclement days of the new century. I prayed whenever I saw the occasional sailor swaying down the platform – no doubt returning to their ships after an inebriant Christmas leave – that they would not choose my compartment, would not bother me.

I put my second class return ticket in my top inside pocket. My fingers searched the pocket's inner lining to ensure it was secure. I am what Dr Freud would call obsessional in these matters. The few coins change from eighteen shillings and three pence went into my trouser pocket. Before lifting my briefcase next to the portmanteau in the overhead luggage rack, I removed that morning's correspondence.

The first regular brown envelope I opened was from Ignatius Shore, telling me that he and Amelia had decided to report Mortimer Blakely missing to the Dutch police. The second more official looking manila envelope was from Benjamin Levi. He advised me, by return, never to mention the name of Evans-Gordon to him "because if that bloody Tory ever gets elected for Stepney he will be the first to push through the poisonous Aliens Bill". He wrote that he personally had never heard of Arnon van Grunsven, alias Howard Greenstock, but he would make enquiries through the numerous contacts he still had in London's Jewish community. "What are you getting yourself into now, James?" was his closing line.

What had I already got myself into, I wondered, as the train steamed on towards Portsmouth and the ferry crossing for the Isle of Wight.

I knew I would be away from York for some time – I wallowed in the knowledge – York had suddenly become work and trouble; York was associated with my unrequited affection for Winifred Holbrook. I sat comfortably back escaping into my recently purchased Alfred Wallace's *The Malay Archipelago: The land of the orangutan, and the bird of paradise. A narrative of travel, with sketches of man and nature.* The train stopped at Guildford station. Lost in Wallace's wonderful book, I took little notice of the interruption. A minute or two later a tall fair-headed man dared to walk into my compartment, shutting the door carefully behind him. I presumed he had just got on the train. Not wishing to make eye contact, resentful of the man's presence, I could not help noticing he was carrying a briefcase identical to mine. He slid his case on the rack above my head before taking the seat opposite. I thought little of it at the time. We sat there in silence until the man got up as the train pulled into Havant station. I began to scrutinise him surreptitiously, there was something not quite right about him. His coat reeked of cigar smoke. His blond hair was long and unkempt. He had a rather dissipated effeminate look about him – the face of a pretty woman gone to seed. Reaching over me, his long arm retrieved the briefcase with case.

'I think you've taken my case,' I told him. I recognised the sickle scratch mark in the leather surface.

'Sorry, they look the same.' The cracks running from his eye corners wrinkled deeper.

He was not English. He was not French or Italian either. There was a comical slurring "sh" like a drunk to his accent that I could not quite place.

'Yes, they are identical,' I was forced to agree.

With another "shorry", the man immediately replaced my briefcase back up on the rack and took his own down before disappearing through the compartment door.

'Phew!' I acknowledged to myself aloud. What a near thing that was, my briefcase was full of confidential notes about the Hobb case. Then the question occurred to me, why hadn't my fellow passenger used the rack above his own seat? Wasn't that rather strange? Then again, perhaps the man was merely keen not to let his own briefcase out of sight.

For a winter's day the weather looked set fair for my crossing from Portsmouth Harbour to Ryde on the Isle of Wight. The iron hull paddle steamer, the *Alexandra*, was already in dock with only minutes to spare before her departure. Other passengers glowered down on me from the deck as I clattered up the gangplank, struggling with my luggage. It was as if they somehow held me responsible for an imaginary delay in the steamer setting sail. The gangplank was drawn back as soon as I landed on deck, chains clanked as the boat was freed from her moorings. I checked my half hunter watch, my recent Christmas present from my mother. Two o'clock, we were sailing right on time.

The Solent reminded me more of a giant lake than a strait with its jerky ruffles of water. This stretch of water appeared benign enough but I

171

knew from sailing friends that the tidal flow and currents were deceptively dangerous between the Isle of Wight and the mainland.

Undaunted, the ferry paddled on amid talk that her Majesty's yacht might be making the same journey for her post-Christmas break at Osborne House. Most of the people around me seemed to be locals returning home. A pompous looking man in a loud suit and slouch hat was describing the previous year as being an *annus mirabilis* in terms of weather. I was surprised at his use of Latin: he looked to be more a connoisseur of equine pedigree and the racecourse than a classical language student. Nevertheless, he was treated as a man of substance, judging from the quiet respect given to him whenever he spoke. I soon gathered that because of the previous summer's heat, springs were low and ponds were dry on the island. The drought had led to catastrophic crop failures. This was so alien to my northern experience of climate, they might as well have been talking about India as the Isle of Wight.

I could not prevent my thoughts returning to last summer's lush and golden corn fields around York on the day I had visited Kirkdale with Winifred and Lucy. That glorious day was burnt into my memory. What a coincidence seeing Lucy and Howard Greenstock, or whatever he was called, across the road in London like that. I still wasn't sure then what it all meant but logically I knew it meant something, was a key to something.

The man in the slouch was telling his disciples about the monsoon that had hit Portsmouth on the 23rd July, a deluge of rain that had flooded Portsmouth two feet deep.

'Ay, there's no accounting for the happenings of last year,' pondered one man, wiping the edge of his nose on his coat sleeve. 'What about that plague of octopus we had off the coast of Devon? We fishermen were pulling out nothing but octopus in our nets.'

An old lady, seeing my interest in the to and fro of local conversations, told me she worked as a cook on Hayling Island and had witnessed the Isle of Wight floating in the sky last summer. I laughed, thinking this was just an old woman's rant until a weather-beaten man, a farming type, assured me it was true.

'A mirage, sir, that was what it was,' said the man, a spotted handkerchief creeping out of his top pocket.

'Well, whatever it was called, I've never seen the like across the water,' said the old woman, pulling her shawl tighter round her face against the rising breeze.

The paddles began to slow as we pulled into Ryde Pier. The man in the slouch had somehow managed to push his way to the front of the queue, or maybe people had just parted for him like the Red Sea, I hadn't really noticed. However he achieved it, Slouch Hat was first to disembark down the gangplank as one by one we subordinates followed on.

All was soon forgotten as I admired the pier head's cream and green decorated octagonal pavilion with its mosque like dome. They say we have given much to India, I say we have taken much from India in the way of architecture.

'Nice, isn't it?' The man whom I took to be a farmer was standing behind me. 'I particularly like that ornate wrought iron work, don't you?'

'If the rest of the Isle of Wight is as grand as this,' I replied.

'Oh, it is, much grander.'

'Then I am in for a good time.'

'There's a five hundred seat concert hall in there, reading and refreshment rooms and upstairs a sun lounge. Why don't you go and take a look for yourself?'

'No, no, not with all these bags to lug around. It is better that I get the tram straight into town.'

'I could look after your luggage for five minutes, if you like,' offered the farmer. 'Trams go up and down this pier all day long.'

'I think not,' I told him firmly It seemed as if everyone wished to relieve me of my luggage or was I being oversensitive?

The farmer dissolved into the background as I mounted the electric tram for the journey down the pier. Advertising boards for local trades, whisky, ales and stouts, Bovril and Oxo adorned the track – commercial pictures at an exhibition. As the tram gathered speed I saw him, thought I saw him standing on the opposite walkway appearing to be gazing across at a Pears' Soap hoarding. He nodded. How could he have the effrontery to be nodding at me in such a familiar way? I turned to see if anyone was seated behind me. The man I had taken to be a farmer sat two rows down. He was smiling but not at me. He was smiling at the man outside on the walkway, the foreigner who had tried to exchange his briefcase for mine on the Portsmouth train. Then he was gone, we had moved on, away, faster now. Was I fatigued enough to be imagining all this or was it real?

The Royal Esplanade Hotel was thankfully just that, it stood on the Esplanade across the road from Ryde Pier. Juggling my briefcase and portmanteau, I scurried across like a frightened mouse seeking shelter. If I was being followed, the resources needed for such surveillance were terrific. They must have been shadowing me all the way from York. But why, what for, what had I done to warrant such attention?

With a few furtive glances round the foyer, I saw there was no one. Judging it to be safe, I booked in at reception. Noting my impatience to be off, the hall porter regarded me suspiciously as he hailed a boy to take me and my luggage up to room thirty-five.

The bed and room appeared to be spacious enough. I tipped the boy a few pennies before examining my new surroundings in greater detail. There was a small artificial balcony outside my window, again like the pier's pavilion, decorated with wrought iron railings. Wrought iron had become the rage even in the industrial North, if one considered spa towns such as Ilkley and Harrogate truly representative of the North. The basin, jug and bedding seemed clean enough. I tested the bed, firm. A couple of seascapes hung on the walls giving me a taste of that holiday feeling at last. This overnight stay would suit me fine. I felt safe, relaxed, my troubles seemed to be behind me for now. My eyes flickered, wanting to close.

One, two... Nine! A clock on a floor below had chimed nine times on the periphery of my dreams. It was late evening and I had not eaten or drunk yet. Without changing my bed rumpled clothes, I splashed water on my face at the basin before rushing downstairs. Neither dressed nor in the mood for a formal dinner, I walked into the bar and order beer and a beef sandwich. The young barman, with an interesting mole to one side of his nose, was more than happy to oblige for an extra two penny pieces.

'Hello again,' said a voice at my ear, making me jump as I ravenously collected my order. 'Didn't expect to see you again.'

I was speechless. It was the farmer with the spotted handkerchief. I finally managed to summon up a 'how did you get in here?' Never realising how rude I sounded until I saw the barman's and farmer's astounded expressions.

'Like how did they let me in here?'

'No, no, I didn't mean…'

'I work here,' interrupted the farmer.

'He's the acting chef,' added the barman; a hint of fear in his eyes.

'Why, only "acting"?'

'Just until Mr Halliwell gets right,' explained the barman. 'We are short, it being winter and all.'

'I cooked that piece of beef in your sandwich,' said the farmer; who was really the chef, be it temporarily. 'The beef you are about to stuff in your mouth, sir.'

'Sorry,' I apologised. 'You took me by surprise that's all, seeing you in here again like this. A beer for Mr…' I hesitated.

'Mr Walker,' helped out the barman smiling now, pulling on the pump.

'A beer for Mr Walker in recompense for my previous rudeness.'

'Think nothing of it,' said Walker, pacified, already supping on his ale. 'I've finished for the night. Might I join you at your table, sir?'

I nodded, now in too weak a position to refuse the man anything. We chose a small round inglenook table. The table had thick moulded iron legs: we are known as the age of Empire, perhaps we should be known as the Second Iron Age.

'Did you enjoy your half-mile tram trip along the pier?' asked Walker.

'Is it that long?'

'It is and progressive for the island. So much so that last year a rail company wanted to build an overhead electric light railway from the Esplanade down to Seaview.'

'Seaview?'

'Yes, Seaview is a snobbish kind of place three miles east from here down the coast. On the fifth of June, the good people of Seaview decided they didn't want to be connected to Ryde. Permission to build was finally refused in October at Ryde Town Hall. I was outraged at the *County Press'* comment "it is well known that the superior classes frequent Seaview in order to obtain freedom from vulgarity, and the construction of the tramway would enable an undesirable element to visit the place".'

'Outrageous, I agree.'

'Seaview doesn't want undesirables but Ryde has to put up with them.'

'I hope you don't consider me to be an undesirable, Mr Walker?'

'No, sir, not you.' Walker brushed his hand across mine.

I flinched, withdrawing my hand quickly.

'Don't take on so, sir.' Walker's voice was low, coaxing. 'We are all men of the world, now aren't we?' His flabby lips locked round the glass as he moved his head back to drink. I sat there repulsed, watching his Adam's apple lift and fall as each drop of liquid passed down his gullet. He reached for my hand again.

'Are you pursuing me?' This time I removed both my hands off the table and onto my knees.

'Pursuing, sir?'

'In the Whitman sense.'

'Whitman?'

'Yes, Walt Whitman, the late American poet. He has a following of male devotees in Bolton, Lancashire, known as the College, devoted to his free homoerotic work, *Leaves of Grass*. They are men who disguise their attraction for one another under the guise of comradeship and something known as cosmic consciousness.'

'Cosmic, what?'

'Cosmic consciousness. Higher spiritual awareness to you.'

'A deceit.'

'If you like "a deceit".'

'And are you one of these deceptive types of men, sir?'

'I do not know you. I do not even know your Christian name, if you have one.'

'Charlie,' said Charlie Walker, 'and you could get to know me better if you like.'

'Could I really?' I kept my voice neutral.

'Yes, and we could test out some of that cosmic consciousness.'

'Another pint, Charlie,' I offered, belching beef sandwich. He nodded and within a minute was downing a second glass.

'Thank you, it's hot work in them kitchens.'

'Where are you originally from?'

'I've been working on a farm at Ventnor.'

I couldn't help smiling at this. 'And now you're a chef.'

'They were desperate.'

'Now tell me, Charlie, did you know that man who nodded to you from the walkway of the pier this afternoon?'

'Ah, this is all about jealousy, is it?'

'Did you know him?'

'I don't know what man you're talking about,' slurred Charlie.

'I believe him to be a foreign gentleman. He nodded across to you when we were travelling down the pier on the tram. He was standing opposite a Pears' Soap advertisement.'

'Pears' advertisement, you are joking, sir? Soap, I hardly ever touch the stuff.'

Chapter Nineteen

Charlie never did tell me where he was originally from.

I woke up alone the next morning with a thick head and doubting my sanity. The only further information I had got out of Charlie Walker was a case by case history of his romantic adventures with other men. That *Leaves of Grass* – I'll have to give it a try sometime, he had told me. Charlie had got six pints of beer out of me in exchange for his yawning confessions. When pressed further about the man on the pier, he had continued to deny any knowledge of or association with him.

Was I imagining this was the same foreigner who had tried to exchange his briefcase for mine on the Portsmouth train? I thought he had got off at Havant station. If so how on earth had he found his way on to Ryde Pier before me? Then a rather alarming thought struck me: when he got off at Havant station perhaps he had simply reboarded the train in another compartment to later follow me across the Solent. Just suppose he was not nodding at Charlie at all but at me, letting me know he was still there.

That old question of paranoia, my paranoia, had surfaced again as I unravelled myself from the bed sheets to face a new day and a new client. I paid my bill and left my portmanteau with the hall porter so I could make a quick exit after breakfast. I had eaten a sandwich cooked by a farm labourer who did not believe in soap. I prayed Charlie Walker had nothing to do with cooking my breakfast. I kept a furtive eye open, above my haddock and eggs, in case he should appear. I dreaded seeing him again.

Fifteen minutes later, I was scurrying away from the hotel in the same manner I had arrived. I took the train to Newport to await the carrier, George Shotter and Son, in St. Thomas' Square at noon. Before too long a vehicle, the like of which I had never seen before let alone travelled in, rumbled round the corner. It was a two horse van with a hard top and sides, a blessing for passengers against wind and rain. Although, as luck would have it, I was just enjoying an early spell of winter sunshine warming my face.

'Mr Cairn? The Reverend George has sent me to fetch you.' The driver, who I took to be Mr Shotter himself, nodded his introduction. He was a stout elderly fellow with grey hair and a dark neat cropped beard.

He helped me aboard with my luggage, and we lurched forward. I settled back doing my best to conjure up erotic situations with Winifred while dispelling any thoughts of those with the dissolute Walker. There was no contest.

Shotter's hard sprung contraption thankfully had windows on either side. I soon diverted my attention on to the more aesthetic pleasure of the island's landscape, to see what it had to offer. The countryside, on either side of the narrow lanes we travelled down, was decidedly pastoral and gentle. Small fenced meadows, arable fields now resting, marked our way. In the distance I would occasionally glimpse the purple downs rolling up to the blue sky. The lanes between Newport and my destination at Hobb's parish just east of Brighstone could at best be described as uneven. Indeed, the more miles we put in between us and Newport, the more difficult our route became. The island was opening out and becoming less tame but still had nothing of the brutal wildness of Yorkshire. I began to smell and sense the sea – the sky is always different above the sea wherever you are.

'Anvil Rectory,' shouted out the driver, as hooves and wheels crunched over gravel and up a crescent drive. We finally came to a rattling bouncing rest in front of an ivy-clad Georgian grange.

'Good journey?' George Hobb was waiting on his front steps to greet me.

'Fine,' I replied, stepping out of Mr Shotter's van, bags in hand. 'Why *Anvil* Rectory?'

'I believe there was a smithy attached to the house at one time,' shrugged Hobb. 'Now, tell me what is your impression of the Isle of Wight so far?'

'Interesting.'

'How interesting?'

'Well, I spent my first evening at your recommended hotel being propositioned by a chef, who wasn't really a chef, who didn't use soap.'

Mr Shotter shot me a horrified look. 'Begging your pardon, sir, but I think it is ill-judged to speak of such low things before a man of the cloth.'

If only you knew, I thought, saying instead, 'Do forgive me. I am so weary after my journey from London I fear my tongue has quite run away with itself.'

'Don't take on so, man,' Hobb told Shotter, 'The cloth does not insulate clergymen from the ways of the world nor should it.'

Nor does a dress, I fought back an almost irrepressible desire to laugh out loud.

The driver peaked his cap and climbed back into his vehicle. With a "gee up" Shotter and Son were on their way.

'Come in, come in, Mr Cairn, and tell me of any more conclusions you have drawn about our island other than it is frequented by homosexual chefs who do not wash.'

'You don't regard yourself as being of the same persuasion then, sir?'

George Hobb looked puzzled. 'You know I don't.'

'My overall impression of the Isle of Wight is rural,' I said, deciding George's sexual orientation too heavy a subject for our initial reunion. 'And though I don't usually like the word *pretty*, pretty is the word I would use to best describe it.'

I wined and dined on half a dozen of the finest oysters I had ever tasted that evening at the Rectory.

'They melt down your throat with a pure aftertaste of the sea,' I enthused to Hobb.

'They are in season,' he replied modestly. 'I hope you are saving yourself for the cream of celery soup, lemon sole and partridge breasts to follow.'

I sighed, 'You are spoiling me.'

'Nonsense.'

'A good hock this too,' I lifted my glass to the candle light. 'A good colour.'

'More?' offered Hobb, twisting the cork stopper with a screech. I shook my head. Mrs Mew brought in course after course. Mrs Mew was Hobb's widowed cook and housekeeper. His secret treasure, he called her.

'God!...Please forgive me for taking the Lord's name in vain,' I immediately murmured. 'But these partridge breasts are excellent.'

'Help yourself to another one.' Hobb pointed to the serving dish in the middle of the table.

'Some apple cake, perhaps?' suggested Mrs Mew later.

'I am replete, Mrs Mew. Such a feast on top of all those sandwiches and pastries for high tea.'

'See, she is offended if you will not have a spoonful of her special apple cake,' said Hobb.

Mrs Mew did indeed look offended. A woman of middle years, she was dressed beneath her white apron in a pale fern and fleur fabric that had seen better days. But what was really unusual about Mrs Mew was her headscarf affair which was in a matching material to her bustled dress. I wondered if the Reverend was ever tempted to delve into his housekeeper's wardrobe – from the look of Mrs Mew I doubted it somehow.

'One spoonful,' I acquiesced.

'You certainly must make a good living here, George,' I commented with Mrs Mew out of the room fetching dessert.

'Oh, we don't dine like this everyday. Today is special.'

Looking round at the rather faded decor of the dining room, I believed him. The patterned William Morris wallpaper was rubbed and worn. The cornice round the ceiling was cracked in places.

'How long have you lived here?'

'Almost twenty years. Perhaps it is time I moved on.' Sadness crossed Hobb's face. 'Perhaps I will be forced to move on.'

'I hope not. That is why I am here.'

'They got rid of William Fox as curate at Brighstone, you know. I believe it was the vicar's wife who said he put the bones first and the parish next. She could have been right about that. They sent him to some piddling little parish down the road. The living at Brighstone had been six hundred and ninety-six pounds. The living at Kingston had a mere rectory value of only two hundred and six-five pounds. I think Fox must have loved this area as much as I do, otherwise he would have gone back to his roots at Millom in Cumberland.'

'Did you know him well, George?'

'Yes, as a young curate he taught me a lot.'

'About bones?'

'Of course. I considered him to be a great man. He even honoured me once or twice by including me on his fossil collecting expeditions to the Wealden of Brook. I'll take you there tomorrow, if you like.'

The apple cake and cream was delicious. Needless to say I ate more than a spoonful. Long after Mrs Mew had retired, Hobb and I sat before the drawing room's blazing hearth. We talked on and on into the night, enjoying a bottle of rich Madeira.

'Tell me about your wife, Mrs Hobb.'

'Myra died six years ago next month. Consumption of the lungs. She was forty-one.'

'It must have been a devastating loss.'

'Yes, it was. In compensation I inherited a dressing room of desire,' Hobb joked bitterly.

'Did your wife know of your predilection?'

'I think so,' admitted Hobb. 'Though I only dressed up when she was out or away.'

I thought better of mentioning Hobb's missing daughter, Helena, at present. Helena, who might have run away after seeing the horror of her flour-faced father pasted into her dead mother's dress.

'Something strange happened on my journey here,' I confessed to him instead. I do not know if it was the warmth or the wine or my need to confide in someone, but I decided that that someone, of all people, was vulnerable George Hobb. 'A foreign chap, who I suspect might still be following me, tried to switch his briefcase for mine on the Portsmouth train. In that briefcase I hold all my notes relating to your forthcoming trial.'

'You think it is because of me, my case?'

'I don't know what to think. All the paperwork has already gone through to the Director of Public Prosecutions office because of the difficulties of the case. It is accepted that I will be representing you unless you decide otherwise. I do not see what they can hope to achieve if it is they who are harassing me.'

'Who are *they*?'

'The Establishment,' I conjectured.

'Are you sure you are being marked?'

'Yes, I am. Too many inexplicable occurrences have happened to me or around me recently.'

'Could there be another explanation, other than my case?'

'Well,' I sighed, 'I have made one or two friends in the Women's Suffrage Movement and the Peace Society.'

'The Peace Society? But we are at war,' pointed out Hobb. 'I've heard that Lord Roberts and Kitchener have already set sail for South Africa with massive reinforcements to replace General Buller.'

Africa, I wasn't sure I wanted to hear about Africa at this time of night – too many historical nightmares awaited me upstairs.

'I met two friends of yours in York just before coming away.' I decided to change the subject.

'Oh?'

'Kathleen and Marina.'

'Really,' said Hobb unfazed. 'And how are they?'

'OK, in the circumstances.'

'What circumstances?'

'You know, George, you were in a poor way when I first visited you in the Castle at York.'

'Let's not talk about that, not tonight.' George hung his head as Marina had done.

* * * * *

Morning light broke into my bedroom through chinks in the heavy damask curtains. I drew them back on their matching frayed silk cords. Fluff hung in the air waiting to land on the room's heavy mahogany furniture. A thin layer of dust clung to the skirting boards. Though comfortable, the room lacked a mistress's hand; a guest room, I suspected, that had not seen a guest for sometime. Resting a knee across the window seat, I looked out on a long green swathe an even fairway of garden – borders of winter flowering shrubs peopled the course. Here and there the white faces of *Helleborus niger*, the Christmas rose, smiled up at me. Tuesday, January 9th, and the weather was no mild. Judging from the flora down there in the garden the climate must be regularly like this. And though perhaps not a mistress's attention to detail within the house, someone of ability was tending the garden outside, I could not believe my luck. After the tumult of London and Ryde, I had landed in heaven. I hauled my watch chain out of my dinner jacket pocket like an anchor into reality. It was already nine o'clock. I guessed I had missed breakfast.

To my embarrassment, I realised that Mrs Mew must have been in the room while I slept because an ironstone jug of tepid water was already set out for me on its willow patterned tray. I prayed I had not been snoring.

Taking my travelling shaving set from the portmanteau, I took my time over my ablutions at the tiled washstand. I had no regrets about missing breakfast as I still felt stuffed like a pig from the previous night's fare.

No one appeared to be about when I eventually got down stairs to the single chime of half past nine. The Rectory was eerie quiet. Atmospheres can inhabit houses as much as people do. The first living soul I saw was the indomitable Mrs Mew framed in the kitchen doorway. Without as much as a "good morning", she nodded towards the breakfast room.

'Boiled eggs, kedgeree perhaps,' offered Hobb, lowering his morning paper. 'Mrs Mew has laid it all out for us over there on the sideboard.'

'You've not waited for me, George?' I asked horrified.

'Of course, old boy.'

'Then I'll help myself to one boiled egg perhaps.'

'I trust you slept well.'

'I did and refreshed myself this morning with Mrs Mew's thoughtfully provided jug of water.'

'We have a well but unfortunately no piped water out here in the country.'

'We townsfolk are spoilt,' I said, placing half a dozen slivers of toast on a plate with my egg.

'See here, our local *County Press* reports that the Suffolk Regiment has suffered casualties at Rensburg.'

'There are always casualties in war,' I replied, nipping off the top of the still warm shell.

'We've captured another German boat, the East African liner, *Herzog*. She was apprehended outside Delagoa Bay by the gunboat, *Thetis*. Would you credit it, she had German, Dutch and Belgian ambulances aboard for the Boer?'

'I'll credit anything,' I replied, mopping up some of the running egg yolk with a toasted soldier.

'It seems as if the whole of Europe is set against us in this second African war along with your comrades in the Peace Society.'

'They are not my comrades. Let me take a look.'

Hobb reluctantly relinquished his paper. I glanced through our failures and minimal battle successes: the news was the same whatever paper you read, barely disguised bad news. Then a small article at the bottom of the same page arrested my attention. It came under *General News Items*.

'Listen to this, George,' I said. 'Louise Masset, a French governess, was executed at Newgate this morning for the murder of her illegitimate child aged three and a half years. Billington was the executioner. To the relief of all, she confessed her crime, her last words being "What I am about to suffer is just, and now my conscience is clear". She walked to the scaffold without assistance and death appeared to be instantaneous. Outside the prison between two thousand and three thousand persons had assembled and the appearance of the black flag was greeted with loud cheers.'

'Whatever is the matter?' asked Mrs Mew, appearing with a tray of fresh toast and tea.

'Sorry,' I said, still preoccupied with the fate of the French governess. But it was not me Mrs Mew was addressing.

'You look as if you've seen a ghost, Reverend,' she told Hobb.

And he did. If I had not been so engrossed with the fate of Mademoiselle Masset, I might have noticed Hobb's pallor sooner myself.

'It's all right, Mrs Mew. I just felt faint for a moment. It is passing.'

'Can I get you anything? Salts perhaps?' she suggested. Hobb gave her a dismissive wave.

'Did I upset you, George, by reading that article out loud?' I asked, as once more Mrs Mew merged into the background like a bit player. 'After all Mademoiselle Masset might have redeemed herself in the eyes of God with her confession, and be smiling down on us now from your Heaven.'

'*Redeemed*, my *Heaven*,' yelled Hobb 'Have you any idea what pressures society puts on these poor women abandoned by feckless men?'

'I do, as a matter of fact.'

'Sorry, sorry, of course you do in your profession,' said Hobb; his anger subsiding as quickly as it had risen

'And in yours too, I don't doubt.'

'But this is all a lot more personal than that, James,' explained Hobb; using my Christian name for the first time ever.

'I am a good listener.'

'I'll tell you about it as soon as we are safely away from here,' he whispered.

Chapter Twenty

'Do you really expect me to travel in that?' I asked, horrified.

'Why not?'

'What is it?'

'I think it is known as a governess cart. It looks as if "governess" is going to be the operative word today.' The lines already ingrained in Hobb's brow deepened.

'Look, George, I'm really sorry if that story of the French governess upset you. I never meant…'

'It wasn't just that. Anyway are you going to climb aboard this thing or not? I would like to get going.'

I looked doubtfully at the grey harnessed pony waiting as still as a Royal Doulton figurine; at the small cart, a baby cart; at its two disproportionally large wheels; at Hobb grinning down on me like an idiot from his sideways seat.

'This vehicle will never carry my weight,' I complained.

'It's new and Bolter is young and new,' said Hobb confidently.

'"Bolter"?' I gave the pony derisory acknowledgement and a pat. Bolter reacted to neither. He remained firmly rooted to the spot.

'Go on, Mr Cairn.' Mrs Mew was full of encouragement. She had ventured out especially to enjoy the spectacle.

With the help of Hobb's boy, who was standing by, I struggled up onto the tiny seat facing Hobb. The cart listed alarmingly down on my side like a canoe with an elephant on board. Hobb, who now appeared to be seated a foot higher than me, jerked the reins and Bolter jerked into action. Off we set down the crescent drive, crablike.

'I don't believe I'm doing this.'

'Believe it,' said Hobb; as some shoeless urchins appeared from their Shorwell cottage garden to hurl stones and abuse at us. Bolter did not veer from his course ahead one iota. 'I'll be round to see your mother in the morning, Jem Laidlaw,' Hobb shouted back at the tallest boy. Murmuring in a lowered aside to me, 'Father drowned just before Christmas out in the

Channel. The wife is suffering from melancholia and the kids have been running amok ever since.'

'Can't more be done?'

'I understand her unmarried sister-in-law has been summoned from Scotland.'

After high banked lanes, some hedged on top claustrophobically, we joined the more open expanses of the Military Road above Marsh Chine. It was a straightforward run from there to Brook, despite me having to make the occasional cumbersome dismount to open a gate. Over all, dare I say, we picked up speed with Bolter revelling in a better surface.

'The Military Road links Freshwater in the west with Chale in the east, along the south western coast of the island,' explained Hobb. 'It was constructed some forty years ago as part of a defence network.'

'Though straighter and flatter, it reminds me of a coastal road in east Yorkshire. It has the same lonely feel to it.'

'And where is that?'

'The road between Whitby and Staithes.' I suddenly felt nostalgic for all that had gone before. It hit me like homesickness.

'But that is the North Sea, this is the English Channel.'

We both fell silent, mesmerised by the *clip, clip* of the pony's shoes on the paved road.

'We're here,' Hobb finally announced victoriously. 'Journey's end. This is where we leave Bolter.'

'Where are we exactly?'

'Brookgreen. Bolter will be happy here for an hour or two chewing away on this good grass.'

Stationed well back from the cliff edge, I could see nothing but ocean stretching into sky.

'So, where are we going?' I asked.

'Looking for dinosaurs of course.'

Approaching the path going down to the shoreline, we could see the tide was not quite on the turn yet. We decided to take the cliff top walk to Grange Chine, intending to return along the sand back to Brook. The visibility was clear, clearer than most summer days and the view spectacular up to the white Needles off Alum Bay and across west to the purple blur of Dorset – Lyme, once the home of that prolific dinosaur hunter, Mary Anning.

'William Fox used to travel here by donkey,' said Hobb, contradicting my unspoken Anning treachery. 'He was more familiar with Wealden sands and clays than anyone who has ever lived.'

'Tell me, what is Wealden actually?'

'They are a series of thick estuarine and freshwater deposits of the Lower Cretaceous. The name Wealden comes from its development in the Weald of Kent and Sussex.'

'So this island shares the same geology with the mainland.'

'And part of France, until the Universal Flood came and cut us off.'

'So, we are back to that. You don't really believe in the Universal Flood, do you, George? Remember that story I told you about William Buckland and Kirkdale Cave.'

'I do believe something must have happened to make us an island.'

'But you said the Wealden was formed by freshwater deposits, did you not?'

'Yes, at one time all this,' said Hobb with a flourish of his arm, 'was part of one marshy land mass of braided rivers and vast lakes. Dinosaurs would come to feed here, get stuck in the mud and die. Then their bodies were further compacted and covered by rising sea levels.'

'Or sinking land. I remember in Gideon Mantell's book he talked of the Weald sinking into that now chalky ocean.'

'Once a watery ocean.'

'What are you telling me, George? That Cretaceous dinosaurs became preserved like earlier Jurassic life forms? Through a similar process they became fossilised like my baby Ichthyosaur find?'

'I believe so.'

The erosion of the land on top of the cliffs at the Wealden of Brook was dramatic. Great fissures zigzagged like earthquakes. Again I was reminded of Yorkshire's east coast but this was worse, much worse. Blackberry bushes had colonised the soil as if attempting to hold it together like a poultice. I sensed there could be a landslip at anytime. But, perversely, I felt safe here, safer than I had felt anywhere in months. This was the open territory I was at home in. If anyone was following me along this cliff, they would be exposed easier than the Reverend William Fox exposed his Iguanodon foxii. Then again, it would not be hard to push a man – two men – over the cliff and claim accidental falls due to unstable ground. I was under no illusion that my stalker would know exactly where I was and with whom. Nay, the whole world knew I was about to defend the notorious Reverend George Hobb of the Isle of Wight. Notorious – who George? He did not look too notorious to me that day.

'My daughter worked as a governess over there,' he said, pointing to a castellated building peeping above a heavily wooded hillock to the left of us in the distance.

'Oh, and is she no longer there?' I feigned innocence.

'She is quite gone.'

'Gone? Gone where?'

'That I do not know. I wish I did. She visited me one day, must have been about eight months ago now, and then simply vanished. I have had no word from her since.'

'And have you looked, written to her employer?'

'Of course. I've searched everywhere for her'

'What's the name of that house?'

'Bampton Brook Hall. It is famed as the site of a previous medieval hall where an English prince poisoned his mistress.'

'That isn't anything new,' I laughed.

'Sir Clive and Lady Bampton live there now. Helena looked after their two children.'

Bampton, Bampton, the name rattled around in my memory like a caged monkey. 'Wasn't it Sir Clive Bampton who finally stood bail for you?'

'Yes, that was as much a surprise to me as it was to you.'

'You said your daughter went missing about eight months ago, wasn't that around the time of your arrest in York?'

'Helena disappeared several weeks before I came up to Yorkshire. I was on the verge of giving up my ministry, the archbishop dissuaded me. It was the stress of her leaving like that. I don't know if you will be able to understand this, James, but whenever anything big goes wrong in my life my only real relief is dressing up.'

'Some people take to drink, you put on a frock,' I commiserated. 'Tell me, George, did Helena's running off have anything to do with your interest in couture?'

'No,' said Hobb solemnly. 'She never saw me dressed up. Now can we walk on for a while, there's more to tell.'

'More? What more?'

'Four months before the last time I saw her, Helena had come to the Rectory terribly distressed. She was obviously in a state of advanced pregnancy. She refused to tell me who the father of the coming child was, said the shame would only damage my standing in the parish. She told me then that she was going to London to have her baby.'

'So the last time you saw her she was no longer pregnant.'

'No, and how ever hard I pressed she wouldn't tell me if she had been safely delivered of the child, let alone if it was male or female. She flatly refused to reveal the whereabouts of my grandchild. Despite my reassurances that I would help bring him or her up, irrespective of local gossip or any perceived scandal costing me my living.'

I looked back to the forbidding pile of Bampton Brook Hall dominating its surrounding parkland below. Those castellated black walls and high turrets seemed bent on repelling all invaders. But somehow, with a sense of deep foreboding, I suspected the answer to Helena's disappearance would be found there.

We walked on in silence, each absorbed by his own thoughts. Hobb was a fast walker. It was no effort for his light wiry body to cover the ground. I soon began to pant, trying to match his stride. Being a gentleman he did not draw attention to my lack of fitness, nor did he drop his pace.

'Perhaps we should start discussing your case,' I ventured.

'Not now, not here, with all I have to show you. You don't really believe that I brought you to the Isle of Wight solely to discuss my case.'

'What am I to think then?'

'Enjoy the here and now,' said Hobb, dismissing all speculation. 'Grange Chine, this is where we go down to the beach. See, the tide is going out.' We made our way past a lifeboat station – needed and numerous on this coastline due to the treacherous rocky seafloor below the cliffs – and down through a gully, a split which looked like the remnants of an ancient mudslide now reclaimed by trees and scrub. 'This is Fox's beach,' announced Hobb proudly.

I took off my socks and boots, enjoying the sand between my toes. 'This is wonderful,' I gushed.

'This is January,' replied Hobb shivering. 'I had no idea you were such a child of nature, James.'

'January is much milder in the Isle of Wight than Yorkshire.' I persisted on in bare feet carrying my socks in my boots.

After fifty yards, Hobb stopped at what I took to be a large lumpy rock under the cliff. It was about two feet across. He asked if I knew what it was. I stooped down to examine it closer. It had three large protuberances with a smaller sharper one running off at an angle. I shook my head.

'This is the footprint of an iguanodon. See, three toed with a hoof-like claw at the back. During the Cretaceous this particular dinosaur walked across Wealden clay, leaving its imprint to be filled like a mould by sand.'

'But it just looks like any other rock on the beach.'

'You have to know what you are looking for. William Fox taught me to see. This sandstone sculpture has survived for approximately one hundred and ten to a hundred and forty million years.'

Down the beach the shallow sea shimmered tangerine across the sand. The backdrop of cliff rocks glowed the same tangerine in the afternoon light in contrast to the distant chalky mass of the Needles.

Boom! There was a sudden thunderous report from above that made us both jump.

'Run!' screamed Hobb, as the first warning pitter patter of shale began to fall. 'Run towards the sea.'

An avalanche of earth, twenty yards in width, broke away and tumbled down on the spot where we had been only a minute before. Had we remained there, we would have been buried alive.

'That was close,' said Hobb.

'Good grief!' I was verging on hysteria.

'The cliffs here are particularly unstable.'

'You tell me that now.'

'There goes our iguanodon footprint lost for another thousand years.'

'Never mind the iguanodon.'

'You saw for yourself the surface erosion. There is a layer of slimy clay part way down that mass. Imagine throwing tons of soil on top of a layer of blancmange then pouring storm water over it.'

'But I thought I heard an explosion, didn't you?'

'It could have been the earth cracking open. Then again it only takes vibration from an odd clap of thunder to bring some of this down.'

'Who is that?' I said pointing upwards.

'Who? Where?' asked Hobb.

'See, there on top of the cliff.'

'I can't see anybody,' blinked Hobb.

'I am sure I saw someone.'

'It's unusual to see anyone along here at this time of year.' Hobb sounded doubtful.

'A figure staring down on us.'

'Perhaps it's the shock.'

'No, no, there was someone up there. It was only possible to see them when we moved out to the shoreline.'

'Perhaps it was our guardian angel,' announced Hobb glibly.

'Yes, perhaps.'

'Well, they've gone now.'

'Indeed.'

'I know who it was. It was the ghost of my friend, William Fox, exposing us a new deeper surface layer to explore. Come on, James.' Hobb led the way across to the landslip.

'Is this safe?'

'Perhaps not but sometimes a fresh fall can reveal dinosaur bones.'

We stared up at the excavated cavern of shale and mud, expecting to see at any moment the protruding bones of the giants who had once ruled the plains. We stared long and hard until we were almost imagining them. Our scrutiny was in vain until I glanced down at my naked feet which were beginning to turn blue.

'What's that?' There among the grit of the recent landfall was what looked to be a piece of paper an inch or two long by an inch wide. I stooped down and picked it up.

'So, what is it?' enquired Hobb.

'I think I've seen one of these before at an inquest following a fatal mining accident in the northern coalfields. It looks like a fragmented wrapper from a cartridge explosive. A cartridge, I presume, that failed to detonate.'

'Are you saying?' Hobb gawped at me.

'Yes, it was an explosion not thunder we heard to bring this lot down. And, yes, it looks like someone placed two cartridge explosives up there, one went off this other one didn't.'

'But who? Why?'

* * * * *

'Did you find any bones?' asked Mrs Mew, as soon as we got through the Rectory doorway.

Hobb shook his head. He had been silent and circumspect ever since we had rushed back to Brookgreen to collect the pony and cart.

'Tea, a tray of tea in the drawing room would be lovely,' I told Mrs Mew.

'I've been wondering how many people I told that we would be going over to examine the Wealden clays in Brighstone Bay today,' said Hobb, sinking back into what I took to be his usual comfy chair from its worn appearance. 'Mrs Mew knew of course,' Hobb hesitated, 'and the boy was there when we set off.'

'And?'

'And,' Hobb drew out the word. 'The other day I visited Sir Clive Bampton. For two reasons really. The first one was I wanted to know if he had heard anything from Helena and, secondly, I wanted to thank him for standing bail for me. I told him that you would be staying with me in the next few days. He generously offered to loan me Bolter and the governess cart to take us to Brighstone Bay, the same cart that Helena used to ferry his children around in.'

'So, that wonderful vehicle isn't yours at all.'

'I thought you would have realised that, James. It isn't quite my style.'

On the little table between us, Mrs Mew carefully put down the tea tray and a few remaining slices of her apple cake.

'You're not seriously suggesting that Sir Clive Bampton might be involved in this in someway?'

'No, no, of course not. But he is a mining engineer. His family made their fortune diamond mining out in Africa. Perhaps he might be able to tell us more about that piece of explosive cartridge wrapper you found.'

'When do you have to take Bolter and the cart back?'

'Saturday morning.'

'Tomorrow is Wednesday. Tomorrow and the next day I would like to spend preparing your defence. Friday can be free. Then perhaps you might like some company for the journey back to Bampton Brook Hall,' I suggested, licking sticky cake crumbs from my fingers with relish.

'I'll send word, with the boy, to Sir Clive straight away that you will be accompanying me. I'm sure he will be delighted to meet you.'

'And I him.'

'You don't really think someone tried to kill us today?'

'Us or *me*, I'm not sure,' I shrugged. With all imminent danger passed, I could feel my eyelids begin to droop, tiredness suddenly overwhelmed me. Excusing myself, I went up to my room to rest before dinner. I lifted open the small sash window to one side of the house. I had never examined the view from here before. Leaning forward, I could almost touch the branches of an apple tree – winter bare now. Was this the source of the famous apple cake? Why couldn't things remain this simple, feel this good?

A now almost unwelcome disturbing picture of the ripening summer cherry trees at the Holbrooks' house in Belle Vue Terrace filled my imagination. Next the image of Winifred Holbrook herself took hold. Winifred from whom I had fled. I had escaped to an uncomplicated respite in my mother's house, with its neat little garden containing an apple tree like this one. Although my mother's tree had been overwhelmed, infiltrated by frost crystals.

Lowering myself down onto the single four-poster, I reached for the bedside table and took up Alfred Wallace's *The Malay Archipelago* which I had not quite finished yet. Again my eyelids felt heavy, too heavy to read.

Hoarfrost, cold, a chill ran down the back of my neck. I leaped from a world of half-slumber into a real and terrible possibility. Just suppose I had unwittingly led these people – these potential killers who I suspected were following me – to my mother's house.

Chapter Twenty-One

Friday morning saw Hobb fixed over the previous night's special edition of the *County Press* in the breakfast room. Unused to guests it was obviously a habit hard to break. We had worked as a team over the previous two days preparing for his forthcoming trial, now I felt as if I was an unwelcome breakfast distraction as before. I have found you can divide folk into two temperamental categories: morning vivacious people or night vivacious people, Hobb definitely fell into the latter.

I cleared my throat. 'I got word from Trotter this morning. The trial date has been provisionally set for April.' Hobb did not react. 'George, I said the trial has been set for Monday the ninth of April.'

'It's January the twelfth today,' replied Hobb obliquely. 'Listen to this, the Boers have been repulsed at Ladysmith and Lord Roberts and Lord Kitchener have finally arrived in Cape Town.'

'Good,' I responded dismissively, swinging one leg over the other in irritation.

'And the bank rate has been reduced today from six to five per cent.'

'As you don't have any money, George, that can hardly be of any concern to you.'

'That's true,' he readily agreed. 'James, you'll find this really interesting in light of what happened to us on Brighstone Beach the other day. A landslip occurred at Whitby yesterday. Three lives were lost and two houses were destroyed. You see, landslips are not uncommon occurrences when cliffs are formed from little more than compacted mud.'

'But you heard the explosion too, George. And what about that fragment of cartridge wrapper we found?'

'We haven't had that verified yet. It might have been from a bonbon wrapper.'

'"A bonbon wrapper",' I repeated in disbelief.

'I'm just saying that perhaps we shouldn't have read so much into it.'

'I expect you think I am suffering from paranoia too.'

'Para what?'

'Paranoia, it is a delusional disorder in which you imagine you are being persecuted. It is a condition first described by a Doctor Karl Ludwig Kahlbaum. Kahlbaum, I believe, only died last year.'

'So now you are telling me you are knowledgeable in psychoanalysis.'

'No, although I am interested in it.'

'I expect it helps when dealing with me.'

'It does a little, George.'

'Have you ever heard of François Timoléon, abbé de Choisy?'

'Who?'

'François Timoléon, abbé de Choisy. He was a beautiful French nobleman and cleric born in the mid-seventeenth century. It is said that his mother, fearing he would die by the sword, dressed him as a girl until he was eighteen.'

'How confusing for him.'

'Later he became a diplomat, writer and ordained priest.'

'In manly apparel, I take it.'

'No, as a matter of fact he would often revert to female dress.'

'Entrenched.'

'Yes, entrenched,' sighed Hobb. 'It is believed he co-wrote *Histoire de la Marquise-Marquis de Banneville*, a love story between a man who dresses as a woman and a woman who favours the attire of a man.'

'Do you feel you have a lot in common with the abbé then, George, even though he lived in a distant century?'

'No, James, what I am trying to tell you is there are men like me throughout history and more than you would credit. There was Charles-Geneviève-Louis-Auguste-André-Timothée d'Éon de Beaumont in the following century.'

'Trust the French, what a mouthful.'

'In 1756 d'Éon joined a secret network of spies called Le Secret du Roi which worked exclusively for King Louis XV. He was sent to Russia to intrigue against the Habsburg monarchy and it is claimed he disguised himself as a lady to do so. Returning to France, he became a captain in the dragoons and fought in the latter stages of the Seven Years War. He worked in the French embassy in London and was eventually exiled there after claiming the new French ambassador had tried to drug him. Despite d'Éon always wearing a dragoon's uniform, it was rumoured around London that he was really a woman. So much so that a betting pool was started on the Stock Exchange about his true gender. D'Éon refused to offer himself for examination, saying it would be dishonouring, and the wager was abandoned.' George paled. Was it at the memory of his own humiliating examination? 'D'Éon claimed he was physically a woman and demanded the French government recognise him as such. The King, who was under threat of exposure from d'Éon's spying revelations, granted the now "her" funds for a new wardrobe. She returned to France believing she would live out the rest of her life there dressed as a woman. But following the French Revolution, d'Éon lost her pension and fled back to London. She died there in 1810. The doctors who examined the body discovered that the Chevalier d'Éon was anatomically male. But was she really a man, James, I ask you that. What was she in here?' Hobb jabbed at his forehead.

'A friend of mine who works as a physician at The Retreat in York told me that a German doctor, Hirschfeld, has done work in this area.'

'Yes, Magnus Hirschfeld.'

'You know of him then.'

'James, when you are like me you read everything and anything you can get your hands on to give you greater understanding into why you are like you are. French, German, it doesn't matter, you learn the language. Under the pseudonym Thomas Ramien, Hirschfeld wrote a pamphlet *Sappho and Socrates* a few years back. In that pamphlet he credited Nietzsche with the inspirational idea "what is natural cannot be immoral".'

'But is effeminacy, homosexuality natural?' The old fear rose with bile in my gullet.

'Ah, Károly Mária Kertbeny's "homosexual".' Hobb smiled. 'I sometimes think these things trouble you more than they do me, James.'

'Nonsense.'

'What is normal and natural to me might not be to you.'

'Normality is what is adhered to by the majority.'

'There I think you are wrong. Normality is what the majority *appears* to be adhering to. But back to Magnus Hirschfeld. An interesting man. A small rotund Jewish physician who likes dressing up. He believes that people like me, like him –"sexual intergrades" – are born that way and cannot be changed.'

'Really, I'd like to make a note of that.'

* * * * *

Free Friday – George was insistent on taking me to see Brighstone village itself. This meant another humiliating ride in the sagging governess cart past the stone throwing Laidlaw children's Shorwell cottage. Luckily, they were nowhere to be seen. Perhaps they had heeded George's warning that he would tell their mother.

'George Shotter's, the carrier's house is up that road to Moortown,' announced Hobb, above the noise of our trundling cart.

'I wish he was carrying us now,' I retorted, as the thatched cottages of Brighstone came into sight. 'You can hardly call this an entrance, George. I feel like a war refugee fleeing as best I can with nothing, not even a proper vehicle.'

'And you think you would have made more of an entrance arriving in Shotter's van, do you?'

'No, but it was better than this.'

'Raag-boh,' screamed Hobb joyously. 'Raag-boh.'

'Stop it, you are showing us up. What's more, you're not far from the truth. We have a rag-and-bone man back in York who passes down Gillygate every day. He rides on a similar contraption to this, sinking down on one side under his weight.'

'Don't be so sensitive, man,' Hobb told me. He pulled Bolter up outside a cottage gate on North Street, suddenly with all the deference of a man pulling up in front of a shrine.

'Myrtle Cottage?' I read.

'Yes, Myrtle Cottage.'

It seemed I was expected to have some knowledge of this building. The cottage was enchanting; a quintessential English country cottage with a red pantile roof and green leaf flora running riot over its chalkstone walls.

'This is where William Fox lived when I knew him,' announced Hobb with undisguised pride. 'He lived here for about twenty years in all. This is the home of the fossil collector who discovered Polacanthus foxii, Hypsilophodon foxii, Eucamerotus foxii, Iguanodon foxii and Calamospondylus foxii. He is also credited with finding Aristosuchus. This is the home of the man who rubbed shoulders with John Hulke, Sir Richard Owen and the like.'

'Yes, I know,' I said. 'I have been privileged enough to see his collection in the British Museum of Natural History.'

'You *do* know then.' Hobb jerked the reins and Bolter trotted off down North Street with renewed energy. We pulled into the yard of the New Inn where, Hobb told me, they would provide our pony with good stabling for an hour or two.

With eyes everywhere and little talk, we walked down a street of twittering birds towards the Church of St Mary's the Virgin. Birds there might be, but there was not another human soul to be seen. It was then that I saw a dying pigeon on the grass verge outside the churchyard.

'Poor thing,' said Hobb, as the bird's eyes began to glaze over. 'I expect a hawk dropped it.'

Although I tried to convince myself that this was primitive thinking, I could not dissuade myself that the dying bird was a bad omen.

I ran my hand in fascination over the church's rough hewn outer fabric. Walls reinforced with a mishmash of local stone – undressed stone picked up from the beach – connecting St Mary's directly with its landscape and congregation. The tower was 14th to 15th century. Like St Gregory's Minster there was a sundial above the porch.

'It is the original sundial from 1721,' explained Hobb avidly.

'Not Saxon then like St Gregory's.'

'"Go your way into HIs gates with Thanksgiving",' quoted Hobb.

'I don't suppose Arnon van Grunsven ever got to see this one,' I muttered.

'Who?'

'Oh, just someone I know who is an expert on Saxon sundials.'

'You do know some interesting people, James.'

'You could say that.'

Inside the church the font looked to be 15th century, and there was a wonderful Good Samaritan stained glass window that did not look very old at all.

Kee, Kee. We were outside paying homage over William Fox's grave when I saw and heard the two buzzards above us. Lost in his own reverie, Hobb paid them no attention at all.

'The pigeon killers,' I pointed up to the sky.

'Not seen you in the village for sometime, Reverend,' came a voice from behind us.

'Rollo, how are you? James, this is Rollo Dale, sexton of St Mary's.'

I shook Rollo's hand.

'I don't see why you spend your time mourning the likes of he, Reverend,' Rollo nodded to Fox's simple stone mounted cross. A small oak sapling planted at its side, an umbrella waiting to explode and protect in years to come.

'Because he was a great man.'

'He was not liked here.'

'I find that very sad.'

'There'll be another grave to dig soon over there.'

'Oh, no. Who?'

'James Buckett. There is no man better thought of in Brixton.'

'I am so sorry to hear that,' Hobb told him. 'Mr Buckett was the first coxswain of Brighstone lifeboat, James. He was awarded the silver medal for his part in rescuing twenty men from a Norwegian steamer.'

'The *Woodham*, iron screw,' helped out Dale. 'That was some twenty-six years ago. The old fellow is well into his nineties now and failing fast. It is a full moon in three day's time. I shouldn't wonder that James Buckett isn't called to the Lord by then. The moon pulls the best to Heaven when its belly is big.'

'Why does Mr Dale here use the name Brixton and you Brighstone?' I whispered to Hobb.

'Brighstone, Brixton, like a shy author this village has undergone several noms de plumes over the centuries, am I not right, Rollo?'

'You are that. Folks call it one way or the other. They can please their selves as far as I am concerned. By the way, a chap was asking after you the other day, Reverend.'

'Oh, and who might that be?'

'I didn't know him. He was a stranger. A foreigner, I think. Wanted to know where you lived and if you were married. Seemed very nosy to me. I told him nothing.'

We left Rollo tending the graveyard. We did not speak. I had the feeling that someone was following us a few yards behind, someone who could easily overtake us but was desisting from doing so until the time was right. It was a very unnerving sensation, a sensation of innate fear. It was the feeling a rabbit must get while being harried by the stoat.

'How about a stiff drink,' suggested Hobb, as we walked into the yard of the New Inn.

'Everything all right your way, Reverend?' asked the pub landlord, Job Hawker. A larger than life character with a wild white beard and watch chain dangling over his corpulent frame.

'Yes, why shouldn't it be?' asked Hobb, more tetchily than usual.

'I just wondered because there was a fellow in here asking questions recently. Dutch, I think he was from his accent. Dutch, like the seamen we used to get putting into Weymouth. Shall I make that a double tot of rum, Reverend? Your friend, here, looks as if he could do with one too. He's gone the colour of my beard.'

* * * * *

'They did not like him very much down there in Brighstone, did they?' We stood on a knoll, very much like the Clifford's Tower mound back in York but below us the landscape was patchwork rural rather than red brick urban.

'They banished him here.'

'Despite the fact that his congregation must have been small and you told me the living was poor, I can think of worse places in the world to be banished to.'

St James' Church, Kingston, Reverend Fox's final stand as it were, overlooked the manor-house to the south of the Shorwell road. With its high vantage point across the vale, I suspected it had been built on a pre-existing prehistoric site. A church to appease pagan followers on their journey to Christ.

Although I had felt extremely threatened on hearing about the enquiries being made about Hobb (and by association me) in Brighstone, Hobb had insisted we did not allow it to curtail our itinerary. He remained sceptical, telling me I was making too many assumptions on what he considered to be too little evidence.

'St James' was remodelled by the architect R. J. Jones about eight years ago,' he said.

'But it looks thirteenth century to me.'

'Absolutely, he kept it in period.'

I watched the weather-cock spinning on the pantile roof. Anything would spin at this elevation. Before we had started the climb, we had happened to meet the lady of the manor who told us it was a view to die for up here – the lady had not exaggerated.

'Shall we take a look inside,' suggested Hobb.

The building was a plain rectangular structure without a dividing chancel arch. After closer scrutiny, only the double hollow lancet windows in the north and south walls, the lower portion of the east window, and a trefoil credence in the south wall seemed original. There was a fine 16th century brass to a Richard Meux, dated 1535, with his arms, and I noticed a pipe organ by Gray and Davison had recently been installed. Like Brighstone, I was impressed with this small church's equally fantastic stained glass windows – windows telling gospel stories – one window particularly caught my eye as being rather Catholic in taste with its depiction of Christ on the cross.

Creak, squeak, a long drawn-out yawning sound. Hobb and I swung round as the heavy door slowly opened. We froze, waiting to see what would happen next. Who was there? Someone was there.

Nothing; no footsteps; no one – just the occasional creak from the plank door swinging gently on its iron hinges in the breeze. We moved towards it as one to investigate further. Peering out, peering across the graveyard, there was no one.

'You can't have shut the door properly behind us, James,' remonstrated Hobb.

'It must have been a sudden gust of…' My voice trailed away. I smelt it first – then I saw it lying there on the porch step – a cigar butt still burning red. With the trace of cigar smoke in our nostrils and panic in our hearts, Hobb and I took off down the tumulus.

I kept telling myself not to be stupid, it was undignified to run away like this. Then I stopped, turned round and began to climb back up to the church.

'What on earth are you doing now?' Hobb cried after me.

'Evidence,' I shouted down to him.

Every nerve in my body jangled on edge being back at that church alone. I was alert to any sound, any movement, as I knelt down and stubbed the cigar butt out on the cold stone step with a shaking hand. To make sure it was completely extinguished, I formed a string of spittle between my fingers and cocooned the ash. Was I being watched? Placing the cigar butt in the middle of my balled up handkerchief, I fled the scene as quickly as I could.

'You all right, James?' asked Hobb, as I stumbled up into the governess cart. Hardly a vehicle for a quick getaway.

'Yes,' I said, fumbling in my pocket for the handkerchief, opening it out on my lap as Bolter began to trundle away. I examined the cigar's yellow label and smelt carefully before confirming it as a Sumatra leafed Balmoral.

'Balmoral, is that a British manufacturer?' asked Hobb.

'No, I know this label well. My head of chambers, Carlton-Bingham, smokes this brand. It's Dutch, a fine Dutch corona.'

Chapter Twenty-Two

Bampton Brook Hall was more a castle than a house. The only thing it lacked was a keep, moat and drawbridge. It had huge ornate locks for keys and gaining entrance was not at all easy. Hobb had to give his card as proof of identification before the footman would allow us into the baronial enclave. I could see Hobb chafing over this humbling procedure: a clergyman, dressed as a clergyman, he was unused to having his way barred to anywhere.

The footman's slender fingers toyed with Hobb's card as we hovered on the threshold. The thought occurred to me that he was actually toying with us, we playthings of no consequence. He had the fine dark features of an Italian youth, a Donatello David. I was spellbound.

With a haughty jerk of a centrally-parted fringe, we were summoned to follow. He escorted us across the hall, across the black and white marble chequerboard floor as if we were already captured pawns.

'I was never attracted to boys, only dresses,' Hobb muttered to me as we trailed in the footman's arrogant wake. 'I see you are a man of tempered passions, James.'

'No, I am a man who has seen in court too many times where untempered passions can lead.'

'And where is that?'

'There is nothing wrong in admiring beauty in others whether it is man or woman.'

Hobb smiled politely as footman handed over to butler.

'The Reverend George Hobb and Mr Cairn, Your Ladyship,' announced the butler down an echoing salon.

Hobb and I stood at one end of a room the size of an elongated ballroom. I could see in the distance a small gowned figure rising to her feet. We approached and Lady Bampton, placing her needlepoint with precision on a side table, received us with far less condescension than her footman had done.

'Peters, will you inform Sir Clive that the Reverend and his guest have arrived?' she instructed the butler.

I don't know really what I had expected but Lady Bampton's youth cancelled out most imaginative predictions. A delicate looking woman in her twenties, bedecked in jewels. She was pale and blonde whereas Winifred was of a deeper complexion. But because of their similarity of age I could not help drawing comparisons. Both were equally attractive women but Winifred had an immediate weightiness to her disposition that appeared to be lacking in the ethereal Lady Bampton.

'Ah! I see you have already been introduced to my lovely Ellisia.' From his slicked back waxed hair and moustache down to his pointed shoes, the first impression of Sir Clive Bampton was that he was obviously a dandy. He was tall and slim, and though fit looking and well-preserved, he must have been well into his forties. I judged him to be around Hobb's age. He was much older than his bejewelled wife. 'Still no news of Helena?' he asked Hobb.

The despondent Hobb shook his head, whispering, 'No, no news.'

'Women, eh. She'll turn up in her own good time, you'll see,' assured Sir Clive, with all the assurance of one who if it did not happen would make it happen. 'I see our house guest has not come down yet.' He turned to his wife.

'No, dear. I'll send Peters up to fetch him right away.' Ellisia Bampton reached for the bell.

'How was the cart, George?' chuckled Sir Clive.

'A godsend, thank you,' replied Hobb.

I flashed him a hostile glance for his sickening servility.

'And how did you like riding in the governess cart, Mr Cairn?' asked Sir Clive.

'It served its purpose.'

'Did it really and what purpose was that?'

'To see the island's outstanding countryside.'

'I have heard you are a great man for the countryside, Mr Cairn,' said Sir Clive, in an intimate tone that surprised me.

'Yes, he is,' echoed a familiar voice from the far doorway. 'James Cairn is a great man for the countryside and country.'

I squinted down the salon. 'Doctor Holbrook, what on earth are you doing here?'

'Cedric and I are old friends,' explained Sir Clive.

'But… but this is too much of a coincidence,' I stammered.

'Yes, perhaps it is.' Sir Clive smiled his controlled and controlling smile again.

'How is Winifred?' I asked Holbrook.

'Ah! The lovely Winifred,' chipped in Sir Clive; a finger straightening his moustache. Sir Clive, I felt, was one of those men incapable of having anything but the most superficial interest in women.

'Winifred is well.' Holbrook's expression fell dark, grave. He appeared to be collecting himself, pausing for what seemed to be a whole minute. The worrying thing was that not even Sir Clive saw fit to interrupt him. 'I have some bad news, James.'

My heart beat seemed held in suspense. I could not utter a word. I did not want Holbrook to say anything more. I did not want to hear anymore, know anymore.

'Please, let us all be seated,' Sir Clive suggested. We sank down onto the nearest chairs for what I sensed was not going to be a bedtime story.

'Lucy Alexander hanged herself a few days ago in lodgings in Clerkenwell, James.'

'But I saw her. Saw her in London only the other week.'

'Well, it's true. We tried our best to keep it out of the papers. Winifred is inconsolable, beside herself with grief.'

'Poor Winifred.'

'There'll be an inquest of course. One is being arranged as soon as possible.'

'I can hardly take this in. Lucy was such a positive person, so full of life. But how did you know I would be here today, Doctor Holbrook?'

He cleared his throat. 'As you know I had read in the papers that you were representing the Reverend George Hobb and that he came from the Isle of Wight, and when I called at your chambers they told me you were holidaying over here.'

'"Holidaying"?'

'That is what they said. It wasn't hard to put two and two together. I knew Sir Clive had a house on the Isle of Wight and, as we are old acquaintances…'

'Come, come, Cedric, we are more chums than acquaintances,' objected Sir Clive.

'Whatever we are,' sighed Holbrook. 'The rest of my arrangements were conducted through telegrams as I felt the matter to be urgent.'

'Telegraphy, it would have to be on the Isle of Wight,' I murmured, still flabbergasted by Holbrook's news and presence here. No one spoke – a minute's silence ensued for Lucy.

'Does anyone know anything about this Italian scientific chap who's set up at the Needles Hotel?' Sir Clive broke the spell.

'Guglielmo Marconi,' Hobb helped out.

'Yes, that's him. He's hauled a bloody great – forgive me, my dear (said with a conciliatory bow to his wife) – a hundred and sixty-eight foot mast onto the cliff above Alum Bay. He's even been sending messages across to the royal yacht and Her Majesty at Osborne House. He's trying to perfect something called wireless signals. Can't see it taking off myself, can you?'

'I think it already has,' pointed out Hobb apologetically.

'Well, we'll see. Perhaps I should explain how Cedric and I first came to know each other.' Sir Clive crossed his long legs. He was working hard in the salon of sorrow. He was no longer affecting the demeanor of cheery chappy. 'My father was one of the last Whig ministers in Palmerston's government. There was a split in policy, he lost his seat, and decided to go into mining, diamond mining instead. As a young man I was sent out to Africa to manage my father's mine in Griqualand West, once part of but now bordering the Orange Free State. Cedric here, was the Medical Superintendent of Mines. We were little more than wild lads then, roaming the veld, were we not, Cedric?'

'Little more,' nodded Holbrook. His thoughts probably focused towards poor Lucy's blonde braided plaits swinging free in a dingy Clerkenwell apartment than on the shifting sands of the Karroo.

'It is amazing to think that back in the sixties, Boer children played innocently with precious stones on the banks of the Orange river as if they were marbles. One such farmer's son was fifteen year old Erasmus Jacobs, he would keep stones in his pocket like toy charms. His mother happened to mention to a neighbour, Schalk van Niekerk, that her son possessed a stone that had a particular shine to it. After wiping it clean with a dusty cloth, Van Niekerk offered to buy the stone but Mrs Jacobs told him "You can keep the stone, if you want it". Those were the woman's actual words, can you believe it?' At this Sir Clive ran a hand across his brow. 'Van Niekerk later entrusted the stone to a travelling trader who failed to sell it. The trader, O'Reilly I think he was called, brought it to the notice of Lorenzo Boyes, acting Civil Commissioner of Colesberg who grandly declared "I believe it to be a diamond". Bets were taken if it was or not. One local apothecary bet Boyes a new hat that it was merely a topaz. The stone was sent by mail in an ordinary paper envelope to the colony's foremost mineralogist, Doctor William Guybon Atherstone, where it is said it rolled out across his floor. On finding it, the kneeling doctor must have taken a deep intake of breath. Eureka! Aptly-named, Atherstone held in his hand the biggest and most extraordinary stone he had ever seen: a twenty-one and a quarter carat diamond. The brownish yellow diamond, The Eureka Diamond, was within the year sparkling in its showcase at the 1867 Paris Exhibition. It was the first diamond to be found in The Orange Free State.'

'Hence Lady Bampton's fantastic necklace,' I made a flattering, if tactless, gesture towards Her Ladyship's jewellery.

Another uneasy silence followed.

Pit-a-pat. Pit-a-pat. We all turned to the light tread of feet. I was saved further embarrassment by two little girls, rosy-cheeked twins dressed like shepherdesses, skipping down the long salon towards us. Struggling on behind them was a woman with a pointed nose and a baby in her arms.

'Since Helena left, the children have had a nanny rather than governess,' explained Sir Clive. 'We felt it more expedient with the new baby.'

Dressed in a dove grey silk skirt with a white ruffled blouse, the narrow-waisted, long-legged nanny smiled. Her smile was polite if tight.

'She reminds me of one of those haughty white secretary birds back on the veld, does she not?' Sir Clive winked at Holbrook.

But I was not looking at Holbrook, I was looking at Hobb staring fixedly at the baby. Ellisia fidgeted uncomfortably on her sofa. Her jewellery tinkled and flashed: blood garnets, green peridot, rare blue jasper and above all a myriad of diamonds – a rainbow of colour.

Jink, jink. The necklace swivelled on her long alabaster neck. Sir Clive was the last to notice his wife's irritation.

'What is he or she called, your ladyship?' Hobb asked Ellisia, pointing to the baby. Ellisia swallowed hard but did not answer.

I must admit I was unsure of the baby's sex myself. It was dressed in a long, fashionable white gown with a petticoat and bodice beneath. The delicate tiny face was swathed in an embroidered woollen bonnet.

'We've called him Tom, Thomas after my father,' interjected Sir Clive. 'Please be good enough to take the children to the nursery now, Nanny. We do not want to fatigue them with all our grownup talk. Cook will bring them up a tray shortly.' He dismissed his children and the secretary bird with a wave of his hand. Sir Clive, the magician.

'Perhaps Lady Ellisia might care to join them?' suggested Holbrook; presumptuously, I thought. 'Rather than having to sit here listening to all this boring men's stuff and nonsense.'

'Yes, my dear. Perhaps the children will settle better with you there,' acceded Sir Clive.

Obediently, Lady Ellisia uncurled from her embroidered sofa and left us without a word.

'Tell me more about your father, Sir Clive,' I asked, attempting to ease the growing tension. Hobb was still staring at the spot where the baby had been.

'My father always believed that Whigs, and later the Liberals, should represent manufacturers rather than royalty. He saw industry as a positive influence, a tool towards a better society for all. He also knew that the working man would finally find his voice, possibly form an alternative party, and it would be better to enfranchise him sooner rather than later. Unless there was social reform, he feared the Liberal Party would lose the workers' majority vote forever.'

'And it is happening already with the rise of the Independent Labour Party,' added Holbrook. 'The masses are turning to socialism.'

'Indeed,' agreed Sir Clive.

'And how do you feel about that, sir?' I asked Sir Clive.

'Feel? I feel anything is better than the lot we have in power at present.'

'Even revolution?'

'Look, James, my father and I were empire builders not warmongers. The Tories are turning the gold and diamond fields of Africa into a bloodbath. Unless they put an end to this siege of Kimberley soon, find a political solution to live side by side with the Boer, we as a family are in danger of losing everything.'

'Are both you two gentlemen against this war?' asked Hobb incredulous.

'We are not against it per se,' replied Holbrook.

'We are against the way it is being conducted at present,' chimed in Sir Clive.

'Or not conducted,' added Holbrook.

'I hate war, all wars,' I said.

'Sometimes you have to fight for what is yours, it is inevitable,' said Hobb.

His enthusiasm for this war in Africa surprised me. I would have thought he was a pacifist. Ah well, onward Christian soldiers. I decided to change the subject from the morality or immorality of war on to something nearer to home and immediate.

'Being a mining expert, sir, could you tell me where this might have come from?' I passed Sir Clive the fragment of cartridge explosive wrapper I had found on Brighstone Beach.

'How did you say you came by this?'

'I didn't, sir. There was a coastal landslip not far from here and I found it among the debris on the beach.'

'Not English.' Sir Clive turned to Holbrook and asked what he thought. Holbrook nodded expressionless. 'Where were you precisely, James, when this landslip occurred?' Sir Clive rolled the wrapper between his fingers.

'We were a few yards up the beach from Grange Chine,' explained Hobb.

'Yes, if we hadn't moved quickly, we would have both been directly beneath the fall,' I added more emphatically.

A look passed between Sir Clive and Dr Holbrook that I could not quite read.

'We do use similar sorts of cartridges in our own mining operations of course. But judging from the wrapper this definitely isn't one of ours,' said Sir Clive, handing it back to me.

'Didn't Martial Bourdin, that French anarchist chap, use a similar explosive to try and blow up the Royal Observatory at Greenwich?' Holbrook asked him.

'Ah, the warlike pudding.'

'The what?' We all exclaimed.

'I believe that is the correct translation of his name.' Sir Clive smiled. 'But Bourdin used an explosive bomb rather than a cartridge that needs a detonator. He never reached the observatory, blew his own hand off and a hole in his stomach with the thing instead in Greenwich Park. He died of his wounds without speaking half-an-hour later.'

'Are you saying anarchists might be responsible for trying to bury James and me alive?' asked Hobb.

'That is a big leap of imagination, if I might say so. Without more information we are accusing no one, you understand,' said Sir Clive. 'But Cedric, here, has already told me about some of the troubles you have been having lately up in Yorkshire.'

'I am sure that you yourselves have read about these subversive cells at work in our country from time to time,' added Holbrook.

'But who are these people? Are we talking about disillusioned Establishment forces loyal, disloyal, to the elected government...?'

'Puh! "Elected",' interrupted Holbrook.

'Or foreign agents loyal to God knows what?' I continued.

'That we have yet to find out,' said Sir Clive.

'Until then you must remain extremely vigilant, James,' warned Holbrook. 'Show your mettle.'

'I know. I suspect that I am being followed. Then there is this on top of everything else.' I held the cartridge wrapper up to the window light.

'Perhaps these people think you know more than you do,' suggested Holbrook. 'Somehow there must be a link between you and them.'

'And that is why you are here today, isn't it? Not just to tell me of Lucy's death.'

'Quite,' he admitted. 'I fear we all might be at risk.'

'So my concerns have foundation?'

He nodded, asking, 'By the way, are you going back via London?'

'Yes, I am going to book into the Midland Grand Hotel near St Pancras.'

'A good choice, James. Very wise not to involve family,' added Holbrook.

'How do you know I have family in London, sir?'

'I believe Winifred must have mentioned it.'

'Now how are preparations for your trial going, George?' Sir Clive turned to Hobb, turned the conversation.

* * * * *

'Those two aren't prepared to tell us much, trust us,' said Hobb, as we began the long walk back to the Rectory.

'That landslip was no accident and they know it,' I said.

'Did you notice how close Sir Clive and Doctor Holbrook were?' asked Hobb.

'Yes, they knew each other far better than they were letting on.'

'And they seemed to be in full political agreement on everything.'

'I couldn't believe it when I saw Doctor Holbrook there.'

'I couldn't believe it when I saw that baby boy there.'

'You don't think...'

'Helena told me some time ago that Ellisia Bampton was too fragile to give birth to another child after her twin girls were born. Sir Clive was left without the possibility of an heir.'

'You don't really believe...'

'For an articulate man, James, you can sometimes be annoyingly repetitious. I hope you will fare better in court.'

'I always fare better in court.'

'There was something about the features of that little chap. A resemblance to... Thomas they've called him, have they not?' mused Hobb.

'It couldn't be possible, could it?'

'Anything is possible in this life. But what did you think to Bampton Hall itself?'

'Internally no expense has been spared. The walls outside are Gothic revival. A folly but nevertheless a pleasing folly.' We both turned to look back at the hall, partially hidden in foliage, only its rising battlements silhouetted against the sky.

'I've got you labelled now, James,' said Hobb. 'You are a disciple of Ruskin. An aesthetic who never quite likes getting involved, getting his hands dirty, or, God forbid, sloshing around in the mire with the rest of us pigs.'

'I think you do yourself a disservice there, George,' I laughed.

'And now you've found yourself in a real sticky patch.'

'You are absolutely right. My life up to date has been one of calm repose and detachment.'

Hobb, bless his heart, was not in tune with irony. 'Things happen to test us,' he declared.

'I'll have to leave soon,' I told him. 'There's Winifred.'

'Ah! "The lovely Winifred",' quoted Hobb. 'That's Doctor Holbrook's daughter, I take it.'

'Stepdaughter.' I don't know why I offered Hobb this private information. It suddenly struck me of all the people in my life at the moment, I trusted this cross-dressing priest more than anyone. 'I can hardly believe this is happening to me,' I reluctantly, finally admitted: no irony here.

'Well, it has and it has to be dealt with. I haven't brought you much luck so far, have I James?'

'I might have been under this threat before knowing you. Indeed, it is more probable that I have brought this trouble to your door. Then there is my mother and sister whom I stayed with on my way here. While not wanting to alarm them, I am concerned about their safety too.'

'Stay away,' Hobb advised me firmly. 'Doctor Holbrook is right about that. Stay away until this is over.'

Chapter Twenty-Three

Back in Euston Road, London, I walked into the Midland Grand Hotel, opposite St Pancras railway station, and signed in with the bedroom clerk for a night's rest before my journey up to Yorkshire. For the first time, in a long time, I did not feel as if I was under surveillance. I cannot fully explain the feeling but something, someone, who had been there stalking me no longer was. I felt the tension that had been building up on the Isle of Wight had suddenly evaporated.

Building – solid buildings – the train station, along with the Midland Grand, had been designed by George Gilbert Scott who was, like Ruskin, an advocate of Gothic revival architecture. In the case of the Grand I saw it was pointed Gothic. Another Scott achievement was The General Infirmary in Leeds. It was not hard to see that all three buildings had been created by the same hand. A more uncomfortable association with Scott's genius was the North Riding Lunatic Asylum at Clifton. York seemed to have a preponderance of such institutions. If things went on as they had been back on the Isle of Wight, I felt sure my legal colleagues would be booking me a bed.

Who else would truly believe in this predatory phantom of mine? Hobb believed in it because he was there. Sir Clive Bampton and Dr Holbrook seemed on board because, in some way I had not worked out yet, not only were they aboard they were manning the ship.

I felt guilty at not contacting Marie and my mother. But in spite of the feeling that the danger I was in had somehow diminished for the time being, I was sure this scenario had not fully played out yet. Lucy Alexander was dead. I was determined to protect my kith and kin at all costs.

There was another vow I made. A few years ago, Digby West had persuaded me to spend a week with him stalking deer in Sutherland. I was a practised and extremely good shot but I was never comfortable seeing those fine stags dance, buckle and slowly fall to the ground because of the incompetence of other members of the party to make a clean kill. *Monarch of the glen* might have become something of a cliché after Landseer's famous painting, but that is just what these lofty antlered beasts are. I swore there and then in the coffee room of the Grand Hotel that I would never again stalk the deer – my fate and theirs had become linked – predator had become prey and it was not a comfortable position to be in.

'A smile at last, sir,' said a young waitress, laying my coffee cup down on the table. 'You must be thinking of something extremely comical.'

'If I told you what is amusing me, I doubt it would mean very much to you.'

'Try me, sir.'

'Have you ever heard of Sir Edwin Landseer's painting Monarch of the Glen?'

'I've seen it, sir.'

'Seen it?'

'Yes, sir. Wasn't it used for a Pears' advertisement at one time?'

'Was it?' I was immediately reminded of the man opposite the advertising hoarding on the tramway at Ryde.

'Yes, sir. A magnificent painting.'

'Did you know that it was commissioned for the Palace of Westminster as part of three panels, and the Commons refused to pay the hundred and fifty pounds for it?'

'That will be how it finished up with Pears. Politicians can be so short-sighted, can't they, sir?'

The coffee room swept along the whole curved wing of the hotel. It was approximately a hundred feet long by thirty feet wide, almost the size of the salon at Bampton Brook Hall but not quite. The ceiling was extremely high though, I estimated it must have risen to about twenty-four feet above ground level.

The room was full of residents and non residents. A man sitting alone at a nearby table smiled across to me. He must have been listening to my conversation with the waitress because he asked me in an obvious American drawl 'You English don't reckon too much to your politicians, do you?'

'Do you Americans?' I asked.

'We have Republican William McKinley in the White House at present,' he replied drily. 'I am a supporter of the Anti-Imperialist League. That doesn't always make me too popular with my fellow Americans.' My conversationalist was in his mid-sixties and had a mass of longish white hair

215

and a drooping mustachio. There was something familiar about this man but I couldn't quite place him.

'But America is a wonderful country,' I pointed out. 'Full of opportunities and youthful ambition.'

'That's fine as long as all that youthful ambition is put to good use at home. I take it you have visited my country, young man.'

'Oh, yes,' I crooned. 'My name is James Cairn, I'm a barrister.' I reached out my hand.

'My name is Samuel Langhorne Clemens. Nice to meet you, James Cairn.'

My hand trembled in Mark Twain's hand – the hand that had written The Adventures of Tom Sawyer and Huckleberry Finn – Carlton-Bingham was never going to believe this.

* * * * *

I started to pad happily back to my room on the deep-piled Axminster. There was a stooped figure blocking the corridor ahead. The man appeared to be looking through my bedroom keyhole. Coming to an abrupt halt, I checked the room number. Forty-five, there was no mistake it was my door.

'What on earth are you doing?' I challenged him.

'Must have got the wrong room,' he mumbled.

'The rooms are all numbered.' My pulse was beating wildly. I could hardly breathe. What did he want? Had he come to assassinate me?

'My eyesight isn't all it should be,' he said, lifting his monocle.

'I've seen you somewhere before, haven't I?'

'The Natural History library,' he replied. 'I was sitting at a desk opposite you. You were engaged in a deep conversation with Mr Alfred Wallace, I believe. I must say, Mr Cairn, you do keep rather strange company.'

I remembered that the threatening letter accompanying the extortion photographs had accused me of keeping unfortunate company. Could this man be its author? Another guest – or was he an accomplice? – squeezed past us. I thought of appealing to the man for help. When in doubt – I did nothing

'Rather than spying through the keyhole, you might as well come in.' I tussled in my pocket for the key. I would never find out who this character really was if I just let him drift back into the night. I would never find out what was going on.

'This will do it.' To my amazement the monocled assassin produced a thin metal device and slickly turned the lock.

'Have you already been in my bedroom?' I was aghast.

'I was just on the point of breaking and entering when you appeared.' The man was blatant, assured, no doubt accomplished in the martial arts. 'After you, Mr Cairn, sir.' He stepped aside.

My motto has always been if you cannot beat them wait until they are off guard. While he conducted a physical search of my room, I prepared two tumblers from a bottle of cognac I had bought in Portsmouth.

'Find anything?' I asked, passing him a drink.

He shook his head. 'Not yet.'

'Maybe I could help if I knew what you were looking for?'

'This job takes skill, years of training. I am looking for something that might endanger life, poisons, explosives, that sort of thing.'

'My life or someone else's?'

'Yours of course.'

'Has Doctor Holbrook sent you?'

'Doctor who?'

'Sir Clive Bampton perhaps? British intelligence even?'

He took a gulp from the tumbler and handed it back to me still almost full.

'Don't worry, Mr Cairn, I'm a friend.'

'Friend?'

'Sent by friends to look out for you until you leave London.'

'Which friends exactly?'

'By certain people who still have sympathies for the Rosebery position, you understand.'

'I'm not sure that I do. At first Rosebery appeared to give conditional support for Gladstone's Irish Home Rule Bill, while backing imperial expansionism in Africa to the hilt. Not exactly the most consistent of prime ministers.'

'Perhaps not, but Lord Rosebery knew what was good for Britain. Who cares about the bog Irish anyway, go for gold.'

'Or diamonds,' I suggested.

'Just so, sir,' he agreed.

'I wouldn't have marked out a man of action as an Archibald Primrose man.'

'Yes, a pretty name, isn't it for an ex-prime minister?' He smiled. I could see he would not be drawn any further. 'I can reassure you that this operation is being conducted at the highest level, Mr Cairn, and I urge the upmost secrecy on your part. Tell no one, trust no one.' With that the monocled assassin bowed and left.

* * * * *

Tell no one – I felt as if I was living a fiction, inhabiting an unreal world.

'Puh! Coffee with Mark Twain,' scoffed Gerald Fawcett.

Back at Bootham Chambers my colleagues had not believed my story of having coffee with Mark Twain, they were hardly likely to believe my story about the monocled assassin.

'Perhaps we should invest in a telephone,' I suggested, changing the subject.

'Andrew would never give his consent to that,' said Leacock, pre-empting the opinion of our absent boss.

'The expense,' sneered Fawcett.

'This chap Marconi is doing a lot of work on the Isle of Wight with his wireless telegraphy to improve our speed of communication,' I pointed out. 'We must keep up with the times. There are already over a hundred names in the York Telephone Directory. The Lord Mayor's business number is there too.'

'Oh, if J. Sykes Rymer and Son are in then we must follow,' again sneered Fawcett.

'Mr Levi told me his chambers in Leeds were considering investing in the speaking telegraph,' helped out Trotter.

'Mr Levi?' Fawcett turned up his nose in disapproval. 'The Jews have to be the first to everything.'

Turning my back on Fawcett's prejudice and my campaign to modernise Bootham Chambers, I went to my room to send Winifred a card of condolence instead. Mrs Holbrook replied by return saying her daughter was staying at Scarborough with friends. Plenty of sea air, a cure all since Brontë times, an attempt to lift Winifred's spirits following Lucy's untimely death. But not quite the romantic reunion I had envisaged. Here I was back to walk the streets of Bootham alone with neither a friendly nor a sympathetic ear.

Bootham itself leads out of York to the village of Clifton, which has a lovely village green on which I have shared a picnic or two with several of the local lasses. Clifton is also the site of the North Riding Lunatic Asylum. Oh, God, isn't that where I said my colleagues might have me incarcerated with my wild tales? Gerald Fawcett I was sure would not hesitate to have me committed. The monocled assassin was right, it was better to keep my mouth shut.

I was extremely tired and dispirited when I got to my Gillygate residence after my first day back in chambers. It was my maid's night off. However Kate had carefully propped up a letter in the silver tray on the hall table to make sure I did not miss it.

The letter was in my sister's modern and unmistakable hand.

> Petersham Place.
> Wednesday 17th January 1900
>
> Dear James,
> It is with regret that I have some unfortunate news for you. Lucy Alexander was found hanged in a basement flat in Clerkenwell the other day. No one in the movement believes that Lucy would take her own life. The newspapers are full of it. They are saying Lucy was pregnant. Arnon van Grunsven has gone missing.
> Personally, I think he has a lot to answer for.
> Your loving sister,
> Marie

I went to bed early that night sharing my sister's misgivings. I could not believe that Lucy would take her own life either. She was too much of a plucky fighter, a feisty little character. I had known women to take poisons because of unwanted pregnancies, sometimes to fling themselves into lakes, but in my entire professional career I had never heard of a woman hanging herself with the risk of slow strangulation. No, hanging was a male option. I could see the newspaper headlines now: *Pregnant Suffrage Woman found Hanging*. So much for Dr Holbrook's attempt to keep it out of the press.

I heard the rope creaking from a meat hook down in the kitchen somewhere. I forced myself to investigate. A pink carcass swung to and fro, to and fro. Was it a pig? No, it had the swollen puffed face of a toad, a giant stretched out toad hanging up there. The eyes bulged out of their sockets, the tongue lolled forward from its mouth. I did not recognise the face of Lucy Alexander at first. I felt sick. Then the picture changed. It was a befrocked George Hobb dangling there from the rope. Whores' lipstick was smudged all over his face, or was it blood? I tried to catch his feet, keep him alive. My hand closed on the smooth leather of a shoe. The shoe came off in my hand. Looking up again and to my horror I saw that the shoe belonged to me. I had changed places. I saw it was me hanging there. I tossed to free myself from the entangling rope, the rope creaked again on its hook. I tossed to free myself from the entangling shroud. Sitting bolt upright in my creaking bed, I felt cold, exposed in the midst of a ball of kicked away sheets.

* * * * *

The next morning in chambers I could not settle into a working routine. I bit my nails to the quick. Had the monocled assassin assassinated Lucy Alexander? Had he meant to do me harm? Had that other guest squeezing past in the hall unknowingly saved my life. Professional assassins do not like witnesses when they are about to commit murder. Who had known I was staying at the Midland Grand Hotel that night? Three men: Dr Holbrook, Sir Clive Bampton and George Hobb. Unless, God forbid, I had been followed there.

I got up from my desk and went across to the window. Moving the velour curtain cautiously back an inch or two, I peered round it. Someone could be down there in the street watching me now.

Trotter kept giving me worried glances from the legal research work I had given him to do at the corner table.

'You all right, sir?' he asked.

'Fine, fine,' I lied.

I paced and fretted on until one firm knock on the office door made me jump as if to an explosion.

'Come in,' I shouted.

'Business, always legal business. I've more business in York and thought I would drop in on you, James. I hope you don't mind,' fussed Benjamin Levi.

'Not at all.' I shook Levi's hand and indicated a seat, regretting Fawcett wasn't here to witness the scene of me giving succour to a Hebrew.

'Besides,' hesitated Levi, looking pointedly across at Trotter. 'I have a rather private and sensitive matter I wish to discuss with you.'

'Trotter, would you be good enough to leave Mr Levi with me for a minute or two?'

Without a word, Trotter bowed and left the room.

'I'll not shilly-shally any further about the reason I have come to visit you in person, James. You asked me to make enquiries about an Arnon van Grunsven who sometimes uses the alias Howard Greenstock.' I nodded. 'He is a Jewish postgraduate student at Oxford University, studying the unlikely subject of Anglo-Saxon history.'

'I know that. I first met him at St Gregory's Minster in Kirkdale.'

'Minsters, churches, I have not time for such things.' Levi shook his ringed hand dismissively.

'But Van Grunsven was an expert on Orm Gamalson's sundial.'

'Orm who?'

'Orm Gamalson. He was a northern chieftain of possible Viking descent who rebuilt St Gregory's…'

'Bloodthirsty Vikings sprouting horns, Saxons long gone, what real interest can these things have for a Sephardic Jew?'

'But the Saxon sundial above the minster porch is believed to one of the oldest examples in the world.'

'I don't doubt it,' mumbled Levi. 'Nonetheless, I must warn you, James, that Van Grunsven comes from a very powerful Dutch family.'

'Warn me, warn me why?'

'He is a man better avoided. The Van Grunsvens own one of the few diamond mines left in Dutch hands in the Orange Free State. They have a monopoly on the industry at the moment. They deal in an exclusive market. Meanwhile hundreds of diamond traders and cutters in Amsterdam are dependent on the arrival of British sights.'

'Sights?' I queried.

'Sights are galleried packages of diamonds. They look like ordinary small parcels but contain a fortune.'

'What are you getting at Benjamin?'

'The British are at war with the Boer in Africa. The Boer are descendants of Dutch trekkers. If the British win the war it could ruin the Van Grunsven business. But, I understand, the Boer at present have the upper hand. Van Grunsven diamonds are still getting through unhindered, while Cecil Rhodes' workers are having to hide down their Kimberley mine shafts away from heavy Boer bombardments. Indeed, is it not so that Rhodes himself is battened down manning that big gun of his?'

'The Long Cecil,' I helped out.

'Yes, The Long Cecil,' ruminated Levi. 'Africa is a very complex picture. Other powerful Jews have thrown their "pot" (I think Benjamin meant "lot" here) in with Cecil Rhodes' company. Alfred Beit was a partner in Rhodes' company which bought out Barnato's mining interests in 1888. Barney Barnato died, a couple of years back, in peculiar circumstances returning home from Cape Colony. He disappeared overboard near Madeira. Suicide it was claimed.'

'You don't sound too convinced.'

'Well, his family aren't. They do not believe Barney would ever have taken his own life. They do accept, however, that he was depressed about the Jameson Raid which had taken place over the New Year weekend of '95, '96.'

'The Jameson Raid, I remember that. Leander Starr Jameson made an incursion into the Boer held Transvaal with a small force of men in support of a British settler uprising.'

'Yes, the Uitlanders. I understand that the British Colonial Secretary, Joseph Chamberlain, though initially sympathetic to the cause had a change of heart. He felt if it succeeded it would ruin him. He travelled hotfoot from his Highbury home down to London to influence the outcome. The

Uitlander insurrection was curbed and Leander Starr Jameson and his six hundred men caught.'

'Wasn't Cecil Rhodes' brother, Frank, imprisoned by the Boers for conspiring against the Transvaal Republic?'

'Yes, that's right. Colonel Frank Rhodes was convicted of high treason, jailed in the most appalling conditions, and was due to be hanged. Within a few months he was released on payment of a hefty fine and joined his brother in the second Matabele War taking place just north of the Transvaal. The power of money. Cecil Rhodes, Alfred Beit, even Barney Barnato were implicated in the Jameson Raid. Many believe Cecil Rhodes, then governor of the Cape, was the mastermind behind the entire plot. Ultimately, that was more about gold than diamonds, gold found in the Transvaal.'

'Barnato could have been returning to London with a lot of damaging information then.'

'Indeed,' sighed Levi. 'And a fortune of inheritance in the bank.'

'Do you think he will win at Kimberley?'

'Who, Cecil Rhodes? You English always win in the end but war is never good for us Jews. Let me tell you this, James, if that hothead Arnon van Grunsven has his way things could get a whole lot worse for my people in this country.'

'What does he intend doing?' Alarm bells began to ring.

'Right wing fanatics like Evans-Gordon describe Jews as foreign invaders bringing crime and disease with them. He needs only the slightest excuse to push through that obnoxious Aliens Bill. Then only rich Jews, who can deposit their money on these shores, will be welcome here. But what is even more alarming is this growing band of Gentiles, secretly calling themselves the Brotherhood, who appear to be intent on Jewish annihilation.'

'Van Grunsven, what is he intending to do?' I persisted.

'I will not betray my people further. Although I will reassure you of this, James, the Jewish community has the apparatus for dealing with their own.'

'I have heard Van Grunsven has gone into hiding.'

'No, James, not another word.' Levi stood up to leave. Feeling enough of his dignity and integrity were still intact, he draped his coat over his shoulders like a magician's cloak.

Although I had not got another word out of Benjamin Levi – not even his usual warning of *do you know what you are letting yourself in for* – I had hardly drawn breath when there was a second knock on my door. This knock though was more hesitant, softer, the returned Trotter perhaps.

Ignatius Shore stood in my doorway looking in a bad way. He looked older, more careworn, not as dapper.

'Mortimer still has not made contact since those last two postmarked letters before Christmas. We are now extremely concerned for his welfare. He didn't even come home for the festive season and Mortimer loves Christmas above everything. Amelia is becoming more hysterical each day over her brother's absence. Brother and sister are very close, in some ways they are more like husband and wife, a married couple. They were orphaned at a tender age and have always looked out for each other. Amelia feels sure Mortimer is in some kind of trouble.'

'Perhaps he has met someone in Holland, a Dutch woman perhaps, and he dare not tell her.'

'No, no, I don't think so, that isn't Mortimer's character at all. He is the most honest open chap I have ever known.'

'How can you say that? How much do we really know about anyone when it comes to emotional feelings?'

'I know Mortimer, Mr Cairn,' insisted Shore. 'We've worked together for years. I am extremely worried. What can I do? I feel so guilty about allowing that sensitive letter to get into the wrong hands at the Fox.'

'Nonsense, how could you have anticipated anyone snatching it up like that? Anyway, that happened months ago. Mortimer's second letter arrived after that, remember?'

'I know and yet I am still very uneasy. Suppose that incident, that first snatched letter, in some way put Mortimer's life in jeopardy. I haven't dared admit to Amelia what happened. The Dutch police haven't come up with anything yet either.'

'Ah, the Dutch police. I have heard different regions hardly talk to each other. Do you really think they will have much interest in finding a missing Englishman? You'd be better going over there looking for him yourself, a detective to find a detective.'

'But there is only me left in the office, Mr Cairn.'

'There is Amelia. I am sure she is more than capable of holding the fort for a few days in your absence, especially if it is part of an effort to find her brother.'

'But Hull to Rotterdam.' The delicate Shore looked horrified at the prospect of a rough North Sea crossing.

'I'll go then,' I said.

'You will?'

'I haven't much on at the moment,' I admitted. And I hadn't, merely a family starvation defence for the ten year old son of imprisoned pickpocket, William Huddleston. Charlie Huddleston had been caught lifting a turnip from a market vendor's stall for his Mam. 'Get me return train tickets and tickets for the ferry. I'll go in a fortnight's time for a week. I hope you will not be charging my chambers for any expenditure incurred.'

Ignatius Shore left beaming. He had got what he came for.

'Trotter! Trotter!' I screamed down the corridor to no avail. Where was the man? He must be hiding in a cupboard somewhere sulking again.

Chapter Twenty-Four

What had I let myself in for? – this seemed a recurring theme lately. Ignatius Shore managed to get me a Wednesday ticket on a small cargo, passenger steamer bound for Rotterdam. The North Sea churned. I am sure waves must have been breaking over the deck had I been on top to see them. But I was not, a green, clammy nauseous shadow of myself was below decks. Confined to my cabin, I felt terrible. I felt terrible until after I had vomited, vomited and vomited.

My stomach emptied of all contents, arriving in Rotterdam was a relief.

'Ever since the Dutch built the Nieuwen Waterweg, the new seaway, Rotterdam's approaches have become more accessible,' explained a merchant seaman as I drooped over the side. 'Rotterdam is one of the few ports in Holland deep enough to accommodate steamers' paddles.'

'Really,' I said, still feeling unwell and drained of enthusiasm. 'Ports always look the same to me. The boat could have turned round and be back in Hull for all I know.'

'No, no,' disagreed the seaman. 'Rotterdam is a wonderful place. You must visit the Spanish Quay and the Fish Market.'

'Fish Market,' I said doubtfully. My stomach giving a lurch at the conjured smell of fish.

'Not seen you on deck much during the sailing, sir.'

'Sick. My first experience of such a rough crossing,' I was forced to admit, shamefaced.

'Oh,' he said and smiled.

Feeling I was still rolling with the waves – or not rolling with the waves – I swayed across to find the Port of Leuve mentioned in Mortimer Blakely's letter. I found port and hotel almost immediately. I remembered the hotel's name now. It was painted in big letters on the tall narrow gable end and it was not a Dutch name either.

QUEEN's – HOTEL

CAFÉ RESTAURANT

BREAKFASTS & DINNER

The Queen's Hotel, how reassuringly English. No doubt the reason why the lone traveller Blakely would have chosen to stay here. No doubt the reason I had failed to absorb it at a glance before it was snatched away. Breakfast and dinner, my stomach heaved again at the thought of them.

I booked in. The concierge was of average height and dark haired. The man did not look Dutch at all, although he spoke English with an obvious Dutch accent as he helped me up the stairs with my luggage. After my North Sea crossing, I expect I looked like a man in need of help.

'Will this room suit you, sir?' he asked; plonking my case with a thud on the polished oak floorboards and proudly indicating the interior of a heavily furnished bedroom.

'Very nice,' I replied. If I had been absolutely honest anything would have suited me as long as it had a stable bed. I decided now was not the moment to interrogate the concierge about Mortimer Blakely and dismissed him with a few cents for his trouble. Though only four o'clock in the afternoon, I undressed and got into bed. That is where I stayed until first light of the following day broke through my deep sleep.

I had a wonderful view of the Leuve from my bedroom window. Its calm waters sparkled in the sharp winter light. An early boatman was sculling down the waterway, no doubt enjoying having an unhindered course all to himself.

Breakfast was comprehensive with the addition of continental cheeses and ham. I decided when in Holland – my stomach had almost recovered from its sea crossing but wavered away from anything fried – and I was not disappointed with my Dutch Gouda and Leyden cheeses. A tomato, the freshest farm butter I had ever tasted, with several slices of rye bread complemented the dish. And the coffee, the full flavoured coffee was out of this world. I finally threw a piece of French Brie de Meaux into the mix, garlanded in grapes.

Occasionally, I peeked round the palms and ferns of the breakfast room in the hope of seeing Mortimer Blakely. No such luck. No Mortimer Blakely. No spending the rest of my week holidaying.

Coming out of breakfast, I decided the concierge was still the best man to approach regarding the whereabouts of Blakely: concierges of small hotels usually see all the comings and goings. I found the Queen's standing alone at his desk, now was my best opportunity.

'Could you tell me if a Mr Mortimer Blakely is still staying in the hotel?'

The concierge's smiling expression turned to one of anger. I stepped back. 'Is Mr Blakely known to you, sir?' he asked.

'Yes, he is. I have come to Rotterdam to look for him. His family have not heard from him in months.'

'Then you are a friend of Mr Blakely's family.'

'Yes.'

The concierge reached under his desk and passed me a piece of folded paper. 'Then perhaps, sir, you might see they pay this.'

The paper was the hotel's bill for several hundred guilder. 'I'll pay it,' I told him reaching for my wallet. 'I'll pay it right now if you will tell me all you know about Mr Blakely's last movements.'

'There's not much to tell. Mr Blakely was with us for a few weeks only and then he was not.'

'Did he take his luggage with him?'

'Oh, yes. He said he was going to Amsterdam for a day or two and would be coming back to settle his bill.'

'And you believed him?'

'Why not? He told us he was a business man.'

'A business man?'

'Yes. He said he traded in diamonds.'

'In diamonds?' I was beginning to sound like an incredulous parrot.

'We had no reason to doubt him Mr Cairn. He entertained Mr Da Silva to dinner here on at least two occasions.'

'Mr Da Silva?'

'Yes, Mr Da Silva is a gentleman who has a jewellery shop in the Arcade.'

I paid Mortimer Blakely's bill and asked the concierge if he would be good enough to write the address of Mr Da Silva's shop on the receipt. All smiles now the man would have gladly signed his own mother's death warrant.

* * * * *

The Arcade in Rotterdam reminded me of the newly completed County Arcade in Leeds with its pillar-like structures. Jacob da Silva's jewellery shop enjoyed one of the Arcade's more privileged sites at the end nearest the fountain. I rang the bell.

'Mr Jacob da Silva?'

'Indeed.' Spoken in perfect English.

'I am looking for a diamond ring for my wife,' I lied.

'Then, sir, you have come to the right place.' Jacob da Silva lowered his white, long, elegantly coiffured head of hair over a display case. In seconds his tall frame retrieved a tray of rings and he rose to face me with similar grace. 'If you should choose any rings from here then I am sure Mrs...' He waited.

'Roberts,' I said, for some reason Lord Roberts' surname sounded the right chord. 'Mrs Amelia Roberts.'

I watched carefully, Da Silva did not baulk at the name Amelia. Announcing calmly instead, 'Then Mrs Roberts will not be disappointed.'

'I quite like that one,' I said, pointing to a large coloured diamond. The diamond stood alone in its antique scroll setting. The ring would have been diminished by the presence of other stones.

'Ah! The fancy yellow. Sir, has good taste. This is the very best example of a top quality stone that I am able to show you. It is pure, flawless. It is the only one I have in stock.'

'What is your favourite diamond, Mr Da Silva, clear or coloured?'

'This yellow diamond is near perfection but if money was no object I personally love the Indian blues. Mark my words, coloured diamonds will come into their own in the future as long as there are enough to mine and market.'

'A friend recommended your shop to me.'

'Ah! A friend.'

'Yes, Mr Mortimer Blakely.'

Da Silva's hooded lids closed. This time I could see I had got a reaction. He reached for a handkerchief and rubbed it under his hooked nose, a nose that was not out of place with the rest of his chiselled features.

'Why, I have not seen Mortimer Blakely for many months.'

'No, I believe he went to Amsterdam.'

'Ah! Amsterdam.'

'Do you know why he might have gone to Amsterdam?'

'On business I expect.'

'Did he say what business?'

Jacob da Silva shook his head. 'He told me he worked in the diamond industry but of course it did not take me five minutes to realise that was untrue.'

'So, why did you keep having dinner with a liar?'

'He was a interesting man and I wanted to polish up my English.'

'If I might say so, Mr Da Silva, your English is already excellent.'

'Ah! Well,' said Da Silva, lifting his hands as if in apology.

'So, you don't know where Mortimer Blakely might have been heading for in Amsterdam.'

'He was very interested in Jewish diamond trading in that city. He often brought up the subject. So many Jews involved in the trade, always Jews,' Da Silva began to ramble. I half listened.

'Did you give Mortimer Blakely any names, addresses?' I interrupted.

'A few,' admitted Da Silva.

'Can you remember them?'

'Ah! I'll do my best,' again the lifted hands. He took a piece of paper out of one of his drawers and began pencilling down information about Jewish traders known to him in Amsterdam. He also gave me a letter of introduction. As I was leaving he called me back. 'There is one name I have forgotten to write down on that list, and it is a name that Mortimer mentioned once or twice. Indeed on more than one occasion, he asked me if I knew this family.'

'Please write it down here then with the rest.' I passed the list back to Da Silva. His elegant hand trembled momentarily as he made the addition.

'You did not come in here to buy a ring for your wife at all, did you, Mr Roberts?'

'It really is a lovely ring but I'm afraid I'm not married.'

'Mr Blakely wasn't in the diamond trade but he was certainly Jewish, I suspect crypto-Jewish.'

'Are you sure?' This was a surprise.

'I am as sure Mr Blakely was Jewish as I am that your name is not Roberts.'

As my boots began to beat a retreat down the hollow echoing Arcade, I took the opportunity of glancing at Da Silva's Amsterdam list. The names and Dutch addresses meant little to me until I got to the afterthought at the bottom of the page. Boots and heart were now in high-speed unison.

I decided to calm myself with a cup of tea and walked into one of the city's pavement cafes. Although it was mid-February, the cafe had a few tables and chairs outside. In this respect Café Rotterdam appeared to be operating under the delusion that its location was the South of France. Nevertheless, the sun was shining and had a little spring warmth to it. Had we finally begun to cast off winter in Northern Europe, I wondered. I suddenly felt optimistic. It was one of those odd February days that heralded something better was waiting round the corner.

Wrapped up in my Inverness tweed overcoat, I rejected the cafe's gloomy interior to sit outside and enjoy the goings on in the street: the horses and cabs, people flying about their business as if there was no tomorrow, even one or two bicyclists performing their precarious balancing acts between pedestrians. But what impressed me most of all were the road sweepers, mainly men, who were more attentive to their task with their twig brooms than any I had ever seen in England. The Dutch struck me as a very organised, neat and clean people.

I did find similarities with my home country though: the *clip, clip,* noise of passers-by, in their formidable clogs, reminded me of the Pennine towns of Nelson and Colne as cotton workers beat out their tracks to and from the mill. Strange, I thought, how there is always a need to reference a new experience to an old. Perhaps it is a way of pinpointing our position on earth. Rather like a librarian who files certain books away under particular categories so they can be easily found. My tea arrived. I paid the waitress there and then as I was eager to make a quick escape once I had emptied my cup and explore Rotterdam with only an afternoon left to me.

I watched as a newly arrived chap lit up his cigar at a window seat inside the cafe. An even better reason for sitting outside unless I wanted my overcoat to stink of tobacco for the rest of my stay in Holland. Despite the glass pane between us, smoke managed to waft out through the open door.

Without ever having had the desire to smoke anything myself, I must admit I find the smell of cigars rather pleasant especially with coffee. I was used to my boss Carlton-Bingham regularly lighting up over his morning coffee. At the same time I do have this niggling apprehension about smoking. My father's younger brother was addicted to a meerschaum pipe for most of his life, and I was forced to witness his deathbed suffering. At the age of forty-two, William Cairn had a growth on the tongue. His airways were so restricted, he struggled to breathe to the end. Surely in the not too distant future a connection will be made between smoking and diseases of the lungs and airways. The botanist, John Hill, over a century ago, made a correlation between snuff taking and cancer of the nose. I am sure these associations between tobacco and ill health are not too farfetched.

However, the man beyond the window did not appear to be nearing his end, nor did his expression convey any thoughts of death on his optimistic, broad Dutch features. He had a dark complexion, beard and, although he was seated, he appeared to be built like Grutte Pier, or Pier Gerlofs Donia to give him his proper name, a 16th century Frisian pirate and rebel who was reputed to be seven and a half feet tall. My man of myth smiled an acknowledgement to me through the glass. I then remembered the incident of the smoking Dutch cigar butt left in the porch of Kingston Church. Balmoral was the brand. I searched the Dutchman's table for his cigar packet. Justus van Maurik spelt out the red lettering on the yellow packet. Thank goodness for that. I was being ridiculous, thousands of men must smoke cigars here in Holland. Millions of men must indulge in the smoking habit all over the world. I was placing far too much significance on one paltry corona butt.

So, back to my afternoon, what did I want to see? By my last sip of tea I had rejected the Embankment for the Spaanse Kade, the Spanish Quay – I liked the name. As I got to my feet to leave, Grutte through the glass gave me another smile. I gave him a cheery wave and left a tip for the waitress.

The Spanish Quay did not disappoint. To one end there was a fine columned bridge with gaslights. Many small boats with sheet sails were docked all along the quay. Some bigger vessels, river barges, had washing hung on lines across their decks. They appeared to be occupied homes. I had never seen anything like this before, no previous experience to relate to this.

I was enjoying a second open air cafe in as many hours, quietly taking in the atmosphere of the quay, when I realised someone was standing at my shoulder. I turned and my mouth fell open in disbelief. Cigar-less, Grutte smiled down on me.

'Sir, are you following me?' My shoulder twitched as if to shake the man off like some medieval devil. Whatever my outward appearance, however much I tried to convince myself otherwise, after what I had learnt from the jeweller, Da Silva, I was in a highly nervous state.

'May I join you for a while?' A deep baritone request expressed in impeccable English.

I pulled out a chair. Examining the dregs of coffee in my cup, Grutte ordered two fresh ones from the hovering waiter. February on the Spanish Quay must have been a quiet month.

'You've not answered my question yet.'

'What was your question? I've forgotten.' Grutte smiled nonchalantly.

'To get here you must have been following me.'

'That is not a question but a supposition.'

'Come, man, you didn't just happen to find me here.'

'My name is Derk.' He offered his large hand.

'Well, Derk, why are you following me?'

'We are back to that are we? You English men.'

'What do you mean we English men?' The coffees' arrival was opportune.

'I thought you wanted me to follow you,' finally admitted a more conciliatory Derk.

'You thought what?'

'You waved at me like this.' Derk flopped his hand.

'I never wave like that at anyone, certainly never to another chap.'

'I thought you liked me. Were lonely perhaps. Needed a little company during your stay in Rotterdam.'

'I beg your pardon!' Not again, I thought. Not another Charlie from Ryde. What was it about me that attracted these men? Was I made more vulnerable to their attentions because I was a man travelling alone? I girded up, I could see from the expression in Derk's eyes he was about to tell me something I might not want to hear.

'You fresh faced Englishmen with your pretty manners. Such hypocrisy when your country is full of Eton and Harrow Oscar Wildes.'

I said nothing. Derk had a point here. I focused in on one of his big dark eyes. The eye, bulging with rage, appeared to me to fill most of his forehead. Derk was not Grutte Pier at all but Cyclops. I could not resist a smile.

'Have you seen the Embankment yet, the Bridges of the Meuse?' Encouraged by my smile he offered to show me the sights. 'The Fish Market?'

Chapter Twenty-Five

If Mortimer Blakely is Jewish then Amelia must be as well. Irrespective of Jewishness, Jacob da Silva had given me a link between Blakely and Amsterdam, a trail to follow. As the train pulled into Amsterdam Centraal railway station, I was confident I would find Blakely here. The station is a show piece of architecture in itself, a Neo-Renaissance building designed by Pierre Cuypers and A.L. van Gendt. It has a roof span of 40 metres fabricated in cast iron by my fellow countryman the late Andrew Handyside of Derby. The Centraal is situated on three man-made islands, themselves resting on 8,687 wooden piles which have been driven deep into the muddy and sandy soil. Its location was not popular with the citizens of Amsterdam as it effectively cut them off from their waterfront.

Looking round this echoing cathedral of a place, I could not help reflecting that its magnificence would be lost on most weary travellers. But not on me, my journey had been a short and interesting one from Rotterdam. Energy flowing, I surged on with the rest of humanity choosing the Centrum tunnel to bring me up from the platforms like a mole from the depths.

Crossing the bridge from the station, the Victoria Hotel loomed before me. Luggage in hand, I saw no reason to look further. I had rested my head in the Queen's Hotel in Rotterdam, why not the Victoria Hotel in Amsterdam? After I signed in, it was again a concierge who was to prove my main informant. Wilhelm had a comprehensive knowledge of the hotel's ten year history. The hotel opened its doors on August 19th, 1890. It was the brainchild of German architect J. F. Henkenhaf. He strategically placed it across from the Amsterdam Centraal on the corner of Damrak and Prins Hendrikkade, a street named after Prins Hendrik the Navigator, the youngest son of King William II of the House of Orange.

'You know of the House of Orange in England?' enquired Wilhelm.

'Oh, yes, we certainly do.'

'Prince Hendrik had a terrific interest in trade and shipping.' Hardly drawing breath, Wilhelm continued, 'The architect, Henkenhaf, tried and failed to buy numbers forty-seven and forty-five along Prins Hendrikkade, undaunted he built this hotel round and over them where they still remain privately owned today.'

'Has a Mr Mortimer Blakely recently stayed here?' I finally got to ask Wilhelm. He shook his head sadly.

'Many famous people stay here but I do not know the name Mr Blakely.'

'Mr Blakely is not a famous man. Nevertheless, he is a man who is important to me.'

I tipped the obligatory cents to the porter, as he placed my luggage carefully down on a tasselled Turkish carpet – the centrepiece in what can only be described as a luxurious bedroom.

The porter hovered in the entrance. Had my tip fallen short by Victoria standards?

'You know, sir, there are plenty of gentlemen in Amsterdam who would wish to be important to you. Forgive me, but I overheard you enquiring about a Mr Blakely. Why trouble yourself over him? If you wish I could introduce you to many gentlemen down the Geldersekade during an evening of your choosing.'

Forget Lord Alfred Douglas, I looked across at this slim, blond hermaphroditic god Tuisto of Holland and wondered just how many Dutchmen were homosexual. He was, however, slow to acknowledge my disdain.

'There are ladies out there too, if they are more to your taste.' Unable to read me, he had finally decided on compromise.

* * * * *

I managed to get an English paper to complement my English breakfast. To say we had been at war many times with the Dutch over the centuries, we seemed to have made our mark on the country. Quite a few hotels enjoyed English names – I was staying in one – and hoardings slung up high on shop roofs advertised *Old England* and *Quaker Oats*. We dominated most of the world, now we were dominating other countries' skylines.

Speaking of domination, my two day old *Times* reported that on St Valentine's Day Major General John French launched a major offensive to relieve Kimberley. He made a daring charge up a shallow valley – known as a nek in Africa – leading to Kimberley which was held by the Boer blocking his route. If the Boer lines had held it would have spelt disaster for French's entire command. *Aut vincere aut mori* – to conquer or die. After a five mile gallop along the valley, French's cavalry swept down the pass and through Boer lines. Out of a force of five thousand, he lost only one man with twenty others wounded. At 2.30 p.m. a heliograph was sent to the garrison. At 6.30 p.m. the defenders were eventually convinced that French was who he said he was and the garrison was finally relieved after a hundred and twenty-four day siege.

I took in a long, thought provoking mouthful of coffee. Now perhaps British diamonds would start to flow again into cities like this. How would Van Grunsven & Co. respond?

'Telegram, sir,' Wilhelm announced from his little wooden kiosk in the entrance hall as I made my way to face a rain splattered Amsterdam.

'For me?'

'For you, sir.'

My spirits lifted from rain to sunshine. Perhaps it was another communication from Mortimer Blakely and I would no longer have to look for him. It was not from Blakely but a response to my telegram informing Ignatius Shore of my whereabouts. Shore enquired how my enquiries were progressing.

'Not from Mr Blakely, I take it,' whispered Michel, the porter, impudently. 'Have you given my offer to show you round the Geldersekade any further consideration, sir?' I shook my head and just laughed at him. 'And where is sir going today, might I ask?'

'The weather is so foul, I've decided on a visit to the Rijks Museum.'

'By tram, sir, or shall I get you a cab?'

'Thank you, a cab will be most welcome.'

As much as Amsterdam is a grid of canals so it is equally criss-crossed by tram tracks. Each tram is drawn by a single horse and carries about a dozen or so passengers. I regarded some of these poor draught animals doubtfully as Michel tried to hail a driver.

'Don't worry,' drawled a passing American. 'These streetcar horses are regularly rested and watered. I know how sensitive you British are about the welfare of animals.'

'This gentleman is. This gentleman is sensitive about humans too,' trilled Michel eagerly from beneath our shared umbrella.

The American stopped and turned. 'That's good to hear, fella,' he told Michel.

'How did you know I was British?'

He looked down at my feet. 'Without sounding too presumptuous that, my friend, is rather obvious. Your shoes are made by Church & Co. of Northampton.'

'That's an impressive observation.'

'Where are you bound for?' he asked me, the rain pouring down his face.

'The Rijks Museum.'

'Where else. That's where I'm headed too. As you British say, might we go Dutch on a cab together?'

Tom, he was called. Tom from Baltimore, married with three children – thank goodness for small mercies. I introduced myself as James from Yorkshire, unmarried, with an interest in art and architecture. When holidaying surnames do not seem important.

'Who's your pal with the umbrella?'

'Michel is not my pal, he is one of the porters at the hotel I am staying at.'

'That must be the Victoria.' I did not reply. 'That's where you were both standing outside at any rate. Come on. Don't be so stuffy. You're in Amsterdam now.'

'I'm not being stuffy but everybody in Holland seems to presume if you're English you must be a pillowman.'

'Blame your Mr Wilde for that.'

'I think Oscar Wilde has already taken the blame for much more than he was entitled to.'

'You sound well-informed.'

'I have some knowledge of the law. But tell me, I'm curious, how did you, an American, recognise my shoes as Church's?'

'Why, one of Thomas Church's original styles of shoes, the Adaptable, won a gold medal at the Crystal Palace Exhibition some fifteen years ago.' I stared at him in amazement. Tom laughed and explained that he was a shoe manufacturer in Amsterdam on business. He told me he was staying at the

Hotel Prins Hendrik across the way from the Victoria.

'A shoe manufacturer interested in art, how very interesting.' My recent history was making me suspicious of everyone.

'Why, aren't we allowed to be interested in something other than footwear?' Tom smirked. I was admonished. 'I've been told there is a picture by Jan Asselijn of a threatened swan that is superb.'

'I have to confess that I am not totally enamoured of the Dutch school of painting. I find some of their canvases rather dark, staged and of course that is just what they are. They are of their age, the Golden Age, an age when artists had to produce their work in houses with little window light.'

'Perhaps it would have been more appropriate to call it the Brown Age,' chuckled Tom. This shoe manufacturer from Baltimore was beginning to grow on me. He had humour.

'There is one painting I have come to see above all others,' I told him.

'And which one is that?'

'Wait and see.'

Tom's coat began to steam in the confines of the cab. He must have got extremely wet. We had to travel right across the city to get to the Rijks Museum. Many of the large buildings we passed had some of the Classicism of York. But the tall, narrow Amsterdam canal houses had a character, a peculiarity all of their own, with decorative cornices and openwork festoons on the masonry facades and gables. They reminded me of homemade biscuits piped with icing sugar. Many of these houses had beams with pulleys protruding from their upper storeys. I presumed as a method of raising goods, so avoiding impossible staircases. Pathways ran on either side of the numerous canals and I noticed one or two innovative bicycles peddled these routes. There were more bridges in this city than I had ever seen anywhere.

The tall-hatted cab driver pulled to the side of the pavement on the Stadhouderskade announcing our arrival at the Rijks Museum. I paid him off, and with my new American companion walked into the world of Dutch masters.

Tom could have stepped off a Van Baburen canvas himself. He was only about five feet nine inches tall but every inch of his broad frame appeared to be extremely well muscled.

He had a large chin, and below brown ox-like eyes a boxer's nose inhabited most of his face. Not a man to trifle with, I guessed.

We ambled through galleries of brooding Dutch landscapes. I longed for the lightness, the brightness of contemporary impressionism. Even though I admired Rembrandt's dramatic use of light in his *Night Watch* much of the composition's periphery was in browns, in shadows.

'What do you think of this then?' asked Tom, as we stood before the biblical portrait of a man and woman. The woman wore a rich red dress. Her male consort pressed his flattened hand across her bosom, not in any sexual sense, no, more in the manner of a future father feeling the heart beat of his unborn child. Rembrandt had used a smooth painting technique for the couple's hands and faces, whereas the paint on the man's right golden sleeve had been thickly applied, perhaps palette knife applied.

'*The Jewish Bride*,' I sighed. 'This is more to my taste. See there, how that thickly applied paint gives depth to the painting. Here, I can see Rembrandt's genius.'

'Me, too,' agreed Tom, as we reluctantly moved on.

'What on earth is this?'

'This is what I told you about. This is the painting I have come to see,' said Tom. 'This painting was one of the museum's first acquisitions.'

An aggressive swan, hissing, white wings outstretched against an azure sky, towered above us on a huge canvas dominating an entire gallery wall. Beneath the bird its excrement and furiously scattered feathers made the composition all the more realistic.

'Unbelievably powerful.' I gazed up at the hissing swan in awe. Stepping forward to get some insight into the painter's technique, I was disappointed to see the painting had been adulterated with text. The words "Grand Pensionary" had been written beneath the swan, "Holland" on one of her eggs, and "the enemy of the state" above the dog's head.

'Symbolic too. The swan is believed to represent Grand Pensionary Johan de Witt protecting Holland. See, there, that dog swimming in from the left, threatening the swan's nest, that's the enemy of the state, England.' Tom seemed to derive some pleasure from telling me this. Perhaps he was still living in the days of the American Revolutionary War.

'Nothing has changed,' said a heavily accented voice behind us. I turned – many Dutch faces beamed innocently back at me – there were too many people grouped in a half circle behind us for me to discern who had actually made the remark.

Tom muttered to them in Dutch something like "genoeg" and "manieren" – "enough", "manners".

'Let's move on,' I told him, feeling outnumbered.

'There is a price to pay when you belong to the greatest empire the world has ever known,' said Tom. 'That price is popularity.'

'Forgive me for saying this but you are extremely erudite for a man whose business is shoes.'

'Ah well.' Tom smiled. 'I come from a long line of Dutch American politicians.'

'Hence your linguistic skills.'

'And my surname, De Vries.'

We walked into yet another gallery, a thankfully empty gallery. 'Well, Tom de Vries, you've shown me your favourite painting now guess which is mine.'

Tom looked down the length of the room, meticulously examining each wall. I could hardly contain myself because it was so obvious to me what my choice was – a painting that stood out head and shoulders above the rest in technique, light and composition – a masterpiece by a master.

Tom began to walk slowly towards the end wall. 'That is your choice,' he said, pointing to the Vermeer. '*Woman in Blue Reading a Letter.*'

'It's perfect, don't you think? See how her blue jacket is balanced by the blue chairs.'

'I agree. This is indeed a beautiful painting,' enthused Tom.

'So, how do you interpret the symbolism here?' I asked him. 'That is if you see any at all.'

'For a Dutchman there is plenty of meaning in this painting, James. And remember I will always remain a Dutchman at heart.'

'The lady looks pregnant, does she not? It could merely be the loose fashion of her jacket of course.'

'No, no.' Tom shook his head. 'She is nubile, full-faced, alone and with child.'

'Abandoned then, you think?'

'The map behind her head is of Holland and West Friesland.'

'I believe Vermeer used the same map in an earlier work, *Soldier and the Laughing Girl.*'

'Perhaps the map is a clue to a travelling husband or distant lover,' suggested Tom.

'In Dutch paintings, during the Vermeer period, a woman reading a letter is usually a reference to love. Look carefully there on the table, the box and spilled pearls that might suggest a lover or vanity or both.'

'This picture is unique, James. There is not a fragment of corner, wall or ceiling to detract from the woman, from her facial expression.'

Was this how Lucy Alexander had looked? – accepting the fate of an unmarried mother. Had Arnon van Grunsven written to her like someone had written to the *Woman in Blue Reading a Letter*? Had Van Grunsven refused to make Lucy Alexander an honest woman?

'I must leave,' I told Tom; a shiver travelling the length of my spine.

'How about we get together for dinner tomorrow evening at my hotel and discuss art?' suggested Tom, seemingly unfazed by my abruptness 'Seven thirty OK with you?'

'Why not. But now I must get some air.'

It had stopped raining when we emerged. I decided to walk back along the Herengracht and through central Amsterdam. To my relief Tom chose to ride. I needed time to think, time to reflect. Tomorrow would be a day of reckoning. Tomorrow I was determined to find Mortimer Blakely.

Chapter Twenty-Six

It was Sunday, the day after Shabbat, and while most of Amsterdam slept or prepared for early morning church, the old Jewish quarter around Waterlooplein, Jodenbreestraat and Weesperstraat sprang back into life after its religious day of reflection. Particularly Waterlooplein Market, a haven for Jews and Gentiles alike where anything could be bought when everything else in Amsterdam was shut down. The closer I got to Waterlooplein the stronger the smell of sewage from the canals. The rich were housed along the main canals such as the Herengracht, the poor had dwellings on the minor canals that ran off them. Waterlooplein, Jodenbreestraat and Weesperstraat were not rich areas although a few citizens managed to make a decent living there: shopkeepers, stallholders, street vendors and of course diamond workers. That is diamond workers had made a good living until recently, until ironically the Boer had surrounded Kimberley and rough British diamonds were failing to come through to be cut, polished by Amsterdam expertise. Only one sight package had arrived to a sight holder in Antwerp from Africa, via London, but that had been months ago. Mr Da Silva in Rotterdam had confirmed a similar story told to me by Benjamin Levi back in York. There were Van Grunsven diamonds available but, having a monopoly and just the one mine, these diamonds were extremely expensive and sold only to exclusive dealers.

So, what was really happening? Were the British holding back diamonds from Dutch manufacturers because of the war, were the diamonds just not being mined or getting through, or were greedy London syndicates attempting to buy up the diamonds to control the market?

'So many Jews involved in the trade, always Jews,' Da Silva had told me. (Although I had only been half-listening then, I remembered now.) 'And do you know why?'

I had shaken my head. 'No idea.'

'Apart from moneylending, the cutting and polishing of gems was one of the few crafts permitted to Jews by the medieval guilds of Europe. Likewise, during the Inquisition, diamonds proved to be a portable asset, small enough to be sown into clothes or hidden on the body. My ancestors were forced to flee twice for their lives, first from Lisbon and then from Antwerp when the Spanish invaded.' Jacob da Silva had sighed, sighed as if over a recent memory, sighed with the amazing equilibrium of a man ready for flight all over again.

I smiled at the stallholders in Waterlooplein Market crying their wares. I smiled but I had not come to buy a coat or a cabbage. I had come to buy information.

I knocked on the door of an address in Jodenbreestraat on Da Silva's list. The door opened a fraction. An old woman, dressed from head to foot in black, peered suspiciously through the tentative crack.

'Mevrouw Groot?' I enquired.

'Ja.' Lost for words, lost for a common language, we stood staring at each other. With the impatience of the elderly, Mevrouw Groot soon tired of this impasse and asked me in Dutch what was my business. At least I think that is what she asked me.

'Hayek Groot?'

'Hayek,' she half wheezed and screamed across the yard behind her. Eventually the tiptoe of boots could be heard approaching across the cobbles.

'Hayek Groot?' The old man nodded behind his wife, his chin was almost on her shoulder. The door opened a fraction more allowing me to see the couple more clearly. He, too, was dressed head to foot in black. I had lived in London and York long enough to know Groot was a traditional orthodox Ashkenazi. 'Do you speak English?' I asked him.

'Small,' he replied.

'Do you know where I might find Victor Toledano?'

'Weesperstraat. Not today, tomorrow.'

'Where on Weesperstraat?'

The old man's livid hand drew a 45A on the back of mine. 'Tomorrow,' he repeated; before closing the door against real or imaginary enemies.

Tomorrow it would have to be then. Mortimer Blakely's Weesperstraat contact would have to wait until tomorrow. Being Jewish I expect Blakely felt entirely at home in this atmosphere – the bustle of commerce and trade – I was beginning to rather like it myself. I wondered why Ignatius Shore had never mentioned that his partner was Jewish. Did he know? Perhaps it didn't matter. Perhaps Blakely was so crypto-Jewish, he had hidden his Jewishness from even his partner.

I decided to buy some tulip bulbs for a window box at my Gillygate home. Holland, after all, was renowned throughout the world for her tulips. I was standing talking to the stallholder in broken Dutch as I got out my money to pay, when I felt a tug at my sleeve. I looked down. A dusty street urchin was standing waist high at my side. He pushed a piece of tightly balled up newspaper into my hand.

'Van Hayek,' he said and was gone.

"Van Hayek?" – from Hayek – it took me awhile to register he meant the old man I had just visited. I took my bag of tulips and paper cutting to a nearby bench beside the Amstel. Although it was Sunday, some bigger barges were still plying their trade up and down the river. The Amstel gave its name to Amsterdam and is the biggest waterway running through the city. It was a fitting venue for what I was about to learn.

LICHAAM VAN MAN GEVONDEN IN DE AMSTEL

Relying on my limited Dutch, I gleaned from the *De Telegraaf* cutting that a man's body had been recently recovered from the Amstel. Why had Hayek Groot sent the boy to find me with this? I had not mentioned to old Groot that I was looking for a missing man. The Amstel looked black. I realised once you fell in there was no means of escape: no steps, no lifebelts and the stone sides were perpendicular and high. Suddenly, I was hit with a terrible foreboding. I immediately got to my feet. After several enquiries I was directed to the nearest police station in the Jonas Daniel Meijerplein.

The Politie were not blessed with officers fluent in English. However they did look official if jaded in their tired blue uniforms. The cloth did not appear to be of the same quality as their British counterparts, indeed in places blue was turning to grey. But it was the badge on their helmets that caught my attention – the three crosses of Andreas, the insignia of Amsterdam.

After half an hour's wait, one of the boys in faded blue informed me that they had finally located an interpreter, a superior officer with many years service who was involved with the body in the Amstel case.

'Inspector Hugo van Meegeren.' The inspector clicked his heels.

'James Cairn from England. Pleased to meet you.' I gave him a curt little bow in complimentary Prussian fashion.

'So, what can I do for James Cairn from England?'

'I have come about the drowned man fished out of the Amstel.' I told him. 'When was his body recovered?'

'The day before yesterday.'

'Have you identified the man yet? Do you know his nationality?'

'No, to both questions. We found no means of identification on him.'

'No personal papers in his pockets?'

'None.'

'Do you not think that rather strange?'

'Suicides sometimes just want to disappear.'

'You do not suspect foul play then?'

'There was nothing to suggest that. No marks on the body, no bruises or suchlike.'

'Where is the body now? In the public mortuary?'

'The what?'

'The mortuary, the place you keep bodies before burial.'

'We do not have such places in Holland. The deceased is being kept in hospital.'

'What hospital?'

'The New Jewish Hospital. There is no other hospital in central Amsterdam.'

'Would it be possible for me to see the body?'

'Do you think you might know him?' The inspector looked more interested. I nodded. 'Then you might be able to make a formal identification and clear this matter up once and for all. I will accompany you to the hospital, if I may.'

'One hundred and twelve, Nieuwe Keizersgracht,' Van Meegeren told the cab driver.

The New Jewish Hospital resembled what the Americans would call a tenement house. It was a plain building with high chimneys and occupied a gable end in a block of other residencies.

We were greeted in the hall by a starched lady in a nurses uniform. She seemed unimpressed even by Van Meegeren's splendid helmet. 'Hoe kan ik helpen?' she asked.

'Het verdronkene lichaam,' replied Van Meegeren. I was glad he had come with me after all. 'Commissaris Van Raalte verzendt zijn achting.'

She shrugged and led us up and down corridors as white as her apron.

'What did you say to her?' I asked Van Meegeren, puffing with tension.

'I asked her to show us the body and told her that Commissioner Van Raalte sends her his regards.'

'Van Raalte?'

'Mr E. W. van Raalte is our elderly Jewish police commissioner. You seem surprised, Mr Cairn.'

'In England the police force is not a favourite Jewish calling. Doctors, barristers, solicitors, yes.'

'Do you realise the police station you have just visited in the square is in honour of the first Jewish solicitor to qualify in Holland? – Jonas Daniel Meijer.'

'Really?'

'Yes, really. And what is your profession, Mr Cairn?'

'I'm a barrister.'

'So, if this man is who you think he is, what is your relationship to him?'

'A colleague.'

'A colleague,' repeated Van Meegeren. He looked relieved. This suited him fine: no embarrassing emotional outbursts usually from just a colleague.

Without ceremony, the starched nurse pulled back the sheet covering the body. The eyes stared emptiness from the bloodless face. The head was bloated like a blown up football, the head was bald.

'Mortimer Blakely,' I sighed.

'Are you sure?' Van Meegeren asked. I nodded. I no longer possessed enough energy for words. 'He's a Jew too, I see.'

'Yes, he's in the right place,' I sighed. Da Silva had been right all along. Even though corpulent and bloated by canal water, Mortimer Blakely had obviously been circumcised.

How will I tell Ignatius Shore? How will I tell Amelia? Was all I could think of when I got back to the police station in Jonas Daniel Meijerplein to fill in a statement.

'Tell me, Mr Cairn, what business brought your colleague to Amsterdam?'

'Shoes,' I said. Shoes was the first thing that came into my head.

'By shoes, do you mean clogs?'

'That's right, Mr Blakely was here to buy industrial clogs.' For the life of me I do not know why I invented this deceit. I was lying on instinct.

'An unfortunate accident,' said Van Meegeren.

'Or someone pushed him.'

'There is no proof of that. Perhaps Mr Blakely had a little too much to drink one evening and then plopped into the cold water.'

Blakely had been pulled out of the Amstel early on Friday morning. I arranged for Blakely to be buried at the Orthodox Ashkenazi Cemetery at Zeeburg on the outskirts of the city. Now the body had been identified, it could be buried forthwith in accordance with Jewish tradition.

* * * * *

'Plop! – into the cold water. Was that how it happened?'

'What's that you said?' asked Tom de Vries, pouring the wine. I made no effort to reply. I did not know who I could trust anymore. 'How can I put this, you seem a little preoccupied this evening, James?'

'It's nothing.' I said. Adding benignly, 'I bought a bag of tulips today.'

'Tulips, you have to be so careful what dealer you buy them from.'

'It was a stallholder in Waterlooplein Market.'

'Waterlooplein, so that is where you found yourself today.'

'It was about the only place open for business.'

'Yes, it would be,' replied Tom thoughtfully. 'Do you know, James, in the middle of the seventeenth century tulip mad Calvinists would pay more for a single bulb than the price of a house.'

'You are a mine of information regarding Dutch history for an American.'

'A Dutch American.'

'Sorry, I was forgetting.'

'Ah, the famous *snert*, pea soup,' said Tom, as we eyed the steaming dishes the waiter placed before us.

The soup was heavy. The strongest flavours to hit my senses were celery, pork and of course green split peas. I hardly had space left for the Friesland beef. Tom seemed to cope better with his *Boerenkoolstamppot* with *rookworst*, mashed potatoes and kale with sausage. We said very little as we tucked in. Apart from our shared love of art, discussions on which we had soon exhausted, we seemed to have little in common. Tom the family man was a matter-of-fact American whereas I – well, what am I?

I was pleased to say goodnight to Tom before the gulf between us widened. I think I saw relief on his face too. There is nothing sadder than two men thrown together with little in common attempting to connect.

Walking back across the congested waterways between the hotels Prins Hendrik and Victoria, I marvelled at how alive the water was with boats even at that late hour while the streets above were relatively empty. The only quiet piece of water was the landlocked rectangle of the Damrak itself. Forgotten now, here was once the medieval city's busiest canal until it was partly filled in, cutting it off from the river Amstel and the fish markets of Dam Square. I decided to get the most out of the evening left to me and follow the Damrak's old course to the Amstel and the famous Blue Bridge.

Whereas my (what Tom would term) "commuter" area round the Centraal was dead at night, in contrast Dam Square was fizzing with life and youth. While tempted to join one of these Dutch al fresco parties, a greater incentive was to see the bridge before I returned home I decided that my time in Amsterdam had become limited. I must give my appalling news to Amelia and Ignatius Shore in person as soon as possible, there was no other way.

I cannot deny I was still enjoying sucking up the ambience of this cosmopolitan city, while the image of poor Blakely was never far from my mind. Particularly, as I stared down into the Amstel from the Blue Bridge. Even if it had been an accident – even if Mortimer Blakely had been a strong swimmer – again, I could see no way of getting out of this river alive once you had fallen into it.

Absorbed in what was a terrifying thought for a non-swimmer, I was slow to recognise a presence at my side. A tall man, a very Dutch looking man with long, blond unkempt hair had sidled up to me. He had a rather dissipated look about him. He seemed familiar but I could not quite place him.

'Hello, Mr Cairn, do you remember me?'

'I'm not sure that I do.'

'The Portsmouth train, the mix up over our briefcases.'

'Who are you? What do you want?'

'You've been asking a lot of questions, Mr Cairn, too many questions. You've even been seen in the company of Jew boys.'

'So, what's that to you?' I asked, suddenly riven with fear.

'Everything.' Briefcase Man calmly lit a cigar – a cigar from a yellow packet – though the two packets were similar this was not a Justus van Maurik but a Sumatra leafed Balmoral, I was in no doubt. He blew a cloud of smoke into my face.

'Hello, James.' Another voice.

I was put into shadow by a giant standing between me and the gaslight on the bridge. I spun round to see this second man's face. It was the giant Grutte Pier from Rotterdam.

'Derk, what on earth…?'

He did not answer me. Instead he grabbed and pinned my arms behind my back with his giant paws. 'Leeg zijn zakken,' he told Briefcase Man.

As Briefcase Man began to empty my pockets of money and identity, my whole life ran before me. Perhaps this is how death comes in a dream. This is how Mortimer Blakely must have met his end at the hands of these two cowardly rogues – the modus operandi was the same – the coincidence too great. And, of course, one man would not have been able to tip a big man like Blakely over the bridge's parapet and into the water, but two men and one a giant. All my bulk and rugby training came to nought against this. I had to think of a more subtle ruse to save my life, give something a try.

'I have left word with Inspector Hugo van Meegeren at the police station in the Jonas Daniel Meijerplein that if something should happen to me.'

'Shut up,' said Briefcase Man. Derk just laughed and pushed me closer towards the side of the bridge.

Out of my eye corner I could see Briefcase Man's pointed ears were pricked up like a fox. I sensed Derk behind me looking right and left, checking that no one else was about. I did not want to die. I was not ready to die. I braced every muscle in my body against being tipped over that parapet into the Amstel. How ironic was this when I had had a lifetime's fear of water.

Derk hesitated. I could hear and feel running feet vibrating along the bridge from the far end. Derk loosened his grip. Now I was determined not to die.

'Let him go, let him go,' someone was screaming.

Derk and Briefcase Man seemed paralysed at first. I jabbed two fingers into Briefcase Man's eyes. He screeched like a cat before bounding away. That is when Tom de Vries swung at Derk with the crushing force of a professional left hook. Nothing was held back in Tom's punch. Derk's sizable jaw cracked as he was felled to the ground. Stunned for a moment, he struggled and scrabbled to get to his feet like a clawing crab. Tom gave him a kick on the backside to help him on his way as he made off after his cohort who, from his speed of flight, must have been well on his way towards Rembrandtplein by then.

'Those two men killed the man I came here to find.' Was the first thing I gasped at De Vries.

'I know.'

'How do you know?'

De Vries leaned forward on the parapet and looked down to the river. 'I'm sorry, James, I was too late to protect Blakely.'

'You knew about him?'

De Vries nodded. 'He was followed as soon as he stepped off the boat in Rotterdam.'

'As I presume I was.'

Again De Vries nodded. 'Although tonight was pure chance as you had told me you were going straight back to your hotel. According to you, you should have been tucked up in bed by now.'

'I changed my mind.'

'Oh! I know that.' De Vries grimaced, rubbing his knuckles pointedly.

'Luckily for me.'

'Yes, luckily for you, as soon as you left the Prins Hendrik I decided to have a cigarette outside. I watched you looking down into the Damrak and when you moved off I realised you were not alone. You had company.'

'Where did that punch come from?'

'I was the middle-weight champion of Utrecht in my youth.'

'Not Baltimore then?'

'No, but I have spent time in America.'

'You are not a shoe manufacturer either, are you?'

'No, but everything will be explained later.'

'How can I ever thank you?' I asked, as my legs began to buckle under me. 'You definitely saved my life. Those men meant business.'

Tom de Vries shrugged and shook out another French cigarette from his packet. 'Those men are in the killing business. Come, I am in need of a coffee as I am sure you are. A friend of mine has opened a new cafe, De Kroon, in Rembrandtplein. I am sure he will oblige us even at this late hour.'

De Kroon had atmosphere. Although Tom's friend was on the point of closing, he made us a wonderful coffee equalled only by the one I had for breakfast at the Queen's Hotel in Rotterdam.

'You English have no idea how to make coffee,' boasted Tom.

'You must have been to England then. Recently?' I asked.

Tom laughed at this. 'Not very subtle, James.'

'You said Mortimer Blakely and I were followed ever since we got off the ferry in Rotterdam. Why and by whom?'

'Various agencies will have been monitoring your movements. You must understand, James, your country is at war with the Dutch in Africa. My government does not like any financial repercussions this war might bring.'

'For the diamond industry?'

'Yes, diamonds are part of it. As I think perhaps your friend, Da Silva, has already told you hardly any British diamonds are getting through to Dutch sight-holders at present.'

'Then perhaps the Boer should not have laid siege to Kimberley.'

'Or the Jameson party made an incursion into the Transvaal. But you are not listening to me, James, I said hardly any "British" diamonds are getting through.'

'But Dutch ones are? Van Grunsven diamonds are?'

'Correct. Van Grunsven & Co. is one of the few African mines still in Dutch hands.'

'I know all about that.'

'I know you do.'

'What I don't know is how the hell you first identified me on that rainy day outside my hotel?'

'Yes, I haven't quite forgiven you for that. I got soaked waiting for the Englishman to emerge from the Victoria wearing Church shoes.'

'So, it really was the shoes. But why so much interest in me? I am not a spy nor am I a government agent.'

'It isn't you personally who is being targeted, James. Nor was Blakely.'

'But two Dutchmen have just tried to murder me and they succeeded with Blakely. One of them followed me from Rotterdam, the other I recognised from England. How can you say Blakely and I were not targeted?'

'There are so many different interests involved here. The picture is extremely complicated, international. I think your friend Blakely was killed because he discovered something in Waterlooplein. They attempted to murder you fearing you were on the point of making the same discovery.'

'Are you saying this is a Jewish plot?'

'No, I am not saying that at all. But I am warning you that somehow, through some connection, you have been drawn into a dangerous game between two different radical factions who will stop at nothing to achieve their aims. Have you ever heard the story of Lieutenant Van Speyk, James? He threw a light or lighted cigar into a gunpowder barrel rather than let the Belgians take his ship. To most Dutchmen he is a hero. I think he should have avoided such a situation in the first place.'

'So, whose side are *you* on?'

'Oh, like Van Speyk, I am very much for Holland.'

'More coffee?' offered De Kroon's proprietor, obviously wanting to close.

'Regards to Sir Clive Bampton should you bump into him in England,' was Tom de Vries' parting shot to me outside the Victoria Hotel.

'You know Sir Clive?'

'Tread carefully, my friend.' He began to walk away.

'But what about those men who have just tried to kill me?' I shouted after him.

'James, you need not worry about those two gentlemen anymore.'

Chapter Twenty-Seven

The pebble that young Erasmus Jacobs innocently found on the shore of the Orange river has led to this.

I deliberately had not told Tom de Vries, or whatever his name really was, about my appointment with Victor Toledano on the Weesperstraat. I suspected Tom was a Dutch government agent but then what was Sir Clive Bampton, and how did Tom know him? I was determined to get to the bottom of Mortimer Blakely's death now, now I knew the detective had definitely been murdered.

If this wasn't a Dutch Jewish plot to gain a monopoly on African diamonds, what was it then? Somehow I had to get to the Van Grunsvens here in Amsterdam. I felt they held the key to everything. I had Jacob da Silva's letter of introduction in my pocket. Victor Toledano and the Van Grunsvens were at the end of his list of contacts.

'Mr Cairn, I was expecting you.' Victor Toledano spoke fluent English. Da Silva had told me that Toledano had spent a year or two with the diamond traders of London.

'But how?'

'Word gets round this area faster than the plague.'

I offered him Da Silva's letter of introduction.

'No need for that,' he said, waving away the letter in my hand.

'So, how is trade?'

'No good diamonds are coming through,' complained Toledano. His small office was dusty in an equally dusty diamond factory on 45A Weesperstraat. He put a small magnifying loupe to his eye. 'See, this is a clean five carat diamond, I have not seen the like in months.'

'My word. Five carob seeds. One carob seed roughly equals nought point two grams, does it not?'

'You know about this old method of weighing, I'm impressed.'

Because of the excellent way the stone had been cut, it was a jewel of many subtle colours. I looked down on Toledano's production floor and marvelled at how such a work of art had emerged from this down at heel enterprise.

I nodded at the sparkling gem still held between Toledano's thumb and forefinger. 'How on earth do you begin to cut that, dare to cut it?' I asked him. I was becoming genuinely fascinated by diamonds, perhaps if I had been rich enough they could have replaced my passion for palaeontology.

'It is a process of splitting, cutting and polishing. Diamonds have a crystal structure that is layered. I have to study carefully to know the best places at which to cleave it to get most use out of the rough stone. One bad stroke with the cleaving blade and the stone will shatter. Another method we occasionally use is sawing with this taut wire covered in diamond powder and oil. Then my men polish by hand, this takes time, much time. *Voilà* – a perfect brilliant cut diamond.' He briefly held the stone up to the window before stooping down to place it in a safe under his desk. 'Shush!' he said, lifting his finger dramatically to his lips. 'I have heard a whisper around the city that Joseph Asscher is working on an entirely revolutionary cut. But then, my friend, does any of this matter?' Toledano flung his hands out in appeal. 'When our brothers in London are not sending us diamonds.'

'Well, perhaps…' I began.

'Puh!' interrupted Toledano. 'Here in Amsterdam we workers now have a trade union and there is an association of diamond traders, but tell me, Mister, what good are they if there are no diamonds?'

'Aren't you getting Van Grunsven diamonds?'

'Ah! Van Grunsvens.' Toledano raised his thick black eyebrows – curtains on a stage – again lifting his hands emphatically. 'We have had a few pique two stones packages from them.'

'"Pique two"?'

'An inferior grade. Very difficult to deal with, distinct inclusions. Better for small stone production. For some reason Van Grunsvens seem to be holding their best stones back. I do not understand why. With this war in Africa, I would have thought now was the time for Van Grunsvens to grab the market. But no, they seem to be holding back. Maybe by holding back they think the price of diamonds will explode. Maybe they have learnt this from your Cecil Rhodes. Don't get me wrong, Van Grunsvens are supplying but the quality of stone is not good.'

'This is news to me. I understood that the Van Grunsvens dealt in exclusive diamonds for exclusive markets.'

'No, that rumour is untrue.'

'Perhaps their seams are exhausted. Perhaps they are hoping the Boer will win the war. Saving their diamonds and guilder to take over British mines.'

'No, I don't think so. You will win. It is as if they are, as you English say, waiting for "the rainy day" that might never come.'

'Are they Sephardi?'

'They are Sephardi. I am Sephardi. Sephardi, Ashkenazi, what has that to do with anything when it comes to business?' I smiled. I could hear the echoing sentiments of Benjamin Levi.

'Could you give me directions to the Van Grunsvens' house?' Da Silva had given me an address in the Plantage. But how did I get from here to there, I wondered. I was beginning to lose my bearings in more senses than one.

'Don't worry,' said Toledano. 'We have so little business on at present I will take you there myself.'

'No, no, I wouldn't dream…' I was surprised and taken aback. Why would Toledano want to accompany me to a supplier who was not supplying him properly?

'Zeeman! Zeeman!' he screamed to his foreman. 'U neemt over.'

We left the deprivations and decay of Waterlooplein, Jodenbreestraat and Weesperstraat to walk into another world. We left the bustling cramped life in these areas – which I rather liked – for the spaciousness of parkland and large daunting houses. The Van Grunsvens lived a mile or so beyond the New Jewish Hospital where I had viewed Mortimer Blakely's body.

Victor Toledano said very little on our journey, until we walked through the big iron gates of a baroque mansion: 'Our big fear is, Mr Cairn, that once this war is over Britain will regard us as Boer sympathisers and refuse to let us manufacture her diamonds.'

'Well, aren't you? Aren't you Boer sympathisers? You are supplying them with volunteers, ambulances and God knows what.'

'Puh! Ambulances. And don't you think those poor farmers need them? When they are fighting with sticks against the might of the British army.'

'I think many of them are armed with more than sticks.'

'War, we Jews have no time for war. War is wasted time. Haven't you heard we are only interested in making money?' Again this Dutch Sephardim spoke with all the matching irony of Benjamin Levi. Countries and centuries of different experiences might separate them but they are still one people, I noted.

It suddenly struck me why would these people send out two Gentile thugs to murder – to drown one of their own – one of the tribe? None of this made sense. However, walking down Van Grunsvens' long drive through a ceremonial guard of lifeless statues, I suddenly felt convinced that I was closing in on the truth.

"There is something you should know about the Van Grunsvens, Mr Cairn, before you go in there.' Toledano blinked nervously. 'That rumour you heard was partly true. The biggest part of their business isn't their African mine, it is trading in high quality diamonds. They have a long heritage as Court Jews, Jews who regulated the traffic of rough diamonds from London to Amsterdam and then distributed the finished article to the royal courts of Europe. Today they trade in flawless diamonds, or at least nothing short of V.V.S. stones, stones with very, very small inclusions. The Van Grunsvens trade all over the world. Sorry, I lied to you. But Van Grunsven & Co. hardly mine anything these days. You were right in supposing their seams are almost dry. But in addition to that, this war in Africa is killing their main trading business, killing all our businesses.' Toledano turned to leave as two men, doubling up as footmen but looking more like wrestlers, skipped down the villa steps to meet me. 'Sorry, Mr Cairn,' muttered Toledano for a final time.

The two pugilists escorted me into a magnificent drawing room. Smaller than the salon at Bampton Hall but equally sumptuous in decoration. In every alcove, adorning every shelf, there was a porcelain figurine of exquisite quality. I wished George Hobb was with me to see this.

'Mr Cairn, we finally meet.' A cultured accented voice rose from behind one wing of a high-backed winged armchair. The armchair was tastefully upholstered in colourful satin. I walked round for a better view. In the midst of all this finery sat a tiny figure, wizened, slightly curled. A frizz of long white hair contrasted with the red, gold and green floral fabric.

'How do you know who I am?'

'Toledano. He was pre-warned yesterday to expect a visit.'

'Hayek Groot?'

'Ask questions in the Waterlooplein and it does not take long for word to reach us here in the Plantage. Even the elderly know what is good for them. Who puts the bread in their mouths.'

'I know your son, Arnon van Grunsven,' I said by way of introduction.

'Then you should know Arnon is not my son. He is the son of my late brother. Take a seat, Mr Cairn, and forgive me for not rising. I have experienced weakness of the legs recently.' Arnon's uncle pointed to a matching winged chair near the hearth. 'Tamir, some pastries for our guest,' he told one of the pugilists. The other one remained standing guarding the door. 'Now how can I help you, Mr Cairn?'

'Mortimer Blakely.'

'Mortimer who?'

'Blakely.'

'Am I supposed to know this man?'

'He was drowned a few days ago in the Amstel.'

'I am sorry to hear that. Was he a fellow countryman of yours?'

'And yours,' I told Arnon's uncle bluntly.

'You mean he was a Jew.'

'I mean just that, and he was murdered.'

'By whom?' asked the old man. I did not attempt to answer but watched for the slightest change in his expression. There wasn't so much as a guilty twitch. 'By me?' he cackled in disbelief. 'You think I murdered this Blakely? Why should I murder him?'

'He had found something out about Van Grunsven & Co. Something you didn't want the world to know,' I suggested.

'Now what could that be?' The blue, the surprisingly blue eyes sparkled with mischief.

'That is what I want you to tell me.'

The old man placed his gnarled hands beneath the rug covering his lap. Tamir's arrival with a tray of tea and pastries gave him an excuse not to answer. Tamir passed us both cups of milk-less tea. For a big man he was surprisingly delicate.

'Baklava, dipped in syrup and honey,' offered Van Grunsven. 'Perhaps a ma'amoul filled with dates, walnuts and cinnamon might be more to your liking.'

I could not resist trying one of the small ma'amouls cakes. It was sweet and spicy, I had never tasted anything like it back in England. Van Grunsven observed me cat-like. I began to feel like Adam taking the forbidden fruit. He took out his pocket watch and checked the time with the quarter chime of a porcelain carriage clock on a nearby table. Van Grunsven obviously was a collector of everything porcelain.

'What time is it?' I asked.

'A quarter to two.' This knowledge somehow seemed to empower Van Grunsven even more. 'I believe my nephew has closer friends than you in England, more powerful political friends.'

'So, he has mentioned my name to you?'

'Arnon tells me everything.'

'Did he tell you about his girlfriend who died recently?'

'Arnon has many girl friends.'

'Lucy Alexander was a particularly intelligent and gifted woman.'

'"Alexander", I take it she was not of the faith.' Van Grunsven gave a dismissive sigh. 'Arnon would never have married her.'

'Tell me more about these powerful political friends of Arnon's in England.' I took a sip of tea to demonstrate to Van Grunsven that I was still at ease and unafraid.

'There are many here in Holland who believe in total allegiance to their country as well.' Again the old man checked his watch. 'I can see no harm in telling you now. Did you hear of the major strike of diamond workers we had in Amsterdam about six years ago? It and their demands nearly brought our industry to its knees. Now all these workers are members of the ANDB, Algemeene Nederlandsche Diamantbewerkers Bond, the diamond workers' trade union. Socialism is becoming a curse among our people as I hear it is with the artisan class in your country. That and this war in Africa is destroying our country. If your country wins this war, the diamond industry in Amsterdam could be ruined forever. You British are all liberal imperialists at heart. I despise you for it, just as much as I despise socialism. People in business want to see political strength not weakness.'

'So these English friends of Arnon's believe in exclusive nationalism,' I persisted.

Beads of sweat had begun to form on his wrinkled upper lip. Again he checked the time before hissing, 'They are growing and eventually you will know them as the Brotherhood.'

I could not believe the spiel I was hearing spouting out of the mouth of this foolish old man. 'You do realise, Mr Van Grunsven, that you are talking about an extremely dangerous organisation?'

'I'm talking about people who are prepared to help Arnon and our trading interests. I am not long for this world but I want to leave a business worthy of the name for Arnon to take over.'

'But these people hate Jews. They want to rid our country of Jews.'

'Only poor Jews, socialist Jews who add nothing to your economy,' objected Van Grunsven.

'It was these same anti-Semites who killed Blakely, wasn't it?'

'I do not know who killed Blakely. I do not want to know.'

'Then you are an ostrich, sir, with the misguided belief that these men share your ideals. Are you going to allow them to silence me too?'

'That will not be necessary,' said Van Grunsven coldly.

'Or compromise me?'

'It is well past two o'clock. You are already compromised, Mr Cairn.' From beneath his rug, Van Grunsven drew out an ancient pistol – lethal looking despite its age – and pointed it with shaking hands at my face. Out of my eye corner, I saw Tamir straighten a little at the door. 'Now we wait,' said Van Grunsven.

I looked round, away. Tamir and his friend, guarding my escape, stood motionless like the statues in Van Grunsven's garden. For a second time in Holland, I was sure I was about to die. I felt like someone finally about to be ejected from the party of life.

'*Rat-tat…*!' I nearly jumped out of my skin. We all jumped and ducked. I was sure Van Grunsven had pulled the trigger. '*Rat-tat-tat*!' – again and again. No, someone was hammering on the front door. *Boom*! *Crack*! It now sounded as if a tree trunk had been taken to the door. Tamir and his friend ran out to investigate. Next came the sound of scuffles and moans. Tamir and friend did not return. For the first time that afternoon Van Grunsven's shrunken mouth fell.

'Mr Cairn, fancy finding you here.' Inspector Hugo van Meegeren stood in the middle of the room wearing a sarcastic expression on his face. His impressive helmet was slightly knocked askew. Apart from when Tom de Vries had saved my life on the Blue Bridge, I had never been so glad to see anyone in my entire life. A posse of policemen stood behind him.

'How did you know I was being forcibly detained here?'

'I didn't.' Van Meegeren turned to Van Grunsven. Van Grunsven had concealed the pistol back under his rug. I was about to enlighten Van Meegeren to the fact, when the inspector announced to the old man that 'Arnon is dood'.

Van Grunsven seemed to curl up tighter in his winged armchair, trying to hold himself together. He looked more like a foetus than a man. 'When?' he wheezed more than whispered. 'How?'

'Two o' clock. We have just received a telegram from England. Arnon was shot dead on the steps of the London Stock Exchange. It appears he was about to detonate a bomb. Did you know anything about this, Joseph?'

'I knew nothing.' It was obvious Van Grunsven was lying.

'Nevertheless, I will need to take a full statement from you later, Joseph,' insisted Van Meegeren, looking questioningly across at me. He and I knew it would take my evidence to pursue a prosecution against Joseph van Grunsven. The old man had held me at gun point against my will but at the same time he had lost his heir, and it was obvious that he was dying. I wanted to go home.

Escorted by a young policeman, I was relieved to walk away from the mansion of misconceived dreams. Outside in the parkland, a man tipped his cap to me from behind a statue of Hermes. I looked hard at the face beneath the Dutch peak. It was Tom de Vries.

'Have a safe journey home, James Cairn,' he shouted.

As I hurried on I heard the report of a pistol shot from the mansion behind. I knew straightaway that Joseph must have taken his own life. I looked back to Hermes. There was no one there.

Chapter Twenty-Eight

Despite my misadventures in Amsterdam, I considered it a lovely and interesting city. It was with some sadness that I said farewell to the languid curve of the Herengracht, before throwing my bouquet of flowers into the Amstel in memory of Mortimer Blakely.

Thankfully, the return ferry crossing back from Rotterdam to Hull was smoother than my arrival. Nevertheless, I found myself haunted by the story of Barney Barnato who had "slipped overboard" off Madeira. I, too, was returning to my homeland with possibly dangerous information about the great and the good. I kept looking over my shoulder. Arnon van Grunsven and his uncle were dead, but the Brotherhood was very much alive and I still did not know who was involved in England. I am sure the Jew-hating Brotherhood had set Arnon on his fateful path, promising him support in his bombing campaign but really intending to discredit him – discredit all Jews as murderers – once he had succeeded. I would not have been at all surprised if the Brotherhood had murdered Lucy Alexander. She knew too much and I am sure she would not have approved of Arnon's violent intentions. But then who had shot Arnon before he completed his mission? It would have suited the Brotherhood for him to have blown the Stock Exchange to smithereens. "Reasonable" public opinion would soon have turned against the Jews.

Many voices began to play in my head.

"The Jewish community has the apparatus for dealing with their own," the words of Benjamin Levi. I wondered was it the Jews themselves who had foiled the Van Grunsven plot.

"This operation is being conducted at the highest level, Mr Cairn," the words of the monocled assassin.

"Regards to Sir Clive should you bump into him in England," Tom de Vries had made a point of saying. Sir Clive Bampton – powerful and political – again I looked over my left shoulder only to be met by the smile from a pretty girl under a French parasol.

* * * * *

The day before his trial, George Hobb arrived in York carrying a letter to me from the noble Sir himself. Another paper cutting from Amsterdam's *De Telegraaf*. The accompanying letter gave no comment just a simple translation on the rich note paper bearing the Bampton crest.

TWO MALE BODIES PULLED OUT OF THE HERENGRACHT

Two men died following a tragic accident, when a horse bolted and fell into the Herengracht, pulling its cab and passengers behind it. The cab driver, Mr Jan Petersen, managed to jump off his vehicle before it entered the water. Through the quick actions of two boatmen, the horse was cut from its harness. The horse was later recovered alive from the canal by a crane. The two men who drowned within the cab have yet to be identified.

"James, you need not worry about those two gentlemen anymore." Tom de Vries' words came back to haunt me. Through non-judicial means – means I did not believe in Mortimer Blakely's drowning had been avenged. Briefcase Man and Derk from Rotterdam were dead, I was sure of that now. I wondered if Derk had been his real name: Derk in old German means the people's ruler. What was even more strange was the fact that Sir Clive Bampton felt no further explanation was necessary Sir Clive was no longer attempting to conceal that he was heavily implicated in this affair.

Too many people had died. Too many people had been hurt. I will never forget the scene in Low Petergate when I had to tell Amelia that her brother would not be coming home, tell Ignatius Shore that his partner was dead.

* * * * *

Making history. It was the final Monday of the old Lenten Assizes. A condition of Hobb's bail had been that he would spend the night prior to the trial in the Castle Gaol. Husband poisoners, horse stealers, child murderers and now a clergyman whose only crime was his love of wearing dresses – George followed them all on that long walk across the expanse from prison to the courthouse. He would be the last ordinary citizen accused of a "serious crime" ever to make that walk. Within months the Castle was about to close as a civil prison to become a military one.

All right for some! The two prison warders accompanying Hobb told him that the governor, Edwin Taylor, would be moving to Northallerton Gaol at the end of July. George hoped, as he dragged his feet those last fifty yards, that he would not already be there awaiting the arrival of Taylor.

He paused a moment before the courthouse entrance. The two warders allowed him a moment to reflect on the life that had brought him to this. They knew the Reverend was an "old poof" but they liked him. He spoke well.

Yesterday, Robert Brown had shown him the layout of the courtroom and explained some of the procedures to expect. On their way out, Brown had told George all about the pediment on the 18th century courthouse above them, told him the meaning of the carved laurel wreath, fasces and staff. The fasces dated back to ancient Rome and consisted of a bundle of birch rods and an axe bound together with leather bands. The fasces symbolised authority – George did not have a very high opinion of authority and had often found its power corrupting. The staff supported on its end a Phrygian cap, symbolising liberty – now George could do with some of that. Brown had said that these emblems were widely used in the previous century in America and post-revolution France.

George's imagination moved on, as he moved towards his fate between the two warders. He shivered at the thought of all those pale victims bowed beneath the guillotine. *We'll do our best to avoid the blade* – that time had come – George felt his legs giving away beneath him.

The two warders supported him up the steps into the dock. An array of strange faces lifted to greet them from the well of court. The two warders were used to prisoners getting the shakes like music hall stars on their first night.

I turned and saw George Hobb's face appear above the hand rail of the dock. I have never seen a living man so pale. There was a slight tremor to his proud chin. He looked expectantly towards me. I took out the gold locket he had given me to identify his daughter should she choose to attend his trial. I carefully checked the likeness with the bursting to capacity public benches above. No one up there was a match for Helena. So much so, I wondered how on earth Hobb had ever spawned such a beautiful creature. Displaying the locket in my open palm, I shook my head. Hobb's chin dropped to his chest.

A bloody good start this is, I thought.

Eustace Frere nodded pleasantly across from his station to mine. We were about to lock horns over a cause célèbre that could make or break either of our careers.

'All rise,' shouted the clerk of assize.

The full form of Mr Justice Summer walked out on to his elevated dais in a cardinal scarlet gown. But Summer was no cardinal and his countenance reflected no light. The courtroom fell silent. This judge was unknown to me. He was not the usual judiciary of the North Eastern Circuit. Carlton-Bingham said he was a judge from the capital whose parents loved the seasons. Despite taking up a considerable amount of space on the bench, where ever he came from Augustus Summer looked impressive.

'George Hobb, you are charged on indictment that on the twenty-second of May, 1899, you solicited, procured and committed an abominable and detestable crime against nature. Are you guilty or not guilty?' asked the clerk of assize.

The courtroom gasped into life. There was a buzz particularly on the press benches.

'God, they are intending to make an example of this poor old sod after Wilde,' said one of the journalists from the local *Evening Press*.

'Sod, being the appropriate word,' replied a wit from the *Evening News*. Saul Winlock was a journalist from London whom I knew only by reputation.

'Silence!' screamed Summer, already outraged by those he took to be unruly northern rustics.

'Are you guilty or not guilty?' repeated the clerk of assize.

'Not guilty,' whispered Hobb.

'Speak up. What is your plea?' bullied Summer.

'Not guilty.' Hobb calmly lifted his voice without losing face.

'Members of the jury, the prisoner at the bar, George Hobb, is indicted and the charge against him is…' The clerk of assize's little moustache rose and fell with relish and self-importance. He was a weasel of a man.

I was hardly listening to the indictment made against my client, I knew it off by heart already. I was more concerned about how Hobb would stand up to all this. Rather like a surgeon wondering if his weakened patient would survive the knife.

'What proof have they? Where is the proof?' hissed Trotter.

Swan-necked Eustace Frere slid gracefully to his feet. 'May it please your lordship, members of the jury, I am the prosecutor in this case. Regrettably, there are some extremely distasteful aspects to this crime that we will be forced to confront.' Frere fastidiously smoothed his gown with a slender finger as if he was smoothing away the unpalatable. He had the sort of hands that my client might covert – women's hands.

'Yes,' said Summer. 'Should any gentlemen up there on the public benches not wish their wives', sisters' or daughters' delicate ears to be contaminated by the filth they might be about to hear in this courtroom, then I suggest they escort them out now.'

There was a clearing of throats, a stir and shuffling of positions but nobody made a move. Hobb looked across at me again, beseeching, desperate. If all women were ejected from the court, Helena might be barred from coming in.

'If that isn't prejudicial against our case, nothing is,' muttered Trotter.

'My lord,' I objected.

Summer lifted a finger to his lips to silence me. 'You will be able to put your client's case soon enough, Mr Cairn. Please continue,' he instructed Frere.

'What is this, Frere and Summer, the pantomime act?' hissed the serpent at my ear once more.

'Shush! It will be you who kills this case for us,' I warned Trotter. 'Anyway, I didn't think you had much sympathy for Hobb.'

'I don't have any truck with his dressing up in frocks, if that's what you mean.'

'The Crown intends to prove that on the evening of Whit Monday, the twenty-second of May, 1899, the Reverend George Hobb was seen attempting to importune other men for immoral purposes in York city centre. So bizarre and offensive was Hobb's behaviour that evening, both inside and outside the Star public house on Stonegate which he visited as a customer, he caused a riot and the police were called. Prior to this riot, to his visit to the public house, we have evidence that the prisoner had on more than one occasion been successful in his wicked designs. Permit me to call that evidence before you.'

'What evidence are they talking about, sir?' asked Trotter, looking down the witness list.

'No idea,' I shrugged.

'Call William Tuck! Call William Tuck!' Rang down the corridors of justice before a heavy tread could be heard creaking the wooden floorboards of the court.

'He's the landlord of the Star pub, I know him well,' murmured Trotter.

The clerk of assize held out the Holy Book towards one of Tuck's large red hands, hands more used to rolling out barrels than pressing the bible.

'I swear by Almighty God that the evidence I shall give shall be the truth, the whole truth and nothing but the truth...' King Athelstan's Anglo-Saxon oath echoed across the centuries.

Frere stood, hands on lapel-less gown like a competent headmaster taking control. 'Mr Tuck, you own a public house in Stonegate, do you not?'

'I do, sir.' Tuck puffed out his chest. He was a colossus of a man whose huge girth rested comfortably on the edge of the witness box.

'You are acquainted with the man in the dock, George Hobb, are you not?'

'I am, sir.'

'Tell the court what happened on Monday, the twenty-second of May, 1899.'

'It was a Whitsuntide holiday as best I remember. We were extremely busy serving customers at the bar when he comes in wearing a dress.'

'Let it be recorded that the witness is pointing to the prisoner,' said Frere, patting his dark blonde wig – his 100 per cent horsehair wig – which needed no patting because it was perfectly in place.

'Him over there caused a riot.'

'How did Hobb cause a riot?'

'Well, my regulars objected to him drinking alongside them. We eventually had to evict him. But a mob outside had got word of it and drove him back inside with stones. Smashed two of my front windows. I was forced to barricade the doors and send one of the locals for the coppers. I have never seen the like. I thought the mob would tear my place apart. I don't run that sort of premises.'

'What do you mean that sort of premises?'

'A place for mollies and suchlike to meet.'

'So why didn't you turn Hobb out earlier?'

'As I've already explained, I was so busy that night by the time I realised what was going on it was too late. The mob would have killed him if I'd not let him back in.'

'I have no more questions of this witness, my lord.' Frere glided back down into his seat. Although apparently much less ferocious and not under threat, prosecuting counsel did remind me of Jan Asselijn's mute swan at the Rijk.

'Mr Cairn?' Summer's brows lifted expectantly to me.

'So, Mr Tuck, I have you to thank that I have a defendant left to defend.' I smiled, the landlord nodded. 'Tell me, Mr Turk, if you don't in your own words encourage "mollies", why did you serve drink to the Reverend Doctor Hobb in the first place?'

'I didn't. It was a young lad who we had set on as an extra barman for the evening what served him. The young lad took him for an odd looking female. I didn't take a good look at Hobb until it was too late.'

'But had you heard that the defendant had been accosting other men outside your premises?'

Turk hesitated. Frere frowned, hunching forward in his seat. Perhaps he was about to become Asselijn's threatened cob after all.

'Not personally. The police told me afterwards.'

'What police?'

'Constables Goater and Robins.'

I delved into my papers, asking, 'But it was a Constable Gruelthorpe who was the arresting officer, was it not?'

'Constable Gruelthorpe was one of the officers who arrived to sort out the riot, true enough. But it was Constable Herbert Goater who told me that Hobb had been trying it on with other men outside my pub earlier.'

'What did he say?' asked Summer, a hand to his ear.

'He said, my lord, that he was told by a Constable Herbert Goater that the defendant had been seen trying it on with other men outside his pub,' I was forced to reiterate.

'By "trying it on" do you mean Hobb was attempting to solicit other men for sexual purposes?' Summer asked the witness. Tuck nodded. 'Answer "yes" or "no",' insisted the judge.

'Yes,' said Tuck. There was a murmur of disapproval in the court.

'Do you know any of the policemen involved in this case well, Mr Tuck?' I enquired.

'Constables Goater and Robins often drink in the Star after their shifts, but as far as I know they weren't directly involved in this investigation.'

'Only in gossiping about it, it would seem.' His lordship failed to pick me up on the quip. Tuck's heavy features registered nothing. 'Tell me if I am wrong, Mr Tuck, but you seem rather familiar with the law and policing?'

'I walked the beat for a year or two myself.'

'Really, how interesting. And at what time did you send for the police and barricade your doors on the Whit Monday in question?'

'Must have been around nine o'clock.'

'How long would you say the defendant had been drinking on your premises?'

'The lad, our temporary barman, told me he had been in about an hour.'

There jumped up. 'Objection, my lord, inadmissible hearsay.'

'Upheld,' agreed Summer. 'If it is important to confirm a period of time with any accuracy, Mr Cairn, you will have to call the witness concerned.'

'I will, my lord.'

'I am glad to hear it.' Summer gave me one of his most beguiling smiles.

'So, if the riot started about nine o'clock, it must have still been daylight outside.'

'Yes, it was.'

'So anything that happened earlier outside your premises would have happened in the full glare of daylight? No more questions.' I took my seat before the incisiveness of my question had struck home with William Turk.

Frere was on his feet again.

'Yes, Mr Frere?' asked Summer.

'May I ask the witness if there are not a lot of side alleys and enclosed courts in Stonegate?' he asked.

Clever, I thought, but not clever enough.

'A few,' muttered the by now bewildered ex-policeman. 'And the Star itself is set back in its own yard.'

'If my recollection is correct, there are also hundreds of overlooking windows in that neighbourhood to risk any unlawful liaisons in broad daylight, my lord.' I planted my feet and my point firmly. Frere fluttered back; not an angry swan at all but a petulant wallflower.

'Call Francis Gruelthorpe...' *Gruelthorpe, Gruelthorpe,* echoed and splashed off the walls of the chamber.

'Were you and some of your fellow officers called to an affray outside the Star public house in Stonegate on Monday, the twenty-second of May, 1899?' asked Frere.

'We were, sir.'

'What time was this?'

'About half past nine in the evening.'

'And what did you find when you got there?'

Gruelthorpe's little black book shook in his hands as he checked for the relevant facts. 'About twenty or thirty men had gathered outside the pub. They were throwing stones, apples, anything they could lay their hands on at the building. I believe the pub landlord, William Tuck, had barricaded the doors fearing they would break in. When the crowd saw me and my fellow officers, they turned their missiles on us.'

'What did you do then, Constable Gruelthorpe?'

'We pulled out truncheons and blew our whistles for reinforcements,' replied Gruelthorpe as if this was self-evident. 'We hoped the loud whistling would disperse the crowd.'

'Did it work?'

'No, not really, not until more officers arrived. The crowd was very angry, very vocal. We were forced to use our truncheons on a few of them.'

'Eventually you restored order though?'

'Yes sir, we were then able to extricate the prisoner from the pub.'

'How did he look?'

Gruelthorpe hesitated before finally admitting, 'A mess, sir.'

Masculine laughter rang round the courtroom.

'Did you caution him there on the street?' continued Frere.

'No, we handed the prisoner over to our colleagues at Jubbergate Police Station.'

'Thank you, Constable Gruelthorpe.' Frere quit the spotlight, I entered the stage. Gruelthorpe visibly tensed knowing that I was the enemy.

'Tell me, Constable, if I have got this correct, following the riot outside the Star public house, you merely asked the defendant if he would voluntarily accompany you to the police station?'

'Yes, sir.'

'Which he did?'

'Yes, sir.'

'Tell me, Constable, why didn't you arrest the defendant then and there on the street?'

'We... I...' Gruelthorpe was flustered.

'Could it be that you did not know what to arrest him for? Because the defendant had done nothing wrong. You did not know what to charge him with.'

'He was wearing a dress,' spluttered Gruelthorpe.

'"He was wearing a dress", is that all? It wasn't as if George Hobb was walking the streets of York naked, was it?'

'Objection, my lord. Counsel for the defence knows perfectly well that the appearance of Hobb in a dress caused an affray in the City of York that night. Innocent people could have been hurt in the uproar.' Frere twizzled one of the three buttons on his bar jacket in agitation.

'Forgive me, my lord, I was under the misapprehension that it was the Crown's submission that the reason for the riot in Stonegate was because George Hobb had been trying to procure other men there earlier that evening.'

'Mr Cairn, I am going to uphold counsel for the prosecution's objection in this instance.' Augustus Summer's lips curled with pleasure. 'And do try to use less inflammatory language.'

'Who detained the defendant at Jubbergate Police Station?'

'I believe the duty sergeant, Sergeant Howell, cautioned him.'

'No, who did you actually hand George Hobb over to? Who was responsible for him during his confinement in a cell overnight?'

'I believe Constables Goater and Robins were the custody officers that night.'

'And custody is something Goater knows all about having once worked as a warder at the Castle,' hissed Trotter disparagingly.

'And that is their duty usually?' I asked Gruelthorpe.

'Sorry, sir?'

'Constable Goater and Constable Robins normally look after the cells, do they?'

'No, not necessarily. They sometimes offer if we are short of custody officers back at the station.'

'I see.'

Gruelthorpe precipitously began to gather his helmet and little black book thinking he was about to be dismissed.

'Just one more question, Constable Gruelthorpe. Have you ever, at anytime, seen the defendant physically attempting to solicit other men for immoral purposes on the streets of this city?'

'No, sir, not exactly.'

'Is that a "no" or "not exactly"?' asked Summer.

'No, my lord. But if a man wears a dress surely it can be assumed that he is advertising his availability to other men.'

'It can be "assumed", can it? Not necessarily,' I interjected, reasoning that any further pressure or analysis regarding Hobb's susceptibility would be lost on Gruelthorpe and the rest of the court at this juncture. 'No more questions,' I told the relieved constable.

Chapter Twenty-Nine

Trotter and I met Robert Brown in the Fleece on the Pavement. Brown had been detained by other legal work but was free to attend court with us that afternoon. Brown and Trotter began to share a bottle of Merlot but I abstained. I wanted a clear head for that afternoon's work. So far it had been an uphill battle against Frere and the judge. Summer, I was sure, had been brought in by the Establishment to get a conviction if at all possible. And it was possible, very possible, according to the evidence so far that the jury would find for the Crown and convict Hobb.

'A prison sentence would ruin the Reverend,' bemoaned Trotter to Brown.

'Thank you for your faith, Trotter,' I put in.

'It's not that I don't have faith in you, sir. It's that they have stacked the cards against us. This trial is not fair.'

Brown said very little but he looked worried. This was more than a client's trial to him, George Hobb was a dear friend.

'Excellent beef,' I said, clinking my narrow water glass against their big bowls reflecting purple red.

'Good this,' said Trotter, rubbing it in, raising his glass to the window.

'Yes,' I sighed. 'The Bordeaux were almost completely ruined by the phylloxera infestations only a few years ago.'

'I remember hearing about that,' said Brown, 'Didn't they now their industry by grafting native vines onto pest-resistant American rootstock?'

'That's right, you do know your wines,' I complimented Brown.

'And now we have an infestation of another kind.' Trotter was taciturn of late. He examined the contents of his glass gloomily. I had noticed ever since learning about the murder of Mortimer Blakely, Trotter's temperament had been fretful. I was concerned. I suspected he felt responsible for bringing Blakely to my attention in the first place.

'So we will have to graft our vine onto something new,' suggested Brown. The company fell silent.

The Fleece was a tall narrow building rather reminiscent of the canal houses in Amsterdam. It was well-patronised by the legal profession being near to the law courts. I was nodding across to a few familiar faces when I noticed Benjamin Levi sitting at a corner table alone. I blinked in disbelief. He smiled. I beckoned him over.

'I didn't know you had a case on at the moment,' I said, indicating a vacant chair between Trotter and Brown.

'I don't. I have come to see how you fare, James.'

'Were you in court this morning?' I moaned.

'No, I couldn't make the morning sitting.'

'We have been appointed Augustus Summer.'

'Then it will be difficult, extremely difficult.'

'You know him then?'

'Only by reputation. He's an Establishment man through and through. A beak intent on sitting in the Old Bailey trimmed in the finest ermine and silk with a knighthood waiting for him in the wings.'

'I see,' I said, and unfortunately I did only too well. My heart was bleeding over the possibility of an unjust fate for George Hobb – a good man – a man with ambition only to do the right thing.

'I like this place,' said Levi. 'I believe Merchant Adventurers dealing in wool used to drink in here. Now that is what you have to do during this trial, James, be adventurous.'

* * * * *

Frere glowed proudly across at me as a tall, rather elegant man stepped up to be sworn in for the afternoon sitting.

'I swear by Almighty God that the evidence I shall give…' Not a falter from this witness. This was a man of substance, used to giving evidence.

'Doctor Edmund Cross, you are a police surgeon attached to the City of York police, are you not?' began Frere.

'I am, sir, and a registered medical practitioner in this city.'

'I really feel that this witness's medical testimony might cause offence to many ladies present,' interrupted Summer. 'I strongly advise once more that all members of the fair sex take this opportunity and quit the court now.'

I looked up to the public benches. This second warning was too much for most men. Reluctant wives rejected the assistance of their spouses' arms as they were guided to the exits.

'It's a good job that the twelve men and true aren't women. Those fishwives in the public only came to hear as much salacious gossip as they could.' Trotter's undertone was without sympathy.

'I do believe you really are a woman hater, Trotter. It wouldn't do if Winifred Holbrook were to hear you.'

'Miss Holbrook, now I like her. She wouldn't be seen dead at a trial like this.'

'But obviously her step-father would.' I nodded up to Dr Holbrook, who was regaining his seat at the end of one of the benches at the back. Within minutes the public gallery was empty of women.

'Tell me, Doctor Cross, were you called to examine the prisoner, George Hobb, at the Castle Prison on Thursday, the twenty-fifth of May, 1899?' resumed Frere.

'Yes, I performed a thorough examamination about eleven o'clock that evening.'

'Please tell the court what you found.'

'The prisoner had much bruising about his person.'

'And?' asked Frere.

'I examined the prisoner's anal canal and found bruising and minor cuts there too.'

Frere flipped his Geneva tab collar in distaste before asking, 'Would you say these were consistent with sexual activity?'

'Yes, I also found his anus to be infundibuliform.'

'"Infundibuliform"?' queried Summer.

'Funnel shaped, your lordship,' explained Cross.

'Would you say this physical anomaly is further confirmation of the debase practices of a passive sodomite?' asked Frere.

'Yes, I would,' replied Cross quietly.

The court fizzed with outrage, heterosexual indignation.

'No more questions.' Eustace Frere had played his trump card.

Staggering to my feet, I had to mentally regroup quickly. 'Your criterion for this intimate examination comes from the influential treatise of our good friend Doctor Auguste Ambroise Tardieu, does it not?'

'Yes,' agreed Cross, seeing no trick here.

'This work was published as long ago as 1857, was it not?'

'I believe so.' Cross nodded.

'Hardly an up-to-date procedure, would you say?'

'It holds as well today as it did then.'

'It was devised to identify prostitutes and suchlike, was it not?'

'Yes.' Again Cross nodded a cautious affirmation.

'I hope, Doctor Cross, you are not suggesting that the Reverend George Hobb has been subsidising his stipend with money made from prostitution.'

'No, no, of course not,' blustered Cross. 'I am saying his body shows signs of passive homosexual activity.'

'Homosexual, here we have a new word originally coined by the Hungarian journalist and writer Károly Mária Kertbeny back in 1869, have we not?' Cross made no attempt to respond. 'Now becoming increasingly known in the English language as a person sexually attracted to his own sex, is that not so?'

'Yes,' sighed Cross.

'This is all very interesting but where is it leading, my lord?' asked Frere.

'Mr Cairn?' Another Summer appeal.

'Passive activity, you say, Doctor Cross, as opposed to aggressive activity?'

'Aggressive behavior in this respect would be hard to elicit from a medical examination.'

'Tell me, Doctor Cross, how would you be able to differentiate medically between passive homosexual behaviour on the part of my client or him having been subjected to a violent assault?'

'I...' More bluster and fluster. 'Well, I wouldn't be able to,' Cross finally admitted.

'Objection, my lord. There is no evidence of an assault being made on the prisoner. This is not why we are here today,' interrupted Frere.

'Upheld,' agreed Summer.

On the ascendancy, Frere defiantly flung his gown back like a tail as he regained his seat.

'It's a fix,' said Trotter. 'This whole trial is a charade.'

'Nevertheless, we will have to play along, play the game, provide proof that is irrefutable,' I side-mouthed to him, a finger to my lips. 'My learned friend for the Crown has made a valid point, my lord. But might I ask him where is the solid evidence that my client has solicited, procured and committed an abominable and detestable crime against nature with another person? Where is this person?'

'Person or persons unknown,' muttered Frere.

'Surely, Mr Cairn, this is what we are trying to establish,' said Summer.

'Forgive me, my lord, I thought the objective of this trial was to prove my client's guilt or innocence not to detect fictitious people.' Summer frowned. He did not like this at all. I did not wait for his response. 'Tell me, Doctor Cross, why did you conduct your examination on the defendant so late in the evening?'

'It was the only convenient time.'

'It wasn't to avoid any objections from the defendant's solicitor, was it?'

'The law has the right…'

'To assault and violate George Hobb's person against his will.'

'Mr Cairn,' warned Summer.

'It is the law,' mumbled Cross lamely.

'I know, I know,' I exclaimed, holding up my hands. 'All sexual offences give the State the unusual power to undertake intervention directly into people's bodies,' I recited like a parrot. 'But where is the sexual offence here, Doctor Cross? Wearing a dress?'

'I was instructed to examine the prisoner. I was only doing my job,' replied Cross.

'And why shouldn't you? We use that same power against the hijras in India so why not against Her Majesty's subjects here?'

Cross, looking cross, said nothing. It did not matter, my question was rhetorical anyway.

'Hi… what?' asked Summer, attempting to pencil it in his notes.

'Hijras. HIJRAS,' I spelt out. 'They are a male sect in India who dress and behave like women, my lord.'

'Do they really?' I could see it was beyond Summer's imagination to understand why anyone in society could possibly wish to be a powerless woman.

'Karl Heinrich Ulrichs invented the term *Urning* in Germany in the 1860s for a male-bodied person with a female soul. In Germany the physician Magnus Hirschfeld has expanded on this theme and refers to an intermediate sex, a third sex if you like, my lord.'

'I am not sure I do like,' sneered Summer, dabbing the end of his nose with a handkerchief. 'But you certainly seem to know a lot about it, Mr Cairn.' Guffaws from the press benches. They were loving this. 'Are you suggesting that the prisoner is one of these *Urnings* rather than homosexual?'

I looked across to my pallid client. 'Yes, I am, my lord.'

'Have you any more questions for this witness?'

'No more questions, my lord.'

'Another display of Summer's ambition for the finest ermine and silk,' muttered Trotter.

Speaking of silk, if not pure silk there was a rustle of taffeta, much layered taffeta, as Frere's next witness crossed the floor.

'I swear by Almighty God that the evidence I shall give...' It was impossible to tell if the elfin cheeks were blushing or not, they were so heavily coated in rouge. She looked like one of George Hobb's friends in drag but the high-pitched squeaking voice was definitely feminine rather than effeminate.

'Isn't that...?' I indicated to Trotter.

'I don't know her,' he replied; his eyes popping out on stalks.

'Is that Frere's star witness?' scoffed Brown from the seat behind. 'Can't he do better than drag the Cutty into court.'

'Who is she, the Cutty?' asked Trotter, still open mouthed at the sight of the boyish figure lost in flounces in the witness box.

'You recognise her, James,' said Brown, tapping my shoulder. 'She usually stands in shop doorways along Feasegate plying her trade with a cutty in her mouth.'

'Cutty?' asked Trotter.

'A four inch working man's pipe with a thick bowl,' explained Brown.

'I know her as Tobacco Alice. Her modus operandi always starts with "can you spare a twist of baccy, luv?",' I laughed.

'That's her, right enough,' agreed Brown.

'If counsel for the defence has something to say perhaps he would like to share his comments with the rest of the court,' reprimanded Summer.

'No, not at this stage, your lordship.' I bowed and scraped an apology.

'Careful here, James,' warned Brown.

'Are you Alice McMahon?' asked Frere.

'I am, sir.' (Almost the squeak of a mouse.)

'Do you live in John Bull Yard, Layerthorpe, in the city of York?'

'I do, sir.'

Just as Frere was purring into action some uncouth wit shouted down from the gallery, 'Ask her what she does there.'

'Usher! Remove that man immediately,' shouted Summer. 'This is intolerable. Any more outbursts like that and I'll remove the public from the court.'

'He's already removed all the women,' muttered Trotter.

But here my clerk was wrong: I noticed a few women had crept back into court during the afternoon session, perhaps they had come to provide Tobacco Alice with moral support.

'How old are you, Miss McMahon?' resumed Frere.

'Nineteen, sir.'

'And I believe you have one conviction for loitering to the annoyance of the public.'

'I was only waiting for me friend,' objected Alice. 'When this bugger of a policeman comes along and arrests me.'

'Please moderate your language, Miss McMahon,' snapped Summer.

'When were you convicted of loitering?' asked Frere.

'Must be two years back.'

'But this offence was so minor that you did not receive a custodial sentence, am I right in thinking?'

'A what?'

'You did not go to prison for loitering, Miss McMahon?'

'No, I didn't.'

'Tell the court exactly what happened on Monday, the twenty-second of May, 1899?'

'I was waiting for another friend outside a shop in Feasegate.' Laughter from both the public and press benches at this. If not to Trotter, Tobacco Alice was obviously well-known to most York residents. 'When this old geezer comes along wearing a dress. What a spectacle he looked.'

'Could you tell the court what time you first saw the man dressed as a woman?'

'About a quarter to eight in the evening.'

'Do you see the same man here in court today?'

Alice scrutinised the room for at least a minute and appeared to recognise no one.

'Have you ever seen the man standing over there say?' Frere pointed directly at the dock.

'Objection, my lord!' I bounced to my feet. 'My learned friend is blatantly leading this witness.'

'Upheld,' agreed Summer reluctantly.

'Problem is,' said Alice, 'he's not wearing a dress today.'

'Nevertheless, have you seen him before?'

'Yes,' nodded Alice. 'Although he looked such a sight then. He looks better today as a man. The old sod was trying to pick up fellas right under me bloody nose on my pitch.'

'Sorry, your lordship,' apologised Frere smoothly. 'Although Miss McMahon occasionally uses language of the streets, she is an extremely straightforward, truthful young woman. I have no further questions for this witness. That is the case for the prosecution.'

'Miss McMahon.' Thinking she had said her piece, Alice almost jumped out of her skin at the sound of my voice. 'A moment ago you referred to your "pitch". Would you be kind enough to explain to this court and members of the jury what a "pitch" in this sense actually is?'

'Well, well...' For the first time Alice fell into real confusion but she was a woman used to fighting her way out of tight corners. 'It's where I make a pitch for baccy.'

I had not underestimated her. 'You mean you beg?'

'I do, sir, for me pipe smoking.'

'And you have just told this court that the defendant in the dock over there was sharing your pitch, your shop doorway, around a quarter to eight on the evening in question, is that not so?'

'I did,' she confirmed solemnly.

'Tell me, Miss McMahon, when you were first arrested for loitering which police station where you taken to?'

'Jubbergate.'

'About what time of year was it?'

'Spring, spring like now, I think.'

'I expect spring is a clement season to begin pipe smoking.' I heard Levi's toothy chuckle from the gallery above as I took my seat. He might not laugh at his own jokes but he was laughing at mine.

'Might I point out that Miss McMahon's reputation is not under scrutiny here today, my lord.' Frere was on his feet in re-examining mode. 'Miss McMahon, perhaps you would clarify for the court how many men you saw Hobb pick up that evening right under your nose?' he asked her.

'Two or three.'

'"Two or three",' repeated Frere loudly. The court groaned at such depravity.

'She's lying through her teeth,' spluttered Brown.

'No more questions.' Frere sank back in his chair smugly as Alice McMahon slunk away – a cat with claws, claws that had drawn a little blood.

'I think the time has come for cool reflection. Might I remind both counsels and members of the jury that the sole purpose of this trial is to get to the truth.' His lordship reared on his dais like a big bird in full scarlet plumage. He must have been smarting over my earlier remark about the objective of the trial. His out of context response had come a little late in the day and would be lost on most people. But not on me, not on me.

'My lord, as the sole purpose of this trial is to get to the truth, I would like to recall Miss McMahon tomorrow.' Augustus Summer nodded to the usher. I turned to Trotter. 'Get a warrant if necessary to examine the custody books at Jubbergate Police Station for the year 1898 until today.'

The hunched form of Benjamin Levi approached me in the corridor outside.

'Very entertaining if it wasn't so serious.' Levi's undertone spluttered in my ear. 'I think I'll come tomorrow.'

'It was you who had Arnon van Grunsven killed on the steps of the Stock Exchange, was it not?' I whispered back.

'I never lie under oath but I am not the one on trial today. If I can be of any help to your client, Hobb, you only have to ask. By the way, I was so sorry to hear about your friend Lucy Alexander and the child.'

Chapter Thirty

'I wish to share with the court that because of my legal obligation to defend a man who I believe, with all my heart, to be innocent of this charge, I have personally received threats of blackmail and physical violence by "person or persons unknown",' I announced, mimicking Frere's words. I could see the various journalists writing down my opening statement with gusto. This is what they had been waiting for, this was original copy. 'Indeed, sadly, a private investigator hired by my chambers to track down these miscreants lost his life in the process.'

Gasps. Augustus Summer's court erupted. It was no longer his court but mine. It was my stage from now on.

'Silence! I will have order in court,' shouted Summer, struggling to regain control.

'Silence!' echoed the usher, fearing the court was beyond Summer's control.

'I was warned to leave "the poofs without representation". Let me assure those who sought fit to give me this advice, let me assure the court, I will not be silenced. I will not be silenced in the name of justice and truth. Justice will be more than seen to be done in this court today. Justice will be done.'

Someone began to clap in the public gallery. I looked up. I looked again, I did not believe my eyes. Winifred Holbrook, dressed in mourning black from head to toe, was stood on her feet clapping. Benjamin Levi in the far corner rose to clap too. They orchestrated an explosion. Dr Holbrook remained statuesque. He was seated several places away from Winfred. I wondered why they were not sitting together.

'Silence! I'll have no further outburst in this court. Please let counsel for the defence conclude his opening statement,' appealed Summer moderately, somewhat subdued. Even he was learning how to woo the crowd.

'George Hobb has been a hard-working clergyman all of his life, a man of extraordinary kindness and charity. According to his governing body, the Church of England, he is a man of the highest intellect and, they believed, integrity. This man's integrity has now been called into question by the allegation that he committed an abominable and detestable crime with, the prosecution maintains, person or persons unknown. The defendant does not deny that he has an unusual obsession for wearing female apparel. But he has never meant to cause offence to anyone and his private inclination to occasionally dress as a woman has never interfered with his pastoral duties back on the Isle of Wight. Indeed, no one on the Isle is aware that the defendant has this predisposition. No, rather than risking the prejudices and embarrassment of his parishioners, George Hobb chose to risk ridicule and abuse in a setting where he is unknown. Your lordship, members of the jury, permit me to call the evidence for the defence before you. I call the defendant, the Reverend Doctor George Hobb.'

'Sorry, sorry,' mumbled George to himself, to the air. He shuffled nervously from one foot to the other. He looked as if he had terminal anaemia.

'Are you George Hobb of Anvil Rectory, near Brighstone, on the Isle of Wight?' I asked him.

'I am.' He bowed his head, he was barely audible.

'Speak up,' insisted Summer.

'You have heard some of the evidence so far against you?'

'I have,' sighed Hobb.

'Can you tell the court why you were not attending to your parish duties at this holy time?'

'I was suffering from both a spiritual and nervous collapse.'

'Can you tell us why?'

Hobb hesitated, looked up to the public gallery. 'My daughter had gone missing.'

'Do you remember going into the Star public house in Stonegate, on Whit Monday of last year, wearing female apparel?'

'I do,' admitted Hobb with an even deeper sigh bordering on a groan.

'Do you remember being served a drink there by a young barman?'

'Vaguely.'

'"Vaguely" will not do. Please answer "yes" or "no" to counsel's questions,' interjected Summer.

'Yes, then,' said Hobb.

'At what time was this?' I continued.

'It must have been about eight o'clock because I had already eaten in my room at the Fox.'

'Is that the Fox in Low Petergate?'

'Yes.'

'Do you know or have you ever conversed with the witness Alice McMahon in Feasegate?'

'I have never seen that young lady before outside this courtroom.'

'Did you ever enjoy the company of other men in Star Yard off Stonegate?'

'No, I did not.'

That was good enough for me. I took my seat.

'Are you really asking this court and gentlemen of the jury to believe that you don't dress as a woman to attract other men?' began Frere.

' Yes,' replied Hobb. 'Although in my experience people will believe what they want to believe.'

'Reverend Doctor Hobb…,' began Summer.

'That is a definite "yes", your lordship,' interrupted Hobb, before the judge could complete his reprimand.

'Why do you dress in frocks then if it is not to attract others?' persisted Frere.

'I dress in frocks to please myself.'

'This is all very hard to understand.'

Back on my feet again. 'My lord, may I suggest that my learned friend was not listening to my explanation of Karl Heinrich Ulrich's theory of the *Urning*, a male-bodied person with a female soul. He is confusing an *Urning* with a sodomist.'

'Mr Frere is not alone in his confusion,' announced Summer.

'Perhaps, my lord, we will have a term in the not too distant future which will clarify the Reverend George Hobb's need to dress as a woman.'

'I hope so, Mr Cairn, I truly hope so.'

'Are you saying Alice McMahon was lying when she said she saw you soliciting other men in Feasegate?' resumed Frere.

The Reverend hesitated before replying 'I am afraid she was'.

'Why would she do that?'

'A good question,' I muttered to my table.

'I have no idea,' said Hobb.

'It comes down to your word against hers, doesn't it?' Frere gave Hobb no time to answer. 'You were examined by the eminent police surgeon, Doctor Edmund Cross, were you not?'

'Yes, sir.' Hobb lowered his head, I could see his hands trembling on the railing.

'Have you any explanation for the physical findings of Doctor Cross?'

'I am not a doctor of medicine.' The last vestige of colour drained from Hobb's face.

'No, you certainly are not, sir. But do you not agree that his examination showed that you had been recently involved in an act of gross indecency?'

'Objection, my lord,' I intervened. 'The defendant has already denied the indictment made against him.'

'All the same, it would be interesting to hear the Reverend Doctor Hobb's response to counsel for the prosecution's accusation in person. You after all, Mr Cairn, put your client forward to testify.'

Hobb looked across at me helplessly before telling the court in a faint voice, 'I am not interested in or seek other men for illegal sexual congress.'

'Speak up, man, I can't hear you,' Summer's voice boomed above the floor of the court.

'I am not interested in or seek other men for illegal sexual congress, your lordship.' Hobb sounded near to hysteria.

Frere flounced back into his seat. Satisfied, flushed with success following his encounter with Hobb.

'Are you Robert Fry of Fossgate in the city of York?' I asked the pimpled youth with a bulbous nose. Not an unlikeable face for all that.

'I am.'

'And were you working as a temporary barman on Whit Monday, 1899, at the Star in Stonegate?'

'I was.'

'Do you recognise the defendant in the dock?'

'I do, sir, but with difficulty as he was all painted up and dressed in frills when last I set eyes upon him.'

'Can you tell the court and gentlemen of the jury at what time George Hobb came into the public house?'

'I can, sir, because I remember checking the pub's clock. It was eight o'clock. William Tuck had set me on for only four hours until eleven. I had three hours left to work.'

Frere appeared disinclined to challenge Fry. Fry stepped down with a heavy self-conscious tread and grinned manically. He looked like a child who had just performed a brief turn before party guests.

Florrie Cary was back in the box – the witness box not the dock – so was her feather hat. Keen and eagle-eyed she surveyed the court, but this time not with the blinking stare of a defendant caught in the dazzling light of justice. No this time Florrie's expression was assured. At the risk of bringing back unpleasant memories of her own indictment for shoplifting, she was true to her word and had agreed to step forward as a character witness for George.

I glanced up to see if Winifred was still there as Florrie was sworn in. She was but half a dozen ruffians were pushing their way onto the bench next to her step-father. One or two even squeezed in next to her. She pulled a face but to my surprise Dr Holbrook did not seem to mind. He merely adjusted in his seat. I was calling Goater and later Robins for examination, were these their supporters, fellow off duty police officers perhaps?

'Mrs Cary, you are the landlady of the Fox, Low Petergate, are you not?' I gave Florrie a reassuring smile.

'I am, sir,' said Florrie; very correct, very formal, feathers nodding as she spoke.

'I believe George Hobb was staying with you at the time of his arrest, was he not?'

'He was, sir, and he always acted the perfect gentleman.'

'Except when he was in drag,' muttered Frere's clerk; a theatrical aside for the whole court to hear. There were loud roars from the men next to Dr Holbrook. Judge Summer chose not to restore order.

'So the defendant never caused you any trouble?'

'Never, George never bothered no one.'

'Mrs Cary, can you tell the court at what time you provided the defendant with dinner on Whit Monday of last year?'

'I served him dinner in his room at precisely seven o'clock.'

'Thank you, Mrs Cary.' Florrie looked disappointed that I had no further questions for her. She was used to being on show, she liked being on show, except of course when she was in the dock.

'Tell me, Mrs…' Frere hesitated, looked down his witness list. He had forgotten her name. He wanted Florrie to know he had forgotten her name, wanted her to know she wasn't important. 'Mrs Cary,' he began again. 'How can you be so certain about the time you served Hobb his dinner?'

'Because I always serve my live-ins dinner at seven sharp, before we get too busy downstairs.'

'But this was a Bank Holiday Monday, was it not?'

'Doesn't matter what day it is. I always serve dinner to them upstairs at seven.' Florrie's huge bosom lifted with indignation. She would not be moved. I silently applauded her as she climbed down from the witness box.

Herbert Goater nodded an acknowledgement to Florrie as she quit the courtroom and he entered it. Her expression cut him dead. Not a good start for Goater.

'There looks to be some history between those two,' whispered Brown.

'I don't doubt it,' I replied, before turning my attention to Goater. 'Constable Herbert Goater, you are stationed at Jubbergate Police Station, are you not?'

'I am.' The eyes that lifted to mine were dead, expressionless. Here was a man who did not like me, that was apparent. The feeling was mutual. God knows what my expression revealed. I had a score to settle with this man before the trial of *Regina v Hobbs* was over, I was sure of it.

'Constable Goater, did you tell William Tuck, landlord of the Star in Stonegate, that the defendant had been seen soliciting for immoral purposes in his yard before the riot there at nine o'clock?'

'I might have said something of the sort.'

'But how could the defendant have been soliciting in the yard of the pub in Stonegate, when one of the Crown witnesses has told us he was standing with her in Feasegate at a quarter to eight. Added to this another witness has just testified that he served George Hobb a drink inside the Star at eight o'clock that evening.'

'Objection, my lord. Forgive the pun but Feasegate is but a stone's throw from Stonegate,' pointed out Frere.

'It is not disputed that Feasegate is but a stone's throw from Stonegate. Nonetheless, perhaps counsel for the prosecution would be good enough to explain to the court how George Hobb could enjoy his evening meal in Low Petergate at seven o'clock, stand in a shop doorway in Feasegate at a quarter to eight, importune two to three men for unlawful congress and be buying a drink at the Star all within a quarter of an hour.'

'Because he's a dirty old bugger,' someone shouted from the gallery above.

'A filthy poof,' embellished someone else.

I saw Winifred trying her best to edge away, disassociate herself from these musical hall Johnnies. She pulled the veil firmly down on her small black tricorne hat, whereas before it had been pushed back off her face.

'Silence!' Summer thumped on the table with his fist. 'I'll not warn the public again,' he threatened. 'I think counsel for the defence has made his point, pray continue.'

'I have here, my lord, copies of entries taken from the Jubbergate Police Station custody book.' The usher took Exhibits 45 and 46 to the clerk of assize, who in turn passed them to the judge and then on to the jury. 'I draw the jury's attention to Exhibit Forty-five with an entry date for April, 1898, and Exhibit Forty-six which has an entry dated for Tuesday, the twenty-third of May last year. Constable Goater, your name is on this second entry as the arresting officer of the Crown's witness, Alice McMahon, for loitering to the annoyance of the public, is that not so?'

'Yes. What of it?'

'This second detention of Alice McMahon was the day after you arrested the defendant?'

'It could have been.'

'Yes or no?'

Goater gave a reluctant 'yes'.

'You kept Miss McMahon in a cell overnight, is that correct?'

'Yes.' Goater's brow ruckled.

'As this was the second time Miss McMahon had been arrested, why wasn't she charged?'

'We thought a night in the cell was enough.'

'She wasn't just loitering though, was she? She was soliciting for business in a public place, was she not?'

'Perhaps.'

'This second time she would have gone to prison, wouldn't she?'

'Magistrates tend to be lenient regarding such offences these days.'

'Miss McMahon wasn't to know that though, was she?'

'Who knows,' shrugged Goater.

'Constable Goater, did you strike a deal with Miss McMahon that you would drop all charges against her if she testified against the defendant who had been arrested the previous day?'

'My lord!' exclaimed Frere.

In full flow I ignored him. 'Wasn't this whole story an elaborate fabrication from beginning to end against Hobb?'

'Mr Cairn.' Summer's voice, Summer's intervention too late. I had placed the seed in the jury's mind. Even the thugs in the gallery kept silent.

'Tell me, Constable Goater, do you know a Marcus Hale and Kenneth Bright?' I asked. Again puzzlement. Beads of sweat had begun to form on Goater's top lip. 'You should do because you arrested both men in the autumn of last year. I draw the court's attention to Exhibit Forty-seven.' The usher placed a copy of the entries for Hale's and Bright's detainment under Goater's nose.

'I have locked up many men in my time.'

'I am well aware of that Constable Goater. Although I should have thought you would have remembered for example young Marcus Hale. You, personally, dealt with his arrest and detainment only last autumn.'

'Oh, yes, I remember him now and his friend. *Men*, you say? They were two mollies I thought they were females at first, all dressed up in fancy gowns and powdered faces. Friends of yours, Mr Cairn, are they?' scoffed Goater. An eruption of appreciative handclapping and jeers came from the gallery at Goater's sarcasm.

'I will remind the witness that he is not here to question counsel. He is here to answer questions put to him,' rebuked Summer; mildly, I thought, in the circumstances.

But none of this really mattered. Gently, gently, I was corralling the wolves unknowingly into a corner. I resumed my examination. 'Can you tell the court how long it took you to discover that Marcus Hale was not a woman but a man?'

'I am not sure what you mean.'

'I cannot put it plainer, Constable Goater. How long was it before you realised you had arrested a man and not a woman?'

'It dawned on me slowly.'

'As you have just told the court you have locked up many men in your time. You are an experienced officer. And you were a warder at the Castle Prison across the way before you joined the constabulary, were you not?'

'I was.'

'So perhaps you can share with us, provide this court with an estimate of how many men you have roughed up a little in the confines of their cells?'

'I…' Goater looked flabbergasted. He turned as white as Hobb in the dock.

'Objection!' Tiresome Frere again.

'Mr Cairn, I must warn you that you cannot make an accusation against a witness unless you have proof to substantiate it.'

'Oh, I do and I will, my lord. No more questions for now, Constable Goater.'

Taking my seat, I did something then that I had never done before. I gave Trotter a pat on the back for obtaining those vital custody book entries.

'No trouble, sir. Sergeant Howell was more than obliging,' whispered Trotter.

'I bet he was,' said Brown. 'He did not want to be associated with Goater's antics and finish up in court.'

'When I met him, I got the impression that Howell would like to be rid of both Goater and Robins. I expect he is happy that someone else is doing the job for him,' I told them, as Frere was coming to the end of his cross-examination regarding Goater and his exemplary career in both the prison service and police force.

I was too sick of the sight of Goater to attempt any tongue in cheek retorts. Now was not the time anyway.

'I would like to recall Alice McMahon, my lord,' I announced instead.

'Call Alice McMahon… McMahon!' Such a loud encore for such a diminutive figure.

'Might I remind you, Miss McMahon, you are under oath,' I began. 'If you tell the truth now to this court and to the gentlemen of the jury, I am sure his honour will show some leniency for any previous inaccuracies in statements made by you under duress.'

Duress. Duress. The word buzzed round the courtroom like a trapped bee.

'Did he say "duress"?' asked Saul Winlock. The veteran London reporter must have been getting a little hard of hearing.

'Again I would like to draw the jury's attention to Exhibit Forty-six. Miss McMahon, would you be good enough to tell the court what happened following your arrest by Police Constable Herbert Goater on Tuesday, the twenty-third of May last year?'

'What happened?' McMahon looked around for guidance. Her eyes suddenly big with fear.

'Please answer counsel's question,' Summer told her.

'Did you know Constable Goater before this date?' I helped out. 'I'd seen him about town.'

'Following your second arrest for loitering, you were kept overnight at Jubbergate Police Station and set free in the morning without charge, is that correct?'

'Yes.'

'Why, was that?' I asked. Again the hesitation, again the big eyes. 'Miss McMahon,' I prompted.

'Copper said if I did a good turn for him, he would do one for me.'

'The "copper" being Constable Goater, isn't that so?'

Lost for words, McMahon nodded.

'Answer "yes" or "no",' prompted Summer.

The 'yes' that came was barely audible.

'It's like drawing blood from a stone,' muttered Brown.

'What good turn did Constable Goater offer you?' I asked her.

'He said they'd let me go.'

'If you did what?'

'If I said I had seen some old poof touting for business in Feasegate,' finally admitted McMahon to a collective gasp.

'The "old poof" being the defendant, George Hobb, isn't that so?'

'Yes.'

'Have you ever seen that man over there in the dock before?'

'No, only in this courtroom.' The mouth drew in, in a face much older than her years.

'So he never stood shoulder to shoulder with you in your shop doorway soliciting for men.'

'No,' said with hung head.

'My lord, I move that this witness's previous testimony be struck from the record.'

'Clerk of assize.' Summer nodded to the clerk to take the appropriate action: he had no other option. 'I shall take this opportunity to remind this witness that perjury and attempting to pervert the course of justice are extremely serious offences. A police investigation will be set into motion immediately following this sitting. Do you wish to continue cross-examining this witness, Mr Cairn, when you yourself have discredited most of her previous testimony?'

'I do, my lord. I firmly believe Miss McMahon has learnt her lesson and is now being completely truthful with the court. She could have some further vital information to offer.' I turned back to the witness. 'Tell me, Miss McMahon, were you ever assaulted at Jubbergate Police Station?' McMahon looked perplexed. 'By Constable Goater or anyone else?'

'Him. He came into my cell during the night and fooled around a bit. I was half asleep at the time to tell you the honest truth.'

'By "him" you mean Goater?'

'Ay, I do.'

'Did he force himself on you?'

'What?'

'My lord, this is outrageous,' squealed Frere.

'Not heard from him for some time,' chuckled Trotter.

'Mr Cairn, is this line of questioning of a witness who has already perjured herself absolutely necessary?' enquired Summer.

'Yes, my lord, it is fundamental to the defence's case. You will see the justification for it very shortly.'

'I hope so, Mr Cairn, I do hope so.' I almost sensed Summer was warming to me.

'Did Constable Herbert Goater force you to perform a sexual act with him?' I pressed on.

'No, he said I wasn't his type. Said he might catch something from me.'

'Thank you, Miss McMahon.' I watched her slink away, knowing I had never cross-examined a creature so bereft of dignity and self-esteem. A creature whose situation was made all the worse by the likes of loveless men like Goater.

My stomach growled. Fortuitously, Judge Summer chose that moment to adjourn for lunch.

Chapter Thirty-One

Marcus Hale walked into the courtroom looking immaculate. He wore tight highly creased trousers with a short lounge jacket that emphasised his narrow waist. The low-cut patent leather pumps on his feet were topped with a large flat bow of grosgrain ribbon. He moved across the floor with the light soundless steps of a principal dancer. While his thin soled pumps remained soundless, the derisive whistles and catcalls that followed him were not.

A "quiet" came from a second usher who was now stationed at the back of the public gallery. The court officials were preparing for trouble.

Undaunted, Marcus Hale smiled briefly across to the dock. This was the first time anyone had smiled at George Hobb in days. Hale then nodded to him indicating the public gallery. At first I thought he was taunting his detractors until I saw the dazzled expression on my client's face. I took out Hobb's locket from my small waistcoat pocket to check the likeness. There was no doubting it this time. Helena was truly stunning. She beamed reassurance down on her father from beneath coral egret plumes. Golden ringlets framed her face. Her full lips mouthed to her father that it would be all right now. I hoped she was right.

'The evidence I shall give…' Although Hale's high voice lisped through the oath, each word was clearly enunciated.

'Are you Marcus Hale of Nunnery Lane?'

'I am, sir.'

'And you share the defendant's habit of appearing in drag from time to time.'

'I do.'

'"Drag"?' queried Summer.

'Dressing in female apparel, my lord,' I explained.

'My lord, I object to the obvious dubious nature of this witness. This trial is becoming nothing more than a circus.' Frere on his dainty little feet again. Frere on ground ever getting weaker.

'I think perhaps my learned friend should be a little more circumspect,' I retorted. 'After all has he not brought before this court a lady of "dubious nature" who initially lied under oath?'

'Please continue, Mr Cairn,' directed Summer.

'Thank you, my lord. I can assure the court and gentlemen of the jury I do not intend to prolong my questioning of this witness.'

'Glad to hear it,' mumbled Frere.

'When you are in drag, Mr Hale, you are known as Marina, is that correct?'

'Yes.'

'And as Marina you were arrested by two police officers on the ninth of October last, were you not?'

'I was.'

'I should like to draw the jury's attention to Exhibit Forty-seven again, a copy of an entry made in the Jubbergate custody book. I see here the arresting officers were Police Constables Goater and Robins.'

'Yes.'

'And you were arrested with a friend, is that not so?'

'I was.'

'Although you were housed in separate cells for the night?'

'Yes.'

'Known as solitary confinement, I believe.'

'Yes. They threatened to throw away the keys.'

'Who threatened that?'

'Police Constables Goater and Robins.'

'Really, my lord, is this waffle relevant?' asked Frere. 'It is merely tittle-tattle.'

To my surprise Summer did not answer him but put a silencing hand up instead.

'Although I know this is extremely difficult for you, Mr Hale, would you tell the gentlemen of the jury what transpired during that night of your arrest?'

Hale gave a quick nervous glance across to Hobb in the dock before taking a deep breath.

'While Constable Robins stood guard at the door, Goater came in and assaulted me.'

'How did he assault you?'

'He sodomised me.'

The court was in uproar.

'He did right,' a thug shouted from the gallery.

'Serves you right,' shouted another.

'You were asking for it, you little poof,' shouted another.

But the ground swell of reasonable opinion was rising against the thugs. Victorian society was outraged. Pressmen were on their feet, fluttering like lemmings towards their deadline – the journalistic cliff face of the final edition.

'Clear those men from the public benches immediately,' shouted Summer to the ushers, fearing a riot. As if from nowhere the gallery above was swarming with policemen. It was a good job because one or two ushers would never have been able to deal with the ensuing mayhem. Both Winifred and Helena were hanging on to their hats as if in a gale.

I looked across to Hobb. Slow tears were running down his face. I looked at Hale in the witness box. His silk cravat was stained with tears too.

'Tell the court what happened the next morning?' I asked him, once peace was restored, suddenly aware that my own throat was nervously dry.

'They let us go.'

'Without charge?'

'Without charge.'

'I think the court is indebted to this man for the courage he has shown in the interests of justice to come forward. I have no more questions for the witness.'

There was a lull in the proceedings as if the court was having to adjust to Marcus Hale's appalling account of his ordeal. Total silence was followed by much embarrassed blowing of noses, clearing of throats, scraping of chairs. I saw Augustus Summer was scribbling furiously at his notes.

'Perhaps Goater got his name from sodomising goats,' suggested Trotter sotto voce.

'In the Ancient Egyptian temple of Mendes, the goat was viewed as the incarnation of the god of procreation. As a ritual of worship, the male priests would fornicate with female goats, and the priestesses would do likewise with male goats,' I told him.

'How disgusting!' retorted Trotter. 'It makes you wonder.'

'Wonder what?'

'How many men Goater assaulted when he was a warder at the Castle Prison? It makes you wonder if he molested our ex-client, Daniel Robertshaw, poor simple man that he was.'

I lifted a hand to silence him. 'Please, Trotter, I am trying hard not to think of that.'

'Well, it looks like Police Constable Herbert Goater is about to get his comeuppance,' put in Brown, ever the pragmatist.

'I for one will be glad if I never have to go inside that Castle place again. It is full of ghosts,' said Trotter.

'Not all of them pleasant,' agreed Brown, until he was interrupted by the clerk's call.

'Constable John Robins, did you know anything about Constable Goater's arrangement with Miss McMahon for her to make a false allegation against the defendant?' I began.

'No, sir, I did not.'

'Did you collude in any way, either knowingly or unknowingly?'

'No, I did not.'

'Constable Robins, did you aid and abet an act of gross indecency being committed against Marcus Hale during the night of the ninth of October, 1899 .?'

'I did nothing,' interrupted Robins

'At Jubbergate Police Station.'

'It was all him.'

'Try to remember you are in a court of law,' remonstrated Summer.

'By "him" do you mean Constable Herbert Goater?'

'Yes, he did it alone. He was always at it, especially if he was in drink.'

'Was he drunk on the night in question?'

'He was often drunk on duty, sir. He would call in at the Coach and Horses near the station before his shift.'

'And the Star in Stonegate afterwards, I understand.'

A refreshing titter wafted through the oppressive atmosphere.

'Mr Cairn,' remonstrated Summer.

'Constable Robins, do you remember arresting George Hobb on Monday, the twenty-second of May, 1899, in the evening?'

'Yes, he had him too.' Robins began to blubber.

'Who had whom?'

'No, no, James. My daughter. Not here in public,' screamed Hobb, before crumpling back in the dock.

'He's fainted. He's fainted.' A sympathetic murmur went round the courtroom. Helena strained over the balcony in anguish to try and see her father. I saw Winifred's arm move round her waist, protectively round a stranger's waist. I would have expected nothing less from Winifred Holbrook, she was perfection.

'This is terrible to hear, terrible to see,' said Trotter.

'Usher, a cup of water for the defendant,' ordered Summer. 'We are not as inhumane in here as it would seem they are at Jubbergate Police Station.'

'You were saying?' I asked Robins, momentarily thrown.

'Goater forced himself on the Reverend in the cell that night. Smashed him up something awful. He knocked him unconscious before... It's right played on my mind ever since, him being a clergyman and such.'

You could hear a pin drop. The court held its breath. That is when I noticed Robins look up to the public benches. The thugs had gone, ejected. His eyes were fixed on Dr Holbrook. Cedric Holbrook turned away, turned to examining his fingernails. Robins' look – Holbrook's lack of acknowledgement was a connection in itself – the final pieces of the jigsaw were falling into place.

'Talk about spilling the beans,' muttered Brown. 'There aren't any left in the sack, are there?'

'You might be surprised,' I side-mouthed back to him.

'Are you all right for us to proceed, Reverend Doctor Hobb?' Summer asked my insensible client. 'I don't think we will be much longer now.'

'Am I to understand that you, Constable Robins, did nothing? You stood by and watched your fellow officer, Goater, commit a most detestable assault on a man of the cloth?' I asked in disbelief.

'He would have beaten me up too,' Robins whimpered.

'I have no more questions for this witness.' I spat each word out with contempt.

'Nor I,' said Frere.

Again there was much blowing of public noses, rustling of papers on both the crown's and defence's tables as Frere and I attempted to put our closing statements into some order. No one had been expecting this rather abrupt end, least of all me. To my way of thinking the prosecution case had been shattered. But, then again, you can never tell for certain how a jury will react. The jurymen sat up in their seats expressionless but expectant. I nodded encouragingly at my client – Hobb had revived a little – propped between his warders.

'Your lordship, members of the jury,' began Frere. 'I am sure you are relieved that we are coming to the end of this trial. A trial where you have been forced to sit through many unpleasant details regarding the prisoner's abnormal obsession. Details that you would not wish your scullery maid to hear, let alone your sisters, wives and daughters. I suggest that any assault that was perpetrated against the prisoner was because he was dressed like a woman. In short, everything that happened to him he brought upon himself. May I further suggest to you that the wearing of a dress solicits male attention, welcomed or not. The Vagrancy Act 1898 clearly states that it is an offence for a male person persistently to solicit or importune for immoral purposes in any public place. The street is a public place, an alehouse is a public place. Both William Tuck, the licensee of the Star in Stonegate, and Constable Gruelthorpe of this city testified that George Hobb's frock caused a riot.'

The gentlemen of the press could not stifle their titters. Again Levi's toothy laughter came down from the gallery.

'I wonder if Mr Levi would have enjoyed this trial half as much if he had chosen to prosecute it,' muttered Trotter.

'Doubt it,' retorted Brown.

'Finally,' Frere sucked in the airless room. 'The eminent Doctor Edmund Cross gave evidence that the shape of the prisoner's anatomy was consistent with that of a passive sodomite. It is up to you, gentlemen of the jury, to decide whether the prisoner sought to seduce and was experienced in the abominable seduction of other men.'

Frere bowed out and I bowed in.

'Firstly, I dispute the Crown's assertion that an alehouse is a public place. It is a house licensed to sell alcohol. The licensee can refuse to serve any customer with drink if he so chooses. The Reverend Doctor Hobb was served his pint of ale at the Star in Stonegate and no questions asked.' I kept my voice controlled, low and full of *gravitas*. 'I would like to draw the gentlemen of the jury's attention to the evidence of the Star's barman, Robert Fry, who said he had served the defendant at eight o'clock. Mrs Florrie Cary, the defendant's landlady, said she served him dinner at Low Petergate at seven o'clock. Through the discredited witness, Alice McMahon, the prosecution wanted you to believe that the Reverend Doctor Hobb solicited and engaged in unlawful acts with persons unknown within an impossible period of time. Why, after enjoying his dinner at Low Petergate, he would barely have had time to smile at anyone on his way to Stonegate for eight o'clock, let alone seduce them. Far from proving that these offences ever took place, the prosecution has failed to provide us with an attested venue. Where did the defendant take these supposed clients to? – alleyways in Feasegate, Stonegate, Coppergate or any other gate? I suggest to you, gentlemen of the jury, that they do not know where these offences took place because they are an invention, a fiction. A person committing such offences in broad daylight would have to be an imbecile. George Hobb is certainly not that. He is a man of letters. A man who holds several degrees from London University. Doctor Edmund Cross said he was only doing his job. Indeed he was. But that has been, and will be in the future, an excuse to cover a multitude of sins. Many mandates are introduced and upheld by government, governing in ignorance. Why did Doctor Cross not think to ask the prisoner how he came by these intimate injuries? No. Regrettably that fact has had to be teased out in this courtroom. The testimony given of a sexual assault being committed against the defendant at Jubbergate Police Station, totally discredits Doctor Cross's "Infundibuliform" theory which I suspect might be a physical variation common to many. Constables Robins and more particularly Goater, I can hardly bring myself to mention their names, to say they abused their power is the least of it. I am sure his lordship has already set into motion the mechanism for dealing with them.'

'Indeed I have, Mr Cairn.' Augustus Summer nodded his accord.

'In the Middle Ages, the goat was associated with the Devil as one of his preferred forms, often in connection with sexual deviance. Who is the sexual deviant here? A man who likes wearing dresses or a man, aptly named may I say, who abuses his position of power to sodomise other men? I will leave the jury to reach its own conclusions regarding this distasteful subject. However, the Reverend Doctor Hobb is not a sexual deviant in the defence's opinion. Perhaps the correct term for his mental state has not been properly defined yet. We are on the epoch of a new science, the science of the mind, being investigated by doctors especially in Germany and Austria as I speak. Perhaps, as the science stands today, the best description of my client is Karl Heinrich Ulrich's "a male-bodied person with a female soul". George Hobb has never actively gone out seeking the company of other men, indeed he is a good family man, a man more comfortable in the presence of women than men. So much so, his daughter is here in court today to support him.'

There was a kerfuffle in the public gallery as people tried to identify Hobb's long suffering daughter. I hoped she remained concealed under her egret feathers.

'Silence! Let counsel conclude his closing statement,' said Summer, fist poised once more.

I glanced round at Brown and remembered my evening in that bleak terrace house in Coppergate – the street of the cup makers. I realised now that perhaps Brown's scholarly father had unknowingly put my fingertips on the trophy. 'I refer your honour and members of the jury to the case of fifty-eight year old Percy Jocelyn, the disgraced Bishop of Clogher, who in 1822 was caught with his trousers down in a love tryst with a common soldier thirty-six years his junior. The coupling, I understand, took place in the back room of the White Lion public house...'

'Should be *pubic* house,' shouted a wit from the gallery.

'This particular White Lion pub was in St Alban's Place, off Haymarket, in London. Jocelyn tried to escape but his trousers were still down round his ankles, and he was arrested. Although dressed as a clergyman, he refused to reveal his identity. Once in custody his identity was soon discovered and caused a sensation in the London clubs and drinking dens of the day. The moral of this tale is that Percy Jocelyn broke bail and was never seen again, although it is believed he ended his days as a butler in Edinburgh.

Percy Jocelyn and George Hobb – both clergymen – here the comparison ends. Jocelyn was a predatory sodomist who ran, the defendant is merely a man confused as to his gender and remains. Unlike the infamous Bishop of Clogher, the Reverend Doctor Hobb has returned from the Isle of Wight to face trial because he is innocent of the charge made against him and wishes to clear his name.'

Again someone clapped in the gallery but I dared not look up this time.

'Counsel for the prosecution quoted the new Vagrancy Act 1898 to you. In your deliberations, gentlemen of the jury, consider this: who are these men whom the defendant importuned for immoral purposes? Where are they? Where are the witnesses to such abominable acts? Where is the evidence?'

'Members of the jury,' began Summer. 'You have listened with great patience and attention to this case. The learned counsel on both sides presented to you in an eloquent manner the points which will call for your consideration. I therefore do not deem it necessary to go through the minutiae in detail as I am sure they are still fresh in your minds, and I do not wish to detain you long from your important deliberations. However, I must point out that I have never presided over a trial where so many witnesses have proved false.

There has been both conspiracy and perjury involved in this case which will be dealt with by another agency in due course. I suggest that you disregard the two testimonies given by the witness Alice McMahon, and also the testimony of Police Constable Herbert Goater. Both witnesses' testimonies are unsound. It is my duty to remind you that the prisoner must be given the benefit of any reasonable doubt there is in this case. The prosecution has to satisfy. The defence has merely to show there is a reasonable doubt as to the prisoner's guilt. You have heard the prisoner's answer. He told you that he does not dress as a woman to attract other men but to please himself. Counsel for the prosecution quoted The Vagrancy Act 1898 to you. Now please allow me to quote Section Eleven of the Criminal Law Amendment Act 1885.'

'Oh, no, here we go, Labouchere Amendment,' groaned Brown.

'"Any male person who, in *public* or *private*, commits, or is a party to the commission of, or procures, or attempts to procure the commission by any male person of, any act of gross indecency shall be guilty of a misdemeanour, and being convicted shall be liable at the discretion of the court to be imprisoned for any term not exceeding two years, with or without hard labour".'

'I think his lordship is having a go at you here, sir, over your public or private alehouse argument,' whispered Trotter.

'I think you are right, Trotter. The old Oscar Wilde get into gaol clause,' I replied; a finger to my lips.

'You have to decide today if the Crown has provided enough evidence that the prisoner committed such an offence, enough proof for me to sentence this otherwise respectable clergyman to two years in prison possibly with hard labour. Members of the jury the fate of this man is in your hands. Let me end as I began by saying, if there is any doubt, he must have the benefit of that doubt. If there is none, let your verdict be equally clear and let justice be carried out. Will you consider your verdict?'

* * * * *

Finally, I had a minute to myself to mull over the trial, to wonder if we had done enough, suspecting any other judge than Augustus Summer would have already thrown out this case due to a lack of evidence.

One minute I was enjoying being alone the next I sensed someone was there.

'There you are. The great advocate of Jews, poofs and socialists,' ridiculed Holbrook, beginning to pee in the urinal next to mine. 'You must feel extremely proud of yourself, James.'

As if by stealth the gentlemen's room filled with other feet, other low threatening voices. Unlike Holbrook, these men did not address me directly at first as if they were waiting for a signal. Too late, I sensed my vulnerability. The ambushing lions had gathered.

'Poof lover,' sneered a man behind me. A man I recognised as one of those ejected earlier from the public gallery.

'Rather pretty himself, ain't he? With his wig and long flowing gown,' said another band member with a deep scar running down his left cheek.

Another was stretching over my shoulder, presumably to get a better look. 'Very pretty,' he confirmed in a gruff lecherous voice.

'Fancied you from the start, Mr Cairn,' said another. I looked up, it was Jake, Holbrook's butler.

I was surrounded, hemmed in. The stench of urine and filth triggered a memory. I began to sweat, shake. An almost uncontrollable rage began to well up inside me. Some of my clients referred to this as "the red mist" and I knew what they meant. I knew I could kill.

'Two reputable policemen are about to face criminal charges because of you,' snarled Holbrook, in a voice I did not recognise as his.

'Yes,' said one of the thugs, taking me unawares and thumping me hard in the kidneys. 'That's for Goater.'

I doubled over, the pain was excruciating, I began to retch.

'You see, James, I am already exposed so I don't care anymore.' Holbrook's cool breath wafted against my ear.

'Indeed you are, Cedric.' Another voice, a posh voice. Still crouched on the floor, I did my best to locate it. Sir Clive Bampton, arms crossed, leaned casually against the tiled wall. Half a dozen police officers flanked him. The gentlemen's room was now crowded to capacity.

'I was expecting you. Can't you let a fellow take a piss first?' Holbrook spat into the trough.

'Indeed I can. I have all the time in the world, Cedric, as you yourself will soon have. Take them away for questioning. Get them all out of my sight,' snapped Sir Clive to the officers.

'One day you will see I was right. One day we will take over the world.' Holbrook's words echoed off the tiles as he and his men were dragged out.

'Not you, Cedric. You will hang. Her Majesty's government does not take kindly to traitors,' Sir Clive shouted after him.

'Thank you. Matters were beginning to get rather ugly there,' I groaned, trying to straighten up.

'You all right, James?' asked Sir Clive; as if he had been so intent on arresting Holbrook and his thugs, he had only just noticed me.

'I'm a little winded that's all. I need some air.'

'So do I.'

Sir Clive helped me outside the courthouse into the light. That is when I saw him, not in light but in the shadows. A man I immediately recognised. He lifted the monocle from his right eye in an ironical salute.

'You,' I said.

'Yes, me,' he smiled. 'I get everywhere. Everything go smoothly, boss?' the monocled assassin asked Sir Clive.

I did not hear Sir Clive's answer. At that moment Winifred walked past me without a word. She obviously must have put two and two together regarding her step-father and his thugs, and had no stomach for the Hobb verdict anymore. I could see her eyes were cast down behind the thin veil. She looked neither to the right, nor the left, nor straight forward to where several Black Marias were parked against the pavement. Their horses were pawing the ground impatient to be off. She did not even lift her gaze at the sound of an equine snort, the lash of a whip and the metallic squeak of springs as the Black Maria carrying her stepfather shuddered into action at the head of the queue. I knew then that there was too much sad history between us. If only I had not stepped into that chain defining moment outside the Mansion House, things might have been different, we might have met in more auspicious circumstances. Then again, too, Lucy Alexander might still have been alive.

'Sir, the jury is returning.' Trotter was out of breath as he stomped up to us.

'That was quick,' said Sir Clive.

'They often are these days,' I explained. 'It means nothing.'

'But surely George will get off.'

'Who knows,' I shrugged. 'With juries anything can happen.'

＊ ＊ ＊ ＊ ＊

George back in the dock. His whole life and reputation hanging on one or two words. That metaphoric blade still hanging above his head. I looked up to the perfect face under the coral egret feathers, it was motionless.

'Members of the jury, are you agreed upon your verdict?' asked the clerk of assize.

Journalists adjusted themselves on the hard press benches, it had been a long sitting. Mr Justice Summer's left eyelid twitched.

'Yes,' replied the foreman of the jury.

'Do you find George Hobb guilty or not guilty?' A collective intake of breath.

'Not guilty.'

Augustus Summer rose from his dais like God. The press were off their benches like Olympians. Again George Hobb's legs gave way and he crumpled back into the dock but this time out of joy. Handshakes all round. Handshakes with Trotter and Brown. Frere, cool and contained as always, bowed and glided away without a word.

'Thank you, James. Words can never be enough,' said Hobb, on the stone step beneath the pediment – the pediment with the Phrygian cap symbolising liberty. 'Forgive me, I am forgetting my manners, may I introduce you to my daughter. Helena this is James Cairn, a man who is as much a friend to me as he is my barrister.'

I took Helena's gloved hand in mine. She smiled. We smiled.

'How can I ever repay you for this?' asked her father.

'Well, there is my fee,' I laughed. 'But I am sure we can reach an amicable agreement, George, as you entertained me so well at Anvil Rectory. How about you accompany me on that promised trip to St Gregory's Minster and Kirkdale Cave?'

'Oh, I will. I will really look forward to that.'

'Perhaps the three of us could go before you both return home,' I suggested.

'Helena!' Sir Clive Bampton appeared out of the blue, on cue, a habit with him. 'I thought I might see you here.'

'The same cannot be said for me,' replied Helena with surprising coldness.

'You look more beautiful than ever.'

Ignoring Sir Clive's flattery, Helena asked, 'How is Tom?'

In that moment, that look, everything was confirmed. I looked across at George, he knew it too. The French saved their wine industry by grafting native vines on to pest-resistant American rootstock. Is that what Sir Clive had done with his and Helena's child to maintain his family name with a male heir?

'He thrives,' replied Sir Clive.

Chapter Thirty-Two

The late afternoon sunshine blinked temptation. I loved water and took myself off to sit and think by it as I had done in Amsterdam. Spring had come round again but it would be another year before my Dutch tulip bulbs flowered. Spring in the air, a spring in my step as I walked down Marygate making for the river to clear my head. I claimed a form on Marygate Landing with all the physicality of a game of musical chairs. The river Ouse was calm, low. Her spate and winter temper gone. She was at peace with the familiar quack of a mallard hen, a brood of seven in her wake, seven bobbing balls of down tickling the river shallows. She was at peace with the imperious procession of Her Majesty's white swans gliding mid-stream.

My thoughts turned to George Hobb who at least had the courage to follow his inclinations – the courage and dignity to be seen swimming against the current – however bizarre. Oh, that I should have the same courage.

But what becomes of those acted on *without* love, robbed of conviction? What will become of Helena, the Holbrooks, Marcus Hale and the rest?

Too many people have drowned in this story.

Back at Bootham Chambers the next day, I was busy clearing the backlog of work that accrues after a big trial. My office was hot and stuffy so I created a through draught by opening my door and a window.

'Got an invitation to Dollis House, July time. Do you fancy being reacquainted with your old friend Samuel Langhorne Clemens?' Carlton-Bingham shouted through the open doorway.

'You are teasing me?'

'No, I am not. Do you want to come?' Before I had given my answer, he disappeared.

The next interruption was Trotter's reverentially bowed head and raised hand about to knock on the open door. After much unnecessary bobbing and scraping, Trotter showed Sir Clive Bampton in. While Bootham Chambers had been graced by its fair share of dignitaries, few had been titled. Hence the reason for my clerk's new toadying demeanour. If only, I thought, if only

I received such deference from Martin Trotter the world would be a better place.

'Thank you, Trotter, that will be all.'

Trotter backed out like a penitent leaving the holy presence. I noticed Sir Clive looked ill at ease, not his usual smooth self at all. I guessed it must have been more than Trotter's servility upsetting him.

'I have something to tell you, James, before you read it in the newspapers. Cedric Holbrook is dead. He killed himself. We were about to indict him for treason. Thankfully, the rest of the Holbrook family had gone off to stay with friends in Scarborough, I believe, immediately following the end of the Hobb trial. I know you are extremely fond of Winifred. I think you deserve an explanation.'

I lifted up my ammonite paperweight and rolled it about in my hands, struggling to collect my thoughts.

'Do you know how I met Winifred?' I asked. Sir Clive shook his head. 'She had tied herself to some railings outside the Mansion House. I helped stop her being seriously assaulted by Goater, of all people, and a mob. Doctor Holbrook invited me to Heslington for tea and cakes, in thanks I presumed.'

'Winifred was always fully committed to the cause.'

'Which cause?'

'Votes for women of course.'

'So, how did Holbrook really regard his stepdaughter's suffrage when he held such extreme political views on everything else?'

'I would hazard a guess that women's suffrage was merely a joke to Cedric. He would have indulged Winifred rather than have taken it seriously.'

'He targeted me though.'

'Primarily your association with him through Winifred would have been pure chance. Then Cedric learned you were defending Hobb. To a man like Cedric, George is a degenerate.'

'I am finding it hard to grasp any of this. It was Holbrook who sent me a socialist pamphlet written by Philip Snowden.'

'Philip Snowden?'

'Holbrook implied that Snowden was a friend of his.'

'Know thy enemy. They were political poles apart. Snowden was anathema to a man like Cedric.'

'Was Holbrook a Quaker then or not?'

'He purported to be one for his wife's sake. Cedric Holbrook the free thinking Quaker, I don't think so.' Sir Clive's laugh was dry and brittle.

'He even advised me to quote Hirschfeld in the Reverend's defence.'

'All part of an elaborate subterfuge, I'm afraid. I have known him for years, as you know, right back from my days in Africa. He fooled us all, James, even his own family. He manipulated everyone. If he could use both you, the liberal advocate, and Van Grunsven, the Jewish anarchist, to further his cause then he would.'

'But it was the Jews themselves, not Holbrook, who shot Van Grunsven, wasn't it?'

Sir Clive put a finger over his lips. 'We don't talk about that.'

I suddenly saw the whole picture as clearly as I had seen Vermeer's *Woman in Blue Reading a Letter* on the wall of the Rijks.

'Was Holbrook a member of this newly formed right-wing organisation?'

'One of the founding fathers. The Brotherhood has sympathetic wings all over western Europe and especially here and in Holland. It is an organisation set on propelling Jews, homosexuals, free thinkers and all non-Arians into the abyss. I believe it was Cedric who originally recruited the unknowing Lucy Alexander to spy on Van Grunsven. Maybe Lucy did take her own life when she discovered the man she had genuinely fallen for, against her better judgement, was about to blow up the London Stock Exchange. But more likely the Brotherhood regarded her as a loose cannon, an ardent socialist who knew too much, and they murdered her making it look like suicide. We'll never know for sure. What I am absolutely certain about is that the Brotherhood actively encouraged Van Grunsven in his objective. Should Van Grunsven have succeeded it would have discredited his race. One more step towards the Aliens Bill. One more step towards the mass expulsion of Jews from this country.'

'So, finally, to save the tribe the Jews were forced to kill one of their own.'

'As I just said, that is something we never talk about, James.'

'So was it Holbrook's men who tried to kill me, tried to kill me and George that day on Brighstone Beach?'

'Did you never consider it strange how he happened to turn up on the Isle of Wight when you were there? A busy medical man, he travelled all that way from Yorkshire just to warn you Lucy was dead. What was wrong with a telegram? I thought that part of his story was a little weak myself.'

'But you two were friends.'

'We were. That is why I allowed him to stay under my roof for a couple of nights at short notice. Cedric had not been to Bampton Brook Hall in years. Although we did meet up once or twice a year at my London club.'

Where you fed him with what you wanted him to know, you clever bastard, I thought.

'So *was* it Holbrook who orchestrated that explosion on Brighstone Beach?' I persisted

'The picture is far more complex than that. Several different groups were involved. Some linked to each other, some not. Some for your protection, James, some for your demise. I can tell you that the cartridge wrapper you brought back from Brighstone Beach was one the Dutch particularly favour in their mining operations.'

'The Dutch, why would the Dutch want to kill me?'

'Mortimer Blakely. I believe it was Blakely who finally sealed his and your fate. Perhaps they feared he had told you more than he had before they murdered him.'

'But what had Blakely found out? He was supposed to be investigating who was trying to blackmail me, nothing else.'

'Perhaps because of that he had stumbled on something far more sinister. A protracted Boer War, and the strangulation of Jewish diamond interests in Holland suits the fraternity. More than anything else the Brotherhood fears the rise of socialism, particularly among working Jews, it gives those workers greater protection. And democratic socialism is certainly taking hold among the Jewish diamond workers of Amsterdam, as I expect you found out for yourself. Look at the ANDB – the diamond workers' trade union.'

'Diamonds seem to be at the centre of everything. Arnon van Grunsven's uncle told me he hated the unions.'

'Then there was the Van Grunsven plot itself. I'm in no doubt that Blakely got wind of that, too, from the Jewish diamond community he mixed with in Amsterdam. A plot of international importance. The bombing of the London Stock Exchange by a Dutch national would not only have divided Jew from Gentile, it could have sparked off another Anglo-Dutch war.'

'But how would an Anglo-Dutch war suit the Brotherhood?'

'They don't have a chance of seizing power in either Britain or Holland as things stand. Both countries are too economically sound at present. But a war, a big war, would change that – destabilise both economies – lead to waves of discontent, dissatisfaction.'

'It's already started in London's East End and Amsterdam's Waterlooplein.'

'Indeed. Mark my words, the Brotherhood will rise up and surge to power on storm waves.'

'What a frightening prospect.' I took out a tightly balled handkerchief from a side drawer in my desk. 'Take a look inside,' I told him.

'What is it?' he asked; his long fingers fastidiously unravelling the handkerchief.

'That is the butt end of a Sumatra leafed Balmoral corona left burning on the porch step of St James' Church, Kingston. Its owner must have been following George and me all day.'

'Of course, I know that church well. It's in a very lonely location. But, James, no agent in his right mind would have left you such an obvious clue unless he was merely warning you off.'

'Well, I should have taken heed. The Dutchman, who smoked this brand, tried to push me into the Amstel as he had Blakely. But then you knew all about that. You sent me the *De Telegraaf* cutting, remember?' Sir Clive did not reply. 'Tell me, Sir Clive, how did Doctor Holbrook kill himself?'

'He threw himself into the river Ouse in the early hours of this morning.'

'Rather like Barney Barnato.'

'No, Barnato drowned in the sea off Madeira.'

'By the way, I almost forgot, Tom de Vries sends his regards.' I tried to keep my voice neutral, even.

'Did he really?'

'Yes, he saved my life.'

'That's Tom for you.'

'Holbrook knew too much, didn't he? No trial. No tell.'

'A just ending, don't you think?' Sir Clive's smile gave nothing away.

Author's Note

1899 – 1900. Queen Victoria's life and long reign are almost at an end. Her legacy is an empire on the epoch of great change. The century has been shaped by technological innovation – the train, the car, the telegram – but still the cart or hansom is the transport accessible to most. Philosophers such as Jeremy Bentham, John Stuart Mill and Karl Marx have challenged the old order. In natural science, Charles Darwin and the wonderfully modest Alfred Russel Wallace have discovered evidence that contradicts accepted religious teaching. Richard Owen, Darwin's bête noire, has built his "cathedral to nature" in Kensington. The Natural History Museum acquired 500 specimens from the collection of the Isle of Wight palaeontologist, William Fox, after his death in 1881. Fox is one of the great unsung amateur pioneers in the world of dinosaur discovery, having many named after him including *Iguanodon foxii*.

England has experienced the decorative Aesthetic Movement of the Wildes and James McNeill Whistler. Post Dickens, she has drawn to her shores great American writers such as Mark Twain and Henry James. Yet England is at war again. Her women are at war against a male dominated establishment at home. Her soldiers are away fighting against the Boer in Africa. The rumble of native drums can be heard along the Thames as Irish, German and Russian immigrants flood her banks. The sun might never set on the British Empire but there are storm clouds brewing on the horizon – France and Germany are rearming.

One of the characters mentioned in *Mortimer Blakely is Missing* is Archibald Philip Primrose, 5th Earl of Rosebery. Dubbed "Miss Prim" at Eton, he epitomised the rather dandy Victorian aristocrat. He was a Liberal Imperialist, a man firmly behind British colonial expansion while remaining solidly anti-socialist. He served in three of Gladstone's governments, later becoming Prime Minister himself in March, 1894. Intriguingly, he married Hannah, only child of the Jewish banker Baron Mayer de Rothschild in 1878. Hannah unfortunately died from typhoid fever in 1890. It has been speculated that Rosebery was bisexual. Like Oscar Wilde he was harassed by John Douglas, 9th Marquess of Queensberry, because of his alleged homosexual relationship with one of Queensberry's sons, Francis Douglas, Viscount Drumlanrig (Bosie's eldest brother), who was his private secretary. It is suspected that Queensberry was only placated after the Establishment closed ranks over the Rosebery affair, and Wilde stood trial for sodomy. Francis Douglas died from a shooting accident, possibly suicide, only months after Rosebery became Prime Minister.

It was partly due to the failure of liberal politicians, like Rosebery, to embrace full working class enfranchisement that the liberal party lost the working class vote. Instead the working man found his voice through such men as the brilliant orator and Christian Socialist, Philip Snowden, and founder member of the Independent Labour Party, Kier Hardie. Both Snowden and Hardie championed Women's Suffrage. But it was not until The Representation of the People Act 1918 that all male householders over twenty-one, and women over thirty, got the vote. At the beginning of the twentieth century, there were a million more women in England and Wales than men. Equality, equivalence, is never easily won: it took until the 2nd July, 1928, for women rate payers over the age of twenty-one to become enfranchised.

Nothing is new to history, history itself is cyclical. There was a severe economic depression that began in 1873 and lasted for twenty-three years. This was the precursor of the Great Depression of the 1930s, which in turn led to a surge in international fascism, but the seeds of British fascism had been sown a lot earlier than that in London's East End.

As a species we are not always kind. Xenophobia exists in every country. In England and Scotland poor Irish Immigrants, following the potato famine of the 1840s, were racially abused and depicted as Darwinian apes in anti-Catholic periodicals. However, no other race on earth has been persecuted more than the Jews – historically the whipping boys of Europe. In the 1880s thousands of Jewish refugees arrived in the East End fleeing murderous pogroms in Russia. The pressure for homes and jobs created a tension between them and the local population. Major William Evans-Gordon, campaigned in Stepney on a platform of limiting Eastern Europe immigration before the 1900 General Election (known as the khaki election). He was successful for the Conservatives, becoming closely involved with the British Brothers League which was officially formed in 1902 along paramilitary lines. Evans-

Gordon was instrumental in pushing through the notorious Aliens Act 1905, requiring steerage passengers on ships to establish that they were in good health and had the means to support themselves before entering Britain. The great and the good (and healthy) in first or second class were exempt from examination. Winston Churchill crossed the house to vote with the Liberals against the bill saying "the simple immigrants, the political refugee, the helpless and the poor – these are the folk who will be caught in the trammels of the Bill, and may be harassed and hustled at the pleasure of petty officials without the smallest right of appeal to the broad justice of the English courts" (quoted in *The Times*, 31st May, 1904).

Towards the end of the nineteenth century, Britain was engaged in the Anglo-Zulu War and the Boer Wars. These were simply conflicts over the acquisition of African lands rich in mineral wealth, particularly gold and diamonds. It was a time of intrigue and political manoeuvring on "The Dark Continent". From the 14th October, 1899, to the 15th February, 1900, the Boer surrounded the Kimberley Diamond Mine, owned by Cecil Rhodes. Two years before this, Rhodes' partner in De Beers – the one time acrobat Barney Barnato – had mysteriously disappeared overboard and drowned off Madeira on his way back to England. Did he fall? Was he pushed? Did he jump? Besides his riches, Barnato carried with him intimate knowledge of the failed British incursion into Paul Kruger's Transvaal known as the Jameson Raid – an act of war that the then Colonial Secretary, Joseph Chamberlain, denied any complicity in. And here is another military and political absurdity: the Boer were originally Dutch trekkers, the Boer were preventing British diamonds getting to Amsterdam to be cut and polished by Jewish workers, who in turn had trekked to Holland from all over Europe. I was fascinated to learn in one of Amsterdam's diamond museums a reason for the long Jewish association with the stone: diamonds are a small precious commodity which are easy to conceal and transport when you are fleeing at short notice for your life.

Victorian Britain had its own fears to contend with: fears of revolutionary ideas and anarchistic principles brought across by migrants from the Continent and Russia. When on the 15th February, 1894, a Frenchman, Martial Bourdin, blew himself up near Greenwich Observatory – this served as further confirmation to the British Establishment that the enemy was now truly within.

There was a police station in Jubbergate, York, until 1892. Most of the settings in *Mortimer Blakely is Missing* are authentic, traces of which can still be found today.

This explanation of the historical background to my novel is rather like some beast that has been skulking in a fictional undergrowth and has now been forced out on to the great plain. So, mindful that history can be perceived very differently whether viewed through the eyes of the lion or wildebeest, I have done my best to remain impartial and simplify many nineteenth century complexities for readers who are graciously giving up their time to open *Mortimer Blakely is Missing*.

Acknowledgements

First and foremost I am extremely grateful to Jeremy Mills and his team at Jeremy Mills Publishing for their belief and professionalism in producing not only *Mortimer Blakely is Missing* but my previous amended novel *Dangerous Waves*.

I am indebted to Isla Gladstone and Stuart Ogilvy of the Yorkshire Museum for giving up part of their morning to guide me through the complexities of their fabulous natural science collections. Likewise to Peter Thorpe of the National Railway Museum, York, for his expertise on local Victorian timetables, and Joanne Shanks and Georgie Myler of York Archives and Local History Team for their research on my behalf into Jubbergate Police Station.

One spring morning I was lucky enough to chance upon the extremely modest Professor S.A.J. Bradley at St Gregory's Minster. Professor Bradley took the time and trouble to give me highly accomplished Anglo-Saxon translations of some of the inscriptions there and a detailed explanation of the famous Orm Gamalson's sundial.

Author Lee Jackson kindly furnished me with information about a murder committed in Victorian London. Lee was big enough to help a fellow professional out. Unfortunately, this does not often happen. I am very impressed and grateful, Lee.

I would like to thank all the people I met on the Isle of Wight for their warm welcome. Particularly Martin Simpson, known as the Isle of Wight's Fossil Man, for his kind words and encouragement regarding a subject that he is an expert on while I am merely a passionate amateur. I also enjoyed a visit to the excellent Dinosaur Isle Museum where I found all the staff to be extremely helpful and informative – thank you guys.

This book could not have been written without the help of such official bodies as the Isle of Wight Record Office, Newport, and Amsterdam City Archives where I met and was helped by the knowledgeable Peter Kroesen. Guus Meershoek supplied me with some insight into historical policing in Amsterdam and the position of Jews in that city. The Diamond Museum, Amsterdam, was a treat to visit, and the Rijksmuseum with all their fabulous

Dutch paintings was a total indulgence as was the celebrated apple cake at the Jewish History Museum. In short, thank you to all those people who did not have to help me but chose to do so.

Now available in the same series

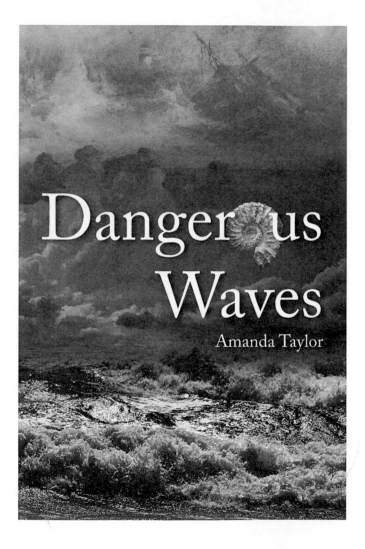

'... a tremendous mystery with twists and turns that keep you gripped until the final page. I couldn't put it down.'
– Kay Mellor

Author Profile

Educated in Leeds, Amanda Taylor did some magazine work and won a National Poetry Prize. She played squash for Yorkshire for nine years. Despite living in the middle of a grouse moor, about as far away as you can get from the sea, Amanda completed a successful relay swim of the English Channel and maintains that working out her plots helps the tedium of all those training miles. This is her second novel.

Visit her website: **www.amandataylorauthor.com**